28 DAYS

A NOVEL OF RESISTANCE
IN THE WARSAW GHETTO

28 DAYS

A NOVEL OF RESISTANCE
IN THE WARSAW GHETTO

David Safier

Translated by Helen MacCormac

Feiwel and Friends

New York

A Feiwel and Friends Book

An imprint of Macmillan Publishing Group, LLC

120 Broadway, New York, NY 10271

"Kolysanka Dla Synka W Krematorium"
("Lullaby for My Little Son in the Crematorium")
Words: Aaron Liebeskind
English translation taken from liner notes
by Peter Wortsman translation © Folkways Records

Our books may be purchased in bulk for promotional, educational,
or business use. Please contact your local bookseller or the Macmillan
Corporate and Premium Sales Department at (800) 221-7945 ext. 5442
or by email at MacmillanSpecialMarkets@macmillan.com.

Library of Congress Cataloging-in-Publication Data.

Names: Safier, David, author. | MacCormac, Helen, translator.
Title: 28 days : a novel of resistance in the Warsaw Ghetto / David Safier ; translated by
    Helen MacCormac.
Other titles: 28 Tage lange. English | Twenty-eight days
Description: First U.S. edition. | New York : Feiwel and Friends, 2020. | Originally
    published: Hamburg : Rowohlt Verlag, 2014 in German under the title, 28 Tage
    lange. | Summary: In Warsaw, Poland, in 1942, Mira faces impossible decisions after
    learning that the Warsaw ghetto is to be "liquidated," but a group of young people
    are planning an uprising against their Nazi captors.
Identifiers: LCCN 2019018302 | ISBN 9781250237149 (hardcover)
Subjects: LCSH: Holocaust, Jewish (1939-1945)—Poland—Juvenile fiction. |
    Jews—Poland—Juvenile fiction. | CYAC: Holocaust, Jewish (1939-1945)—
    Poland—Fiction. | Jews—Poland—Fiction. | World War, 1939-1945—
    Underground movements—Fiction. | World War, 1939-1945—Poland—Fiction. |
    Warsaw (Poland)—History—Warsaw Ghetto Uprising, 1943—Fiction. | Poland—
    History—Occupation, 1939-1945—Fiction.
Classification: LCC PZ7.1.S2415 Aah 2020 | DDC [Fic]—dc23
LC record available at https://lccn.loc.gov/2019018302

Book design by Ellen Duda

Feiwel and Friends logo designed by Filomena Tuosto

First U.S. edition, 2020

10 9 8 7 6 5 4 3 2 1

fiercereads.com

For my mother and father and for my sister

I

They'd spotted me.

The hyenas had spotted me!

And they were out to get me.

I could tell by instinct. Without actually having seen or heard them yet. The same way an animal in the wilderness can sense when it is in imminent danger, before it has actually sighted the enemy. This market, this perfectly ordinary market, where the Poles bought their vegetables, bread and bacon, clothes, and roses, even, was the wilderness for people like me. A place where I was the prey. Where I could die if they found out who or, more importantly, what I really was.

Don't walk any faster, I thought. *Don't slow down. Or change direction. And whatever you do, don't look back. Don't do anything to arouse more suspicion.*

I found it incredibly difficult to keep moving, pretending to stroll through the market as if I was enjoying the sunshine on an unexpectedly warm spring day. Everything about me wanted to run, but then the hyenas would have known that they were right. That I wasn't an ordinary Pole carrying groceries home to her parents; that I was a smuggler.

I stopped for a moment, pretended to admire an apple on a farmer's stall and wondered if I could risk taking a quick look. After all, there was a chance that I was imagining that I was being followed. But every inch of my body wanted to flee. And I'd learned to trust my instincts a long time ago. Otherwise I would never have managed to survive till sixteen.

I moved on slowly. The old farmer's wife was disgustingly fat. She obviously had more than enough to eat, far too much in fact. She kept on croaking, "These are the best apples in all of Warsaw."

I didn't tell her that every single apple looked amazing. For most of the people forced to live within the walls, even a moldy apple would have been a treat. Not to mention the eggs in my pockets or the plums or, best of all, the butter I was going to sell on the black market for a great deal of money.

I had to find out how many people were after me before I had the slightest chance of ever getting back behind the wall. They couldn't be 100 percent sure yet, or else they would have stopped me by now. I needed to get a look at them without being noticed. Without causing any more suspicion.

I looked down at the cobbled street. The heels of my lovely blue shoes clacked on the stones. They matched my blue dress with the red flowers perfectly. My mother had given me these clothes when we still had some money, and I always wore them when I was out smuggling. All my other clothes were threadbare, and most of them had been mended again and again. If I had been wearing those, I wouldn't have lasted two minutes at the market without being noticed. The pretty dress and shoes were my work clothes, disguise and armor all in one. I took great care of them.

I casually let my heel get caught between two stones. I buckled my ankle a bit and swore out loud, "Oh, crap!" Then I put my bags down, glanced over my shoulder and saw them: the hyenas. And they were smiling.

My instincts hadn't deceived me. They never did, unfortunately. Or fortunately, depending on how you looked at it. There were three of them. A short, unshaven, stocky man with a brown leather jacket and a gray peaked cap was up front. He was about forty years old and was obviously the leader. He was followed by a big man with a beard who looked as if he could throw a rock or two, and by a boy about my age who was wearing the same leather jacket and cap and was like a mini version of the leader. Maybe they were father and son? At any rate, the boy didn't go to school—otherwise he wouldn't be able to hang around markets in the morning, looking for someone to hunt.

Behind the walls, we weren't allowed to go to school anymore, because the Germans had banned all classes. There were illegal schools in the underground, but not everyone could go and I left ages ago. I had to feed my family.

This Polish boy could go to school and get educated, but chose not to. Of course, there was a lot of money to be made by a gang of *szmalcowniks*, or hyenas, as we called them—people who hunted Jews and then handed them over to the Germans for a bounty. There were loads of them in Warsaw, and none of them cared if the Germans shot every illegal person found on the wrong side of the wall.

It was spring 1942, and anyone found in the Polish sector of the city without a permit was sentenced to death. And that wasn't the worst of it. There were the most awful rumors about how the Germans tortured prisoners before they put them to death. Men, women, and children alike. They actually tortured children to death! Just thinking about it terrified me, but I wasn't dead yet. And I needed it to stay that way for my sister Hannah's sake.

There was no one in the whole world I loved as much as that little girl. Due to the appalling food rations, Hannah was far too small for her twelve years, and pale as a shadow, except for her eyes. They were big and wide awake and inquisitive, and deserved to see something better than the nightmare behind the walls.

All the power of an endless imagination shone in those eyes. So what if she wasn't very good at most of the subjects taught at the Szulkult underground school, like math, biology, or geography; when it came to telling the other children stories during the breaks, no one could do it better. She made up stories about a ranger called Sarah, who freed her beloved Prince Joseph from the clutches of the three-headed dragon; or about Marek the rabbit, who won the war for the Allies; and the ghetto boy Hans who was able to bring stones to life but never wanted to, because they were always so cross and grumpy. Anyone who listened to Hannah found the world a brighter and better place.

Who would take care of her if I let myself get caught here? Not my mother. She was so despondent that she never left the shabby hole where we lived anymore. And certainly not my brother. He was far too busy worrying about himself.

I looked away from the *szmalcowniks* and let my hand rest on the cobblestones for a moment. Often, when fear gets too strong, I touch the surface of something to calm myself: metal, stones, cloth—it doesn't matter—the main thing is to feel something else apart from fear.

The bright stones beneath my fingers had been warmed by the sun. I took a deep breath, grabbed my bags, and set off again.

The *szmalcowniks* were following me. I could tell. I could

hear the sound of their footsteps speeding up, although the market was full of so many other sounds: the voices of the sellers praising their goods, buyers haggling over prices, birds chirping, or the sound of cars passing on the street behind the market. People strolled past at a leisurely pace. A young blond man wearing the same gray suit most of the Polish students wore whistled away to himself. I could hear everything, but the sounds were muted somehow. All I could hear properly was the sound of my breathing, which was getting hectic, although I wasn't going any faster whatsoever, and my heart racing more and more from one second to the next. But the loudest thing was the sound of my pursuers' footsteps.

They were getting closer.

And closer, and closer.

They'd catch me in a moment and would confront me. They'd probably try to blackmail me, demand all my money for a promise not to hand me over. And then, when I paid, they'd do it anyway, and take the Nazis' bounty, too.

I'd known that this was going to happen sooner or later, ever since I started smuggling. That was a few weeks after Papa abandoned us. We didn't have any money left to buy food on the black market, and the food rations the Germans allowed us per person were only 360 calories a day. Most of the time, the food they gave to us Jews at the food dispensary was rotten. We got whatever was too lousy to send to the troops on the Eastern Front: spoiled turnips, bad eggs, or frozen potatoes that couldn't be cooked but could be turned into a more or less edible patty with a bit of luck. Last winter, the whole ghetto smelled of those patties on some days. So if I wanted my family to eat, I had to do something about it. My friend Ruth sold her body at the Britannia Hotel and had offered to get me in, even though she did grin and say that my figure was a bit boyish, but I preferred to risk my life smuggling rather than doing that.

Just in case I did get caught by the *szmalcowniks*, I'd concocted a story: I was Dana Smuda, a Polish schoolgirl from another part of Warsaw, who liked to come to the market because it's the only place you can buy a special sweet puff pastry cake with the most wonderful apple filling. It was important that my fake address was a long way away, because otherwise the hyenas would just walk me to my given address and find out that I was lying. I always bought a piece of cake every time I came to the market and put it in my bag to prove my story, just in case.

I also always wore a necklace with a cross. And I had learned a number of Christian prayers by heart, so that I could pretend to be a good Catholic if I had to. Prayers like the Rosary, Sanctus, or Magnificat: "My soul doth magnify the Lord, and my spirit hath rejoiced in God my Savior . . ." As if any sane spirit could rejoice in God these days.

If He were to appear in front of me, I'd throw eggs at Him for sure, even though they were worth a fortune in the ghetto. I didn't believe in religion, or politics, or in grown-ups anymore. All I believed in was surviving.

"Stop!" one of my pursuers shouted. Probably the voice belonged to the leader of the gang.

I pretended that he couldn't mean me. I was just an ordinary Polish girl; why should I turn around to a stranger's command?

I went through everything in my mind one more time: My name is Dana Smuda, I live at 23 Miodawa Street, I love puff pastry cakes . . .

The hyenas blocked my path and crowded in on me.

"You can't get rid of us that easily, you Jew-whore," the leader said with a grin on his face.

"What?" I asked, acting angry. It was a matter of life and death not to look scared.

"Two thousand zlotys," the leader demanded, while his son—it had to be his son, they both shared the same slightly crooked build—looked me up and down in a way that suggested that he was disgusted by me, the Jew, and that he was also using his dirty mind to picture me with nothing on.

"This is a one-time offer: two thousand and we'll leave you alone."

Suddenly I could feel sweat on the back of my neck. Not ordinary sweat caused by, say, the sun shining on a warm midday. No, this was sweat caused by fear. It smells terrible, and I had known nothing about it until a few years ago when my sheltered life ended.

As long as it stayed at the back of my neck and ran down my armpits, it wouldn't betray me, but I had to keep it off my face. The hyenas were very good at registering the smallest sign of weakness.

"Don't you understand, you Jew-whore?"

I couldn't say a word.

I suddenly understood why people in my situation were prepared to give all their money to crooks and criminals, even when they knew they would be betrayed regardless. They clung on to the absurd hope that the *szmalcowniks* would stick to their side of the bargain. If I'd had the money, I might have confessed I was a Jew and given it all to them. But I'd never had that kind of money. So I forced myself to smile and said, "What are you talking about?"

"Don't pretend we're stupid," the leader hissed.

I knew that my innocent little story wouldn't work with him. I might have been able to trick his son and the coarse-looking thug, but not him. He'd probably tracked down loads of Jews in the past few years and heard many stories better than the one about the girl who liked puff pastry. Way better. And he wasn't going to be tricked by a cross necklace, either.

My lies would be useless, worth less than nothing. How could I be so stupid, so badly prepared? It would be my fault if my mother died in our room at 70 Miła Street in a couple of weeks' time, and Hannah wouldn't survive much longer. Maybe she'd get by, begging on the streets of the ghetto. That could work for a bit, but the beggar children would freeze to death in the night when the next winter came, at the latest.

I couldn't allow that to happen to Hannah. Never.

I concentrated on the fact that the necklace and my lies weren't the only things I had going for me. There was one more thing I could bank on: I didn't really look Jewish. My hair was dark, like most of the Jews but also like many Poles. And I had a little snub nose and something that didn't fit the picture of a Jew at all: green eyes.

In one of his rare romantic moments, my boyfriend, Daniel, told me that my eyes looked like two mountain lakes, sparkling in the sun. I hadn't actually ever seen a mountain lake, so I had no idea if they could sparkle green and would probably never find out now.

The color of my eyes made me unusual on either side of the wall.

I fought back my fear and looked the leader of the *szmalcowniks* straight in the eye. The green got to him. And then without planning to, I burst out laughing. The few people who really know me, know that I hardly ever laugh. And when I do, it's never like that. But it sounded real to the *szmalcowniks*, and it disconcerted them.

"You are so wrong," I said, and pushed past the dumb-founded men who obviously had never been laughed at by someone they thought was Jewish. Then I walked away, carrying my bags. It was incredible—my audacity had paid off. I nearly grinned.

But then the stocky leader charged after me, followed by the other two and blocked my path again. I caught my breath. I wouldn't manage another bold laugh.

"You're a Jew. I can smell it," the man barked, and pushed his cap back. "I'm an expert at rooting out vermin."

"The very best," the boy said proudly.

Really? He was proud of a father who blackmailed Jews and then sent them to death?

It was all so unfair: My father had healed people, Poles and Jews. He'd even helped a young German soldier shot in our street during the last days of the invasion. But no matter how many people he had saved or how respected he had been as a doctor, now, when we really needed him, my father was not there.

"Stop bothering me," I threatened angrily, "or I'll call the police!"

The boy and the bearded man were impressed by my hollow threat. The Polish police didn't like the *szmalcowniks*. They were rivals when it came to earning money with the Jews found on the Aryan side. And if the *szmalcowniks* were caught harassing innocent Polish girls, then they'd be in real trouble, and they knew it.

But their leader wasn't going to be intimidated by me. He stared at my eyes, looking for a trace of insecurity somewhere, some sign no matter how small; my green eyes hadn't dislodged his suspicion.

I met his gaze. With all my might.

"I mean it," I repeated.

"No, you don't," he said quietly.

"You bet I do!"

"Well, then, let's go to the police together," he suggested, and pointed to a policeman wearing a blue uniform standing at the fat old woman's stall. He had just bitten into an apple and was pulling a sour face because it didn't taste anywhere as good as he'd expected.

What was I going to do now? I was done for, either way, whether I went to the police or not. There were beads of sweat on my forehead all of a sudden, and the leader noticed and started to smile. There was no more point in lying.

I could hear the student whistling again. I was going to die. Tomorrow at the latest, they'd put me up against the wall. My mother and my little sister wouldn't survive without me. And this guy was whistling a merry little tune!

Should I run? There was no real chance of getting away. Even if I was able to outrun the *szmalcowniks* with my heels on, they would start shouting and calling to people, and there'd be enough Jew haters in the market to catch me. So many Poles despised us. They hated being occupied by the Germans, but they didn't mind if they got rid of the Jews in the process.

And what if I did actually manage to flee from the market? I would never make it to the wall unseen. Not in a million years! I'd never get back into the ghetto. Running away was hopeless. But it was my only chance. I was about to drop the bags with all my precious goods and run for my life when I suddenly found myself staring at a rose.

It was a real rose!

Right in front of me.

Its strong scent actually replaced the bitter smell of my own fear for a moment. When was the last time I'd smelled a rose?

There weren't any in the ghetto. Whenever I went to the Polish market to buy goods, I never had time to look at the flowers. I'd never even thought of it. And suddenly, when I was just about to be handed over to the Germans, somebody offered me a rose?

It was the student.

He was standing beside me, beaming at me with his bright blue eyes, as if I was the most amazing and beautiful thing he had ever seen.

Close up, he looked younger than a student; more like seventeen, eighteen than in his early twenties. Before either the *szmalcowniks* or I could say anything, he laughed and took me into his arms.

"A rose for my rose!"

It was the most ridiculous thing to say, but he was so obviously in love that it didn't sound a bit silly the way he said it.

Suddenly I realized that this boy was trying to save my life. Was he a Jew, too? Or a Pole, maybe? He could even have been German with his blond hair and blue eyes, and his freckles. At any rate, he was a fantastic actor. It didn't matter what he was. He was risking his life for me—a total stranger!

"You're the rose of my life," he said. He sounded so happy.

The hyenas had no idea what to make of him. Could someone pretending to be in love overdo it like this? I had to start playing along if I wanted to convince them and save us both.

But I was too flustered. I tried to take the rose, but I couldn't move. It was as if I'd been paralyzed by Hannah's poison worm Xala from her story about the crazy caterpillars who hated butterflies.

The boy could feel how tense I was and pulled me closer. He held me tight, and his arms were far stronger than I would have thought possible for such a skinny guy. I still couldn't react. I was all fear and surprise, like a dummy in his arms. He increased his antics to cover for me, and all at once he kissed me.

He kissed me!

His rough lips pressed against mine, and his tongue pushed into my mouth as if it had done so a thousand times before. As if this was the most natural thing in the world. I had to answer his kiss. This was my last chance. If I didn't, then everything would be over, for both of us.

The knowledge that I was going to die if I didn't react gave me a new lease of life, and I kissed him back just as wildly.

I had no idea if I liked being kissed, but when the boy finally stopped, I pretended to be over the moon.

"Thank you for the rose, Stefan." I'd made up a name for him in an instant.

"I can't live without you, Lenka!" He had a name for me, too. He must have been relieved that I had started to play along.

The hyenas were pretty impressed by our performance. The young *szmalcownik* even looked a bit envious. He'd probably never kissed a Polish girl like that.

"Are these guys annoying you?" Stefan asked, pretending that he hadn't noticed them before.

"They think I'm a Jew!"

Stefan stared at them as if they were completely mad. But he wasn't laughing like me on my first attempt to get rid of them. He scowled at them.

"Are you trying to insult my girlfriend?"

He was a proud Pole now, whose girl had had her dignity offended. A Jew? No one would dare say something like that to a decent Pole!

"No . . . no," the leader stammered. He stepped back a bit. So did his men.

"Well, they did!" I said in an angry voice. I was only pretending to be offended, but my anger was real enough.

Stefan shook his fist at the *szmalcowniks*. They stepped back again. Of course, they could have simply beaten him up. Three against one would have been no problem for them. But they didn't touch Poles. That would have got them into trouble with the police. They even looked slightly shamefaced to have been so very wrong about me. They didn't bother to apologize, but the leader turned away from us without a word and signaled the other two hyenas to follow him.

Stefan picked up my heavy bags like a real gentleman and put his free arm around my shoulder. We pretended to be two people in love, strolling through the market with me holding his rose.

I did worry that he might run off with my goods. Maybe he was a smuggler, too. But would an ordinary smuggler risk his life for someone like me? And if he did steal the food, wasn't it a small price to pay for my life?

"Thank you," I said to him.

"It was my pleasure," he laughed, and I almost believed him. "You're a great kisser."

He said it with all the authority of a boy who knew what he was talking about, who'd kissed a lot of girls.

"I am if my life depends on it," I whispered so that the passersby wouldn't be able to hear. This wasn't the right time or place to be swapping compliments. "Our lives! You risked your life for me!"

I still couldn't believe it. In a world where everyone only thought about themselves, someone had put everything on the line for me!

"I knew it would work," he said just as quietly. He wasn't play-acting anymore; he was smiling honestly now.

"Well, you knew more than me, then." I gave him an apologetic smile.

"For two reasons," he explained.

"Oh?"

"Your green eyes . . ."

I was flattered, which surprised me.

"And?" I asked.

"Anyone out smuggling in times like this must be a really quick thinker. Or else he'd be dead. Or she would be."

He was impressed! And that pleased me even more and made me feel a tiny bit proud. Of course, I didn't want him to know, so I said, "A really quick thinker or truly insane."

He laughed. A lovely, natural laugh. Nothing like the laughter in the ghetto. Was he a Pole after all? Maybe he really was called Stefan.

"Are you a smuggler, too?" I asked.

He stopped walking, grew serious, and hesitated for a moment, as if he was wondering how much he should let me know. In the end, he said, "Not like you."

What was that supposed to mean? Did he smuggle for the ghetto's black market kings? Was he one of the Polish criminals who supported those people?

Stefan took his arm away.

"It's better if you don't know anything about me," he said, and suddenly he seemed much older than seventeen.

"Oh, I can handle it," I replied.

"I used to think like that," he answered. His eyes had lost the bold sparkle. I would have loved to know what he was talking about, but it was none of my business. He handed me my bags. Good! I wouldn't have to go home without any food.

"We should say goodbye," Stefan said.

All at once, I felt sad. I wanted to know more about him, but I knew it wasn't going to happen. "Yes, we should," I said quietly.

He looked so serious. Was he sorry that we were going different ways, too? But as soon as he felt me watching him, he switched his smile back on.

"When you get home, you need to wash."

"Excuse me?"

"You stink of fear!" he said, and gave me a broad grin.

I didn't know whether to laugh or hit him, so I did both.

"Ouch!" He burst out laughing.

"Mind what you say," I said, "or there'll be more where that came from."

That made him laugh even more. "There you go!" he said. "Never trust a pretty woman."

Damn, I was pleased again!

Stefan planted a kiss on my cheek and disappeared into the crowd. Out of my life forever, probably, without telling me his name or ever knowing that I was called Mira.

And I still held his rose in my hand.

Sometimes when something exciting happens, the feelings don't catch up with you until after it's over.

The rose thorns pricked the tips of my fingers, and suddenly I was overwhelmed by the memory of our kiss. The way Stefan had kissed me. The way I'd kissed him back.

I was shocked. Daniel had never kissed me like that.

Daniel.

I felt guilty all of a sudden. Why on earth was I so overwhelmed by a kiss from a stranger?

Daniel was the only person in the world who gave me any strength. He was the most decent person I knew. And he was always there for me. Unlike everyone else.

I probably wouldn't see Stefan ever again, and even if I did . . . Daniel and me! We were going to go to America together. Someday. We were going to walk down Broadway with Hannah, and see that great city for real. I'd only ever seen it in black and white, in the cinema we used to watch before the Nazis invaded.

Daniel and I had made a New York vow.

I pulled myself together and tried to block off the emotions caused by the kiss. I blamed them on all the danger and excitement, and forced myself to stop thinking about Stefan. The day wasn't over. I hadn't survived yet. The hardest part was still to come. I had to get back into the ghetto. Without being caught by the German guards.

2

The wall the Jewish slave workers had built—it's true, the Jews were forced to build their own prison—was three meters high. It was topped with broken glass and another half a meter of barbed wire. It was guarded by three different units: German soldiers, Polish soldiers, and the Jewish ghetto police on our side of the wall. Those pigs did anything the Germans wanted, just to have a slightly better life than the rest of us. They weren't to be trusted, not even my charming older brother.

Professional smugglers bribed the guards at the few gates that led into the ghetto—guards were always prepared to take money, no matter which group they belonged to. Once the guards had been paid, the carts with the smuggled goods could pass. Often these were stowed under false floors, but sometimes the animals pulling the carts were the goods themselves. Carts could be pulled into the ghetto by horses and back out again by men.

It wasn't as easy for me to get in or out of the ghetto. I didn't have enough money to bribe the guards, and although I was slim,

I was too big to fit through one of the gaps under the wall used by the smaller children who had to help make ends meet. These ragged little creatures were the unsung heroes of the ghetto. They forced their way through cracks and holes, crept through sewers, and even climbed over the wall, cutting their hands open on the broken glass. Most of them were under ten years old, and some no more than six. But if you looked into their eyes you'd have thought they'd roamed the earth for a thousand years. Whenever I saw one of those poor old-young creatures, I thanked my lucky stars that I could give Hannah a better life.

The little smugglers were all doomed. Sooner or later, they got caught by someone like Frankenstein. Frankenstein was our name for one of the more brutal German guards. He enjoyed shooting the small smugglers down off the wall with a cold smile, like sparrows.

In order to get into the Polish part of the city without ending up like a dead sparrow myself, I used the one place that had actually been designed to transport people from one world to another: the graveyard.

We are all the same in death—even if the different religions don't think so—and the Catholic and Jewish cemeteries lay side by side, separated by just a wall. Ruth had told me how to get through. One of her favorite customers, a notorious ghetto gangster called Shmuel Asher, had boasted to her about his smuggling tricks.

I left the market, walked along a couple of streets, and went into the Catholic cemetery. There was hardly ever anyone here, and today it was deserted. The Poles didn't have much time for their dead at present. Maybe people never did.

I headed straight toward the wall. I looked at the graves on the way and was surprised how luxurious some of them were.

Some of the tombs were larger than the room I occupied with my family. And they probably had fewer bugs, too. I was thinking about this when I noticed a blue policeman on patrol in the distance. Whatever happened, he mustn't speak to me or ask for my papers. I couldn't afford a forged passport like the professional smugglers, and I'd be caught at once.

I went on my way without hurrying and stopped at the next grave. I put down my bags, laid my rose beside a wreath, and started to pray quietly. I was a good Catholic girl taking a moment to remember the dead after visiting the market. The man who was buried here was called Waldemar Baszanowski, born on the twelfth of March 1916 and dead on the third of September 1939. He was probably a soldier in the Polish army, shot by the Germans in the first days of the war. I was Waldemar's little sister now. God rest his soul.

The policeman walked past without speaking to me. He left me alone to say my prayers for the dead. Once he'd gone, I let out a sharp breath. I was sorry that I'd have to leave my rose on this stranger's grave. Stefan had used it to save my life, after all. I picked up the rose and toyed with the idea of taking it back to the ghetto. But that was unwise. If I met the policeman again, the rose would give me away. I'd never be able to explain not leaving it on the grave. I could hardly say, "Oh well, the dead man won't mind."

I told myself I had to stop getting distracted by that boy. I left the rose on the grave. "Thank you, Waldemar," I said, and went up to the wall bordering the Jewish cemetery. I looked around, but I couldn't see any soldiers or police, and so I hurried over to a certain spot where the carefully arranged stones could be removed to make a passable hole for the professional smugglers. This was where they brought tons of smuggled goods into the ghetto, including cows and horses. I took out the smallest stone and peered through the hole. As far as I could see, there was no one on the other side, so I started to pull out more stones, as quickly as possible. This was the most dangerous part. I could be discovered on either side as I removed the stones. And there would be no chance of explaining myself or escaping.

My heart beat wildly, and I started to sweat again. I could be caught and shot at any moment. Well, at least I'd be close to my grave.

As soon as the hole was big enough, I squeezed through and started to put the stones back, as fast as I could. I didn't want the guards to notice the hole while they were patrolling the wall and close it for good. And I didn't want the smugglers to suspect that someone was using their secret passage, or they'd pounce on me the next time I went over to the Polish side. Ruth had warned me that they were a nasty bunch of people.

My hands shook. I was more nervous than usual, probably because of my encounter with the *szmalcowniks*. I dropped a stone on my foot and gritted my teeth, so as not to make a sound. I wanted to be gone, but I had to seal the hole in the wall.

To calm myself, I touched the moss growing in front of the wall. It was soft and damp. Once again, I could sense that there was more to the world than just my fear. A bit calmer now, I picked up the stone from the ground—my hands weren't shaking quite as much anymore—and put it in the gap. Only five stones left: In the distance I could hear prayers being chanted loudly all of a sudden. Somewhere, there was a funeral going on. People died all the time in the ghetto. Only four stones left: One of the mourners sneezed. Only three stones: I could hear heavy steps coming from the other direction. Guards? I didn't dare look. Looking would take up invaluable time. Only two stones left: Were the footsteps getting closer? One more stone left: No, they were moving away. The hole was closed. At last.

I turned around and saw that the footsteps came from two German soldiers. They were heading toward the funeral party about two hundred meters away from me. Maybe to torment the mourners. They liked to do that.

I ducked away from the wall, taking my bags with me. Two graves to the left, then two to the right. I stood still to take off my chain with the crucifix, and threw it in with the things I'd bought. Then I reached into a bush, felt for a little piece of cloth, and pulled it out. It was my armband with the Star of David. I put it on.

Now I wasn't Dana the Pole anymore; I was Mira the Jew.

The Germans could do whatever they wanted with me. So could the Poles, and even the Jewish police.

Whenever I put the armband on, I was reminded of the very first time we had had to wear them. I was thirteen then; the ghetto didn't exist yet, but there were other cruelties toward Jews. In 1939, the Nazis had ordered that every Jew had to wear the star.

Of course, the armbands weren't handed out. The Jews had to make them themselves or buy them. On the very first day of this order, I was walking through the freezing November rain with my father and brother, on our way to the market. We still had our good coats, so the cold couldn't get to us.

Until the German soldier appeared.

He walked toward us on the pavement, and we children didn't know what to do. Should we walk past or stop and say hello? A friend had told my father how he had been beaten, just the night before, because he had dared to pay his humble respects to a German soldier. So Papa said, "Lower your eyes."

We walked on, staring at the ground, past the German soldier. But the soldier stopped and started shouting, "What's wrong, Jew, you refuse to greet me?"

Before my father could say anything, the soldier hit him. He hit my father! This honorable man, a respected doctor, the father we looked up to and who seemed so powerful and almighty to us—was beaten.

"Forgive me," he said, while he tried to get up and the blood dripped from his lip down onto his gray beard.

My strong father was apologizing for being hit?

"And what are you doing on the pavement. Your place is in the street!"

"Of course," Papa said, and pulled us into the road. "Barefoot!" the soldier ordered.

We looked at him in disbelief. He took his gun off his shoulder to underline his order. I stared at the enormous puddles in front of us.

"Children, take off your shoes," my father insisted, "and your socks!"

He did so himself and stood barefooted in a freezing puddle. I was too shocked to react at all, but Simon, my brother who was seventeen, got angry. Papa's humiliation made him go red in the face. He went up to the soldier, even though he was small like everyone in our family, and shouted,

"Leave him alone!"

"Shut up!"

"My father saved a German soldier's life!"

Instead of an answer, the soldier took the butt of his gun and struck Simon in the face. My brother fell to the ground, and Papa and I ran to him at once. His nose was broken and a tooth knocked out.

"Take off your shoes!"

Simon couldn't move. He was crying in pain. It was the first time my brother had ever been hit. And it was so brutal.

My father took off Simon's shoes and socks to prevent the soldier from hitting him again. I was terrified and took off my shoes and socks, too. We helped Simon, who was still crying, to get up. Father took hold of each of us by the hand and squeezed our fingers tightly. As if he hoped to give us strength, somehow. We walked through the freezing puddles.

And the soldier shouted, "I hope you have learned your lesson."

We had. Father realized that the Germans weren't making rules anyone could rely on: Greeting, not greeting, it didn't matter, the rules were only there to torment us. And Simon knew from this moment on that he was never going to stand up to the Germans again. One blow, a knocked-out tooth, a broken nose, and his will to fight had disappeared. I had also learned something. As I walked through the icy puddles in my bare feet, and my toes ached with pain and then slowly went numb, my father, full of shame, watched me, and I realized that the grown-ups couldn't protect me anymore.

Papa knew, too. I could see it in his sad eyes. He was suffering far more than I was. I would have liked to cuddle him like he used to cuddle me if I had a nightmare. But this wasn't just a bad dream we could wake up from. The German soldier made us march through the puddles, back and forth. We were a spectacle for everyone to see. The Polish pedestrians looked away, embarrassed, or most of them did. But some laughed, and one man bellowed, "The Jews are in the gutter at last." While we were being humiliated, I pressed Papa's hand and whispered, "I love you, no matter what happens."

Of course, I had no idea what was going to happen.

I could hear the Germans' laughter coming from the funeral. Apparently, they really were having a bit of fun with the mourners. Maybe they were making them dance. I'd heard about awful jokes like that.

Whatever was going on, I couldn't waste any more time. I grabbed my bags and ducked from one gravestone to the next, in the direction of the exit.

One of the soldiers shouted, "Laugh!" And then I heard the tortured laughter of the people by the graveside. I couldn't help them.

This was the ghetto. This was my home.

3

gnore, ignore, ignore.

I hurried through the streets of the ghetto and tried to block out everything, like I always did, so that I could bear it all—the lack of space, the noise, the smell.

Many, many people lived here. We constantly jostled one another, even though I tried to avoid physical contact with anyone. All the ghetto inhabitants did. The fear of catching typhus was painfully real.

And it was so loud, not due to traffic—cars weren't allowed in the ghetto—but because of the sheer number of people living here, talking to one another, arguing. There was always someone shouting. Either they'd been robbed, or conned, or they had simply gone mad.

The stench was the worst thing of all. There were bodies lying in several doorways. This was something I never got used to. Many people didn't have the money or the strength to bury their dead. They simply put them out on the streets at night, so that they would be disposed of like rubbish the next day.

The corpses were stripped of their clothes overnight. I understood why: the living needed coats and trousers and shoes far more than the dead did.

I ignored all the begging children I passed. Some were sitting listlessly on the curb. Others with a bit more strength tugged at my clothes. They'd have clawed one another's eyes out for a single piece of bread out of my pocket.

I wasn't going to let Hannah end up like them.

Ignore. I had to ignore the screaming injustice of it all.

Apart from all the poor and desperate people in rags, there were rich people being carted to the delicatessen shops in bicycle rickshaws. A woman passed by, yelling at her driver to go faster. She was actually wearing a fur coat on a warm day like today. Still, despite the smell, I could breathe more freely here. Despite the cramped conditions, I could move without being terrified the whole time. There were no hyenas lurking in these overcrowded, stinking streets, waiting to hunt me down. I was among my own kind. People who were trying to keep their dignity somehow, despite everything.

They wore decent clothes, kept themselves clean, and walked through the streets with their heads held high. They existed without hurting anyone. Without turning into animals.

The ghetto had not managed to break all of us yet, not by a long shot. There were still good people. I wasn't one of them, of course. The good ones were the teachers, volunteers working in the soup kitchens, and people like Daniel. Especially people like Daniel.

I made my way through the masses and headed toward the little shop belonging to Jurek. The bearded old man was one of the few people who managed to endure the circumstances. He was often in a good mood, not necessarily because he made a living buying goods from me and the other smugglers, but because he had lived his life already.

"I have had sixty-seven great years on earth," he'd told me once. "That's more than most people will ever get, be they German or Jew or Congolese. Even if the last years are more of a struggle, they don't count for much."

As I entered his shop carrying my bags, the broken doorbell rattled instead of ringing and he was glad to see me.

"Mira, my darling!"

I liked the way he called me darling, although I knew very well that he called everyone a darling who brought him decent goods. I took a look at his display counter and made a mental note of the current food prices: An egg—three zlotys, a liter of milk—twelve zlotys, a kilo of butter—115 zlotys, a kilo of coffee—660 zlotys . . . If only I could smuggle coffee. The profits were incredible. But I needed more money first, to be able to buy some on the Polish side. The goods in Jurek's shop were too expensive for ordinary people. Someone working in the German factories within the ghetto earned about 250 zlotys a month. So he could only afford about two kilos of butter and a liter of milk.

Jurek looked into my bags and said, "You really are my darling!"

This time he said it in a way that sounded different. Perhaps it wasn't just meaningless chitchat. Perhaps he really did care for me the most.

After we'd sorted out what I would keep for my family—eggs, carrots, a little bit of jam, and a pound of butter—he took a bite of puff pastry and decided what he was going to pay me. Normally, he gave me half the amount he would get by selling the goods himself. I hadn't found anyone who would pay me more. I was no good at selling anything myself, and the longer I held on to the goods, the more likely they were to be stolen.

Jurek took some money out of the till, which was covered in a thick layer of dust—he didn't care much for cleaning—and put the banknotes into my hand. I counted them to make sure he hadn't slighted me and was surprised: He'd given me far too much money. At least two hundred zlotys too much. I would be able to buy coffee next time, after all. Had Jurek made a mistake? Should I ask? I decided not to. I needed every zloty I could get. If he'd got his sums wrong, then it was his own fault. And he could absorb the loss, anyway.

"I didn't get it wrong," he said, laughing. "It's all right."

Damn! My face was like a book; everyone could see what I was thinking. Or at least crooks like Jurek or the leader of the *szmalcowniks* could. I needed to do something about that!

"You wanted to give me more?" I didn't understand.

"Yes, because I really do like you, Mira . . . ," the old man replied, and stroked my cheek. It wasn't an indecent gesture. It was kind, almost fatherly. He wasn't expecting anything in return for his money. I'd heard a rumor that Jurek had never been interested in women. He preferred men.

"Anyway, money is not going to be worth anything, soon."

Why did he say that? "You mean because of inflation?" I asked, confused.

The prices kept going up in the ghetto, month by month. An egg had cost a zloty at the beginning of the year, and it was worth three times that now.

"No, that's not what I meant." Jurek laughed, and then he said something that frightened me. "You should enjoy life while you still can."

What did he mean? Of course I risked my life every time

I went over the wall and it had been a close shave today—*close* wasn't the right word—but I wasn't going to get killed. I was going to be even more careful and better prepared.

"I'll be all right," I said.

"I'm not talking about that," he sighed. "Things are going to get pretty nasty around here soon."

"What do you mean? What did you hear?"

"Oh, I have been hearing things, bad things . . ." Jurek didn't want to say any more.

"What things?" I asked again. "Who from?"

"From an SS man I do business with."

Although I liked Jurek, I hated the fact that he did business with the SS. "What did he tell you?"

"He was dropping hints, saying that our peaceful life here was going to be over tomorrow." Jurek's laughter turned bitter. "As if you could call this a peaceful life."

"What do you think he means?"

"I've no idea. But I'm expecting the worst."

I was worried. Jurek was usually so optimistic. It wasn't like him to take gossip seriously. There were often rumors that the Germans were about to murder us all. That it wasn't enough if half of us starved to death. But they were just rumors. And Jurek didn't normally pay attention to stuff like that.

"Nothing's going to happen," I said. "The Germans need us to work."

Thousands of Jews worked as cheap labor in the ghetto factories and produced all sorts of things for the Germans: furniture, airplane parts, even German *Wehrmacht* uniforms. It would be foolish to do without them.

"Ah yes, they need us for slave labor," Jurek agreed. "But do they need four hundred thousand of us?"

"And they keep bringing in Jews from all over the place," I continued to argue. "If they'd wanted to kill them, they'd have done it before they left home."

Thousands of Jews from Czechoslovakia and Germany had been brought into the ghetto over the past few weeks. The German Jews wanted nothing to do with us Polish Jews. They thought they were something better. A lot of them were tall with blond hair and blue eyes and looked German; some were even Christians who were simply unlucky enough to have a grandfather they might not have ever known who happened to be a Jew. The Germans had allowed these Christian Jews to bring a priest along, to hold services for them in the ghetto. What must this be like for them? They had gone to church every Sunday, and then they were chased out of their homes, had to wear armbands with the star, and were dragged to this hell, simply because they'd had a Jewish grandfather or grandmother! The God they still believed in had a very strange sense of humor.

"It would make sense," Jurek agreed, "to kill the people where they live."

"But?" I asked.

"The Nazis have their own special logic."

Suddenly, I remembered the soldier beating my father because he had not greeted him. How he would have been struck just the same if he had greeted him. Yes, the Nazis had their own sick logic all right.

And yet, it didn't feel as if something catastrophic was about to happen. "It won't be so bad," I said to myself as much as to Jurek.

Jurek forced a smile. "Does that mean you've decided to give me my money back?"

"I can buy coffee on the Polish side," I said, and sidled toward the door.

That made him laugh properly, again. "Mira, you are my one and only darling!"

I left Jurek's shop and joined the crowds outside. For all the stink and lack of space and noise, the ghetto was so alive that I couldn't imagine it ever dying. For each person who died now, three new ones were forced into the ghetto. As long as there were Jews, there would always be a ghetto.

I decided to let the rumors lie and concentrated on life instead of death: I was on my way home to cook my family a lovely omelet with fresh eggs.

4

I had only gone a few meters when I saw a dirty little man in rags jumping around on the street. It was Rubinstein.

Hundreds of thousands of people lived in the ghetto, but there were three people everyone knew. One was despised, one revered, and one made everyone smile. That was Rubinstein. He pranced about in the street like a clown or like a madman, maybe. He leaped in my direction and stopped right in front of me with a sweeping bow, as if he were a nobleman and me a princess. And he greeted me with his favorite words: "All the same."

Of course, my common sense told me that people were not all the same in the ghetto, but every time I heard Rubinstein saying or shouting these words, I wondered if he might be right, after all. Especially now, after what Jurek had just told me. We all shared the same ghetto hell, the same fear of dying. Didn't that make us all the same? Whether we were rich or poor, young or old, sane or insane?

And weren't the Germans in the same boat, despite all their

power over us? They could still lose this war they were fighting—they hadn't conquered the whole world yet.

Anyway, Rubinstein was the only person in the ghetto who wasn't afraid of the Germans. When he met SS men he jumped around them in just the same way he jumped around us. He would point at them and then at us and keep saying "All the same," until the Germans started to laugh and joined in, chanting "All the same," too. They probably thought it was funny, but perhaps deep inside they could sense that they were just as vulnerable as we were, although they would never admit it.

Perhaps Rubinstein wasn't insane after all. Maybe it was wise not to be afraid of the Germans. Maybe our fear amused him in the same way that his madness amused us.

Now Rubinstein suddenly laughed out loud. I followed his gaze: At the end of the street a group of SS men were out on patrol. Rubinstein was the only Jew I knew who could laugh when he saw SS soldiers. He bounded on a few meters until he landed in front of Jurek's shop and started shouting loudly enough for the old man to hear through the window. "Hitler stinks!"

I could see Jurek flinch behind his dusty till.

"Hitler," Rubinstein shouted, "gave his dog a good old bone!"

Jurek started to panic. The pedestrians around us all hurried away from Rubinstein. I started to feel worried. What happened if the SS men heard this nonsense?

I looked around, but the patrol hadn't noticed the madman yet—he must be mad; why else would he do something this insane? And so I stayed, wanting to see what would happen next, and forgot the most important rule of survival. It is never, ever a good idea to be too curious.

"Hitler is making love with his own hound." Rubinstein wouldn't give up. Jurek grabbed a load of food from the shelf: ham, bread, butter, and dashed out to Rubinstein. He thrust it all into his arms and hissed, "Shut up!"

Jurek was terrified that the Nazis would come and shoot Rubinstein, and then shoot him, too, because someone had been shouting obscenities outside his shop. Even though the old man believed that we were all going to die soon, he didn't want to be executed today.

Rubinstein grinned at Jurek. "I like jam, too."

"You little . . ." Jurek glared at him.

I understood what was going on here: What Rubinstein was doing was the most insane way to blackmail someone.

"I could tell everyone that you'd like to sleep with Hitler, too." Rubinstein grinned even more broadly. The old shopkeeper couldn't say a word.

Rubinstein turned around to face the soldiers, cupped his hands round his mouth like a megaphone, and started to shout. "Jurek wants to . . ."

The SS soldiers looked in our direction. Suddenly, I panicked. I was such an idiot. I should have been gone ages ago.

Jurek put his hand over Rubinstein's mouth and hissed, "You'll get your bloody jam."

The blackmailer nodded happily. Jurek took his hand off Rubinstein's mouth, and the little man pressed a finger to his lips, to show that he was going to be quiet now.

The SS men looked away. Jurek caught his breath, charged into his shop, and came back out with a large jar.

I had never been so happy to see a jar of jam in my life.

"Strawberry!" Rubinstein was delighted and opened the jar

right away. He grabbed a handful of jam and stuffed it into his mouth with pleasure.

There are prettier sights in the world. Rubinstein smiled at me and offered me some, too. I looked at Jurek. I didn't want to be rude, but I hadn't had strawberry jam for ages; it cost almost as much as butter on the black market. The old man looked at me and sighed.

"It's all right, Mira," he said. "At least he's stopped shouting."

As soon as Jurek had disappeared into his shop, I put my hand into the jar and stuffed a huge helping of jam into my mouth. I didn't care if Rubinstein had already stirred it with his filthy fingers. It tasted amazing.

While I was enjoying the glorious, sweet, fruity flavor, I realized that Rubinstein probably wasn't mad at all, he was simply ingenious.

"Maybe I could be your apprentice," I joked.

"Then," the man joked back, "I'll show you how to get the richest Jews to give you a five-course meal."

"I'd really like to be able to do that," I laughed.

A madman's apprentice! And I'd wanted to be a doctor.

Rubinstein put his tongue into the jar and started to lick the sides. Now I didn't think I'd have any more.

"Do you really think that we're all the same?" I asked.

He took his face out of the jar and answered, while red blobs of red jam dripped down his chin.

"Of course I do, and we are all free, too."

Was he being ironic?

"But that's ridiculous," I replied.

But Rubinstein turned dead serious all of a sudden. "No, it's not!"

He wasn't a madman anymore, or a clown. He was suddenly a man who saw the light.

"Everyone is free to choose what kind of human he wants to be," Rubinstein said, looking straight into my eyes. "The question is, little Mira, what kind of human do you want to be?"

"One who can survive," I answered quietly, fending him off.

"I'm not sure that's enough to justify life," he answered. He wasn't laughing at me, but he was smiling. Then he bounded off with his bounty and left me wondering what kind of person I wanted to be.

5

I climbed up the stairs of 70 Miła Street. It was terribly crowded. Not because too many people were heading back to their flats at the same time. No, for lots of people, the staircase was all they had. Whole families slept on the stairs and landings, ate their rations sitting on the steps, and stared listlessly out through the broken windows no one ever repaired. When the Nazis set up the ghetto, they didn't care whether it was going to be big enough for all the people it would have to hold. There weren't nearly enough flats. Which meant that many people lived in every room of every house, and in the rafters, on the staircases, or in the cold damp cellars. And now, in the spring of 1942, the numbers were actually increasing every day, as more Jews were brought in from other countries.

When we were relocated, our family was lucky enough—or rather we had enough money—to get our own room. Before we moved into the ghetto, we'd lived in a spacious five-room flat. But we were forced to give it to a childless Polish couple, who were very happy to have our furniture, as well. All we were allowed to take with us was a handcart loaded with a few suitcases. We pulled our cart through the streets of Warsaw among the silent, ghostlike procession of thousands of Jews on their way to the ghetto. We were guarded by Germans. And stared at by the Poles who lined the pavements or sat at their windows, and didn't seem to mind that their part of Warsaw would be Jew-free from now on.

When we entered the place where we were going to live at 70 Miła Street, my mother burst into tears. One single room. For five people. Without any beds. And a broken window. There were tears in my father's eyes, too. He had spent the few days between the announcement that a ghetto was being set up in the most run-down streets of Warsaw and the start of the resettlement doing everything he could to find an abode for us. He had run from department to department, had bribed officials of the *Judenrat*—the Jewish council set up by the Nazis—and ended up paying thousands of zlotys. Papa had managed to make sure that we wouldn't freeze to death in the streets when winter came.

When we entered that tiny empty room we didn't feel grateful, though. And he never forgave himself for not doing more to help his family and his dear wife who suffered so much.

I had to walk through a larger room to get to our own. An extended family from Kraków lived there. We had not managed to become friends over the past couple of years. These people were quite religious. The women wore head scarfs, and all the men had beards and curled side locks, which went down to their shoulders. While the women did the housework, the men spent the whole day praying. That wasn't exactly my idea of a happy marriage.

The women were washing clothes in large metal tubs and

looked down their noses at me as usual. I was young, I wasn't wearing a head scarf, I had a boyfriend, and I was a smuggler—reasons enough to despise me.

But I'd stopped caring about what they thought a long time ago. And I'd stopped trying to be nice.

Ignore, ignore, ignore.

I opened the door to our room. Mama had drawn the curtains again. She didn't want any sun in the darkness of her life. I closed the door behind me and opened the curtains and the window to air the room. Mama groaned quietly because of the sunlight. But she couldn't manage any real protest. She lay on a mattress we had swapped her favorite golden necklace for during the first winter. The necklace had been a present from Papa on their tenth anniversary.

Mama's long gray hair stuck to her face, her eyes stared into the distance. It was hard to believe that this woman had once been a beauty, or that my father and a Polish general had fought over her. It almost ended in a duel, but she had intervened and saved Papa from being shot.

She had loved him. Loved him incredibly. More than anything in the world. Even more than us children. His death had destroyed her completely. Since then, I'd started to think it was a bad idea to love someone too much.

My boyfriend, Daniel, saw things differently. He thought love was our only hope. He was probably the last surviving romantic in the ghetto.

I took off my best dress, carefully put it on a clothes hanger, and then hung that up on a nail on the wall. I changed into a patched blue blouse and a pair of black baggy trousers, and started to make the omelet. Hannah was due back from the underground school any minute. In fact, she should have been back by now. Hopefully nothing had happened to her. I was always worrying about that child.

Mama never said much, and she never asked me any questions. I still wanted her to share in my life in the outside world, though, so I usually pretended to have a conversation with her where I spoke both parts:

"And how was your day, today, Mira?" I asked.

"Quite successful so far, thank you!" I replied.

"Really, Mira?"

"Yes, really. I made lots of money and have bought loads of food . . ."

I wondered for a moment if I should mention the *szmalcowniks*, but I didn't want Mama to worry about me, assuming that she was actually capable of worrying about anyone anymore.

So instead, without even thinking about it, I said,

"I kissed a boy I didn't know!"

And she smiled. Mama hardly ever smiled. A little explosion of happiness went off in my heart. I desperately wanted her to keep smiling, and so I chatted away:

"It was wild, and passionate and daft . . . And fantastic somehow . . ." Goodness, it really had been fantastic! I suddenly had a desperate wish to kiss Stefan again.

Mama smiled even more. That was so lovely. When I saw her looking like that, I couldn't help hoping that she might be able to be happy again.

Hannah came in at this moment. She could be light-footed and boisterous at the same time. She was an elflike creature, shabby clothes with cropped short hair—she'd had lice last month and I had to cut off all her hair. When I'd fetched the scissors, I'd actually expected her to have a tantrum, but she'd turned the whole incident into one of her stories.

"If my hair grew any longer, I could wind it into twelve long braids. I'd use them like extra arms and capture people. I'd be able to hurl my enemies through the air because of the mighty strength of my hair. And I'd win every fight."

"Well, then," I'd said, laughing, "why don't you mind me cutting it off?"

"Because everyone would notice those braids and they would come and get me. I could use them to beat up soldiers and throw them through walls, even, but the soldiers have guns. And not even my hair can stop a gun. The Germans would shoot me. And then cut off my braids as a warning to everyone who wanted to grow their hair to fight. It's better to lose my hair now, before it turns into a weapon and the Germans find me out."

Hannah didn't want to be strong, she wanted to be invisible. If you were invisible you had more chance of surviving in the ghetto. As soon as I put the plate with the omelet onto the table, Hannah pounced on the food and started gobbling. Mama pulled herself up from the mattress, sat down beside me on the last available chair—I'd used the others as firewood last winter—and we both started eating, more slowly than Hannah. We let her eat more than us, but we always stopped her before she ate too much.

"Why was Mama smiling when I came in?" Hannah asked with her mouth full. Her manners were appalling. But no one had the time or patience to teach this child any manners.

"Tell me, what was going on?" she asked again. A bit of egg threatened to fall out of the corner of her mouth. Just in time, she caught it with the tip of her tongue.

"Mira kissed a boy," Mama explained in her thin voice. "And it wasn't Daniel!"

Before I could explain that the kiss had meant absolutely

nothing at all, except for the fact that it had saved my life, and that I loved Daniel and only Daniel, and that it didn't mean a thing if talking about this kiss made me feel nervous or made me go red, Hannah said,

"Oh, so did I!"

Now it was my turn to nearly drop my omelet.

"You!—You kissed someone?"

"After school." So that was why she was late.

"Who?"

"Ben."

"Does he go to school with you?" I started to smile. I thought that the idea of a twelve-year-old giving my sister a kiss on the cheek was very sweet.

"Nope," she answered.

With all this talk of kissing, Mama was drifting away again, back to the days when my father was alive and they were still happy together.

"Is this boy even smaller than you?" I teased Hannah.

"No, he's fifteen."

Now I really did drop a bit of omelet.

"And he is really, really nice," Hannah said.

"Any boy nearly my age out kissing twelve-year-olds is not nice!"

"And he does French kissing."

"Whaaat?"

"He's a good tongue kisser," Hannah explained, as if this was a perfectly normal thing to say.

She was far too young for this. Not to mention what it might lead to. I looked at Mama—she should do something! Anything! She was Hannah's mother, not me! But Mama got up from the table and went to lie down again.

"Hannah," I said while she grabbed Mama's plate, "don't you think the boy is too old for you?"

"Nope!" she said, chewing away. "Just a bit too shy."

"You kissed him?" I was shocked.

"Isn't that what princesses do?"

"Not exactly," I said.

"Well, they do in my stories!" Hannah gave me a huge smile. If the Nazis didn't manage it first, this girl was going to be the end of me. How could I stop all this nonsense? I needed help. Someone who knew more about dealing with children than I did. Daniel.

6

Janusz Korczak was the ghetto Jew everyone knew and admired. He was famous beyond the walls, in the whole of Poland and throughout the world. He had invented Hannah's favorite story about Little King Macius, and I was sure that had triggered her imagination for storytelling.

The thin old man with a beard ran an orphanage that was an inspiration to people all over the world. The children and caregivers were considered equals. If one of the grown-ups did something wrong, the children could hold a trial and pass a sentence, even on Korczak himself.

At the beginning of the week, I had actually seen this happen. Korczak was on a chair in front of three children sitting behind their little tables like a judge with two assessors.

"Janusz Korczak," a girl of about ten who was the judge said severely, "you are accused of having shouted at Mitek, just because he threw a plate on the floor. Mitek was so scared because of your shouting that he started to cry. What do you have to say in your defense?"

The old man smiled apologetically and said, "I was tired and exhausted. That is why I overreacted. It was wrong to shout at Mitek like that. And I will accept any sentence this high court may decide."

The little judge conferred with her assessors—two even smaller boys—and said, "Because you've pleaded guilty, we will give you a mild punishment. You are sentenced to wipe the tables for one week."

I would have told the children to get lost, but Korczak answered with the greatest respect, "I accept my punishment."

He took the children seriously and gave them dignity, dignity they could find nowhere else in the world.

Daniel had lost his own parents as a child. They died of tuberculosis, and he knew nothing about them. He had spent most of his life with Korczak. Now he was one of the oldest children in the orphanage and shared the responsibility for over two hundred children.

As soon as the orphanage had been moved to the ghetto, Korczak had had the windows to the street walled up. He didn't want the children to be confronted with too much horror every day. At first, I thought it was a naive move, but Daniel had said no. He thought that it was far better for the children's souls that way. And these days, I knew he was right. Whenever I entered the great hall, like now, I was amazed at how safe this world seemed. The beds were crammed together, but they were all made properly, and whenever there was food—every evening—everyone sat together at the big tables and behaved so well. No one gobbled their food like Hannah!

Manners wasn't a foreign word to these children, and thanks to Korczak's lessons, most of them could actually spell it as well!

Daniel was sitting at a table with lots of preschool children.

With his looks, he wouldn't have survived on the Polish side of the city for a minute. He had a mane of black curly hair, a large, distinctive nose, and dark eyes you could get lost in. But he couldn't pass as a non-Jew.

I watched Daniel fooling around with the children. A boy in a baggy sweater was hugging himself with laughter. Above the clatter of the knives and forks, I couldn't make out what they were laughing about. Korczak was sitting at the next table. He looked more gaunt and starved every day. I had to find food for three people. But he had to find food for more than two hundred. Daniel had told me that just last week Korczak had tried to negotiate with the Jewish council for extra rations and received none. So he had had to take donations from the smugglers for the first time. Until now, this honorable man had never had anything to do with those people. But these days, he would have danced a tango with the devil to help support his children.

Daniel saw me and called out, "Children, look who's come. It's Mira!"

I stopped in the doorway. Some of the children waved, but they weren't especially pleased to see me. One little girl, about seven years old in a red polka-dot dress, even stuck her tongue out. I didn't belong to this community, although I'd been turning up regularly for nearly half a year now. No wonder: I'd never really tried to get to know all of Daniel's little brothers and sisters. Hannah was more than enough for me.

I would have loved to go out tonight. There was a play on at the Femina theater—yes, we had theaters in the ghetto—called *Love Gets a Room* about two very different couples forced to share a flat. One pair are musicians; the others work in the Jewish council administration. To start with, they detest each other, but then the two couples fall in love, crosswise, and all sorts of things start to happen. The play was supposed to be funny, touching, and a little bit sad. And it had love songs. Happy ones, sad ones. And a funny one about how you should spend all your money on alcohol. At least that's what Ruth had told me. She had seen it with her favorite customer, Shmuel Asher the crime boss, but there was no point in suggesting a visit to the theater to Daniel. He had no money, and he would never let me take him out. Every zloty not spent on the children in the orphanage was a wasted zloty, as far as Daniel was concerned. And there was no point in arguing about it. I had tried on several occasions and ended up spoiling our evening, every time. That was one of the disadvantages of going out with such a decent boy.

Daniel smiled at me. I knew I'd have to wait until all the children had washed up and gone to bed. The lights were turned off at eight o'clock, but Daniel always spent a few extra minutes with the smaller children who couldn't manage to fall asleep.

I could have helped him and the older children get the little ones ready for bed, but after today I didn't feel like dealing with needy children. I was nowhere near as kind as my boyfriend. And a hundred times less selfless than Korczak, who cleaned the tables just as the little court had decreed. If I had been even a tiny bit less selfish, I'd have taken the tired old man's cloth from his hands and wiped the tables myself.

Instead, I left the hall and headed to the one place where Daniel and I went to have time to ourselves in this overcrowded world. The roof of the orphanage.

This was where we spent our evenings together. Come rain or shine, even when it was freezing. Where else could we have gone? Daniel slept in the huge dormitory, and Hannah and Mama were always at home.

Hannah. How could I stop her kissing older boys?

Having gotten to the attic of the orphanage, I opened a skylight and crawled out onto the dirty brown tiles of the sloping roof. I had to slide down a bit to get to a two-by-two-meter platform. That was our little haven.

I looked across the rooftops of the ghetto toward the wall. I could see a German soldier marching up and down with his gun across his shoulder. Perhaps it was Frankenstein. If I had a gun, I could shoot him down like a sparrow from here. If I could use a gun, that is. And if I was capable of killing someone.

Was I? I didn't think so. I didn't hate anyone that much. I would never understand Frankenstein or those other Nazis.

Anyway, the whole idea was just too stupid for words. Imagine a Jew—a young Jewish *girl*, no less—with a gun! There was no such thing. It was about as likely as a bunch of Germans singing "Shalom Aleichem."

It was starting to get cold so I pulled my brown leather jacket on over my blouse. I loved that jacket. I sat down and let my legs hang over the edge—I wasn't afraid of falling off—and looked into the distance, toward the Polish side of town. I could make out cars and a streetcar and loads of Poles who were still out and about in the evening. I even thought I could hear couples laughing, exiting the cinema without a care in the world. How I missed the cinema!

Sometimes I blamed the Nazis the most for not letting us have films in the ghetto. Theater was all very well, but there was no substitute for cinema.

What kind of films would Chaplin be making now? I wondered. I had loved *City Lights*. The poor tramp who makes sure that the blind flower seller regains her sight. And then she doesn't know that the man in rags is the person who saved her. Not until she touches his hand and realizes who he is. I'd laughed and cried during that film, and when the lights came back on, all I wanted was to see those city lights. I dreamed of going to New York. Daniel always played along, and together we imagined how we would live in America, and how we'd go to the top of the Empire State Building to see where King Kong had taken his woman. Of course, I knew that Daniel would never leave the children or Korczak, who was like a father to him, even if he had promised to go to America with me. Korczak would stay with the children no matter what. Rich Jews from far away had collected enough money to smuggle him out of the ghetto, but he had refused to go. It was as if the children of the orphanage were his own—and what kind of person would ever abandon their own children?

My father.

Last summer, he threw himself out of a window. His nerves were shattered. He couldn't bear the terrible conditions in the Jewish ghetto hospital, and he had stopped working as a doctor. All our savings were gone. Papa had used our last money for bribes to get Simon into the Jewish police.

It broke my father's heart to realize that his son didn't give a damn about his family and couldn't have cared less for his weak father, even though Papa had done everything he could for him.

I was still going to school when he killed himself. Mama worked in one of the German factories. So I was home before her and found him lying in the courtyard in a pool of blood. His head had burst open on impact. In a trance, I went to fetch help so that he could be taken away before Hannah saw him like that. Once the gravediggers had gone, I waited for Mama. She had a crying fit when she heard the news. I couldn't cry. I couldn't comfort her. I hugged Hannah when she came home from school. My little sister cried and cried until she fell asleep in my arms.

I carried her to the mattress and put her to bed, left my mother alone with her sorrow, and went out. I thought Simon should know that his father was dead. So I made my way through the crush of the ghetto toward the Jewish police station.

But halfway there, I gave up. I didn't want to go to that horrible building with all those awful people where Simon was busy making a name for himself.

I didn't want to do anything ever again.

I sat down on the curb. People walked past. No one saw me. Except Daniel. I don't know how long I'd been staring into space. It could have been minutes or hours, but suddenly he was sitting beside me. Being an orphan, he must have sensed that I was someone in need of help.

I hadn't been able to cry. But now that I wasn't alone anymore and didn't have to be strong, a tear trickled down my face. Daniel put his arms around me and kissed it away.

The sun was setting over Warsaw and threw a beautiful red glow across the whole city. Was Stefan out there somewhere watching the sunset, too?

Damn! Why was I thinking about him again? Daniel would be here in a moment, and my head was full of a boy who I knew nothing about. Not even his real name.

If I told him what had happened, Daniel would be glad that my life had been saved. But then he would ask me again to stop smuggling, and I'd say that that wasn't possible, and we would spend most of our precious time arguing. It wasn't worth it.

It would be better if I didn't mention being on the other side today. But then I might have to lie to Daniel for the first time ever. All because of a silly kiss.

"You're lost in thought."

I was startled and jumped. I hadn't noticed Daniel climbing through the skylight. He slid down the tiles and joined me. I stood up.

"Has something happened?" Daniel asked, and put his arms around me.

Go on, Mira! Tell him.

"No, everything is fine."

Oh, well done, Mira!

"Are you sure?" Daniel asked. He wasn't suspicious; he was sensitive and knew me well.

"Hannah kissed an older boy," I said quickly.

He laughed.

"It's not funny!" I said. I wanted to protect my sister's innocence, and he wasn't taking me seriously.

"It really is." He smiled.

"No, it's really not!"

"Don't worry. That sort of thing happens in the orphanage all the time. It doesn't mean anything."

He was trying to soothe me, as if I were one of the children he looked after. He spoke with a certain tone of voice that I found annoying.

"And apart from that," he said, "girls are always a bit faster than boys."

Except for us, I thought.

My friend Ruth had lost her innocence at the age of fourteen, but it was a step I was not ready for just yet. I didn't even know if Daniel was a virgin. And I'd never asked him about his previous girlfriends—I'd have been far too jealous. Selfish me wanted to be his first one.

It was starting to get dark; the moon was only a small crescent in the sky—there had been a new moon three days ago.

Daniel kissed my cheek. This was usually the start of a real kiss.

Daniel kissed my lips gently, lovingly. Not as wildly as Stefan had. But because I was thinking about Stefan, I couldn't return Daniel's kiss properly. Daniel looked at me with his beautiful eyes and asked, "Is Hannah the only thing that's upsetting you?"

After our kiss had gone wrong, it was even harder for me to tell him what had happened. What was I supposed to do when he asked me what that other kiss was like? I could hardly say, "More passionate than yours!"

I had to make sure that kissing Daniel was the best thing in the world. So I cupped my hands around his face, pulled him toward me, and kissed him as wildly and passionately as I could. More fiercely than I'd kissed Stefan. In other words, I made a complete fool of myself. Daniel couldn't keep up with all my passion, and we let go of each other. He laughed awkwardly. "Sometimes you are a real surprise!"

"Is that good or bad?" I asked.

"It's good," he grinned. "I love surprises."

He took me back into his arms and started to kiss me again. His hair tickled my nose, and I scratched it nervously until my hand got in the way and Daniel gave up trying to kiss me.

Daniel and I weren't going to work, until I told him about Stefan.

"Someone . . . ," I started to say.

But then we heard a car.

We were both quiet at once. Jews weren't allowed to drive cars. So it must be the Germans.

We could see all the way down Sienna Street from the roof. A car stopped in front of the building across the street.

Daniel and I lay down in case a German happened to look

up in our direction. I grabbed Daniel's hand. Unlike mine, it felt cool and dry.

While the chauffeur remained in the car, four men got out. One SS man, two soldiers, and a Jewish policeman. The policeman was wearing a blue coat and a black belt. It could have been a brown coat with a brown belt or a black one with a white belt. There was no such thing as a standard uniform for the Jewish police. The Nazis didn't give their underlings uniforms. They had to acquire them somehow, including the mandatory peaked cap with the Star of David. The Jewish policemen got to wear an extra star beside the armband, marking them as Jews who were two times better than the rest of us—or twice as mean.

The policeman approached the entrance of house number four. He was carrying a truncheon. Of course, the Germans didn't let their subhuman accomplices carry guns, either. But the traitors used their truncheons to attack their own people as brutally as they could whenever they carried out the occupiers' orders.

That Jewish policeman could be my brother, for all I knew. I was too far away and the light from the street was too dim. I hoped it wasn't Simon. It was one thing to know that your brother was a pig, but it would be something else to watch him arresting someone for the Germans.

As the men disappeared into the house, Daniel whispered, "It's not your brother."

He knew what I was worried about.

We stared at the house. It had to be awful for the people living there. Their only hope was that the soldiers charging up the stairs would rip open a neighbor's door instead of their own. Somebody was in for it.

Lights went on in a flat on the third floor, and we could see through the window that the soldiers had broken down the door. A little boy hid behind his mother while the SS man pointed his gun at a man's head. He was about fifty years old, wearing an undershirt. The Jewish policeman grabbed him and didn't miss the opportunity to hit him with the truncheon. Although this was awful to watch, I felt a tiny bit relieved: in the lit-up flat I could see that the policeman was not my brother. Barefoot, in his undershirt, the prisoner was dragged out of the flat.

His wife pleaded with the SS man, who nodded after a few moments. Then she followed the men out, taking her child with her. I couldn't understand what she was doing. The men had been after her husband, not her.

"She wants to go with them to Pawiak prison," Daniel whispered, "so she can find out what's going to happen to him."

"Who is he?" I whispered back. The lights stayed on in the empty flat.

"Moshe Goldberg, head of the barbers' union, and one of the leaders of the Bund."

The Bund was a forbidden organization of socialist Jews. They organized soup kitchens and secret schools and printed pamphlets against the Nazis. Papa had never liked the socialists and wanted nothing to do with them. Goldberg was pushed into the street and ended up under a streetlight. He appeared stoic. He didn't want to show any fear in front of his little boy, who was being carried by the mother.

The soldiers would force him into the car in a moment. The chauffeur flicked his cigarette away, looking bored. If Goldberg's family were to fit into the car, too, the mother would have to put the child on her lap.

The SS man went up to the prisoner and gave him an order. A look of sheer horror spread across Goldberg's face.

Beside me, Daniel gasped; he seemed to understand what was going on, while I didn't have a clue. "Oh, God!"

Daniel could still believe in God, despite everything.

I envied Daniel so many things: his selflessness, his decent character, but the fact that he believed in God was what I envied the most. It must be so nice to find comfort in a higher being.

My comfort in this life came from Daniel. I believed in him. I clutched his hand. It was damp now, too.

Goldberg turned around.

Daniel hissed, "Mira, shut your eyes."

But I was too slow; I didn't understand. The soldiers took aim and fired. The bullets hit Goldberg in the back and he collapsed on the curb.

I bit my tongue to stop myself from screaming and held Daniel's hand so tight that I almost crushed his fingers.

Goldberg's wife screamed. The child started to cry. The SS man took his gun and shot them both in the head.

I bit my tongue so hard, I could taste blood. I cried silently and writhed in pain and anguish.

Daniel put his arms around me and held on. I think he wanted me to believe that everything was just a bad dream. And I wanted to believe it, too. I really did. We could hear more shots in the distance. This wasn't a bad dream. The SS man Jurek had talked to had been telling the truth: Our "peaceful" life was over.

7

"Sausages!" the street seller with the grimy beard shouted. "Sausages with mustard!" At the sight of those sausages, my mouth started to water, despite the fact that they were small and shriveled and the seller was using his fingers to spread them with mustard, instead of a knife!

Together, Daniel and I wandered through the summer heat from one food cart to the next. For a small sum you could buy beans, soup, potato patties, or those sausages covered with filthy-fingers mustard. My stomach rumbled loudly. But by now I couldn't even afford the puniest sausage. In the nine weeks since the "Night of Blood," as it had come to be known in the ghetto, I hadn't ventured over to the Polish side once because the SS had started to hunt the smugglers in earnest, as well as the underground activists. To emphasize their new brutal course of action, the Germans now drove a truck into the ghetto each morning and threw the bodies onto the street—the people they had caught on the other side of the ghetto wall the day before. The bodies were a warning.

No one was allowed into the graveyard without a permit now, and because I couldn't afford any forged papers, there was no chance of me even getting a foot inside the gates, let alone through the hole in the wall over to the Polish side. Trying to climb over the wall in any other place was pure suicide these days. If you got anywhere near the wall, the Germans started shooting. We knew SS soldiers sometimes hid ready to jump out and mow down the smugglers with their machine guns. Frankenstein was said to have shot more than three hundred people so far, single-handed. Like most of the rumors in the ghetto, the number was probably exaggerated, but what if he had "only" murdered seventy or eighty people. If a single German monster could kill so many smugglers—or people he suspected might be smugglers—on his own, how many would have been murdered so far by all the guards patrolling the wall? Two hundred? Three hundred? More than a thousand, maybe?

All this didn't exactly encourage me to risk anything new.

But still.

My stomach was rumbling, and my family had practically nothing left to eat.

"I'll have to risk it," I said to Daniel, and sounded far more determined than I actually felt.

Of course my boyfriend knew what I meant when I said "risk it." We'd talked about it thousands of times; there was nothing else left to talk about these days, but we'd talked ourselves out. Which is why he didn't repeat any of his endless arguments to try to dissuade me. I'd heard them all many times before. He didn't warn me that they had started shooting corrupt Jewish policemen, or tell me that last week they'd even killed two women who were pregnant. He just looked at me and hoped that I wouldn't do anything.

"It's easy for you," I said bitterly. "Korczak looks after you. You get fed on a regular basis."

"It isn't much," he answered quietly.

A man beside me took a bite of sausage and clearly enjoyed it. The sight of him made me even more hungry and cross, which is why I snapped at Daniel.

"But at least you get something to eat!"

I was sorry right away. I was well aware that there wasn't enough food at the orphanage to go around.

It's not a good idea to pick a fight when you are starving and you are surrounded by the smell of food. I got a grip and explained things more calmly. "I can only afford the cheapest bread," I said, and showed him the gray loaf I had just bought. "It's just chalk and sawdust; there's hardly any real flour in it at all."

"If you get yourself shot, you won't be able to buy any kind of bread," Daniel said. He seemed to be immune to all the smells of food around us. Being an orphan, he had been used to doing without from an early age and could cope with hunger far better than me, a poor, spoiled doctor's daughter. Why couldn't I be as strong and steadfast as he was? Of course he was right: If I died, things would be even worse for Hannah and Mama. But if I didn't do anything, my family was going to starve to death. When all my money was spent—and that would be by next week at the very latest—we wouldn't even be able to buy the sawdust loaves of bread. What was I supposed to do then?

"Anyway," Daniel started to tease me, "if you go and get yourself killed, I will murder you!"

I had to laugh at that. "You do have a strange way of saying you love me," I said.

"At least I do say so." Straightaway, Daniel tried to cover up the small reproach he'd just let slip by laughing. He was right. I hadn't ever said the weighty words "I love you." Precisely because my mother had shown me just how damaging love can be.

Ever since we started going out together, Daniel had been waiting patiently for some kind of commitment from me. Slowly, my silence seemed to be getting to him.

And it was mean of me. What would it cost me to say "I love you." Just three little words. Daniel was my anchor, after all. Without him I'd have lost my way ages ago.

Tell him now. I took a deep breath, as if I were on the verge of diving into deep water, and said as I let my breath out again, "You know I . . ."

I didn't get any further, though, because—silly me—I couldn't do it.

"You . . . ?" Daniel asked

I was searching for the right words. Why on earth was this so difficult?

"I . . ."

"Thief, thief!" Suddenly we were interrupted by a woman shouting.

A skinny little girl no more than seven or eight years old ran past us. She was wearing a hat that was far too big, a once-white, now very grubby man's shirt, and no trousers. And no underwear, as we could plainly see when the shirt flew up as she ran past, revealing her little bare behind. She was holding an open jar filled with jam. And she dodged through the crowds as fast as she could. The girl was being chased by an old woman in a tattered skirt. I noticed that though she was missing two fingers on her right hand, she had more fingers than teeth!

The girl looked over her shoulder to watch out for the old woman and bumped into the legs of a passerby who started shouting at her. She should be more careful, damn it! He'd string her up from a lamppost if it weren't such a waste of good rope. The old woman managed to catch up. The girl tried to pull away, taking a couple of panicky steps, but the old woman had grabbed hold of the end of her shirt and she lost her balance, stumbled and fell over, jar in hand. All the jam slopped onto the street.

The girl got down on all fours and started to gobble it up like a dog.

I watched the little thief and wondered what I would end up doing once all my money was gone. If I got as hungry as the girl, would I steal from someone? Eat from the filthy street?

Would Hannah?

Could she turn into such an animal?

I imagined my sister on all fours, and shivered in the summer heat.

Daniel put an arm around me and said softly, "You'll never be that desperate."

He knew me inside and out. "No, I won't," I replied. "And Hannah won't be either!" And all at once I was certain; the sight of the girl turned street mongrel had finally convinced me that I had to act to spare my sister such a fate.

I would have to start smuggling again. But not like before. I'd be more cunning this time. And more importantly: I needed help.

Daniel mustn't know anything about this. I didn't want him worrying about me, and I didn't want to argue about it, not even for a second.

"I know that look," Daniel said.

"Which look?"

"The one that tells me you are going to do something really risky."

"I'm not going to do anything," I lied.

"Promise?"

"Promise."

He didn't believe me.

"At the orphanage," he said, smiling, "I always check to make sure the children haven't crossed their fingers behind their backs when they promise anything."

"I'm not a child!"

"Sometimes you are."

There were moments when I hated the way he pretended to be years older than me instead of only seven months.

"If you call me a child one more time, I'll go home right away."

"All right, then," he said. "I want you to stay. But do you promise?"

He looked at me closely.

"Of course I do," I said with a firm voice. I even gave him a little innocent smile to make it all the more convincing.

Daniel hesitated, then he nodded. He'd decided to trust me. Sometimes, of the two of us, he was the naive child. Which made him all the more lovable.

"I must get back to the orphanage and help with lunch," he said, but he didn't want to leave just yet. I gave him a soft little kiss on the lips, so that he would be able to drag himself away. And he smiled, said goodbye by kissing me back, and walked off placated and convinced that I was on my way home to my family in Miła Street. But I was on my way to look for Ruth. At the infamous Britannia Hotel.

8

Even in broad daylight, the neon sign was lit up in red lights. The letter *H* for *Hotel* flickered on and off. A burly bouncer stood beneath the *H*. He wore a long trench coat, despite the summer weather, trying to look like a tough gangster. But he was just a simple thug who had to follow the real ghetto bosses' orders—men Ruth went to bed with every night. It was the bouncer's job to make sure not everyone got into the bar-slash-brothel. Only people with a lot of money who were prepared to spend it on booze and women were allowed inside. And people like me, I hoped, who had a friend who worked there.

I walked straight up to him and said, "Good afternoon, I'm Ruth's friend."

The bouncer pretended not to notice me.

That wasn't quite the reaction I had been hoping for. "I want to see her," I said.

"And pigs might fly."

A bouncer and comedian. A rare combination. Not a good one.

"Ruth is expecting me," I lied.

The guy treated me like I wasn't there and stared past me toward two SS soldiers who were walking along the other side of the street. They had shouldered their guns and were eating ice cream.

I caught my breath. Even though the Germans were concentrating on their ice cream and not taking any notice of us, I was still afraid of them.

I was no Rubinstein who could laugh at them in the face. No one was a real Rubinstein except for Rubinstein.

The bouncer nodded at the soldiers. They nodded back, bored. This simple exchange of greeting was no surprise to me. The Germans got a portion of the winnings from the Jewish racketeers, and of course the soldiers went to the brothel, too. They might be the "master race" but they could still screw a Jew. Did that mean that Ruth did it with Germans, too . . . ?

. . . I didn't want to know.

Although the bouncer made an effort to appear relaxed, I could see the fear in his eyes. Since the "Night of Blood," SS patrols shot Jews for no reason whatsoever. Just for fun. The gangsters were no exception. Neither were children. Only yesterday, three children had been murdered in front of the Bersohn und Bauman hospital. One of the women from Kraków had told me—oh yes, things had got so bad that our devout flatmates had actually started talking to the likes of me. They were scared. The children had just been sitting in front of the hospital, and then the SS men had shot all three of them out of the blue. When I heard this, all I wanted was to keep Hannah locked away in our hovel in Miła Street forever.

When the soldiers moved on, the bouncer released a silent but perceptible breath. I realized that his fear was my chance. I took a step toward him and drew myself up to my full height—I only just reached his chin—looked up at him and grinned. "You know how Rubinstein gets his food?"

I managed to catch his attention. So much so that he stopped ignoring me, and said, "Of course I do—what are you talking about?"

"I could start shouting that Hitler should be shot," I said, grinning broadly. "Or that he is making love to his dog."

"You . . . you wouldn't do that!" The fear was back in his eyes.

"I was Rubinstein's apprentice," I laughed, and took a few wild leaps into the street just like the ghetto clown.

The bouncer had no idea what to make of me.

I landed back in front of his feet and laughed at him, "All the same."

My performance wasn't very convincing, but it didn't have to be. It was good enough. The guy didn't want to take any risks.

"So," he asked cautiously, "is Ruth really a friend of yours?"

"That's why I said so."

"Oh well, it can't do any harm to visit a friend."

"No, it can't," I smiled.

I went past him, up the couple of steps, and entered the Britannia Hotel.

9

I walked past an unattended cloakroom and went through a heavy red velvet curtain into the dimly lit bar area. Apparently, daylight was not wanted here. The atmosphere was smoky and the furniture was pretty shabby considering the amount of money customers spent here. One of the three chandeliers hung crooked from the ceiling, the top of the wooden bar was cracked and splintered, and the tablecloths were so dirty they appeared not to have been changed since before the war. But the men who were drinking vodka at this time of the afternoon hadn't come for the decor. They were here for the young women who were paid to flirt and drink with them. The Britannia girls were really beautiful; none of them were gaunt and hungry like I was. They had womanly curves, and, of course, they were wearing makeup. Most of them were definitely wearing too much makeup, but one redhead sitting at a table not far from the entrance had an elegant shade of red lipstick and rouge. I'd have loved makeup like that, but there was no way I'd ever be able to afford that kind of luxury. I'd have felt jealous if she'd been wearing more than a negligee and black frilly panties, and if she hadn't been in the process of being groped by a man with flabby hands who was kneading her breasts like wads of dough.

Instead of making me feel claustrophobic, the sorid atmosphere lifted my spirits. A female singer, accompanied by a bored-looking pianist, sang in a smoky voice:

Night and day, you are the one, only you beneath the moon or under the sun . . .

American music!

It was forbidden everywhere, but they were playing it here. The music transported me out of the Britannia Hotel, out of the ghetto, out of Poland. Away from war, hunger, and suffering. Across the Atlantic to New York.

In my fantasy, I was dancing down Broadway with Daniel, whirling down the street, like Fred Astaire and Ginger Rogers in the musicals. It didn't matter that I couldn't dance in real life, had never learned how, and would probably fall over my own two feet if I tried. But then I remembered the argument a few moments ago and realized that Daniel wouldn't want to dance with me on Broadway or anywhere else if he found out that I was in the Britannia Hotel at this very moment. All at once, the imaginary dancer turned into Stefan.

I think of you day and night, night and day . . .

I kept telling myself to stop thinking about Stefan, but it never worked. He kept coming to mind all the time, and there was nothing I could do about it. It wasn't fair to Daniel. I tried to order dancing Stefan to turn back into Daniel, but he refused.

The singer stopped singing and the pianist played the final chords of the song, but my daydream wasn't over yet. I was lying in Stefan's arms.

With all my might, I pushed Stefan away and ran to Daniel,

who was wearing normal clothes now, standing in front of a cinema on Broadway where *City Lights* was showing. I hugged Daniel as tightly as I could. Not just because I felt guilty, but because he was my only hope. He was my life; he was the one I loved. And I said the words I couldn't ever say in real life, because I was ashamed of myself and because they were true, "I love you!"

"You're lost in thought, Mira." Someone laughed beside me as the piano player started to play "I Get a Kick Out of You." Ruth stood beside me, wearing a pink negligee, black fishnet stockings, a black suspender belt, and so much makeup that she looked older than sixteen. What the heck. Hardly anyone ever looked younger than they really were in the ghetto.

"But the question is," Ruth said, still laughing, "what on earth are you doing here?"

As I slowly came to, she nodded at a waiter who was whistling along to "I Get a Kick Out of You." He immediately poured her a glass of champagne. Or was it just cheap sparkling wine? I knew absolutely nothing about drinking. Apart from a glass of red wine at Passover, I'd never drunk any alcohol. Whatever she was drinking, it wasn't her first glass this afternoon, judging by her breath and the rather delirious tone of her laughter. "Mira, you aren't looking for work here, are—?"

"God, no!" I interrupted her before she could finish asking. It was too awful to contemplate.

"Good! Because you are too ugly, you know."

"Thanks a lot," I replied.

"So what do you want?" Ruth asked, and sipped her drink.

"I want to join a smugglers' gang!"

Ruth choked on her champagne.

While she coughed away, I asked, "Can't you introduce me to someone who can help?"

She raised an eyebrow.

"Please. For friendship's sake?" I asked, just in case.

I was the only person from the old days who still spoke to her. She didn't want to lose me as a friend. So she replied:

"For friendship's sake."

10

Shmuel Asher's mustache was so thick, a dozen mice could have hidden in it. His face was covered in scars. He was a powerful man, and it was safe to assume that the men who had inflicted those scars ended up looking far worse once he'd finished with them. If they had lived.

Asher was the leader of a group of crooks and thieves called Chompe, and Ruth was his favorite whore. In fact, he was said to truly love her. She'd told me this, bursting with pride, and I'd felt awful. She was so gullible. It was well known that Asher and many other men preferred underage girls.

I was in no danger of being a girl Asher might fancy. I was too bony. We sat at a table in a corner of the bar. Asher had his back to the wall like some desperado in a western who worried someone would shoot him from behind.

The singer was drinking at the bar while the piano man tinkled the keys softly and Ruth slid up and down Asher's lap, pressing her cheek to his. The huge man ignored her attentions and asked me: "How could you possibly be of any use to me?"

"I'm an experienced smuggler," I said, trying to sound confident.

"What sort of experience?"

Ruth suddenly stared at me. If I told Asher about the graveyard, he would know that she had betrayed one of his smuggling routes to me.

Her fear was contagious. I touched the tablecloth. My fingers stroked the little burns in the fabric and touched crumbs of food. I managed to calm down a bit.

"I climb over the wall," I lied. I'd never climbed over the wall in my life.

Ruth was relieved I hadn't given her away.

She smooched Asher's face as he stared at me. "Where do you climb over?"

"Usually at Stawki Street, not far from Pokorna Street," I lied some more.

"There are less dangerous places."

"There aren't any safe places," I said.

"The safe places are where we have bribed the guards," he grinned.

"You bribe the guards and I can't smuggle on my own anymore—that's why I want to join you," I said. This part was true.

"It's pretty brave to walk in here and demand to be a member of my gang."

There was no way I could tell from his expression or the tone of his voice whether he was impressed by my boldness or offended by my behavior.

"We could use someone new. I've lost a few men in the past couple of weeks."

He said a few, but I knew that he meant he'd lost many men.

So this increased my chances of getting work. But it also worried me—in fact, it really scared me. It wasn't even possible for the members of the infamous Chompe gang to survive as smugglers these days.

"But tell me," Shmuel asked as the waiter brought him a cup of thick, tarry coffee. "Why should I choose you of all people to join my gang?"

"Because it'll pay off," I replied.

"A lot of people say that," he said. "Give me another reason."

I tried to think of one. What could I offer the king of thieves?

"Because . . . ," I stammered.

"Because?" he asked, and I was at a loss for words.

"Because," Ruth spoke up all of a sudden, and stroked Asher's cheek, "I'll be especially nice to you."

"You have to be anyway," he replied.

"But it's even better when I love you."

That convinced Asher. He and Ruth seemed to have something else in mind when they used the word *love* than I did. He beamed at Ruth, took a sip of his coffee, and said, "Welcome to the Chompe gang!"

"Thank you!" I said. I looked at him briefly and then turned to Ruth. She was the one I was really thanking.

"You can start tonight," Asher said. "At four thirty a.m. At the corner of Zimna Street and Żelazna Street."

Tonight?

It was sooner than I had expected. Or wanted. I would have to climb over the wall in just a few hours' time. And try not to get killed in the process.

‖

'd entered the Britannia Hotel a starving girl, I walked out a starving member of a gang. The bouncer looked at me skeptically but thought it safer not to speak to me again. And he was clearly relieved to see me leave without any more Rubinstein antics.

The sun blinded me and it took a few moments for my eyes to adjust to the daylight. Now I could start to relax, more or less—even the stench of the ghetto air seemed fresh in comparison to the smoky atmosphere of the bar. And I suddenly realized: Asher hadn't told me what I was supposed to smuggle. Or the names of the men I would meet at the wall.

For a moment, I thought about going back to find out more details. But Asher wasn't the sort of person I wanted to annoy. So I decided to take my sawdust bread and head home. Though not just yet.

Whenever I had the chance, I took a detour through the book market. I enjoyed losing myself in the boxes and suitcases of books for sale: works by the likes of Thomas Mann, Sigmund

Freud, Karl Marx, or Erich Kästner, all authors forbidden by the Nazis. And better yet, there were even books in English. I'd been able to teach myself some English using books, in case I ever got to America.

I'd started with picture books like *Snow White*, *Little Red Riding Hood*, and *Winnie-the-Pooh*. But by now, I could read whole detective novels. My favorites were the Lord Peter Wimsey detective novels by Dorothy L. Sayers, even if she could only transport me as far as England in my mind and not all the way to New York.

I stopped when I came to a large trunk leaning against the curb. It looked as if it had traveled the world more times than I ever would, as far as I could tell from all the travel stickers from overseas stuck to its sides. The trunk was full of English-language books. And it belonged to a skinny man with a thin, wispy beard and bleak eyes. I rummaged through, and amid all the highbrow titles that I wouldn't have understood even if they'd been in Polish, I found a Lord Peter Wimsey novel called *Murder Must Advertise*.

Now all I had to do was bargain well enough to get the book for free. My chances weren't all that bad. Books were one of the few goods in the ghetto that got cheaper by the day. I looked at the bookseller. This man probably hadn't managed to sell a single book so far today. And he was bound to be hungry, just like everyone else. I showed him the book. "I'll give you a piece of bread for it," I said. The man was far too weak to bargain. He fingered his beard and nodded. I was just about to pull the loaf of bread out of my bag and break off a bit when I saw Stefan.

He was hurrying along the sidewalk past the bookseller and didn't look in our direction. For a second, I thought my eyes were playing tricks on me. But by then he had already turned the corner and disappeared into a side street. I quickly stuffed the bread back into the bag, pushed my way past the seller, and ignored him when he said, "—What about a piece of your bread?" I followed Stefan.

Stefan had reached the end of the street and disappeared round the corner. Wherever he was headed, he was in a hurry. I started to run but couldn't call out. Stefan wasn't even his real name. And I was afraid that I'd make him run away. I knew practically nothing about him, but I had a feeling that he was acting illegally.

I charged round the next corner without calling and found myself trapped in a narrow, empty lane. It was blocked at one end by the fence that sealed off the Jewish cemetery. Stefan was nowhere to be seen. Did he go over the fence?

I ran to the end of the lane and stared through the mesh, but I couldn't see anyone in the graveyard. I thought about climbing the fence. But then I'd risk getting caught by the Germans without a pass. I wanted to see Stefan, but I didn't want to risk my neck for the sake of a meeting. It was bad enough having to climb over the wall later tonight. Damn! What had I got myself into? The thought of climbing over all the broken glass and barbed wire made me sick.

After I looked through the fence again, I gave up and walked back down the lane. I kept turning round, hoping to see him. But it didn't happen. I started to think that he hadn't climbed the fence at all. So where did he go?

I stopped, realizing I was really thirsty. My new boss hadn't offered me anything at the Britannia Hotel. A glass of water would be good right now. Or apple juice—imagine that! The taste of fruit and water all mixed together would be heaven. The only kind of heaven I could imagine these days.

I looked at the ghetto buildings around me. They were totally dilapidated in this section, even worse than in the rest of the ghetto. Practically all the windowpanes were broken. So many walls were crumbling, and one house had lost its roof. The German tanks had done excellent work.

I noticed an open door leading into a derelict house that looked ready to collapse sometime soon. Could Stefan have gone in there?

The vestibule stank; there appeared to be people living on the stairs. If one could call that living.

There was a haggard man lying on the first landing, staring into space. He looked ancient, but he probably wasn't even forty. He didn't notice me; there was no point in trying to ask him if he had seen a blond guy running past. Whatever his empty eyes could see, it wasn't in our world.

I went farther up the stairs, past more hollow-eyed people. Although the stink of human waste made me feel sick, I couldn't stop looking for Stefan just yet. For nine weeks, I'd imagined what it would be like to see him again—and been troubled by a guilty conscience because of Daniel. No way was I going to go home without being sure I'd done everything to find him.

On the first floor, there were three flats. Should I just knock and then, if someone answered, ask if there was a blond young man living there?

One of the doors was open a crack; the lock was broken. Probably some gang of thieves had broken in some time ago. Although what could they have been hoping to find here?

I opened the door with a gentle nudge. The flat didn't smell terrible. It just smelled musty.

It appeared empty—no furniture, just broken floorboards and gray wallpaper with a faded flower pattern. Should I go in?

Or should I get home, find something to drink, then get annoyed about finding Stefan only to lose him again? And then worry about what awaited me on the wall with the Chompe gang tonight.

I went.

I didn't hear anything. No footsteps, no sounds of rustling. If anyone was inside perhaps they were asleep.

I opened the first door along the hall and went into an almost empty room. This was where the kitchen would have been in a flat like this, back in the days when only one family had lived here. But this room had no oven anymore, no kitchen cupboards, no plates and dishes. Instead, an old-fashioned printing press stood in the middle of the floor. Piles of newspapers were lying on the floor beside it. Although *newspaper* was too grand a word. These eight-page pamphlets were copies of an underground newspaper simply called *News*. There were all sorts of illegal pamphlets circulating throughout the ghetto, and this was one.

I noticed a commentary on page two: "The Warsaw Ghetto lives in constant danger of being liquidated. All energy must be focused on the great deed we need to perform and which we will perform. We must conduct ourselves in the spirit of Masada!"

Masada was a fortress in Palestine where ages ago a few Jews had resisted the siege of over four thousand Roman legionaries for months. When the Romans, who had suffered countless losses due to the resistance of the Jews, finally stormed the fortress, there was dead silence in Masada. All the residents had killed themselves. Warriors, women, and children.

The spirit of Masada—were the ghetto Jews supposed to fight against the Germans and then kill themselves? "Resistance unto death" didn't sound like an option to me.

"What are you doing?" someone shouted behind me.

I jumped, hoping desperately that the voice was Stefan's, even if it didn't sound anything like him. I turned round slowly. A skinny young man was standing in the doorway leading to the hall. His brown hair was cut exceptionally short, and his eyes were bloodshot. I might have wondered why they were so red if he hadn't been holding a knife.

"I just asked you a question," he snarled. He moved toward me, thrusting the knife through the air like a madman. He didn't look as if he knew what he was doing with it, but he seemed determined to use it.

"I . . . I," I stuttered. What on earth could I say? That I was looking for someone called Stefan although that wasn't his real name, and that I didn't know if he had anything to do with the underground newspaper?

"Answer me!"

This guy shook the knife in front of my face. He probably thought that I was spying for the Germans. Desperately, I tried to think what I could possibly say to make him change his mind.

"Tell me! Tell me, or I'll stab you to death!"

Each time he jabbed the knife at me, he seemed more violent. But somehow he didn't seem 100 percent sure that he was going to kill me. Not yet.

"I'm not a collaborator," I answered. My voice trembled and I started to shake.

"I don't believe you. Why else would you be here except to sniff around for the Germans?"

I was so scared that I couldn't think of any answer except the plain stupid truth: "I was looking for a boy who kissed me."

My attacker was so surprised that he stopped waving the knife for a moment.

"It's true!"

He scowled even more. He didn't believe a word I said. I wouldn't have, either, if I'd been him.

"Do you think I'm an idiot?" he yelled. His face had turned dark red with anger. The veins on his neck were throbbing. The knife! All of a sudden he was holding the knife steady in his hand. No more waving it about. He was ready to stab me now. To murder me. Telling the truth was the worst idea.

"I'll kill you!"

My eyes filled up with tears. "Please don't," I pleaded.

Through my tears, I saw him raise the knife.

I panicked and charged at him, pushing him away as hard as I could. He stumbled against the wall, but managed to keep his balance. He swore in Hebrew, which I couldn't understand. Unlike most of the Jewish children in the ghetto, I'd never learned Hebrew. I spoke Polish and my beloved English.

I tried to push past him toward the door. But just at that moment he stabbed me in the top of my right arm. The blade plunged into my flesh and I screamed.

The pain stunned me. I should have run for my life, but I was frozen, staring at my arm as the blood stained the sleeve of my white blouse in a matter of seconds.

I had never had a wound like this before in all my life. It hurt so much. I thought I was going to die.

I was crying and shaking, and I couldn't see anything properly because I was blinded by my tears. My attacker was grunting like an animal, and I could tell that he was going to stab me again. And again and again. I wouldn't be able to stop him.

"Zacharia!" someone shouted.

Was that Stefan's voice?

"Zacharia, what on earth is going on?"

My assailant backed off. "She's working for the Germans," he snarled.

Relieved, I sank to the ground and cradled my arm. Now Stefan would be able to explain that I wasn't a threat, that I was just a little smuggler.

But Stefan's voice sounded grim. "Are you sure?"

"No!" I wanted to scream, but all I could do was gasp. My voice failed in despair.

"Why else is she here?" Zacharia snapped.

"I'll deal with this," Stefan said in a commanding tone. "You can go." Zacharia obeyed. Reluctantly, but he obeyed. Whatever sort of underground organization this was, Stefan was obviously further up the hierarchy than my attacker was.

"Where were you, anyway?" Zacharia asked, and I heard the anger in his voice. He waited. He obviously didn't like being ordered around like this.

"In the cellar."

That was enough to shut Zacharia up.

Stefan held out a hand for the knife. Zacharia gave it to him and then left the kitchen.

Stefan turned toward me, holding the knife that was stained with my blood.

I tried to stand up. I didn't want to be a whimpering wreck lying on the floor in front of him.

"What are you doing here, Lenka?" he asked.

He'd remembered the name he made up for me at the Polish market. Nine weeks ago!

At any other time, I'd have been so pleased. But his voice was cold, and he was the one threatening me with the knife now. His hand was steady, which made me think that he knew how to use it better than Zacharia did.

His blue eyes seemed to pierce right through me. They were bloodshot, just like Zacharia's. Why was that? At any rate there was no warmth there. Just coldness.

To think that I'd been so enchanted by this guy that I'd chosen to dance down Broadway with him in my dreams instead of Daniel. I felt so ashamed that I forgot the pain in my arm for a moment.

"Am I going to get an answer or not?" Stefan asked. He was holding the knife steady, pointing in my direction.

That was far more menacing than any thrashing about.

"I saw you at the book market and followed you."

"Why?"

"Because . . . ," I answered, but I felt so ashamed. I didn't want to say any more.

". . . I wanted to see you again."

If he was even the tiniest bit flattered, it didn't show.

Of course he wasn't flattered. It was so stupid to keep thinking or hoping stuff like that. Totally childish! I was nowhere near as grown-up as I liked to think.

"You wanted to see me again?" Stefan asked, sounding surprised and suspicious at the same time.

"To say thank you."

He wasn't convinced.

"And instead of saying thank you, you discover our printing press?"

"I saw you at the book market and followed you, but you disappeared."

"So then you stumbled across this house instead?"

"Yes."

"What a coincidence!"

"Yes," I said weakly.

He twisted the knife in his hand. He didn't know what to make of any of this.

"Why would I lie?" I asked. "You know I'm a smuggler."

"Oh, and smugglers never work for the Germans, do they?" he laughed bitterly. "You wouldn't be the first person to be turned in a German prison," he said bitingly. As if he had been betrayed by a smuggler that way before.

"It's the truth," I said. "Should I have lied and made up a better story to convince you?"

He didn't say anything.

Was the man who had saved my life with a kiss going to kill me any moment so I wouldn't reveal the hidden printing press to the Germans? After a while he nodded. He'd made up his mind, but which way?

"A collaborator would have a better story ready," he said, and put the knife back in the pocket of his gray suit. His features softened, and he smiled as if nothing had happened.

"I'll get some disinfectant and treat your wound," he said.

"That would be nice," I answered. I was so relieved that I could have burst into tears. My eyes welled up, but I pulled myself together. I wasn't going to be that pathetic.

Before he left the kitchen he turned around and threatened me again. "If you disappear, I'll be less inclined to believe you and I'll follow you."

But his voice was more friendly than it had been when he was interrogating me. He didn't really think I was going anywhere.

"You could follow the trail of blood," I said, grimacing. Now that the immediate danger was gone, I felt the pain again.

He smiled at that, but then he looked at my arm and his face grew serious. My sleeve was soaked through completely.

Stefan hurried out of the kitchen, and as I listened to his footsteps disappearing down the hall, I started to feel frightened. My wound was bleeding so badly, and I was afraid that Zacharia might come back. I felt totally vulnerable.

But Zacharia didn't come back. He had probably disappeared into the mysterious cellar. That was one place I definitely should not ask Stefan about, if I didn't want to arouse any more suspicion.

Stefan came back into the kitchen with a little bottle, a clean cloth, and a needle and thread. His underground group was prepared for battle injuries.

We sat on the floor, he rolled up my bloody sleeve, and I suddenly realized how deep the knife had penetrated the flesh of my arm. I felt so faint looking at it that I nearly threw up.

"You were lucky," Stefan said.

"Lucky?" That was a strange way of putting it.

"Zacharia didn't damage any muscles."

Considering that then I really had been lucky.

"It will be better in a minute," Stefan smiled at me kindly. He was trying to keep me calm. Or maybe he just didn't want me to throw up all over his shoes.

He dribbled disinfectant into the wound. It burned terribly, and I gritted my teeth. Then he dabbed it with the cloth. Every dab burned as if he were holding a flame to my flesh.

"You're doing very well," he said.

"I wish I could say the same for you," I gasped.

Stefan grinned. He knew I was trying to be funny, not criticizing him.

"At least the cut is clean now, Lenka."

"My name is Mira."

"Then Lenka was a good guess—it's pretty close." He smiled.

"And what's your name?"

"Not Mira." He grinned, and threw the cloth away.

"Idiot," I said.

"No, that's not my name, either," he grinned some more.

"Moron!"

"Some people call me Jerk."

"I can't think why." I tried to smile.

"They can't have a clue about human nature," he said with a glint in his eye. He picked up the needle and thread and said, "I'll tell you my name, but you'll have to be brave first."

"My father used to give me sweets for being brave," I said.

"I haven't got any sweets, but I've got some apple juice if that's any good."

Apple juice? Oh wow!

"I'll take the juice and do without your name," I said as he threaded the needle.

"Oh, you've really hurt me now," he replied, and pretended to look offended.

"If I start asking you questions about what's going on here, will you think I'm a collaborator again, or just nosy?"

He looked at me closely. "Just nosy," he said, and stuck the needle into my skin.

The pain was awful.

Even if he'd sewn a wound or two before, he wasn't a doctor by any means. He was heavy-handed to say the least.

"Well?" Stefan asked, and started on the second stitch.

I nearly shrieked with pain, but I gritted my teeth like I'd done when he'd used the disinfectant.

"You were going to ask me some questions." The needle went into my skin again. Questions . . . questions were good. Questions would distract me. The first one that shot into my dazed mind was "Can you dance?" In my mind's eye I saw Stefan twirling me around to the sounds of "Night and Day" again.

At least I had the sense not to actually ask this out loud. Stefan wasn't a dancer. My hero with the rose would have stabbed me to death if he'd thought I was a spy.

But I wanted him to be a dancer! It was ridiculous. *Mira, you're so pathetic. He's got both feet on the ground while your head is stuck in the clouds.*

"All these questions at once," Stefan was teasing me. "Is it that bad?"

Instead of answering I managed to ask a question at last: "Masada?"

"Masada?" He was surprised and stopped stitching up my arm for a moment.

I needed the break and pointed at the newspaper. "Fight to death?"

"That's right," he answered without hesitating. "The Germans are going to kill us all. No exceptions!"

I studied his face, his eyes. He really believed this.

"That is . . . that's crazy!" I said. Although the Germans had become even more high-handed since the "Night of Blood," the idea that they could kill all the Jews in the ghetto was unthinkable.

Stefan's blue eyes glistened with rage. He did the next stitch angrily.

I cried out in pain.

He relaxed a bit, but didn't apologize, and moved quickly to the next stitch. Thankfully, he was more careful this time. All he said was: "Chełmno."

Of course I'd heard about Chełmno. All the secret newspapers had written about it. In Chełmno, the Nazis were said to have locked Jews into a truck and suffocated them with exhaust fumes. Like most people, I was sure this was a made-up horror story, invented by someone with an imagination like Hannah's, but with a dark and warped mind.

Obviously, Stefan believed that the crazy story about Chełmno was true and not just a dark rumor. I decided not to start an argument.

"What's wrong with your eyes?" I asked instead.

"My eyes?"

"They are bloodshot. So are Zacharia's."

"We stayed up all night to set and print the paper. And we had no lights on, so we wouldn't get caught. We worked by the light of the moon."

Now he cut the thread. The ordeal was over, at last. I looked at his work. It wasn't pretty, but at least I wouldn't bleed to death. And the wound would heal over the next few days. The only thing was—I was going to have to climb over the wall with a damaged arm tonight.

"Let's get you some of that juice," Stefan said, and he was smiling at me again in his nice, cheeky way.

We scrambled back onto our feet. I was thrilled about the apple juice. I stopped thinking about Chełmno or the ghetto being destroyed, and forgot about the dangers I'd have to face tonight by the wall. All my worries were gone because of a bit of juice!

"It's in the next room," Stefan explained.

Just as we were about to leave the kitchen, a woman appeared at the door. She was at least twenty and had the austere, noble face of a queen. Even though she was even smaller than me, she had the aura of a leader who everyone would follow without question. Someone you don't argue with.

"Zacharia told me we had an unwelcome guest," she said stiffly, and looked at me as she spoke. I felt intimidated at once and stared at the floor.

"She's not a spy, Esther," Stefan said.

She kept on looking at me. She obviously had her doubts.

"We can't afford to make any mistakes, Amos."

Amos!

His name was Amos.

That was nicer than Stefan.

Much nicer.

"You know I'm always right," Amos was teasing her.

But Esther wasn't convinced.

"The kid's okay."

Kid! I didn't want him to call me a kid. It was bad enough that Daniel treated me like a child sometimes. Or when I acted like one.

"Well, why is she here, then?" Esther asked.

Now he would tell her that I'd run after him like an infatuated schoolgirl. And show her what a kid I really was. I felt deeply embarrassed in front of this woman who seemed so superior. And even more embarrassed in front of Amos.

"I'll tell you later," Amos said.

I was relieved for a moment.

But then he kissed this Esther person on the cheek.

They were a couple.

Oh, I didn't like that!

And I hated myself for minding.

The kiss didn't really seem to change Esther's mind. Her expression remained stern as she said, "I'm off to the cellar."

"Okay," Amos smiled, and kissed her on the lips this time.

I didn't like that at all.

Esther smiled. Even she couldn't resist Amos's charm completely, not even—or so I supposed—if she tried.

She left the flat, and then I followed Amos into the next room. There were numerous mattresses on the floor; it had to be where Amos, Esther, Zacharia, and all those other people from their group slept. Amos bent down and picked up an almost full bottle of apple juice. He gave it to me and I drank and drank and drank.

"You'll feel sick if you drink too fast," he warned me.

"Do I care?" I asked when I stopped drinking for half a second, to catch my breath.

"No?"

"Right."

He started laughing.

It felt good to make him laugh.

I drank the whole bottle. It was heavenly. Then I wiped my mouth with the back of my hand. And then I suddenly asked: "What's in the cellar?"

"Is that any of your business?"

"No?"

"Right."

Now it was my turn to laugh.

Amos was pleased that he'd made me laugh. He leaned against the windowsill. Behind him through the filthy panes, I saw the graveyard. Because of the dirt on the glass, it looked as if it was raining ashes.

"You should join us," Amos said all of a sudden. He was completely serious. He wanted me to be part of his life. That's the first thing I thought. But I was just being stupid again. This was about politics, not about me.

"I don't even know who you are exactly," I said doubtfully.

"We belong to Hashomer Hatzair."

I didn't know very much about politics, but even I had heard that much about the organization. "So, you all want to emigrate to Palestine," I said.

"This isn't about whether you want to live in Poland or in Palestine . . . ," he said.

"Or America," I added.

"Or America if you want. This is about how we're going to die."

"You really do believe that the Germans might kill us all?"

"Will, not might," he said.

"The only question is how you want to die."

"Would you rather be led to slaughter, or do you want to fight?"

"The last person to ask a question like that was a madman," I said.

"We'll all have to make that decision," he replied, "mad or not, it doesn't make any difference."

"And you've found an answer?"

"I was almost too late," he replied. He looked up at the grubby window toward the graveyard, as if he was ashamed. No, *ashamed* wasn't the right word. It was more like he felt guilty about something.

Even if I didn't exactly know what sort of person I wanted to be, or what sort of person Amos was, I did know that I wasn't going to waste my nights printing useless appeals to resist and fight, getting bloodshot eyes for my efforts. I was a smuggler, not a fighter.

"The ghetto is going to survive," I said. I was certain, but I was also trying to tell Amos that I didn't want to join his group.

He understood immediately and said, "Then you should go."

It was so abrupt and there wasn't a hint of sadness in his eyes this time, although we were going separate ways, presumably forever. He wanted me out of his life. That hurt. Far more than it should have. Though not enough to make me join his stupid group.

"And if you do decide to betray us, I'll find you," he said. He was threatening me again.

His hand slid into the pocket with the knife. I wasn't sure if it was a deliberate move or not.

I shivered.

"I'm not going to betray anybody," I said, and left him standing between all the mattresses. I didn't say goodbye. And I didn't look back. I wasn't going to look at this person who was ready to kill me, ever again.

12

The third person everyone in the ghetto knew apart from Rubinstein and Korczak, the one everyone despised, was a man called Adam Czerniakow. He was the head of the Jewish council, and he was standing less than five meters away, on a podium in the middle of the street, giving a speech. He was almost completely bald with a large nose, wearing a perfectly cut light gray suit and smart polished shoes. A man of impeccable taste.

A small orchestra stood waiting to play. In front of him a group of children and their parents were listening to him speak. The head of the Jewish council was here to open a new playground. "Never forget, when times are hard, or if they get worse—no, especially if they get worse—the children are our future."

He waited for a short moment, and several grown-ups started to clap. Czerniakow seemed to thrive on the little round of applause, as if it had life-giving properties. I suddenly remembered one of the characters from Hannah's stories. There was a million-year-old chemist named Vandal who made children cry so that he could brew an elixir of life from their tears. When I pointed out to Hannah that Vandal could not have lived a million years ago because humans didn't exist then, all she said was, "My story, my rules."

How wonderful to create the world as one pleased. Even if it's only make-believe.

I didn't listen to the rest of Czerniakow's speech. My meeting with Amos had disturbed me. And to make matters worse, the apple juice was rumbling in my stomach. Amos had been right to warn me about that: Drinking too much, too fast could make me ill.

But what really made me feel sick was the fact that he had been ready to kill me. For the first time in my life, someone I cared about had threatened me.

It was true, I did care about Amos. He had saved my life and that kiss had been special.

Well, it meant nothing now.

I'd never care about Amos again.

Let him play Masada with that Esther of his.

Fanatics. Idiots—the lot of them.

Amos would probably have loved to stab Czerniakow, too. Everyone said the head of the Jewish council was a traitor who bowed to the Nazis' demands and did nothing for the Jews. There were only a few people who didn't think so. Jurek, for example, defended Czerniakow. One time when I was slagging off the leader of the Jewish council, he said, "Why don't you all just leave Czerniakow alone? The deluded fool really thinks he's doing what's best for us. He believes everything would be even worse if some corrupt person had the post instead of him. Someone like that tyrant in the ghetto of Lodz. Czerniakow allows himself to be spat on and humiliated by the Germans. All because he thinks he's doing his best for us."

"He hasn't made anything better for us," I answered.

"At least he tries," Jurek had said. "Which is more than most of us can say."

Czerniakow turned round and signaled to the orchestra. The musicians started to play a merry tune, and I wondered if the Jewish council was paying them for the performance, or if the chance to play in front of an audience was enough, even if all they got was a round of applause.

Czerniakow called to the children. "You may start playing now." And the children ran to the shabby playground. As I watched the leader of the Jewish council, the smile slid from his face. The effects of the applause had worn off, and he could not keep up his spirits any longer. Maybe Jurek was right after all. Maybe he was doing everything he could. Maybe he simply didn't have enough power to come up with anything better than a miserable playground.

But no matter what kind of a person Czerniakow really was, his behavior made one thing very clear: Amos was an idiot. If the Germans were really going to kill us all, the leader of the Jewish council would know about it. And he wouldn't be opening children's playgrounds and talking about the future of the children all the while.

Czerniakow patted the head of a dark-haired girl whose parents had allowed her to put on a pretty green dress that was going to be filthy in less than five minutes. Anyone capable of smiling and patting a child like that couldn't possibly believe that the child and the whole ghetto were about to be annihilated. No Jew could be that evil. Nor could anyone else—not even the Germans.

Yes, Amos was stupid if he thought he knew more than the head of the Jewish council did. It felt good to start calling Amos an idiot in my head. *Idiot, idiot, idiot!*

Oh, it was going to be good to forget about him at last. I wouldn't have to feel guilty about Daniel anymore. He was the boy I really loved.

There—I'd said it: I loved Daniel.

Or I'd thought it, at least.

The children and the musicians spurred one another on. The merrier the music, the wilder the children played and vice versa.

What a pity that Hannah was too big for playgrounds. I would have loved to see her join in the fun.

I walked home. And when I reached 70 Miła Street, I couldn't believe my eyes. Hannah was sitting on the front steps kissing a pale, gangly boy at least half a head taller than me. This had to be Ben, the fifteen-year-old she'd told me about.

"What do you think you are doing?" I asked, appalled.

Of course, it was perfectly obvious what was going on. My little sister was far too young to be kissing anyone, but that was exactly what she was doing. Pretty passionately, in fact!

Hannah let go of the redhead, who at least had the decency to go red. Hannah didn't have any such decency. She pushed a strand of hair out of her face, laughed, and answered back rudely. "What does it look like?" I could have slapped her.

"You do it with Daniel, too," she said.

"But I'm older and I don't do it in public and . . . ? Why on earth am I bothering to argue with you?"

"I was wondering," she grinned back.

Now I could have slapped her again.

"P . . . perhaps I should g . . . g . . . go?" the boy stammered.

By this stage, he was so red in the face that he looked as if he was going to burst.

I was angry and wanted to say something horrid back at him, but I wasn't mean enough to make fun of him. "Yes, I think you should," I said.

"Well, I don't think so," Hannah disagreed.

"B . . . b . . . but . . . ," Ben stammered.

"You're staying," she ordered. She wasn't looking at him, though. She was staring at me defiantly.

The boy looked from one sister to the other. He was obviously trying to figure out whose fury would be worse.

Poor lad.

He came to the conclusion that Hannah was the greater danger and stayed where he was. I didn't know what else to do so I grabbed Hannah's wrist and yelled, "You are coming with me!"

"Let go!" she cried while Ben looked as if he might stop breathing any minute. "No!" I said, and dragged my sister up the steps.

"Let go, I said!" She was furious and thumped me on the arm. Right on my wound. I screamed and everything went black for a second. I let go of Hannah and held on to the railing so as not to collapse on the stairs.

"What's wrong, Mira? What did I do?" Hannah sounded scared.

Her voice came from far away.

"I . . . I th . . . th . . . think y . . . y . . . you . . . hurt her," Ben Redhead said.

"I can see that."

The pain ebbed away slowly. I let go of the railing, cradled my arm, and managed to open my eyes. Everything was blurry, but I could see that I'd dropped the bag of bread. Ben Redhead picked it up while Hannah helped me. The pain was more bearable now, but I felt sick.

"What happened to you?" Hannah asked, pointing at the dried blood on my sleeve.

"Later," I gasped, and fought the urge to throw up all the apple juice Amos had given me.

Thinking about Amos made me feel sick all over again.

Hannah turned to Ben Redhead. "It would be better for you to go now," she said.

He thought so, too.

He gave her the bag with the bread and asked, "Will I . . . I see you to . . . m . . . m . . . morrow?"

"Of course you will," she said quickly.

I was too weak to stop them from meeting.

Ben Redhead smiled, looking pleased—this young stutterer really seemed to like Hannah—and hurried off.

"I'll help you get upstairs," Hannah said.

She hadn't panicked. She was doing her best to deal with the situation. My little sister was a lot more mature than I knew. Apart from where boys were concerned, of course. I was proud of her for a moment.

And then I threw up on the stairs.

13

I couldn't eat any of the sawdust bread at dinnertime because I felt ill, so Mama and Hannah shared it between themselves. Although you couldn't really call it sharing. Hannah ate more than two-thirds of the loaf, stuffing it into her mouth, munching loudly, and burping several times. She was doing this on purpose to annoy me. She was cross because I'd stopped her kissing Ben, and I hadn't told her how I'd got the wound on my arm. I didn't want her and Mama to know how stupid I'd been about Amos.

Hannah took advantage of me being weak. "Don't forget, Mira," she said. "You are not my mother. So stop acting like you are." And then she burped even louder.

The rest of the evening, we didn't say a word to each other. And instead of telling us all a good-night story, Hannah just mumbled one to herself. Something to do with two children from the ghetto. A boy and a girl. The boy had red hair and the girl was very upset because no one could see how grown-up she was.

It wasn't very hard to work out who those ghetto kids were

supposed to be. They liked kissing each other very, very much, Hannah told no one in particular.

No, it wasn't at all difficult to guess who she had in mind.

But the children had to hide their love because there was an evil governess. I had a fairly good idea who the governess was supposed to be, too.

According to Hannah, the ghetto children were walking through the book market when they saw a book bound in beautiful red leather. The title *777 Islands* was printed on the cover in green letters. That was all. Nothing else. No author's name. No publisher. No nothing. The children, Ben and Hannah, were fascinated by this foreign-looking book. But the bookseller, a man with a wooden leg, wanted them to work as his slaves for a year before they could have it. So they decided to steal it instead. They ran away with the book, thinking that the one-legged man would never be able to follow them. But he was surprisingly agile, despite his wooden leg—like he was from a different world. The bookseller threatened the children with death and damnation if they didn't give the book back at once. The book would swallow them and they'd end up in the Hell of No Return, he said.

Of course, the two children didn't believe a word he said and kept on running. They were afraid that he'd beat them with his wooden leg if he caught them. They ran into a backyard, saw the trash cans, and hesitated for a moment. When they realized that they had no choice, they jumped into the cans in order to hide. They stayed in hiding until the one-legged man gave up at last and went away. They heard him mumbling away to himself, "The Mirror King will get you, the Mirror King will destroy you . . ."

Once the coast was clear, the children crawled out of their hiding place and studied the book more closely. It was a sort of travel guide. But to a world that didn't exist. 777 magical islands were described in the book. 777 islands full of marvels. Full of danger.

One was covered in carnivorous trees, for example, and another one was inhabited by giants who wrote poetry without vowels—*fff, grr, fff*. The terrifying Scissor Men lived on yet another one. They cut all the travelers who chanced upon their island out of life and pinned them into a giant album, like pictures.

The children turned the pages of the book, and then all at once, it started to glow. They were surrounded by red light, and suddenly they left the ghetto and found themselves on board a magnificent three-master, sailing across the never-ending seas. The sun was shining. The sea breeze filled the sails, and the air was perfectly clear.

Unlike most of the children in stories, Hannah and Ben weren't naive. They knew right away that they had been carried away to the world of the 777 islands. And they were so glad, they jumped for joy. Of course, they knew that this was probably a dangerous world—as I said, they weren't naive—but they weren't trapped in the ghetto anymore.

Suddenly they heard a voice behind them. "What are two stowaways doing aboard my ship?"

They turned round and saw a cuddly little rabbit standing there, wearing an eye patch and a broad-rimmed hat, and holding a telescope.

"I'm Captain Carrot," the little rabbit announced.

Such a silly name! The children found it impossible not to start laughing. So they did: "Captain Carrot . . ."

"This is the most feared name on all the high seas!"

"Sure . . ." The children laughed even more.

Captain Carrot didn't like giggling children, so he said, "You are going to die!"

"Somehow, it doesn't sound scary when a cuddly rabbit says that," Hannah giggled.

"Well, how about I say it!" they heard a thundering voice behind them say. They turned around and found themselves standing face-to-face with a giant werewolf. There were bits of raw meat hanging from his jaws. They didn't want to know what he'd been eating.

"W . . . we should never have st . . . st . . . stolen that book," Ben Redhead stammered.

But Hannah disagreed at once. "I'd rather die out here on the great wide sea than have to live in the ghetto for another second."

My sister stopped mumbling at this point, said something that sounded like: "To be continued, or not, depending on whether we live to see another day," and closed her eyes.

A minute later, she was snoring loudly.

But I couldn't sleep. Hannah's little story worried me. My baby sister would rather be dead than survive in the ghetto.

I'd had no idea how unhappy she was. And then I had made things worse by not letting her kiss Ben. No wonder she had turned me into an evil governess in her story.

"I know how much you do for us, Mira."

I jumped. All at once, my mother was talking to me. She hardly ever spoke. Certainly not at night.

"You think I don't notice, but I do," Mama continued. "I watch you."

She was lying on the mattress next to mine and made no attempt to talk quietly. She knew that nothing could wake Hannah up once she'd fallen asleep. Not even shooting German gunfire.

"You work so hard," Mama said.

Incredible: She'd said more in a few seconds than she usually said all day.

By the light of the moon, I could see that she was smiling. Not in an absentminded way, which usually meant that she was lost in thought, remembering Papa. No, Mama was smiling in the present. Her approval pleased me somehow, although it was a real surprise.

"Do you still feel ill?" she asked.

What was all this about? She never asked me how I felt. On the other hand, I didn't usually come home with a stitched-up wound on my arm.

"Everything is okay," I said. "It's all right."

"Hannah's wrong, you know," Mama continued.

"What?" I asked, confused.

"You are like a mother to her."

"What do you mean?"

"You're the one who looks after her and tries to give her an upbringing."

That was true enough.

"I am so grateful that you are looking after Hannah," Mama said.

No, I didn't want this. "You are our only mother," I said.

"I haven't been for a long time now." Mama sounded sad. "We both know that."

I didn't want her thanks. All I wanted was for her to start being our mother again, damn it!

"I should have been a better mother to you, too."

I sighed. It wasn't the best time for this kind of conversation.

I would have loved to crawl under the blanket and stay there for the next few days, I was so tired. But Asher was counting on me. If the smuggling action failed because of me, they'd make me pay for it.

And Ruth would have to pay, too, for recommending me. And all my family. Asher was fond of making an example, to make sure that no one disobeyed his orders.

I was in way too deep not to go.

Why couldn't I disappear into a magic book and take everyone I loved with me? Or be in England solving crimes with good old Lord Peter Wimsey?

"I love you," Mama said.

A while back, I would have given anything to hear her say this, but not now. After all this time, listening to her just made me sad.

"And your father loved you, too."

"So that's why he only helped Simon, then," I snapped.

"Love isn't easy," Mama said.

I sat up on my worn-out mattress and scowled at her.

"No one can be strong all the time," my mother said, "especially in times like these. You shouldn't judge us too harshly."

I didn't say anything.

"Oh, get off your high horse." Now Mama sat up, too. "Papa did everything he could, he tried everything. But he didn't have any strength left. He was a good man. He'd have had to be a cold, self-centered person to last any longer."

She hadn't just accepted that Father had killed himself. She'd actually forgiven him!

I couldn't do that.

"I know you can't force love," she continued, "but when someone tells you they love you . . ."

Like her now, and Daniel, too.

". . . and if you love that person, then it would be the right thing to let them know."

She had said more tonight than in all the time since Papa's death. I knew that she would feel better if I said I loved her, too.

But I was still angry with Papa, and with her. Why was it my job to comfort her?

Plus I had to climb the wall tonight.

Then she smiled again. She looked sad, but she smiled.

"You can't," she realized, and gently stroked my cheek. She lay back down on the mattress, wrapped herself in her blanket, and closed her eyes.

And I still couldn't say, "I love you."

14

Of course I didn't get any sleep. I was cross with everyone: Mama, Hannah, Amos, and his stupid girlfriend. He'd called me a kid in front of her, and even worse, I'd acted like one. And I was cross with Daniel. He was my friend but I couldn't tell him what I was up to.

I felt so lonely.

But I was cross with myself, too, for following Amos—and getting stabbed by Zaccharia—and for getting into all this mess. And now I was running through the ghetto in the middle of the night, in the drizzling rain, breaking the curfew, which meant that I'd be shot if I met a patrol.

So I'd better not meet one.

It felt strange to make my way through empty streets. During the day, there were so many people about that it was hardly possible to stand still, but now, in the light of an odd streetlamp or two, the streets looked uncannily large and wide.

I approached the meeting point at the corner of Zimna and Żelazna Streets. Every section of the wall was guarded, including this one. So Asher's men must have paid a lot of money to all the guards, both the German soldiers and the Jewish police. I wondered if my brother was one of the policemen involved. Probably not. Ruth had seen him at the Britannia Hotel in May, and he'd told her that he was too important to do guard duty anymore. He'd said he worked in the department that reported directly to the Polish police. Ruth didn't know if it was true, or if Simon had just been showing off like a lot of the customers. At least he'd gone to bed with one of the other girls, not with Ruth. They'd made fun of his poor lovemaking afterward.

I could see the silhouette of the wall at the end of Zimna Street. I knew that it had been built by human hands, but in the dim light of the streetlamps with all the drizzling rain, it was like a force of nature. An unconquerable barrier formed at the beginning of time that would still be standing when all mankind was gone, Jews and Germans included.

At this distance, the barbed wire along the top reminded me of the forest of thorns in one of Hannah's stories. It was about a man made of thorns who could never touch Maid Vera, his one true love, because he always hurt her.

Although I couldn't see the broken glass from here, I imagined it cutting my hands open. The mere idea stopped me in my tracks in the middle of the street.

How was I going to get over the wall with a wounded arm? Already, the area around one of the stitches was so swollen, it felt as if it was going to burst. I'd put on my leather jacket to cushion it, but I doubted it would be enough to protect the wound.

I slunk into a doorway and kept an eye on the street corner Asher had mentioned. No one was there yet. I had to wait.

4:30, 4:35, 4:40. There was still no one anywhere. No smugglers, no Jewish police, no one at all. The sun would be coming up soon, and then my trip over the wall would turn into a suicide mission instead of just a life-threatening one.

Should I go home and risk Asher's wrath? Or should I get closer to the wall to see if any smugglers from the Chompe gang were hiding in the shadows somewhere?

I didn't have any choice. If I gave up and angered Asher, I'd be putting Ruth's life and my family's at risk. Going to the wall risked only my life.

I wasn't cross for getting myself into all of this mess anymore. Now I was plain scared.

I left the doorway and headed toward the wall. Cold sweat trickled down my face and neck, but I forced myself to go on and got as far as the street corner. The wall was less than five meters away. I still couldn't see anyone else. What was wrong? If I'd been supposed to go on a mission by myself, surely Asher would have given me more exact instructions.

Something fishy was going on. The sweat gathered on the back of my neck. I needed to leave. Asher wouldn't blame me for breaking off a mission that had obviously gone wrong before it even got started.

I had just decided to go home when I noticed a ladder lying on the ground. Was it meant for me? Was I supposed to put it up against the wall, climb up, and look over to the other side? To find the Polish helpers waiting to tell me what would happen next? But wouldn't Asher have told me all this beforehand? Maybe not. What did I know about his smuggling tactics?

If this was really what I was supposed to do, I figured, then I wasn't going to be smuggling food into the ghetto. We'd have needed men waiting to load the food onto carts. Maybe I was supposed to climb over the wall to smuggle American dollars, the hardest currency in the ghetto and in all of Poland, probably. Perhaps in the whole world, even.

Whatever my task was, I was never going to find out if I didn't get the ladder and start climbing.

I couldn't afford to hang around doing nothing any longer. The time bought by bribing the guards could run out any second now.

My hands started to shake, and I calmed down only when I touched the rough wood of the ladder. I leaned it against the wall in a dark spot well away from the light of the streetlamp. It was about two and a half meters long, so I would have to pull myself up the last meter—with a wounded arm! But at least the drizzle had stopped. This was one of those situations where every little bit helped. I started to climb up the ladder rung by rung. As fast as I could. If I was going to be a part of this madness, then I was going to get it over and done with as soon as possible.

When I got to the second-to-last rung, I held on to the ladder with my good hand and reached up with my other arm to brush away the broken glass where I was planning to climb up onto the wall. The wound hurt like mad, but I ignored the pain as best I could. The chunks of glass were big, and I had to make sure that I didn't cut myself—I'd forgotten to bring gloves—and that they didn't fall noisily to the ground.

Above the glass, I saw the barbed wire. I remembered stories about soldiers in the First World War who had lost their lives trapped in wire like this. Would I be able to squeeze beneath it if I lifted it carefully? And if so, how was I supposed to get down on the other side? Would my contact person—if there was one—be waiting with a ladder for me? I thought about calling, to see if anyone was there. But no! It was far too dangerous.

I held on to the wall with both hands, and pulled myself up

to check the situation. I peered over to the Polish side between the glass and the barbed wire. Immediately, I recognized what an idiot I was. I had misjudged the whole situation. There had been smugglers on my side of the wall who I'd been supposed to meet, but they'd left the ladder and fled once they'd seen what I could see now. German soldiers were approaching from every direction. They were quiet, controlled, swift, and efficient.

Two hundred meters away from me, the chain of men had already joined up. Why on earth were the Germans surrounding the ghetto? I didn't know, but one thing was certain. I didn't want my head to be a possible target for another second. I climbed back down the ladder as fast as I could, left it standing where it was, and ran through the empty streets, while the sun came up over the wall behind me. I would never make it home without being seen, so I hid in a doorway and fell asleep in the end, totally exhausted.

A couple of hours later, I woke up to the noise on the street. I scrambled to my feet—my arm was still hurting like mad—and set off. I soon realized why the soldiers had surrounded the ghetto. Flyers had been put up everywhere:

NOTICE

By order of the German authorities all Jews living in Warsaw, without regard to age or sex, are to be resettled in the East.

I read this and all I could think of was: Chełmno.

15

Chełmno.
    Chełmno.
    Chełmno!

I saw terrible pictures in my mind. Hannah, Mama, Daniel, and me being forced into a truck along with loads of other people, hounded by shouting soldiers and snarling German shepherds. The doors being slammed shut and us all standing cramped together. In the close space, there's hardly enough air to breathe and our eyes take forever to adjust to the darkness. I can sense the others more than I can actually see them. Instead, I hear panicky breathing and can almost grasp the fear with my hands. Most of the people are wondering where they are taking us. But I know this truck isn't going anywhere.

We hear the motor start, but the van doesn't move. Why should it? It is not meant to move. This is about the fumes from the exhaust. And they are being channeled into the truck!

Initially, the people are baffled; the cleverer ones realize what is going to happen and start shouting. "They are killing us, they are killing us!"

We start coughing, Hannah chokes for air beside me, Mama doubles up with cramps. I try not to be sick but fail. I start throwing up, and the vomit doesn't even hit the floor because it is all so cramped.

People start to panic and push through the smoke toward the door. But it is closed and locked, of course. Anyone standing near the front gets crushed by the others. But no one cares anymore. And Hannah is thrown to the floor. They tread all over her. And she screams and screams and screams.

Until she stops.

I try to pick up my little sister, but I can't get to her, because the mass of people is pushing me away. Everywhere, people are gasping for help and mercy with their final rasping breaths. The first people sink to the floor unconscious.

I can't see Hannah anymore. Or Mama. The exhaust fumes are so heavy. Daniel tries to hold on to me with his last strength. Even dying, he is here for me. But he can't speak because he is choking, too.

I start to lose my senses. I can't even manage to choke anymore. Then Daniel collapses beside me and we fall to the floor. Or rather, on top of other bodies. And people fall on top of us, those who lasted a moment longer than we did. We are crushed by them. And I can't breathe . . . can't breathe . . . any . . . more.

I stood in front of the flyer fighting for air as if I'd already been crammed into one of the trucks.

An elderly man nudged me. "It won't be that bad," he said. Despite the summer heat, he was wearing a coat over his shirt. He probably didn't have a suit jacket left to wear. "The Germans don't have enough field workers in Ukraine and Belarus. That's why we are being resettled."

The way he said it, it sounded true enough. He believed what he was saying. Amos would have started shaking him, no doubt, and shouted at him, "Do you really think the Germans are going to send an old schmuck like you off to work in the fields?"

I was wrong. Amos wasn't an idiot at all.

A jerk maybe,

and a fanatic,

but not an idiot.

He and his friends had seen this coming.

And everyone else had been blind, like me.

"Maybe," the old man smiled at me, "you will be one of the many exemptions, unlike me."

Exemptions?

Yes, there were exemptions.

The notice contained a list of people who would not be deported to the East.

> All Jews employed in the workshops of the German authorities or belonging to the staffs of Jewish hospitals, or belonging to Jewish disinfection squads. Also members and employees of the Jewish council and Jews belonging to the Jewish police...

None of this counted for Mama, Hannah, Daniel, or me. But there was a further exemption in paragraph 2g):

> All Jews who are members of the
> families of persons covered by (A)
> to (F).

I started to feel hopeful again for a moment. My brother, Simon, was a member of the Jewish police, and we were his relatives, which meant we wouldn't get sent to the East, which really meant we wouldn't be sent to the trucks.

I sighed in relief. But then I read point 2g) to the end:

> Only wives and children are
> regarded as members
> of families.

As far as the Germans were concerned, we were not my brother's relatives. His mother wasn't considered a member of his family and his sisters even less so.

So paragraph 2g) was no use. My father was dead and my mother didn't go to work.

So Hannah and I weren't the children of a Jewish person who was exempt from deportation.

And I wasn't someone's wife, either. Maybe I could have found a rabbi who was prepared to marry me to someone because he felt sorry for me. There would be weddings taking place all over the ghetto at this very moment—for the sole purpose of turning someone into a wife or husband in order to save his or her skin. There was no room for love in those weddings. Unless they were all about love. Wasn't marrying someone to save their life the highest form of love?

But who could a willing rabbi have married me to? The only person prepared to marry me would be Daniel. But he wasn't one of the people exempt from deportation. Oh God, what was going to happen to him and all the children at the orphanage? Would Korczak's international reputation be enough to protect them? Would the Germans stop at hounding the world-famous man and his two hundred children out of the ghetto?

Next to me, a woman started to cry, but no one in the crowd took any notice. Everyone was busy weighing their options. Even if most people didn't believe the deportations would end in death, no one wanted to be sent off into an uncertain future with only a handful of belongings. In paragraph 3) it stated that only fifteen kilos of luggage were allowed per person. Even the horror of the ghetto seemed better than deportation to a terrifying and uncertain future in a strange and foreign country.

I didn't care about the crying woman, either. I had to find my brother. Even if the Germans said that he was not a relative according to the order, Simon was our only chance of rescue. He had to help us. He had to get documents to protect us.

I set off in the direction of 17 Ogrodowa Street, the head-quarters of the Jewish police, which also housed the SS. As I ran through the streets, I wondered if I should go home first, just to give Hannah a hug and tell her that everything was going to be all right, although I didn't really believe it.

Hannah must be terrified. And worrying about her friend Ben Redhead, unless his parents were exempt from deportation. Who could stop her being frightened, except me? Mama certainly couldn't.

Then I remembered how Papa had hugged me when we got back home on that cold November day after the German soldier had bullied us. He dealt with Simon's injuries and kept stroking my hair with his rough hands and said, "Everything is going to be all right." But his unhappy eyes showed that he didn't believe what he was saying. The physical abuse had been awful, but Papa's helplessness was even worse. It wasn't fair of me, but the fact he had lied to me, even if he meant well, was the most terrible thing that happened that day.

The idea of lying to Hannah and her being really angry with me was unbearable. So I decided not to go home. Or at least, not until I'd spoken to Simon and he'd used his damned influence as a Jewish policeman—I hoped he hadn't just been showing off to impress the girls at the Britannia Hotel.

It was difficult to get through the streets. Everywhere groups of people were standing around discussing what the notice from the Germans might really mean. As I passed, I heard that the day before, a group of some sixty Jews had been arrested, mainly well-known people including members of the Jewish council. The SS had taken them as hostages and was threatening to kill them if the ghetto population failed to comply with their resettlement demands.

Despite the threat of violence, no one considered the possibility that the *Aktion*, as the resettlement order was also called, would end in the death of the deportees. The general opinion was that about sixty thousand people would be resettled to work, and that the rest would be able to stay in the ghetto. So many people seemed to believe this, and I couldn't stand my panic a moment longer, so I started to wonder if they were right after all. Maybe we weren't all going to be killed. Maybe only a few people ended up in those trucks. Maybe Chełmno was actually made up by someone with a sick mind, and I'd been driven crazy by horror stories while I was reading the notice.

I imagined Hannah and Mama and me harvesting wheat out

in sunny fields in the East. The fields would be beautiful. Better than the ghetto.

The idea of sun and plenty of space calmed me down a bit.

It was impossible not to start hoping again.

No one believed that the Jews would be wiped out, except people like Amos.

Because it was easier not to?

Or because it was just a figment of his imagination? Locking people in trucks to poison them with exhaust fumes . . . surely, not even the Germans could be that sick.

But it didn't matter whether I believed we were going to be killed or not. I wanted to survive. So I had to do whatever I could. Even talk to my own brother. Beg, if necessary. For Hannah's sake. For Mama. And for me, too. I didn't want to. But I cared about surviving more than my pride.

I started walking faster now, and just before I turned down the street to the headquarters of the Jewish police, I saw the priests of the two Catholic churches, All Saints' and the Church of the Most Blessed Virgin Mary, being ordered to leave the ghetto.

Both churches were attended by Christian Jews who didn't think of themselves as Jews at all, but who had been forced to wear the star just the same because of the Germans' insane race policy. Most of the Jews in the ghetto, including me, hated these Jewish Catholics. I didn't mind them getting extra rations from Caritas—but the churches had beautiful gardens and no one was allowed in.

There was only a single tree in the whole damn ghetto, and it stood in front of the Jewish council building. No wonder Hannah's stories were always full of plants and flowers.

One time, Korczak had actually written to the priest of the Church of the Virgin Mary, asking if the children of the orphanage could visit its garden on Saturdays. He wanted them to get out of the cramped ghetto and experience a bit of nature. Some of the smallest children had never seen a garden. But the priest refused to grant Korczak's request. Christian gardens weren't meant for Jews, or certainly not for ones who weren't of the Catholic faith.

What a lousy bastard.

Why didn't someone deport *him* to the East?

No! I didn't want that to happen to anyone.

Not even to some bastard who wouldn't let Jewish orphans smell a flower just once in their lives.

There were maybe sixty people standing in front of the Jewish police building, and they were as loud as a crowd of ten thousand. Some of them were shouting for their relatives to be released from prison, while others needed paperwork to avoid deportation. And then there were people like me trying to find the Jewish policeman they were related to.

The crowd was kept away from the entrance by about ten policemen. They all wore different coats. But with their caps and boots, they still looked like a uniform force. They used their truncheons to beat anyone who came near the door.

Jews hitting Jews—desperate Jews.

It was obvious that I wouldn't get through. The truncheon-wielding policemen seemed to be acting mechanically, not like real people. And they could have been breaking up tables and chairs or chests of drawers for firewood for all they cared, instead of hitting ribs and knees.

So I moved away from the crowd and stood near a couple of trucks with open loading areas waiting to take SS troops through the ghetto.

All at once, the crowd separated like the Red Sea for Moses. And the policemen stopped beating people back. There was a fearful hush when the door opened. Instead of Moses and his followers, a line of SS soldiers emerged.

People who had been trying to get into the building fled in every direction. Everyone knew: Jewish policemen beat Jews up, but the SS shot us.

I couldn't move, I was scared stiff. A group of Jewish policemen marched behind the twenty or so SS men armed with guns and rifles, as escorts. And one of them—dressed in a light-colored coat, brown polished boots, and a peaked cap with a varnished visor that shone in the sun—was Simon.

He looked much younger than the other policemen. Although most of them would be about twenty years old, just like him. And like a lot of the SS soldiers, too. The only one who was older looking was the leader of the German troops, a blond man with a pockmarked face. He looked as if he meant business, and he had a whip in his belt.

It wasn't intended for horses, though.

Simon tried to hide his lack of manliness by looking extra determined. Did he use his truncheon to beat Jews like the other policemen?

The troops marched toward the trucks. Suddenly, I was the only person left standing in their way.

I wanted to run away, but my legs still wouldn't move. I'd frozen on the spot, seeing my brother together with the SS like this . . .

The Germans headed straight toward me. Led by the man with the whip. The soldiers all stared straight ahead. As if I wasn't there. Or as if I were some kind of insect they would simply step on if I didn't creep out of the way.

I wanted to run away, crawl away. I had to!

But I couldn't.

And the soldiers kept on marching toward me.

The clump of heavy-sounding boots rang in my ears. I couldn't hear anything else. The leader with the whip was only a short distance away from me. Was he a major, a lieutenant, an *Obersturmbannführer*? What did it matter, anyway?

His troops marched behind him, followed by the Jewish police. The leader looked at me and noted that I wasn't going to move. He didn't change his step, though, just stared at me coldly. No German was going to make way for a Jew. And suddenly, I realized that to him that was all I was—something in the way. The Jews were in the Germans' way.

What did they want?

Utter supremacy? An Aryan world? Fortune? Or just a germ-free life?

Were we germs they wanted to be rid of?

As I looked into the cold, indifferent eyes of the SS officer, I finally understood that they would kill us all.

The hope I had tried to share with the other Jews in the ghetto was gone forever. This resettlement was not just another resettlement.

And now I was truly paralyzed! I tried to cry out to Simon to help me. He was my brother after all.

But I couldn't make a sound.

The officer's hand moved to his belt. Would he grab the whip? Or the gun?

The whip; please let it be the whip! I actually found myself hoping that he would strike me with the whip!

But his hand went for the gun.

All of a sudden, behind the soldiers, a Jewish policeman broke ranks and charged forward.

Simon!

Was he going to dive in front of the bullet?

Impossible.

But he was charging toward me yelling, "Get out of the way, you little shit."

My own brother calling me a piece of shit!

"Did you hear me? Get out of the way!"

He pushed me aside, violently. I lost my footing and fell to the ground. I landed on my wounded arm and screamed. I was in such pain. I thought my stitches had ripped.

I saw black shiny boots, no more than twenty centimeters away.

I looked up panic-stricken. The SS officer had been forced to stop, with me lying directly in front of him. He pulled the gun out of its holster.

Simon bore down on me and shouted, "Move, move!"

Was he worried about my life or his?

He lifted his truncheon and . . .

. . . started to beat me!

My brother hit me!

He struck my shoulder, and I screamed in pain and anguish. This was my own brother wielding his truncheon on me and shouting, "Move, you little slut."

And the truncheon thrashed down on my chest.

The blow resonated through the whole of my body. The pain was terrible, but I managed to obey and crawled out of the way. As fast as I could. Simon continued to thrash me with the truncheon—I wasn't moving fast enough.

He hit my ankle this time. I cried out. My whole body seemed to explode in pain. Then my brother kicked me and I rolled out of the way.

Once I had been removed, the SS officer pushed Simon out of the way, put his gun back in its holster, and the troop marched on.

Simon's blows had saved my life.

I lay bent double on the ground, holding my shoulder with one hand and my ribs with the other, as if laying on hands could soften the pain. I howled and moaned.

My brother was towering over me, panting, shaking, ugly with anger.

He didn't look a bit like someone who'd just saved my life. The very opposite was true. He looked as if he was about to beat me again. He was furious because I'd put him in a position where he could have been shot.

The soldiers had marched past, the Jewish police following them. Simon had to get back in line, go on his way to help the Nazis carry out their awful mission. He would be involved somehow, and maybe even see children being shot.

Even if Simon wouldn't be shooting, he would be an accomplice.

My brother—who had just beaten me to save my life and hated me for it—was a culprit.

And as I lay on the ground in front of him whimpering, I hated him, too. With all my might. For everything he did to others and for what he had done to me.

He hissed at me, "I'll come home and help, later."

Another time, I might have gasped—"stay away!"

My will to survive was stronger than my pride.

And Simon was the only hope we had.

That made me hate him even more.

He climbed into a truck with the other policemen. As the trucks roared off, no doubt to start rounding up the first Jews to be deported, the exhaust fumes reached my nose.

A whiff of Chełmno.

16

The bruises from Simon's beating hurt terribly. Luckily, the wound on my arm hadn't broken open. But my ankle caused me the most problems. When I got back to Miła Street, I had to force myself to climb the stairs step by step. And by the time I got to the door of our flat, it was throbbing so badly that it felt like some ball-shaped being with a life of its own attached to my leg.

I opened the door. The family from Kraków were a bustle of activity. None of these people worked for the Jewish council, the police, or for one of the official workshops of the Reich. So they were all getting ready for the deportation. The men by praying, the women by packing their shabby suitcases and trying to work out which of their belongings to include in the fifteen kilograms the Germans allowed them to take with them.

I wanted to yell at them, "What does it matter what you pack when you are all going to die?"

And I would have liked to shout at their Orthodox men even more, "What are you praying for? There is no one up there listening to you."

But what good would that have done? They would never have believed me. And even if I managed to convince them of the terrible fate the Nazis had in store for them, what were these people supposed to do?

Fight? Like at Masada? These women? With their praying men? And their good little girls who were helping to pack the suitcases? Or the little boys with the long side locks hanging down in curls, playing with a ball? None of them were fighters.

The only people who could really fight were young men and women. People like Amos or his girlfriend Esther. Or . . .

. . . me?

Not me. I had to look after Hannah.

I felt like sitting down with these men and praying that my sister might survive. I didn't really believe in God anymore, but a small part of me didn't want to give up all hope.

Suddenly I realized that I didn't know a single Jewish prayer by heart anymore.

Only the Catholic prayers I'd learned as a disguise when I was smuggling. Oh, the Orthodox men would be delighted if I joined them and started reciting the Magnificat. I laughed bitterly.

An ancient lady wearing a head scarf saw me and looked dismayed. I stopped at once. I didn't want her to think I was making fun of them. I lowered my head and limped past them and felt like an old woman myself. Not just because of my battered body, but also because it was so hard not to warn these people of their fate. Even if they wouldn't belive me.

I went through the door into the hovel that had turned into a haven all of a sudden. I never wanted to leave it again.

For once, Mama wasn't lying on her mattress; she was sitting at the table instead. Presumably, she had been waiting for me.

After all, I'd disappeared in the night. She must have thought that I'd been caught smuggling. When she saw me, she heaved a sigh of relief.

Hannah looked up from one of my English books—*Alice in Wonderland*. She wasn't simply trying to learn English from the book like me, she wanted to see how the great storytellers constructed their tales, even though she could only understand a tiny part of the plot in the foreign language.

The two of them weren't the only ones who had been worrying about me.

"There you are!" Daniel cried, relieved, but not failing to notice the state I was in.

"Well spotted," I joked weakly. I was trying to make them think things weren't all that bad.

Daniel smiled to please me. One of the great things about him that he knew when to keep quiet. He didn't ask where I'd been or who or what had done this to me.

Although of course he desperately wanted to know.

And he certainly didn't make any accusations along the lines of "I warned you not to go smuggling." He'd never have thought of doing that. He just put his arms around me and held me tight.

I started to cry.

Because my own brother had beaten me up. Because the people from Kraków were going to die. And because I'd read in the German's eyes that I wasn't even human, as far as he was concerned. None of us were. Not even Hannah.

I couldn't stop crying.

Daniel hugged me. Without him I would have broken down completely.

I continued to sob, until he started to say, "It's going to be all right."

"No," I said, and broke the embrace. I didn't want to hear him lie. I didn't want to feel angry with Daniel like I had with my father.

Hannah came over and exclaimed, "You look like someone chewed you up and spat you out."

I actually laughed.

"What happened?" Mama asked. She looked as if she didn't really want to know.

I decided I'd give them an abridged version. I said nothing about the aborted smuggling mission, though I did find myself wondering what I was going to tell Asher. Because, deportations or not, the mafia boss would want to know what had happened.

But he would understand, wouldn't he? Considering the changed situation? On the other hand, the Ashers of this world hadn't got to where they were by being particularly understanding.

Instead, I told them how I'd gone to the headquarters of the police to try to find Simon and that I'd bumped into the SS troops there. I also told them that a Jewish policeman had attacked me—a half truth was the only way to explain my condition—but, of course, I didn't tell them that my own brother had beaten me this badly.

"Did you see Simon?" Mama wanted to know.

"Yes," I blurted. I could hardly control my anger.

Daniel grasped my hand, as if he wanted to take my anger from me. But it didn't calm me down.

"Will he help us?"

"That's what he said," I answered truthfully. And remembered how I had cowered in front of him, whimpering. I gripped Daniel's hand so tight that he flinched despite himself. Anyone else would have let go.

"If Simon told you he'll help us," Mama said, "then he will."

She still loved her son. Although he hadn't come to see us in such a long time. Hadn't given us even the tiniest portion of the extra rations he got as a policeman.

Just like with Papa, Mama could forgive him everything.

My anger moved from Simon to her. I clung on to Daniel's hand. Tighter and tighter. And because he was there, I began to relax. The anger turned into exhaustion. I'd only slept for a few hours after all, and my body was totally battered.

"Would you like something to drink?" he asked.

"That would be good."

"You'll have to let go of my hand, though." He gave me a lovely smile.

A smile, on a day like today, felt wonderful.

"In that case, I'll do without," I replied, and sat down at the table without letting go of his hand.

"I'll get you something to drink," Hannah said, and poured water from a white porcelain jug into a glass.

"Thank you."

"That wound on your arm was there yesterday, wasn't it?" she asked. Why wouldn't she let it be? She still wanted to know how I had been wounded.

"Which wound?" Daniel asked. He was standing beside me at the table, still holding my hand.

"The one we don't want to talk about," I said. There was no way I could tell Daniel about my meeting with Amos and the members of Hashomer Hatzair.

"Ah, that wound," he said, smiling knowingly.

I let go of his hand, and he started to stroke the back of my neck gently. Now at last I started to feel as if there was more to the world than just my fear.

Daniel's kindness and love, for one thing. And I realized that I'd been so full of fear, hate, and exhaustion that I hadn't stopped to think about how Daniel had fared on this terrible day.

What did the German order mean for the orphanage?

"How did Korczak react?" I asked Daniel.

"He tried to talk to the Jewish council . . ."

"And?"

"I haven't heard yet. I wanted to see you first."

"But Korczak will manage to stop the orphans from being . . . ?" I stopped for a moment. It was too terrible to say what I was really thinking. That all the dear children who had been brought up and looked after by Korczak and Daniel, all those clever, lively children were going to die. I decided to use the Germans' word: ". . . resettled."

No wonder they used that word. Resettling sounded bearable. If you didn't see through the word to its hidden meaning.

"If anyone can protect the children," Daniel said, "then it is Korczak."

He said this with great faith. He trusted his surrogate father more than God. As much as the Orthodox Jews next door trusted the Almighty. Far more than Mama trusted Simon. Daniel's trust in Korczak was the greatest trust of all, by a long shot.

If it wasn't so unfair to Mama, I think I would have liked for Hannah and me to be orphans, too, protected by this good, tired, bearded old man.

Daniel stopped stroking me. I knew what this meant at once. "You want to get back to the orphanage?"

"I have to," he said. He loved me, but I had to share him with the children. Especially now. Whether I liked it or not. I was ashamed to admit that I didn't like it at all.

I stood up and winced as I put weight on my damaged ankle.

Then I kissed him on the cheek and he smiled, grateful that I hadn't asked him to stay. We hugged, holding each other tight until he said, "See you soon."

"Yes, see you soon."

Daniel left our hovel, and I realized that we had no idea when we would see each other again.

Before I could start to think about what that meant, Hannah asked, "Are you going to tell me where the wound on your arm came from now, or not?"

"Not," I told my sister, and lay down on the mattress totally exhausted.

Hannah made a face at me. She was offended. She didn't quite understand what was going on in the ghetto. But most of the grown-ups didn't, either. And, even though I thought I knew, I didn't actually know anything.

It would have been the right thing to let Hannah know what was probably going to happen. And I would tell her. Later. When I'd found out if our brother was going to be able to help us. And when I'd had a bit of sleep.

I closed my eyes and asked her, "Tell me a story."

"What?" she asked. She was still cross with me. And getting crosser by the minute.

"About the 777 islands." I sounded like a child wanting to be told a good-night story. Not because I was pretending, but because for once, that's what I really was.

Hannah understood, and we suddenly swapped roles. For once, she was the big sister, mama, whatever . . . and she started to tell me the next bit of the story about the 777 islands.

Onboard the ship, the werewolf stood in front of the two children and bared his teeth. He was just about to seize them when Captain Carrot yelled, "You are not allowed to eat them!"

That was a relief, the children thought.

"You are a spoilsport," grumbled the werewolf.

"The law of the sea demands that they walk the plank and drown miserably."

That didn't sound so good, after all, the children realized.

"Stupid law!" The werewolf was clearly not happy.

"But maybe the bitter rays maul them to death first."

The children had no idea what sort of animals bitter rays might be. Apparently the seas round the 777 islands were full of deadly fish that didn't exist in our world. And the children didn't want to meet them.

The werewolf was sorry to miss a meal, and he started to grumble, but then he said, "Never mind, they are just skin and bones, anyway."

The wolf fetched a plank and attached it to the railing like a diving board. Then he chased the children onto it. The plank bowed a bit under their weight. Beneath them, the waves gently rocked the ship up and down. And beneath the waves they would have to face bitter rays or death by drowning because neither Hannah nor Ben could swim. That wasn't something children learned in the ghetto.

They hugged each other and held each other tight, said things like, "I love you," "L . . . l . . . love . . . you, t . . . t . . ." and "I know what you mean."

And then they kissed each other, like they'd never done before.

That was the moment when I should have opened my eyes and give Hannah another piece of my mind about being too young to be kissing, but I was far too tired.

Captain Carrot was about to push the children off the plank with his sword: "Now meet the bitter rays!"

But all at once the werewolf shouted, "Captain, look!" And showed him the book he was holding carefully in his great paws. "They come from the world of Mainland. The girl must be the Chosen One."

"How can such a little girl be the Chosen One?" the captain snapped. "How can a little girl like that save anyone? How can she defeat the Mirror King?"

Captain Carrot turned and stared at the children, and then Hannah shouted, "But I am the Chosen One."

Everyone was amazed, including Ben, and the captain lowered his sword in awe: "You are?"

"Clever girl," I murmured.

"I will tell you more some other time. Now sleep well," Hannah said, and stroked my hair.

I should have had nightmares about SS soldiers forcing me into a truck, or my brother beating me to death, or even about a rabbit captain with a sword. But I didn't dream about anything. My sleep was as deep as the sea that surrounds the 777 islands.

17

"Let Mira sleep," was the next thing I heard. It was Simon.

"Don't you want to talk to her?" my mother asked.

"I don't have much time," Simon answered.

This wasn't a dream. My brother was here, in this room.

My eyelids felt so heavy. I couldn't manage to force them open just yet. Part of me didn't want to make the effort. I'd much rather fall back into the depths of dreamless sleep than see Simon. But I needed to know why he had come and whether he could help us or not. I ordered myself to open my eyes. But they refused to obey.

"Mira would love to see you," Mama said.

She didn't even believe that herself. She knew what I thought of Simon, although obviously she didn't have a clue that he was the person who had beaten me up.

"No, she wouldn't," Hannah said. She hadn't forgiven Simon, either, for having deserted us in the past few months.

"No, she wouldn't," Simon agreed. And I could tell that he wanted to be gone.

"Well, she will," Mama insisted. "As soon as she hears what you have done for us."

Now I did open my eyes. What had he done?

Simon was standing beside my mattress holding his policeman's hat in his hand. He hadn't even bothered to sit down. As if every second he had to spend with his family was a nightmare. What on earth had we done to be treated like this? Or were we too strong a reminder of all the things he had failed to do for us? Was that what bothered him?

"Mira's eyes are open." Hannah had noticed.

Simon looked at me, startled. He was worried that I'd tell the others about him beating me up.

I was eye level with his boots. The leather was covered in blood. It wasn't mine. He had "only" given me swellings and bruises. He hadn't beaten me until I started to bleed. My eyes moved up his leg, and I saw that his trousers were caked in blood, too. His coat was buttoned the wrong way—he'd always done that, even as a small child—his dark hair framed his face, which was very pale, indicating that he had been through a lot in the past few hours. He wasn't injured, as far as I could tell. So where did the blood come from? Who else had he clubbed for the SS besides me?

I didn't want to be lying on the floor in front of him. Not again. I managed to get up. Everything hurt. My shoulders, ribs, and—most of all—my ankle, which was very swollen. For a moment, everything went black, but I managed to stay upright. Now that I was standing on the mattress, I was level with Simon's eyes. He was a little man in every sense of the world.

"Hello, Mira," he said cautiously, waiting to see how I was going to react.

"Hello, Simon," I answered, and could hardly disguise my anger.

"Tell Mira what you have done for us," Mama said eagerly.

Whatever Simon had managed to do, she felt sure that it would make me forgive my brother. But he'd have to chase the Nazis out of Poland first.

"Yes, Simon," I said provokingly—"why don't you tell us all what you did?"

He looked away from me, ashamed that he had hurt me.

"I got Mama a work permit for Többens' factory."

Többens was a German manufacturer making a fortune with the cheap ghetto workforce. He produced coats for German ladies and children and elegant gowns. The firm even made artificial flowers from leftover material to decorate the dresses. No one earned any money at Többens, or anywhere else in the ghetto. All you got in his factory was a cup of watery coffee and a slice of bread in the morning and another piece of bread at night. But as long as you had a job there, you wouldn't be resettled. Slave labor had suddenly become the best way to survive in the ghetto! Seeing as we were all Mama's children, the work permit would save our lives, too, according to paragraph 2g).

But there was one thing that made the whole idea impossible: Mama would never be able to stand the conditions at Többens. Working a sewing machine for eleven hours would be too much for her. I should tell him. But would Mama be hurt? On the other hand, we wanted to survive. It didn't matter if I hurt her feelings.

Simon had noticed me looking at Mama doubtfully, and knew what I was thinking. "The work permit is forged," he said.

"What?" I was amazed.

"Mamel, a friend of mine, did it," Simon said. "He is very good. He draws maps for the Germans at their command post."

"Oh, I bet he's proud of himself, then," I said bitterly.

"This pass will save your life," he said, "and he has asked for nothing." He said this with a biting undertone.

"So he normally gets paid for this?"

"Of course he does."

"Oh, of course he does," I answered coldly.

"And not badly, either."

"What a nice person," I replied even more coldly.

"If I hadn't got us this," Simon was starting to get angry now, "then we'd all end up . . . ," he took a quick look at Hannah and decided to hide behind the official German term, too.

". . . being resettled."

He seemed to doubt that the Germans were looking for cheap labor for their fields in the East. Or did he actually know something about the Germans' real plans? No. No Jew could possibly support a plan to annihilate the Jews. Not even a member of the Jewish police. Take bribes, beat Jews, and follow nasty orders—those traitors could do all of that, but it wasn't the same as sending our own people to death. If Simon was really sure that the Germans were going to kill everyone they deported, he'd have stopped wearing his uniform ages ago. Or so I hoped.

"Simon is helping us," Mama confirmed, pointing at the forged work permit lying on the kitchen table. And she was letting me know that we should be grateful and stop accusing him.

She was right. Just now, the best thing that could have happened to me, Hannah, all of us, was Simon being a Jewish police pig. So Papa had been right when he spent the last of his money to get Simon into the police.

If I was benefiting from having a brother who was a pig, didn't that make me one, too? I felt so ashamed. And I hated it. I wanted Simon to feel at least as ashamed as I did about all the evil things he did to save our skins and his. So I attacked him. "Where did you go with the Germans?"

He looked at Mama and Hannah uneasily.

"Where?" I pressed.

"They have closed my department," he said. "We are no longer responsible for liaising with the Polish police. We have to help with the resettlement . . ."

He faltered.

I gave him a challenging look. He still hadn't given us a proper answer.

"We were rounding up homeless Jews," he confessed quietly.

I could picture German soldiers and the Jewish police, including Simon, beating the weakest of the weak. The sick, the old, and children. The blood on his boots came from those people.

I started to pray. Yes, suddenly I was praying that this blood hadn't come from a homeless child. For the child's sake, but more for Simon. And for me, as well.

Simon swallowed uneasily. I'd managed to shame him.

But it didn't do me any good.

Simon was suffering because of what he had to do. He was still the poor frightened child. But one armed with a truncheon now.

I didn't feel sorry enough to want to hug him or anything. I was too disgusted by what he had done. But I stopped feeling angry.

"What work could homeless people manage to do in the East?" Hannah asked suddenly, breaking the silence. "They are far too weak."

Mama sat down at the table in dismay. She had finally realized that the resettlement was one big lie.

"They . . ." Simon tried to find an explanation that would save his face somehow without scaring Hannah. "They . . ."

". . . get fed first," I lied. "There is more food out in the fields for them to eat."

"They are right at the food source," Simon confirmed.

Together we fabricated a story for our sister, to stop her being afraid. We lied to her, just the way the Germans lied to all of us Jews to make us behave like obedient children.

Hannah wasn't completely convinced. I'd never lied to her before today. I didn't always tell her everything, but I'd never lied. I didn't want to start acting like a grown-up, but the Germans had turned me into a liar, too. And that drove us apart. I could tell by the way she reacted: She hunched her shoulders and looked away.

"I have to go," Simon said, and put on his hat. He turned back to Mama. "It won't be safe to leave the house in the next few days. I'll bring food."

"Thank you," she smiled and stroked his cheek just like she used to do when he still lived with us. He flinched, waved goodbye to Hannah, and nodded at me as he was going out, in a sad, apologetic sort of way. He was sorry about what he'd done to me. And maybe he was sorry about neglecting to help us all these months. He was about to turn away when I said, "Don't go too far."

His eyes looked even sadder. They filled up with tears, and he said, "I already have."

18

The next night I had a dream. Surprisingly enough, it had nothing to do with soldiers, terror, or death. No, I dreamed something silly. Silly but beautiful. And I was happy in the dream. I dreamed that Daniel was kissing me. It was the kind of dream I wanted to continue dreaming even after I'd woken up, so I refused to open my eyes. The dream world was so much more beautiful than the real one, and because it was so beautiful, it seemed more powerful and intense. And I wanted to stay lying in Daniel's arms forever, kissing him. I didn't want to return to the horror of the ghetto. I kept my eyes closed and traced the sensation of the wonderful dream kiss. Tried to recall every single detail: Daniel's rough lips, the fact that we were naked and curled up close together . . . But the dream faded, and the more I tried to hold on to it, the faster it disappeared.

At least it was quiet all around me. I could only hear Mama's gentle breathing and Hannah's snores. Both of them were fast asleep. I still kept my eyes closed. I could enjoy the peace and quiet for as long as it lasted.

But it didn't last long.

I heard the sound of heavy boots storming our house, but not up the stairs. Instead they went into the back courtyard.

I held my breath and kept my eyes closed, hoping that the nightmare would go away if I refused to acknowledge it. As if that had ever worked!

A voice in the courtyard started shouting, "Everyone out! Now! And no more than fifteen kilograms of luggage."

My eyes were wide open at once. I forgot all about the dream. Instead, I jumped up and dashed to the window, looking out into the courtyard. I hardly noticed Mama and Hannah sitting up sleepily. And I forgot about my aching body. There were ten Jewish policemen standing in the yard!

Their leader was a little man with a mustache that was almost as big as he was. It would have looked ridiculous under normal circumstances, or if he hadn't been wearing a uniform. But in this case, his strange appearance made him seem more terrifying than a huge man with scars on his face would have been.

Half-naked, I dashed out of our hovel into the rooms where the people from Kraków lived. They took no notice of me. They were far too busy gathering up their belongings. Through one of the windows, I could look down into Miła Street. A crowd of Jewish policemen had fenced off the street. Some of them were guarding the doorways while others stormed the houses. No doubt in order to round up the people hiding in their homes, on the staircases and in the cellars. And then to load them onto the horse-drawn carts waiting, which would take them to the *Umschlagplatz*—the collection point where Jews were gathered for deportation—from where the trains headed east.

SS soldiers were standing in front of the carts feeding the horses. They left the Jewish police to round up the Jews. They preferred to look after their animals. The horses probably got better rations, too.

I tore myself away from the view and ran back to our little hole. I stared into Mama's and Hannah's shocked faces. Downstairs, the big mustache was yelling, "If you don't come out, we'll come and get you!"

What choice did we have? There was nowhere to hide. We should have converted a cupboard or prepared one of the rooms in the cellar ages ago. The attic wasn't an option, because the police were bound to search there, too. It might have been possible for Hannah and me to climb up onto the roof despite my wounded arm and damaged ankle, but Mama couldn't.

There was no choice. "Now," I said to the others, "we'll find out how much Simon's permit is worth."

Next door, we could hear the people from Kraków getting ready to leave. Some of the children were crying, but none of the grown-ups comforted them. The fathers simply mumbled their prayers.

Hannah was standing in the middle of our hovel chewing her nails. She'd never done that before. Frantically, Mama started picking up clothes and threw them into a large bag. We didn't have a suitcase.

"What are you doing?"

"If they don't accept the permit, then we'll need clothes for the East." She stroked Hannah's hair. "It gets cold there in the winter. You don't want Hannah to freeze, do you?"

The cold in the East wasn't going to be a problem for us. If Mama guessed this, too, she preferred not to think about it.

I left Mama to pack and Hannah chewing her nails, although her left index finger had started to bleed. I ran my fingers along the rough surface of the wooden table. I needed to feel something that wasn't fear. But then a foreign voice next door started yelling at the people from Kraków, "Faster, faster, faster!"

The voice sounded almost hysterical. Not very old, but harassed and out of control. A jumble of female voices protested; they hadn't finished packing yet. Their men said nothing, and the policeman shouted, "I don't give a damn. Move!"

Some of the women started to cry, too, and all of them—as far as we could judge from the sounds—were forced to leave the flat.

Mama was so shocked that she stopped packing. Although we couldn't hear the policemen's footsteps because of all the noise our neighbors were making, we knew that they would be in our room in a minute.

Out in the yard, a man whose voice I didn't recognize was pleading, "These are my parents; let them stay with me." But parents weren't relatives, according to the Germans. The man started screaming. He was probably being beaten.

Above the sound of his wails, we could hear a women shouting, "But my husband works for Schulz!"

"Do you have a permit?"

"He has it with him at work!"

"Then you come with us!"

"No! No! He's got a permit!"

I knew that voice. Wasn't it the chemist's wife who lived two floors down from us? Or old Schneidel, who used to give Hannah sweets when she could still afford to buy any?

Then, the door flew open and two Jewish policemen stormed into our room armed with truncheons. They were both young, like Simon. One had light brown hair that had stuck to the sides of his head in all the hectic rush, and the other was shaved bald beneath his hat. He'd probably been plagued by lice not long ago.

"Out!" the one with the sweaty hair yelled at us.

I stared at Mama. She seemed unable to move. Why didn't she show him her pass?

"Move!" the one with the hair shouted, while the bald one lifted his truncheon. Hannah ducked to the floor. She was trying to make herself invisible.

But she couldn't.

And Mama couldn't manage to say anything. I burst out shouting, "She works for Többens!"

"Show me the permit!"

Mama still didn't move. I grabbed the piece of paper from the table. The sweaty policeman looked at it. I hoped he wouldn't notice that it was a forgery.

Suddenly, I realized that if Mama was really working at Többens, she should have been in the factory ages ago. Sewing coats and binding artificial flowers, or something. The police would know!

He continued to stare at the paper. Though not as if he was really checking it. More like he was trying to get away from all this madness for a second.

"We must go!" his bald colleague urged.

The sweaty policeman returned from the sanctuary of his mind back to reality. What was he going to say? Was he convinced by the fraud? Or would he make us leave?

He opened his mouth and said . . . nothing.

"Come on!" his comrade hurried him again.

"Your papers are fine," he finally managed to say. He handed the document back to me. It was soggy where he had held it with his sweaty fingers. Had he realized that it was a forgery? Or that Mama should have been at work at Többens? If so, he had spared us on purpose. Perhaps he was relieved not to have to hound another lot of people into the yard. Perhaps it was a sign of humanity.

The policemen charged out of our flat. We stayed where we were.

We could hear police commands outside. And children crying. And women, too. And men. None of us dared go near the window to look down into the yard.

Mama crouched on the mattress and stared at the half-packed bag. Hannah cowered on the floor and bit her nails until they all bled. And I ran my fingers along the table. Back and forth, and back and forth, but all I could feel was fear.

19

About an hour later—or it could have been five minutes or more than a year for all I could tell because I'd lost all sense of time—I opened our door and went into the rooms the people from Kraków would never see again. All the time we'd had to share the flat with them, I'd wished the large family would disappear. Now they were gone, and it was devastating.

It looked as if a tornado had hit the room. Most of the furniture had been knocked over, clothes were strewn everywhere, and there were prayer books scattered on the floor, too. I'd never have thought that the deeply religious men would end up leaving them in all the rush.

I walked through the rooms like a sleepwalker, which is why I bumped my sore ankle against a chair. I was almost glad about the pain. It drew my attention away from the spooky atmosphere.

In the kitchen there was a piece of bread with a bite out of it lying on a plate. My stomach was rumbling. When was the last time I'd eaten anything? Yesterday? No. The day before that. I hadn't eaten anything since I threw up all the apple juice.

I stared at the bread. I'd never stolen anything before. Was it stealing if I took something that had been left behind by someone who wasn't coming back? Would that turn me into a thief?

No.

It wasn't stealing from the living. Was it stealing from the dead? Was that worse?

But the people the bread belonged to weren't dead, yet. They were at the *Umschlagplatz*. Or on a train heading east. On their way to the trucks of Chełmno. Or to work in the fields first. No matter where they were, it didn't help anyone if the bread was left to go moldy. There was no need to feel bad about it.

Of course I felt guilty anyway, but I picked up the bread and bit a piece off.

I chewed slowly and looked round the kitchen. There was enough food here to last us a few days. We wouldn't have to go out onto the streets. Not run the risk of being caught. That was wonderful. I almost laughed outright.

With bread in hand, I went to the stairs. There wasn't a single soul to be seen. I'd never known it to be so quiet. There were abandoned blankets and clothes lying on the landings here, too. And more books.

"It's like a deserted house," I heard a voice calling from upstairs, and I jumped and dropped my bread. I looked up and saw Hannah leaning over the banisters, staring at the shambles.

"Damn, you scared me!" I scolded. But she still stared down the stairs looking disturbed. "Are we the only ones left?"

I hadn't asked myself this question yet. There were so many flats in the building, and presumably there would be people with a permit to stay living in some of them. Right now, they were at work in the workshops and factories and would return to a deserted house tonight. And then they'd find out that their loved ones were gone. There were voices ringing in my ears, "My husband works at Schulz." "Permit?" "He has it with him." "Then you come with us!"

I was sure now that that had been dear Mrs. Seidel begging for release.

"I'm sure we're not all alone," I said to Hannah.

"But we're more alone than we were," she whispered.

I was desperate to make her feel better after all the horror. "Come on," I said. "Let's find some food."

The people from Kraków had not just left bread behind. There was butter and even a bit of ham. And we stuffed ourselves, Mama, Hannah, and me. Watching Hannah eating until she had had enough for the first time in ages made me stop feeling guilty about stealing other people's food.

"Will the Germans be back?" Mama asked. She pushed the larger part of her slice of bread across to Hannah without thinking, although there was more than enough for once. More than we could manage to eat.

"I don't think so," I said. "There are so many houses to be cleared. Why would they come back to somewhere they have already been?"

I felt fairly sure about that, and relieved. I would be able to rest and let my wounds heal as long as there was enough food. If we rationed it carefully, it could last at least a week. If I could find more in the other empty flats, we might last even longer. The best thing was that I wouldn't have to meet any Nazis or see Shmuel Asher for a while.

"Can I have my own room?" Hannah asked with her mouth full.

I had to laugh. And straightaway I thought, *I want my own room, too.*

"Why not?" I said. "Take your pick."

"Then I'd like ours," she said.

She wanted her own space, but no change.

I looked at Mama, asking. She shrugged her shoulders and said, "I don't mind."

"I don't mind, either." Hannah laughed.

"I can take my mattress and move out," Mama suggested.

"There's a room with a bed next door," I said. "You could have that." But she shook her head. "I won't lie in a stranger's bed," she said.

I could understand how she felt.

"It'll be great." Hannah was so pleased

It was crazy. We had food and space. We hadn't been so well-off in ages.

20

Daniel came to visit us as often as possible. Though, unfortunately, it wasn't very often. Each time when we kissed each other goodbye, Hannah said things like, "Not now, there are children present," or, "you're drooling, it's disgusting," or, "can you stop chewing each other's faces?"

Watching us made her miss her boyfriend, Ben Redhead, more than she did already. He hadn't been back. Had he been taken? Or did he think Hannah was long gone on the trains because our house was one of the first to be evacuated? Was he crying his heart out every day? But why hadn't he come back to see if he could find her? Couldn't he bear to know the truth? Or didn't he love her anymore? What did I know about fifteen-year-old boys and their feelings?

My sister got more and more unhappy every single day. She was so sad that sometimes she forgot to eat, but she never left the flat to go and look for Ben Redhead.

"I won't go out into the streets," she explained. "I'm not like the children in the stories. They are always walking into dark

145

forests and haunted houses, even though everybody has warned them not to, and look what happens."

In the ghetto, it wasn't just the Jewish police who forced people to go to the *Umschlagplatz* now. The SS had taken over with groups of helpers from Latvia, Ukraine, and Belarus. Men who had been willing to join forces with the German conquerors as soon as their countries got occupied. For pay, a uniform, and power over the Jews!

These men could let their hatred of the Jews run free at long last. They couldn't understand more than a few words of German or Polish and, of course, no Yiddish. So they ignored the official permits, which meant nothing to them. And they were immune to all the desperate pleas they couldn't understand, "This permit says that me and my children are exempt from deportation." "I work for the Jewish council." "You must ask! Please!" And even if they had been able to understand, they couldn't have cared less. Just as the Germans didn't give a damn if their helpers were ignoring all the certificates and permits they had issued. The permits and passes were the latest gigantic farce.

One was only safe if there was work and housing in the barracks on-site. The German industrialists like Többens and Schulz took bribes from desperate souls who sold their very last possessions to be allowed to work as slaves. For a nine-carat diamond, you could get the whole family a space in the barracks—if Többens deigned to do so. He asked for a hundred thousand zlotys per person. I'd never seen that amount of money in one pile, ever, let alone owned that much. I hadn't met the despicable slave driver Többens yet. I liked to pretend that if I did meet him, I'd spit in his face, instead of giving him my last penny. But the truth is, I would probably have thrown myself at his feet and begged to be a slave in his factory to save my family.

Anyone who couldn't find a job as a slave tried to hide. Or hoped that they wouldn't be among the thousands of Jews deported every day. It was only a matter of time before the orphanages would be next. I still hoped that Korczak and his children would be spared, because the whole world had heard of him. But I knew that it was useless. The world didn't care about us.

"Since Czerniakow's death, Korczak has had no contact with the Jewish council," Daniel said, sounding worried. It was one of our peaceful moments. When we cuddled on my mattress.

The leader of the Jewish council had swallowed cyanide when the *Aktion* started, because he didn't want to help the Nazis send children to their deaths. At least, that is what people were saying. So old Jurek had been right all along. Czerniakow had really believed that he could make some things better for the Jews. And when he realized that it was useless—that his whole life was useless, in fact—he killed himself.

"But Korczak keeps getting offers to be smuggled out of the ghetto. The foreign Jews are actually pressing him hard, and have collected a large sum of money for him. But he says that he would prefer to accompany his orphans to their deaths and . . ."

"Shh," I said, and put a finger on his lips.

I didn't want to talk about death.

All I wanted was to stay lying on this mattress forever. In this room. Secluded from the world. In Daniel's arms.

But of course that wasn't possible. At least not if I didn't want my family to starve.

I'd got it wrong. The food in our house hadn't lasted long, because of course we weren't the only ones raiding the empty flats. On the one hand, there were people like us who had been left behind, and then there were also homeless people who searched through every cupboard looking for food. I actually had to chase two people out of our own flat.

Simon didn't come back once during all this time. He obviously felt that he had done enough for us. Or he was far too busy beating Jews to death. Probably both. No matter what the reason, I had to go and find my brother and make him get food for us.

On the eleventh day of the *Aktion*, I went outside for the first time. My injuries were all nearly healed, and my ankle was no longer swollen. I was surprised when I stepped outside. It was so hot. The sun burned down. Had there been anything green in the ghetto, it would have been parched dry by now.

It wasn't just the heat that made the ghetto seem different from a few days ago. Before there had been a depressing veil of hopelessness hanging over everything, but now there was a heightened sense of fear. Panic-stricken people hurried down the street, looking tormented, looking for work, looking for somewhere to stay. Fleeing from resettlement.

Not far from our house, I saw an elderly man with unnaturally blond hair who looked familiar somehow. I needed a short moment before I realized who was hurrying along.

"Jurek?" I called.

The man looked round. It really was Jurek. His smartly combed hair wasn't gray anymore. It had been dyed, and he had shaved as well. He looked about ten years younger, though, of course, he was still an old man.

He recognized me, but he didn't want to stop.

I ran over to him and barred his path. Instead of saying hello, I simply asked, "You . . . you dyed your hair?"

"I had to close my shop, so I need to find work." He sounded defeated. "The Germans only want productive Jews. They don't have any work for old Jews . . ."

His eyes were jittery. Where was the old man who had been so relaxed about meeting death because he could look back on a lovely, fulfilled life?

When death called, I now realized, no one stayed calm.

"So you dyed your hair!" I couldn't believe it. He had actually put on a little bit of rouge to look younger, too.

"It's not just me," he said. "Look!" And he was right: There were some elderly women with dyed hair just like Jurek.

"Look at those two." Jurek pointed at two boys walking past with their parents. The children weren't much older than Hannah, but they were wearing suits and ties to make them seem older. Old enough for a lifesaving job at one of the factories.

It was spooky. A terrible masquerade to defy death.

And it got even spookier. An old women with a hunchback came up to us. She wasn't trying to hide her age like Jurek was. She was holding an amulet and waved it at us, especially at me.

"A protection charm. It doesn't cost much. A protection charm. It's cheap," she chanted in a horrible voice.

I was far too scared to react, but Jurek chased her away with a sweeping arm movement. "Be gone, you witch!"

The woman cackled and held the amulet directly in his face. "I'll curse you for free," she said . . .

"We're damned already," Jurek answered.

"You're right, there," she cackled again, and limped away.

Jurek's old hand—no amount of makeup could have hidden the protruding veins—shook. And he said, "God won't help us, so we must rely on magic."

I watched the old woman go on her way. Offering her amulet to passersby in the hope of earning a zloty or two.

"Well, what do you still believe in, Jurek?"

"I believe in jam," he said.

"What?" I was stunned.

"If I have to die, then I'll die with a bit of jam," he mumbled sadly, and then he simply walked away.

I watched him go, far too surprised to call after him.

A few minutes later, I realized what Jurek had been talking about. On my way to find Simon, I saw Rubinstein leaping around in front of a new notice. He was shouting, "Catch bears with honey and catch Jews with jam."

He was even dirtier than usual and stank to high heaven. The fact that he was wearing nothing but underwear and rubber boots didn't help. There was a small group of people standing watching who couldn't help laughing. Rubinstein was still good for a laugh, even now.

I didn't understand why everyone kept going on about jam, but then I read the notice the madman had chosen as a backdrop for his performance:

APPEAL

I hereby inform the residents that anyone who voluntarily reports for evacuation on July 29, 30, and 31 will be provided with food, namely 3 kilos of bread and one kilo of jam.
The Commander of the Jewish police
Warsaw. July 29th, 1942

A kilogram of jam per person!

Most of us hadn't seen that amount of jam for years.

And Jurek was going to die for that?

"Lovely, tasty hangman's jam," Rubinstein called, and pretended to be licking jam out of a large jar. The movements were the same as last time, when he'd blackmailed Jurek, only this time he didn't actually have any.

"Who would have thought." The madman giggled. "Who'd have thought that the first days of resettlement would look like the good old days so soon?"

A couple of people actually laughed.

Rubinstein started to shout his greatest hit, "All the same, all the same."

And laughed his loud mad laugh. The people watching joined in and sounded nearly as mad. The whole ghetto was slowly but surely going insane.

As they all laughed, I started to feel angry.

We weren't all the same. Jews weren't the same as the Germans, and Jews weren't even the same as one another.

It was nothing but ridiculous talk from a clown.

I turned away, but Rubinstein saw me. "Where are you off to, little one? I thought you wanted to be my apprentice?"

I didn't bother to answer. I wasn't the sort of person who had time for this kind of rubbish anymore. I had to find my brother and get some food.

I rushed through the ghetto and turned into the street where the police headquarters stood. Then I heard someone shouting, "The orphanages. They are clearing out the orphanages!"

21

didn't even bother to turn around to see who was shouting. I didn't care. And I didn't stop to think that it was probably a bad idea to go to Korczak's orphanage when it was about to be evacuated. Because I was so young, they might mistake me for one of the inhabitants and deport me, too, but all I wanted was to be with Daniel. I wanted him to be spared. I hoped that all of Korczak's foreign supporters had been able to raise enough money to save him and all his children from the Nazis' claws.

I was panting when I got to the orphanage. There were no soldiers anywhere. This meant that I was too late . . .

Oh please, don't let it mean that!

The children couldn't be at the *Umschlagplatz* yet, surely!

Daniel wasn't at the *Umschlagplatz*.

Or that's what I kept telling myself as I walked up to the entrance. I was terrified that there would be no one there when I opened the door, just knocked-over furniture, smashed plates, scattered toys, and a teddy bear torn to pieces, maybe, whose stuffing had been ripped out like some gutted animal.

No matter how hard I tried to convince myself that Daniel was not at the *Umschlagplatz*, my fear got the better of me.

I shuddered as I pressed down the door handle and opened the creaking door. When it stopped making a noise, all I could hear . . .

. . . was nothing.

It was deathly still. Deserted.

Deathly still. I had never thought about what that really meant before.

I held my breath. I hoped I'd been breathing too hard to be able to hear properly. But I still couldn't hear anything. Desperately, I let out my breath. I was just closing the door, about to sit down on the street and start to cry, when I heard a boy calling, "She is going to die."

I dashed up the stairs. Had children been left behind? With Daniel?

I threw open the door to the hall, and there were all the orphans with their backs to me, watching a little play on an improvised stage. Their caregivers were all there, too, and Korczak and Daniel! Daniel!

I burst into tears.

The children closest to me stared, confused. The little girl with the red polka-dot dress who had stuck her tongue out at me last time was one of them, and she stuck her tongue out again. I needed quite a while before I was able to stick out my tongue back.

Onstage, a girl was acting that she was dying of a fever. The boy whose voice I had heard from downstairs was dressed up as a rabbi with a false beard and wearing a black cloak and white prayer shawl. They were surrounded by children of all shapes and sizes who had come to say goodbye to the little girl. "Her suffering will end," the rabbi said. "No more pain or sorrow. She will go to a better place."

The mourners were consoled. The dying girl closed her eyes peacefully and passed away forever. Everyone kissed her on the cheek or eyes or even on the mouth. There were probably a couple of boys who took the opportunity to kiss a girl on the lips at long last.

When the play was over, Korczak started to clap and the whole audience joined in. Especially Daniel.

I wiped away the tears on my face with my sleeve and walked through the crowd of applauding children to my boyfriend. When he saw me, he was startled. Ever since the *Aktion* had begun, we'd only seen each other in our would-be haven in my room. We hadn't met anywhere else since the Germans had started carting Jews off like animals. That was eleven days ago—an eternity.

Daniel stopped clapping only after the little actors had taken the fifth or sixth bow. Korczak stopped just before him and looked at me. He had aged years again. But his eyes still sparkled merrily when he smiled. He said, "It is so nice to see you, Mira," which of course really meant, "It is so wonderful that you are still alive, Mira."

"And you," I said. "And you."

A little girl ran up to us calling, "Dr. Korczak, Dr. Korczak! Elias stole my donkey." She was missing two front teeth, one top, one bottom, which looked adorable, but she was almost in tears.

Korczak smiled. "A donkey needs more donkeys," he smiled. And the little girl had to laugh, even though she felt so angry.

He took her hand in his and said, "Let us go find those two donkeys, eh?" And the pair of them went off.

Now there was just me and Daniel standing looking at each

other, while some of the children started putting out tables and chairs ready for lunch. No one had needed to tell them to do this. The children understood their responsibilities within the community.

"Why are you here?" Daniel asked. He didn't know whether he should be pleased or worried.

I wasn't sure what to say. There were children all around us, and I would scare them if I told him that the orphanage was about to be evacuated. Perhaps it was just another ghetto myth, and I had overreacted.

"I'll tell you on the roof," I decided to say.

Daniel looked unsure. It was his job to help the children set the tables.

"It won't take long," I promised, and he nodded.

As we climbed the stairs to the attic, I thought about what I was going to say. When the orphanage got evacuated—even if it didn't happen today—I didn't want Daniel to be there. He had to stay with me. Stay alive. But would he be willing to abandon the children? Korczak never would. He had already turned down any help to escape. And Daniel adored him. How would he be able to stay behind while his surrogate father and family were loaded into the cattle trucks? How could I make Daniel stay with me?

Love! Surely he loved me more than Korczak, didn't he?

"The play you just saw is called *Goodbye to Sarah*," Daniel said as he opened the skylight in the attic.

He tore me away from my thoughts.

"Korczak wrote it. He is preparing the children for death. He doesn't want them to be frightened, and he wants them to see the end of life as something all-redeeming."

It was the saddest thing I had ever heard.

Daniel climbed through the skylight, and I followed him.

The sun was beating down on our roof. It was good that we were wearing shoes. You could have fried an egg on the hot roof tiles. If you had the luxury of having an egg, that is. It was too hot to sit down. Unless we sat on one of the old planks still lying around. Daniel had been going to build us a little shelter from the rain, but then the *Aktion* started.

"So, why are you here?" he asked.

"Move in with me at Miła Street!" I said, and was as surprised by my words as Daniel was. He stared at me as if I had lost my mind.

"They are going to clear out the orphanages," I explained desperately. But I already knew what he was going to say, "My place is here with the children. With Korczak."

And because I knew, he didn't need to say it.

"I just heard someone shouting that the SS are on their way to get you!"

Daniel looked alarmed. He was more worried about the children than about himself, but of course he feared for his life, like anyone else. He wasn't a saint.

"Come with me," I begged.

"I can't, you know that."

I was furious.

"I don't understand you," I said sharply. "What do they get out of it if you die?"

"My place is by their side."

"That's not an answer," I said. "I asked what good it will do anyone if you die with them."

"They are my brothers and sisters. They need me!"

"I need you, too!"

He realized how desperate I was and put his arms around me.

"Don't . . ." I held up my hands to stop him.

He stood still.

"Unless you come with me . . ."

He didn't move.

My eyes welled up, but instead of giving in to tears, I started yelling,

"Korczak is an old man. He can die if he likes, but not you!"

Daniel was shocked. But I didn't care. "He has no right to take you with him."

"It is my decision."

"That's the point!"

We stared at each other, and my lips trembled because I was trying so hard not to cry.

"It really is your decision," I said quietly, "choose . . ."

I should have said "life."

But instead I whispered, "Me!"

Daniel didn't say anything.

I could see that he was torn.

But not enough to change his mind.

He'd known Korczak all his life. He'd looked after most of the children for years. They were a family with two hundred members; I was just his girlfriend. How could his love for me ever compete with all the bonds he had here?

Before Daniel managed to tell me that he would never choose me, and before I had time to cry, we heard the trucks coming.

We dashed to the edge of the roof. Two trucks had stopped in front of the orphanage. Jewish policemen, SS men, and the Ukrainian monsters jumped down and charged into the house.

"I've got to get to the children," Daniel said without a moment's hesitation.

He tried to get to the skylight, but I jumped in his way. "Maybe they won't look up here! Maybe they won't get us!"

Daniel wanted to push me aside, but I grabbed his arms and yelled at him, "They'll kill you!"

He knew.

"My place is with them."

I now hated this sentence with all my heart.

He got away from me and opened the skylight.

I didn't know what I was doing. I couldn't let Daniel go back down there! He'd die!

I grabbed one of the wooden planks . . . and knocked him out.

22

I t took a moment for me to realize what I had just done. Daniel lay unconscious on the baking roof. The back of his head was bleeding.

Oh God! Did I kill him?

I knelt down beside him to see if he was alive. He was still breathing. And suddenly I was glad that I'd knocked him out. He couldn't go back to the children now. He was going to survive—if the Germans didn't find us up here.

I quickly closed the skylight. Then I lay down, too. Even though the hot tiles burned my skin, I crawled to the edge of the roof to see what was going on. I expected the children to be forced out of the house brutally, but nothing happened. The Germans and their helpers came back out onto the street. Without Korczak. Without the children.

Were they going to spare the children's home? Had I knocked Daniel out for nothing?

On the other hand, the eviction squad showed no signs of leaving. No one climbed back into the trucks. They all waited in front of the house. The soldiers lit cigarettes and chatted among themselves. Jewish policemen wiped sweat off their foreheads. Even now, I couldn't stop myself looking to see if Simon was one of them. And I was relieved to see that he wasn't standing down there.

I looked over at Daniel. He was still unconscious. He was probably going to stay that way for a while. I hoped he didn't have a concussion. I had never attacked anyone, and then it had to be Daniel of all people!

There was nothing I could do for him at that moment. I stayed lying on the roof, so as not to be seen, and watched what was going on below. The Jewish policemen looked like nervous wrecks, but the SS men just seemed bored. One of them told a joke, and the other men laughed. The way they laughed made me think it must have been something indecent.

What on earth were they waiting for? Why didn't they leave? It was all very strange. And it was never a good thing when the Germans started acting strange.

It took almost a quarter of an hour for the door of the orphanage to open again. Korczak stepped out. He had been a member of the Polish army, and he was wearing his uniform. On each side he was holding the tiny hand of a small child. The boy on his left was clutching a worn teddy bear tightly in his other hand. A little blond girl with braids was on his right. She was carrying a doll with a missing leg and was talking to it, as if she were comforting the doll.

Behind Korczak, an older boy stepped out into the street. He was about thirteen years old and was holding a huge flag with both hands. It was King Macius's standard. King Macius was Korczak's most famous creation. The flag was green, with the blue Star of David on a white background on one side. The armbands we were all forced to wear had the same star on them as a sign of shame, but this flag was a sign of pride.

In any other situation, the SS soldiers would have taken the flag away from the boy. But they let him be. Korczak emanated such dignity, even they were impressed.

One after another, all two hundred children left the house. They were wearing their best clothes. Some of them had little knapsacks on their backs, as if they were going on a school outing.

Apparently, Korczak had persuaded the SS men to give the children enough time to get ready. And made sure that they wouldn't be hounded into the streets by shouting soldiers and be even more frightened.

The orphans lined up in rows of four, taking one another's hands, and set off with their caregivers. Korczak walked ahead with the boy who was hiding behind his grubby teddy bear now, and the little girl who talked to her doll kept kissing it over and over again.

The SS and the Jewish police stayed back. Normally they yelled at the people to move, chasing them to the *Umschlagplatz* and beating them if they didn't move fast enough. Or whenever they felt like it.

But these children didn't need to be forced along. Led by Korczak, they headed off in an orderly fashion, along the ghetto streets in the midday sun.

The flag of King Macius fluttered gently in the breeze.

And they reminded me of the little king who strode to his execution with his head held high.

Did the children remember the story, too?

Because they were walking with heads held high.

And singing a song:

"And though the storm engulfs us,
Steadfast we remain."

Some of the Jewish policemen started to cry.
And I cried, too, as the children sang.

23

Daniel woke up in the late afternoon. I was afraid. I'd done the right thing. I knew I had! But would Daniel think so, too?

He sat up and fingered the back of his head. It must have hurt terribly, but Daniel showed no reaction. He just looked at his fingers, which were sticky with blood.

It took forever before he even looked at me. His eyes told me that he could not believe what I had done. But he didn't even ask for an explanation. He got to his feet too fast, and swayed. I went to help him, but he pushed my arms away roughly. I was stunned and moved back.

Daniel had no idea how many hours had gone by, hadn't noticed that the sun was much lower now. He walked to the skylight.

"They are all gone," I said quietly.

He opened the skylight anyway. He hadn't heard me. Or else he didn't want to hear me.

"They are all gone," I repeated a little bit louder. And when he still didn't react, I said, "They . . . they'll be on the trains by now."

Daniel turned back to me slowly. He fought back tears. Tears of rage.

"You had no right!"

"I . . . I," I stammered, and tried to tell him that he had left me no choice.

"You had no right."

"You would be dead . . . ," was all I could say.

"My place was with them."

"I couldn't bear it," I whispered.

His eyes glistened with hatred. As far as he was concerned, it was my fault that Korczak and the children were gone. Nothing to do with the SS. It was my fault that he would have to live without his family from now on instead of going with them to what Korczak had termed a better world.

"I love you," I said to him for the first time.

No one ever hated me more than Daniel did at that moment.

24

walked through the streets of the ghetto in a trance. I didn't feel a thing. No heat, no thirst. I didn't look where I was going, not even to see if there was a roadblock round the next corner. My heart was full of emptiness.

I knew I'd lost Daniel forever.

I only remembered that I had set out to find Simon when I finally reached our door. And I only remembered because my brother was walking toward the house from the other direction, carrying a basket loaded with bread, ham, and cheese. I had no appetite left, although my body must have been craving food.

"We need to talk," Simon said as soon as we met in front of our house.

I didn't answer.

"We've got to talk," he said again.

"You are talking," I answered bleakly, and sat down on the steps. On the opposite side of the street, you could see the sunset behind the houses. A fiery burst of colors. I wanted to drown in it forever.

"We need to find you a hiding place," Simon urged.

I didn't say anything. I was watching the fiery sky.

"God, Mira!" Simon grabbed hold of my shoulders and made me look at him.

"No one is safe. They are going to get everyone!"

His breath stank of cigarettes. When did he start smoking? Why did I care?

"They'll keep searching the houses, again and again," he ranted. "There aren't enough people going to the *Umschlagplatz* voluntarily, not even for the jam, so they are threatening the police now. If we don't catch five Jews a day, we'll be deported."

He got my attention at last. "You . . . hand over Jews?"

"What else am I supposed to do?" he asked in despair.

Daniel wanted to die together with his orphan brothers and sisters, and my brother sent people to death in order to save himself.

What kind of human do you want to be?

"But," he tried to defend himself, "I only take people I don't know to the trains."

What was that supposed to mean? What sort of excuse was that for what he was doing?

"I've seen policemen chase their own parents to the *Umschlagplatz* . . ."

"What?"

"Those pigs said that their parents had lived their lives already," Simon explained, "and that they had their lives ahead of them."

He was calling his own colleagues pigs, as if it made him look better somehow.

"I would never send my own family to death," he said in desperation. "You've got to believe me."

Wouldn't he? Why couldn't I trust my own brother?

166

"Do you believe me, Mira? Do you believe me?" Simon kept shaking me.

He wasn't going to calm down until I lied.

"All right, I believe you."

He let go of me and insisted, "We have to hide you."

Simon wanted to help us, to convince himself that he wasn't a pig like the others. So this was why he'd turned up again after all this time. To ease his conscience. To prove that he was a good person who was only forced to do evil.

We went into the house, and he explained as we climbed the stairs, "I'll bring food every day. I can get hold of plenty."

"Do you have that much money?" I asked, and then regretted it. I had a pretty good idea where the money was coming from. From desperate Jews who paid bribes to be spared.

"I got married," Simon answered.

I didn't understand.

"She's called Leah; she's a rich Jew's daughter. He gave me money to do it. A lot of money."

And as a policeman's wife she wouldn't be deported. Love in the ghetto had come to an end.

When we reached our flat, Simon put the basket of food on the table. Mama tried to hug him to thank him, but he warded her off. He wanted to stop her asking questions about where all the wonderful food had come from, and he didn't want to have to explain that she had a daughter-in-law now, too.

He didn't want to speak to Hannah, either. He wanted to be our hero.

Instead of talking, Simon ran into the kitchen, to the little pantry. Its empty shelves were a silent reminder that we had never really appreciated the times when they were full until it was too late.

"This is a good hiding place," Simon said.

"We won't all fit in there," I answered.

"You will if I take out the shelves. All three of you can sit down then."

"Only with drawn-up knees."

"But you can do it."

"The Germans will look in the pantry," I said.

"Not if something heavy is put in front of it, and you can't even see the pantry in the first place . . ."

He ran into the living room. I followed him over to a huge kitchen dresser. Its glass doors were filthy and cracked, and there were a lot of not very clean cups and plates inside, left behind by the family from Kraków.

"This dresser is big enough to hide the pantry," Simon decided. "You go in there early in the morning before the sun comes up, and I'll push the dresser in front of the door. And when the Germans stop looking after dark, I'll push it out of the way and you can come out again."

"What about air? Won't we suffocate in there?"

"I'll take out the door. That way enough air can get in through the space behind the dresser."

"And what if the Germans see the door and shelves lying around?" I didn't like this idea.

"I'll break them up, so you can't tell what they're supposed to be and take them down to the cellar."

"And what happens if you don't come back at night?"

"You'll be able to push away the dresser from inside. So you can always get out. You just need me to push it back again when you are all in there."

I still didn't want to agree to any of this. It wasn't because I couldn't see the need for a hiding place. And I wasn't worried about spending hours cramped in the dark. Something else was bothering me.

"So we are to put our lives in your hands?"

"I'll bring you food and water every night."

"I just asked you something."

"Do you have any choice?" Simon answered, insulted.

I had no choice. But I didn't want to admit it. So I replied, "There is always a choice."

"The trains," Simon said. "There's your choice."

There was nothing left to say. But I still wasn't ready to agree to all this.

"What happens when you can't fulfill your quota?" I asked him. "Will you give away our hiding place so that you can stay alive?"

Simon was furious. "You think I would do that?"

"Be realistic!"

"That will never happen!" He was almost frantic.

"I find that hard to believe," I retaliated.

"I swear," he said in a trembling voice. Above all, I think he was trying to convince himself. I stopped arguing. Because there was no point. I really didn't have any choice. But for Simon this meant that I trusted him at last. He gave a sigh of relief and started to get the pantry ready. I helped. It was the first time for ages that we did something together. The last time was when we had put on a play for Mama's fortieth birthday. Hannah had written it and called it *Brothers and Sisters Stay Together Forever—Even If They're Idiots*.

I wish!

We didn't say a word while we broke the shelves off the wall: Simon was determined to get this right, and I couldn't stop thinking about Daniel.

I'd saved his life. I held on to that thought. It was all I had. It would have to do for now, to give me strength. I had lost the support Daniel had given me forever. I would have given up when my father killed himself if it hadn't been for Daniel. How long could I cope without him before I gave up now? Let myself be dragged to the trains for a jar of jam? How long would my strength last if no one was sharing theirs with me? How long could I be strong for my sister?

It took several hours to clean out the pantry, demolish the shelves and door, and take everything down to the cellar. Then we moved the dresser into the kitchen. It was past midnight when we were finally done and Simon and I started talking again.

"Where can I stay tonight?" he asked. It was too dangerous to run around in the ghetto at night, even if you were a Jewish policeman.

"Take my mattress," I offered. I didn't want to stay in the room that had been Daniel's and my retreat the past few days. I went to share with Mama. She turned away from me in her sleep. I closed my eyes. I held on to the fact that Daniel was still alive with all my might, even though I'd managed to lose him. There were worse comforts in the world.

A few hours later, Simon woke us up. It was still dark. Of course. We took food and water into the pantry and sat down on the dirty wooden floor. It was too cramped to lie down, and we had to sit with our legs bent. Simon pushed the dresser across the doorway, and we lit a small candle so that we didn't have to stay in the dark. Of course, we would blow it out at the slightest hint of someone coming into the flat.

"I'll let you out tonight," we heard Simon say, "and bring something more to eat."

"You are a good person," Mama said to him.

I laughed scornfully.

Neither my mother nor my brother reacted.

The sound of Simon's footsteps disappeared, and Hannah sighed, "So this is our new home. Smells pretty bad."

The candlelight lit up her sad little face. The rest of our "new home" was hidden in darkness.

"I'm going to miss the daylight."

I would have liked to comfort Hannah. Help make her time in the cramped dark space more bearable, but I simply couldn't. I didn't have enough strength left.

Instead, it was Hannah who stopped me from going mad in the weeks to come. As the world outside in the ghetto got more and more terrible—Simon told us on his evening visits that no one was safe anymore, not the people in the workshops or the members of the Jewish council—Hannah whisked us away to the world of the 777 islands. Really, she only took me with her. Mama disappeared into her own world, to her memories of Papa. Day by day, she became less aware of us, and after five days in the dark pantry she stopped talking altogether.

There were times when I envied her. It would certainly have felt better to live just in my memories of Daniel instead of knowing that I was in a hiding place that could be discovered by the SS at any moment.

In the world of the 777 islands, Hannah had the wildest adventures. Together with her dear friend Ben Redhead, Captain Carrot, and his werewolf sailor, she set off to find the three magic mirrors that would make it possible to defeat the evil Mirror King who already held 333 of the 777 islands in his power. The Mirror King was terribly cruel to his enemies. He locked them away in distortion mirrors where they had to stay forever as twisted mirror images. And this happened to many innocent creatures, too. No matter if they were children, living lanterns, or singing squirrels—the tyrant didn't care.

And all the time, Hannah brought the beauty of the 777 islands to life—the sea was so wide, the sunsets lasted forever, the flowers were every color under the rainbow. I longed to live there. Why wasn't that the real world and ours the imaginary one? Why couldn't our world have been invented by a storyteller living on one of the islands? Someone who told horror stories about the ghetto to the members of his tribe sitting round the fire before they went to sleep? A storyteller would have been able to make up a happy ending for us, and we'd get to live happily ever after once the suffering was over.

Or maybe we were invented, and our storyteller was a very nasty man.

When Hannah's heroes met the Scarecrow Dread on the Island of Fear to get their first magic mirror, Dread used a terrible charm made from straw. It was a charm that forced you to face your greatest fear. Once the fear filled someone's mind, they were usually lost.

Captain Carrot watched his beloved ship, the *Longear*, sink beneath the waves. The werewolf saw his teeth falling out, one by one. Hannah and Ben Redhead had to face the worst fear of all: Hannah saw that Ben Redhead was going to die. And Ben Redhead saw that Hannah was going to die. And they learned that love and fear were very closely linked together.

But they were the first to resist the power of the straw charm because there was something Dread didn't realize. The love they shared was greater than any fear.

25

One morning—or was it already afternoon? We had no sense of time in the pantry—I heard a quiet coughing sound.

"The captain drew his sword," Hannah was just telling us when I heard the coughing again. A bit louder.

". . . and the rattling skeleton said . . ."

"Shh!" I hissed at my sister. But Hannah was lost in her story and continued, "Feel my hatchet, Captain Carrot!"

"Shh!" I hissed more insistently, and blew out the candle. That shut her up at once. We both strained our ears. Was Mama listening, too?

Surely it was just another false alarm. It had to be.

We had had quite a few of those in the past few days. We'd thought we heard doors being opened, or people creeping through the flat. It turned out the door noise was because we'd left a window open to air the place and the draft had moved the doors a little. The other sounds must have been mice.

Another cough.

The kitchen door opened.

I could hear my heart beating. I even thought I could hear Hannah's heart beating. For a moment I was sure that whoever was out there must be able to hear our hearts beating, too, right through our chests and the heavy dresser.

The steps came closer. But they didn't sound like boots. Please let it be some poor person hunting for food, who would be gone in a minute.

Would we be turned in if the person found us?

No way. That would be crazy; he or she would end up being sent to death by the Germans, too. Unless of course whoever it was couldn't care less and handed us over for the sake of an extra piece of bread on the way to the *Umschlagplatz*.

The coughing got closer.

It didn't sound like someone old, more like someone young. Maybe a woman? Whoever it was must be sick. Was it Daniel? I tried to remember how Daniel used to cough. Did he sound like that?

No, the cough out in the kitchen sounded very different. It was stupid to hope that Daniel might have changed his mind and come to find me.

Whoever it was seemed to have stopped directly in front of the dresser. Did the person know that we were hiding behind it? If so, why didn't they try to push it out of the way? Would whomever it was fetch the Germans first?

Hannah and I held our breath. Only Mama continued breathing normally. In and out. In and out. She hadn't even noticed that we had put out the candle and were sitting in the dark. I wished I could make her stop.

"Mira," I heard a pitiful cry from the other side.

I couldn't believe it. The woman—it was definitely a woman—knew my name.

"Mira, are you here?"

If she knew me, then I must know her, too.

She stopped calling. The dresser rattled. Had she found us? Was she going to push the dresser out of the way?

We could hear her sitting down. She must have leaned against the dresser and slid down to the ground. Which is why it had wobbled.

The woman stayed sitting where she was. She continued to cough but she didn't say anything. In my mind I could still hear the sound of her voice, "Mira, are you here?" And all at once I knew who was sitting on the floor leaning against the dresser in our kitchen.

I stood up. Hannah drew a sharp breath but didn't say anything until I started trying to push the heavy dresser away from the opening to the pantry. My little sister whispered, "What are you doing?" but I didn't say, "What does it look like?" It didn't seem right.

I managed to move the dresser far enough away from the door to be able to squeeze through the gap into the kitchen. It took me a few moments to get used to daylight again. I hadn't seen any for the past two weeks, just the light of the moon and stars when we came out of hiding at night. At last I could see the woman properly. It was the person I was expecting to see: Ruth.

She had lost weight, her hair had been shaved off, and her clothes were in rags. The contrast to her appearance at the Britannia Hotel couldn't have been any greater.

I called to Hannah, "It is all right. You can come out."

My little sister crawled out of the pantry carefully, and she, too, needed a moment to adjust to the light. She saw Ruth and was horrified by the look of her, although she didn't say anything.

Ruth pulled herself up from the ground slowly and said, "Do you have anything to eat?"

I fetched a piece of bread from the pantry where my mother was still sitting.

Hannah asked me quietly, "What happens if the Germans come?"

"Then you go back into the pantry, I push the dresser across the entrance, and they just get me."

Hannah didn't look happy. But it was the best I could do if the Germans really came.

Ruth gulped down the bread so fast that she almost choked on it. She coughed, choked, and threw up a small amount of chewed bread, which I wiped away immediately. If the Germans did arrive, I didn't want telltale signs of food to give us away.

I gave Ruth something to drink, and Hannah went back to Mama, who had stayed sitting in the pantry. She helped her get up. Mama should see some daylight, too, even if she didn't seem to react to anything anymore. Hannah wanted to take her to the window, but I told her to be careful. No one must see us from the street. And so they stayed standing in the middle of the kitchen. Hannah looked up to the sun, which was something special to her now, while Mama just stared at the floor.

I took Ruth next door. I wanted to know what had happened to her and make sure that Hannah couldn't hear. But when I asked her, Ruth didn't say anything. I decided that what had happened must be so terrible that she didn't want to answer. She sank to the floor again and leaned against the wall. I sat down beside her. Ruth coughed and coughed. It didn't really sound as if she was sick after all. It was more like she wanted to cough something out of her body—not a sickness, something worse.

She managed to calm herself, and then Ruth said, "Lulay . . ."

"What?" I asked, not understanding.
As an answer she sang a lullaby.
An awful lullaby.

Lulay, lulay—little one
Lulay, lulay—only son

"What's that?" I asked Ruth in the hope that the song had some sort of meaning.

Crematorium black and silent
Gates of hell, corpses piled high . . .

Had she lost her mind? Wonderful, that would make two of them in the flat, then, counting Mama.

Here he lies, my only little boy
Tiny fists pressed in his mouth
How can I cast you into the flames?
With your beautiful golden hair . . .

She definitely sounded crazy. What if she started singing when the Germans came looking for us? Could I risk letting her hide with us? Or would it be better to send her away at once? No matter if she died or not? Could I even think such a thing?

Now little eyes look calmly at the sky
Cold tears, I hear them crying . . .

I couldn't stand this sick lullaby any longer and said, "Please stop singing."

Oh my boy, your blood is everywhere!
Three years old—your golden hair . . .

"Please."

Lulay, lulay—little one
Lulay, lulay—only son

"You've got to stop," I shouted at her.

Ruth flinched and shut up.

I took a deep breath before I asked her, "What on earth was that all about?"

"I heard that song in Treblinka!"

"Treblinka?"

Then Ruth started coughing again.

It took a while before the fit was over and she started to talk. On the second day of the *Aktion*, she had been rounded up and forced into one of the cattle trucks. During the journey, a lot of people had suffocated and she had had to sleep on top of bodies lying on the floor because she was so weak.

It sounded so awful, it could hardly be true.

"Then we finally reached Treblinka . . ."

"A labor camp?" I asked.

Ruth laughed. In the most sinister way. And started to cough again.

"What sort of camp is it, then?" I asked, although I was afraid of the answer.

"You are forced to take off your clothes when you arrive. If you are not fast enough you get whipped. And then you walk naked past mountains of bodies. Thousands of stinking bodies. Swollen bodies. They can't burn or bury the bodies as fast as they gas more people."

I still didn't understand. How could the Germans be gassing thousands and thousands of people in the vans?

"They force everyone into the gas chambers naked . . ."

Chambers? They had built *chamber*s to gas people?

"Afterward, they burn as many as they can and the rest are buried in pits. You can watch the smoke rising in the wind as the bodies burn, and you breathe in the smoke . . . Mira, you breathe in the dead . . . breathe in death!"

Ruth had another coughing fit.

Now I understood. She was coughing because she still believed the ash of the burned bodies was in her lungs.

She was trying to get rid of the ash in her body, but it wasn't possible, no matter how much she coughed and choked. The dead weren't in her body, they were in her mind. Forever. Korczak and the children were among them. I had saved Daniel from that fate. He should have been grateful, instead of despising me.

"The lullaby," Ruth went on, "I heard a watchmaker sing it. For his little son."

The Germans were burning children. Was there no end to their monstrosity? They must be beasts and demons, straight out of hell. Victorious. Come to turn the whole world into hell, bit by bit.

"How . . . how did you manage to survive?"

"I was lucky. Practically no women survive the first twenty-four hours in Treblinka. The strongest men are forced to work. Burying the bodies, sorting the belongings of the dead . . . but there is only one kind of work for women. For pretty women like me."

She had always been so proud of her looks. There was none of that pride left now.

"We were there to serve the SS."

That was what she called luck?

I would have gone to the gas chambers rather than allow those beasts near my body. Although, that's what I thought here and now, but who knows what I would have thought when I saw piles of corpses. Perhaps I'd even have been jealous of someone like Ruth who could stay alive because she was a whore?

"I was the doll's favorite for three days," Ruth said.

"The doll?"

"An SS man. He had such a pretty face that the Jews gave him the nickname 'the doll.' He shot Jews every day just for fun, or he beat them to death."

Enough! It was enough. I didn't want to hear another word about this camp. Just one last thing, "How did you manage to get away?"

I couldn't see why the SS would let anyone get out of that hell.

"Shmuel paid the camp commander some money for me. A lot of money!"

The mafia boss had got her out of there. I was surprised that Ruth had meant so much to him.

"I told you, didn't I?" Ruth smiled weakly. "He loves me."

And I had never believed her.

"But why aren't you with Shmuel now?" I asked.

"He and five of his men have been taken to Pawiak prison." She started coughing again.

I hoped that the coughing wouldn't give us away and lead us all to Treblinka. Because I could never send my friend away.

26

Ruth sat in the pantry with us during the day from now on. We had to squeeze even closer together, and my bent knees started to ache as soon as I sat down. When we came out of the pantry at night, we could only crawl on our hands and knees at first.

Ruth still coughed, and there was no way I could stop her. It didn't matter if I asked her nicely, warned her, or yelled at her. She was going to get us all killed if she didn't stop soon. I started to lose my nerve with Ruth. Not just because I was scared, but also because the coughing reminded me what was going to happen in the end: whips, dogs, and then the gas chambers.

Lulay, lulay . . .

Hannah was the only person who managed to stay sane. She told more and more stories about the 777 islands. Not for ten hours in one go, of course. But again and again. For half an hour or ten minutes at a time. And when she was telling her story, even Ruth's coughing stopped. Ruth was spellbound when Hannah and Ben Redhead managed to snatch the second magic mirror away from the Weather Wizard. Once again the two heroes succeeded because of the power of their love. No matter how many blizzards or hailstones or strokes of lightning the wizard bombarded them with, their love was stronger than any storm.

I bet that Ruth was thinking about Shmuel when she listened to the story. I know I was thinking about Daniel. He had stopped loving me because of what I had done. Where was he now, I wondered? Was he still alive?

He had to be alive.

Hannah and Ben reached Scarf Island. An island where all the inhabitants had to wear a scarf and where you could be hanged for not wearing one. Even Ruth grinned when Ben Redhead, who didn't have a scarf, said, "This whole scarf business is a bum 'wrap.'"

It was the first time that I had been able to laugh heartily since the deportations began. A happy moment—and for once, I didn't care whether the SS heard me or not.

27

Simon kept his promise and came to see us every night. And each time, I was frightened that the day had finally come when he could no longer fulfill his quota of Jews and was forced to betray us.

How would that happen? Presumably he wouldn't chase us out of the house himself, but just tip off the soldiers so they knew where to find us. Then he wouldn't have to look us in the face when they came to get us and we would never know for sure if he had betrayed us or not.

But Simon managed to find other Jews to send to Treblinka. They were gassed instead of us.

Lulay, lulay . . .

Would this madness never end? Hundreds of thousands had been murdered by now. Was the very last Jew to be murdered, too?

Day by day, my hopes shrank that we would manage to survive. I even started to cough nervously, as if I already had the ash of the dead in my lungs.

It was actually Simon who improved the situation! What he told me after two and a half weeks of hiding made me come alive for the first time in a long while: Szeryński, the commander of the Jewish police, had been gravely wounded—by Jews.

Yes, exactly, by Jews.

Jews had defended themselves against oppression. For the first time.

There was no other policeman who deserved to die as much as Józef Szeryński did. The pig was a Jew who had converted to Catholicism long before the war and had never wanted anything to do with the Jews. Of course the Nazis couldn't have cared less, they threw him into the ghetto regardless. A Jew was a Jew as far as they were concerned, even if he thought he was a Catholic. But they were so impressed by Szeryński's organizational skills and his personal hatred of the Jews—wherever that may have come from—that they made him the head of the Jewish police. He carried out every order he was given with burning ambition. Even, or perhaps especially, during the *Aktion*. Day by day he personally made sure that enough Jews were forced into the trains at the *Umschlagplatz*. He sat in a rickshaw, tapping his shoes with his whip in a bored sort of way, and watched the goings-on as if destroying one's own people were just another bureaucratic task.

Now his rickshaw would be empty!

"The person who shot at Szeryński was a Jewish policeman," Simon said ambiguously.

I wasn't quite sure what he thought about all this.

Was he proud that someone from his own ranks had shot the highest-ranking officer and didn't want to admit it? But probably he was just more nervous than usual. The Jewish policemen would have to fear one another as well as everything else from now on.

"The killer rang Szeryński's doorbell this morning," Simon said. "The housekeeper opened the door, and this brute told her that he had a letter he had to give Szeryński personally . . ."

Simon had said *brute*—that must mean that he wasn't pleased that the gunman was a member of the Jewish police.

"As Szeryński came to the door, the brute pulled out his gun. It jammed. Then he tried again and shot Szeryński only in the cheek; it was not immediately fatal. But the killer must have thought that he was dead; at any rate, he leaped onto a motorbike and drove away. In the end, he has got what he wanted. Szeryński is said to be dying."

This was thrilling news.

I was shocked and agitated. In a strange way that I had never known before, I actually felt happy.

It probably wasn't right to be happy about an attempted murder, but I was glad anyway, with all my heart. After all the suffering, somebody had hit back!

"Does anyone know who the killer was?" I wanted to know, half hoping it was Amos.

"They didn't fetch him so far."

I was even more pleased.

Simon was obviously not happy. "It was one of the policemen who went into hiding at the start of the *Aktion* . . ."

And who had a lot more honor than my brother.

"Do they know which group he belongs to?" I asked, and really hoped that it would be Hashomer Hatzair—Amos's group. Then I would have some kind of connection to all of this. I would know Jews who could defend themselves. I had even kissed one of them!

"It was the ŻOB," Simon said with a snort.

"ŻOB?"

"A Jewish fighting organization." He almost spat out the words. I finally understood: Simon had signed a pact with the demons in order to save his life. He had believed that as long as he served them well and spread enough fear and terror himself, he would be saved. But now the beasts were getting more and more unpredictable, sending all those servants who didn't satisfy their demands to the gas chambers. And the underdogs were starting to get dangerous. A Jew had shot the police commander. How safe was an ordinary policeman like Simon in that case?

"The ŻOB is a union of the youth organizations Dror, Akiba, and Hashomer Hatzair," Simon explained.

Hashomer Hatzair—Amos was part of this!

"Those pigs," Simon said, full of anger and fear, "will be the death of us all!"

"What?" I couldn't believe what Simon was saying.

"If they kill even a single German, we will all be destroyed."

"They are doing that anyway," I said.

"But not everyone."

"Don't you know what is going on in Treblinka?"

"Of course I know!" His voice was shaking with anger. "But the Germans won't kill everyone if we don't provoke them. The *Aktion* won't go on forever, and we can survive. We'll belong to the fifty thousand Jews left in Warsaw to work here for them until the end of the war!"

He didn't just hope this, he really believed it. He didn't believe in God, or in himself. He believed in the grace of the beasts and demons. What was the point of arguing? I decided not to say anything. And was secretly pleased that Amos was fighting for our honor. More than pleased. I was filled with pride.

On the same night, Russian planes flew over Warsaw and bombed the city. What a day!

28

The next few weeks in our stuffy dark chamber seemed more bearable somehow. Although our knees and legs ached more and more from day to day, I had found new hope. The Allies must have heard about the crimes of the Germans against the Jews by now. Surely they would—must—come to our aid and bomb the railway tracks to Treblinka soon, so that no more people could be sent to the gas chambers.

When Simon saw us each night, the first thing I always asked him was if there was any news from the resistance movement. My brother was shocked that the ŻOB had set empty houses on fire to stop the Germans from stealing the properties of murdered Jews. I was so pleased by the news that Simon snapped at me, "You'd better hope they don't set this house on fire, too."

Even that thought couldn't dampen my spirits. I imagined joining Amos's group. I would plan attacks together with the other fighters. Not just against Jewish policemen, but against the SS, too. I would walk up to Frankenstein, holding a gun, and say, "In the name of the Jewish people, I sentence you to death for the murder of countless children!" For one long beautiful moment, I would see the fear in Frankenstein's eyes. Then I would pull the trigger and fire a bullet straight into that swine's skull. The Germans had better start worrying. They should be afraid of us. The Jews would get them shaking the way the Allied planes did.

I imagined moving in with the Hashomer Hatzair cell and sleeping in a dorm of mattresses with all the other resistance fighters. I would be one of the bravest ones. Fearing neither death nor torture, I would plan daring missions against the Germans and carry them out. Together with Amos, I would raze the headquarters of the Jewish police to the ground, throw Molotov cocktails at the German trucks, and execute the highest officers. Amos would realize what sort of person I really was, leave his girlfriend to be with me, and we would kiss even more passionately than at the market that time. Far more passionately.

Of course, these were silly fantasies like Hannah's stories; I would never have been able to take Mama, Ruth, and Hannah to join the resistance group, and of course I was terrified of dying and even more scared of the torture chamber in Pawiak prison. There is no way I would have been able to stand the pain in real life. The Nazis wouldn't need to beat the naked soles of my feet before I told them all the secrets of the resistance and betrayed all my comrades. Just that one thump on my wounded arm had almost been enough to make me black out.

And there was no way I could ever kill someone. No matter why. I could burn down houses. But shoot someone? I didn't have the necessary cold-bloodedness for that. No, it had nothing to do with cold-bloodedness. One needed searing hatred.

29

t took two weeks for the planes to come back. My heart started jumping for joy when I heard the drone of their engines. I stood at the window and saw the skies over Warsaw glow red. And I had no fear. The Russians wouldn't bomb the ghetto. We had the same enemy.

I hoped for more and more bombs, hundreds and thousands, the beasts would burn . . . then the first bomb hit the ghetto. I couldn't believe it. This couldn't be, it mustn't be, these were our allies. It must be a mistake, a stray.

More bombs hit the ghetto.

I ran over to the others, and we stared at one another in panic. Where could we go to find shelter? We couldn't leave the flat. No one could know that we even existed.

Desperately, I took Hannah and Mama into my arms, although Mama didn't really have a clue what was going on. Ruth cowered at the other end of the room, under the table, as if that could offer some kind of protection against a bomb. It was no better than my protective arms.

A few minutes later the planes were gone and they took all our hope with them.

No one in the world cared about the fate of the Jews. We were being bombed, instead of the tracks to Treblinka.

The next day the German army surrounded the city in what was called a cauldron—or *Kessel*. We were doomed. There was no escape.

On the sixth of September, in the eighth week of the *Aktion*, Simon arrived at five o'clock in the morning. But he didn't push the dresser back across our hiding place; he was totally hysterical. He couldn't actually speak at first, but then he managed to pull himself together and started talking in jumbled sentences. "All the Jews left in the ghetto have to be outside on the street by six o'clock. Anyone with a numbered tag gets to work; everyone without a tag goes to the trains . . ."

"What sort of tag?" I asked.

"The tags!" he answered as if he'd explained already, and I was just too stupid to know what he was talking about.

"What do the tags mean?" I asked, and Simon realized that I hadn't understood a word he'd said so far.

"There are yellow tags with numbers on them. They get handed out by the workshops and the Jewish organizations. The heads have to decide who is going to live or die. The heads of the hospital, the police, the Jewish council, and so on."

Jews had to choose whose life was worth saving.

The Nazis always managed to dream up something even more twisted.

And it was always the same. Everyone hoped that they would be one of the last forty-five thousand Jews who got given one of the tags. The difference between life and death.

Without that hint of hope there would have been an uprising, I'm sure. But as it was, all the ghetto inhabitants used the time that was left to do anything they could—fight, beg, plea with their bosses—to get hold of one of the tags.

The beasts understood how to break any resistance before it even got started. Except in people like Amos.

"I didn't get a tag." Simon started to cry. "Five hundred tags for two thousand five hundred policemen . . ."

I stood beside my brother and felt terrible. It would have been the right thing to give him a hug, even though I couldn't comfort him. But I didn't want to. The beasts' loyal servant had sent Jews to the camps, and now he was being sentenced to death. He should never have trusted them. Nobody ever should have.

"Hide with us," I said.

I had no idea how that was supposed to work. There wasn't any more room in the pantry. One of us would have to hide somewhere else in the house, and I had no idea where.

"No!" Simon cried.

"No?" I was surprised.

"They have issued new orders: Anyone found hiding will be shot on the spot."

It was possibly still better than the gas chamber. But I was horrified at the thought of being executed like that.

"I am going to report," Simon said. "When the Germans realize that I'm a policeman, and see how young and strong I am, they are bound to keep me alive even without a tag, because I can be useful."

He still believed in the beasts' mercy.

What a pathetic fool.

Simon pulled himself up to his full height, took a deep breath and let it out again, and then left the flat. Without saying anything. He was abandoning us, and I didn't try to stop him. I didn't even call after him to say goodbye. Just as he was no longer interested in our fate, I didn't stop to think about what might happen to him. Instead, I wondered what would happen to us now. In my own way, I had abandoned my brother, too.

But there was no time to think about what I was going to do about food. I heard the stomp of boots.

Soldiers charged up the stairs and forced open the doors of the flats. Panicked, I hurried Hannah, Ruth, and Mama into the pantry.

"What about you?" Hannah asked from out of the dark.

"Someone's got to push the dresser back."

Hannah stared at me, terrified.

"I'll find somewhere else to hide."

"Where?"

I had no idea, but I said, "I'll find somewhere." I started to push the dresser across the opening again, but Hannah said, "Mira?"

"What is it?"

My little sister ran out to me and kissed me on the cheek.

I loved her so much.

One floor down, the soldiers were shouting something in Ukrainian.

I pushed the dresser back in front of the hiding place as fast as I could and hissed to Ruth, "Don't cough, for God's sake don't cough."

I dashed out of the kitchen and tried to think where I could hide. I would run up to the attic. Perhaps I could climb out onto the roof.

I was about to open the door when I realized that the men had already reached our floor. There was no chance of getting to the roof now. And there was nowhere I could hide. They were going to find me and kill me.

Unless, unless . . .

I ran into the sitting room and grabbed an empty suitcase that the family from Kraków had left behind. I threw a few of the clothes lying around into it at random and closed the suitcase. I heard our front door being flung open violently. The SS men shouted their commands, words no Polish Jew could understand, though the sense was perfectly clear.

With suitcase in hand, I ran to the door and reached it just as the men stormed in with their guns drawn. There were three of them, all blond, all of them with angular chins, all in their early twenties. For a second they stopped, surprised to see me.

"I was just on my way to report," I lied.

The Ukrainians couldn't understand what I was saying. The man right in front of me pointed his gun at me. So did the other two. As if it would take more than one bullet to kill a Jew.

With beads of sweat on my forehead, I pointed at my suitcase and repeated what I'd said slowly and clearly. "I was just on my way to report."

The Ukrainians were still pointing their pistols at me; I couldn't convince them. They were going to shoot me in a minute if I didn't do anything. But there was nothing more I could do; I couldn't even think straight, I was so scared.

I could see the Ukrainian in front of me start to squeeze the trigger.

"*Umschlagplatz!*" I screamed hysterically.

"*Umschlagplatz!*"

They must be able to understand that, surely!

The soldier's finger relaxed, and he lowered his gun. The other two followed suit. They had understood after all. I suddenly realized my whole body was shaking. I could only hope that Ruth wouldn't cough. She stayed quiet. Well done, Ruth!

The soldiers made a sign for me to follow them, and I left the flat. I was on my way to the gas chambers. But Hannah, Mama, and Ruth were still safe.

30

I t was a beautiful morning.

It was an awful morning.

Ten thousand Jews were forced to walk along Miła Street in the warm light of the September sun, toward the gates that the Germans had erected. We moved forward slowly. Very slowly. The Nazis and the owners of the workshops were waiting at the gates, and decided according to the tags which way we had to go. One gate meant life, the other one meant death.

Every person caught in this human cauldron was stricken with fear. Including the Jews with the tags. We had got to know the Germans well enough by now to know that they would be the first to break their own rules for no apparent reason. A tag handed out by them was by no means a guarantee of safety.

The streets were lined with Ukrainians, Latvians, and Germans hitting people with truncheons or whips. There was no chance that anyone in the terrible procession was going to fight back. The crowds of people stuck in the cauldron were far too disturbed for that. I could hear a man shouting at the gates, "I don't want to work! I said I don't want to work!"

That surprised me. Someone was actually willing to go to the trains?

"I'll stay with my children!"

Then he went quiet. Probably they'd let him have his last wish. He was just another Jew who was going to be gassed, as far as the Nazis were concerned. With his children! Who cared?

A woman walking beside me in the cauldron was carrying a sleeping baby in her arms. I could see that she was wearing one of the treasured tags round her neck. Her life would be saved. But not the life of her child. The woman noticed me staring at her. She had heard the man shouting to be allowed to go to the gas chambers with his children, too. Quietly, she said to me, "It's always possible to have another child."

I didn't know what she meant at first.

"But if I die with the child, I can't bring new life into the world."

She was willing to leave her baby. And she'd worked out reasons to convince herself. Reasons that sounded more like life than death.

I felt sick.

I looked away and tried to see if I could spot Hannah, Mama, or Ruth anywhere in the cauldron. I didn't see them. Good. There was still a chance that they might be able to survive somehow instead of me.

I didn't bother looking for my brother, though. He must be heading toward the *Umschlagplatz*, too. I couldn't see why the Nazis would allow anyone without a tag to remain alive. The one time their rules always applied was when they were intended for killing Jews.

I was stuck in the cauldron for about two hours before I reached the selection area. When I reached the SS man, I wasn't even nervous or afraid. I already knew which way he would send me. There was no hope left. I felt stunned and as heavy as lead. I didn't look up at him. Without a word, just with a small hand movement, he signaled for me to walk through the gate that led to death.

As I stumbled toward it, the woman with the child was still beside me. The SS man saw her tag, and she was allowed to live. Without a word, she handed me her sleeping baby. I was to take it to death instead of her.

Before I could say anything, she was gone through the other gate. I had the choice of being there for this stranger's child. Being there for it in its final hours, no matter how hard that might be. Or just laying it down there on ground. Where the soldiers would either shoot it or simply trample it to death with their boots.

What kind of person did I want to be?

31

walked to the *Umschlagplatz* with thousands of other people, holding the baby in my arms. I had left the silly suitcase standing somewhere ages ago. There wasn't anything in it that would have been any use to either the baby or me. What do you need in a gas chamber?

The little thing was sleeping in my arms. It hadn't noticed that its mother had given it away yet. How was the woman going to be able to live with her decision? Would she really bring new children into the world in the unlikely event of managing to survive the war? Would they be a comfort to her for having sent her firstborn to the gas chambers?

Lulay, lulay . . .

I wouldn't ever sing that song to the child, no matter what.

As I thought about the woman, I realized that I was never going to be a mother. Not that I'd wanted to be one; I was still too young. But apart from this baby who was going to die, I would never hold one in my arms. Never hug my own child.

Was that the worst thing about dying? To have no future?

When we reached the *Umschlagplatz*, I hugged the child closely. The place was at the very edge of the ghetto and was surrounded by a high wall. There was only a small entrance at one end. Through which we were forced, squashed, and beaten.

The place was totally overcrowded. Everywhere, there were despairing people sitting next to their few belongings. They were squatting in urine and feces. If there were toilets anywhere, then there were nowhere near enough for all these crowds of people. The stench in the air was bitter. I would have liked to put a scarf over my mouth, but I didn't have one.

There was almost no one left with the strength to comfort anyone. Children were crying; couples sat listlessly beside each other. There were bodies everywhere—people who had slit their wrists with knives or razor blades.

The *Umschlagplatz* could rightly be termed hell, but it was just a taste of what was to come. The real hell was waiting in the camps.

The crowds of people pushed me toward the center of the area. The baby I was holding woke up and started to cry. I hoped it wasn't hungry.

I started to rock it gently. "Hush, it's all right . . . everything is fine . . ."

That was ridiculous, of course. Korczak would probably have said something like, "You'll soon be in a better world . . . ," but I couldn't say that. I didn't believe in God anymore. How could I? There would be nothing after death for me or the baby or anyone here.

It would have been better if the Ukrainians had shot me. And if I'd allowed them to kill the baby at the gate. The little thing calmed down and went back to sleep. A small miracle in the middle of hell. I concentrated on listening to the child's breathing. I hoped it would distract me from my fear. I tried to breathe in time with the child. Was it a boy or a girl, I wondered? I didn't dare look to find out. I was afraid I would wake it up again. But I decided I'd give it a name before we died. What would I call it if it was a boy?

Daniel?

Amos?

Captain Carrot?

I started to laugh and cry all at once when I thought of him. I wasn't going to see Hannah ever again.

I saw a doctor in a white coat. She was giving exhausted children something to drink. She looked feverish and haunted herself. I didn't think anything of it at first, but when I looked at the children again—I'd stopped crying about Hannah by this stage and had managed to pull myself together—I realized the doctor had not been handing out water: The little things were lying lifeless on the ground, one in a pool of urine. She had given the children poison. Probably cyanide.

The doctor had put them all to sleep as gently as she could, to spare them the horror of Treblinka. She was even more caring than I had supposed.

If I saw her again, I'd ask for cyanide for the baby and for myself, too.

I pushed my way through to the edge of the space with Amos—yes, I'd decided to call the baby Amos for now, and if it turned out to be a girl, then I'd call her Amy. I concentrated on the child's breathing again and tried to forget about everything else as best I could.

I reached the wall, found a little spot, and sat down exhausted, even though there were feces nearby. The afternoon sun was shining brightly—like some sick joke.

The baby started crying again. No matter how much I rocked it, I couldn't calm it down this time. It had realized that I wasn't its mother, and it was hungry, too.

A gaunt man sitting in a pool of urine next to me said, "Either you make it shut up or I'll thrash it against the wall!"

He was serious.

I stood up and moved away. I popped my little finger into the baby's mouth, which calmed it down for a moment until it realized that my finger wasn't its mother's breast and it started to cry again. And it stank. It needed its diaper changed and to be cleaned, but how was I supposed to do that without another diaper or water or anything?

The crying got to me, and I started to hear all the other noises going on around me because I could no longer concentrate on the baby's breathing. I heard the most despairing wails, "Water, I need water!" Desperate self-hatred, "Why did I leave him? Why?" Useless prayers, "*Schma yisrael adonai elohenu adonai echad*," and screams and yells: "Mama! Wake up! Please wake up!" "Mira, is that you? . . . Mira . . . Mira!"

Mira?

Someone meant me!

I turned round. There was Amos. Wearing the uniform of a Jewish policeman. He wasn't a policeman—he must be in disguise! And he had one of the lifesaving tags! It was bound to be a forgery. What was he doing here? He risked being thrown into the trains, tag and all.

"You've got a baby?" Amos asked me, surprised.

We were on the verge of hell and he wanted to know about the baby?

"It's not mine," I answered.

He nodded, didn't ask anything else and looked around

instead. For soldiers who could catch him? Or for something else?

"What are you doing here?" I asked.

"I'm looking for Zacharia."

The guy who had slit open my arm was caught in the cauldron, too.

"You are going to smuggle him out!" I felt a tiny hope sprouting in me. Maybe Amos could get me out of here, too. Me and the baby. Us.

"I can't find him, though," Amos said, looking everywhere for his friend and getting more and more nervous every minute.

"Take me with you, then!" I burst out.

"I've only got enough money to free one person," he said. "I can only get Zacharia past the SS."

"But you can't find him!" I answered quickly.

Amos looked at me, dismayed. The idea of abandoning a comrade in the resistance for me was not something he could contemplate. But I wasn't going to give up. "Your friend could be on a train by now."

"You don't know that!"

"You don't know, either! And the longer you stay here, the bigger your chances of being gassed, too!"

Amos knew that, too, and he started to waver.

The baby was crying louder and louder.

"You've got to get out of here," I kept saying to him.

He didn't argue.

"But can you really leave without taking someone with you?"

"By someone you mean you?" he asked scornfully. He had come here to save his friend, not some girl he kissed once.

"Yes."

He couldn't make up his mind. Why couldn't he make up his mind?

The baby was screaming right in my ear.

I held it away from me.

"The money is really important for the movement."

"More important than someone's life?"

"Than your life?" he corrected me.

"Is it more important than my life?"

"We can buy arms."

"And that's more important than my life?"

Amos bit his lip. Until it started to bleed. Then he made up his mind, "All right, I'll get you out of here."

I couldn't believe it. I was going to escape the gas!

"But the baby has to stay here."

I stared at the little baby whose face had turned bright red by now.

"I told you, there's only enough money for one person."

Now it was my turn to waver. The child screamed and screamed and screamed. As if it knew what this was all about.

"Come on," Amos insisted, "before I change my mind."

What kind of human do you want to be?

One who is there for her sister! And one who stays alive.

I turned round in panic, trying to find the doctor I'd seen before. She must be somewhere. She could put the child out of its misery! But I couldn't see her anywhere. So I handed the crying baby to a woman standing beside me, just like its mother had done to me. She looked at me, horrified, and asked, "What are you doing?"

"Keep a lookout for the lady doctor. Ask for cyanide."

I didn't stop to say any more. I headed after Amos.

"Wait!" the woman called, and tried to follow us, but we

pushed through the crowd and she lost sight of us. Her shouting and the baby's wailing faded away until I couldn't hear them anymore.

I'd abandoned a child. And I didn't even know if it was a boy or a girl.

32

We paid the SS men a hundred thousand at the gates. So that was what a life was worth—my life. Amos had saved me for the second time.

Once we got out, he bit his bleeding bottom lip even harder.

"I'm sorry about Zacharia," I said.

But Amos didn't say anything. Maybe he could tell I didn't really mean it—I'd be on my way to the death camp if he'd found his friend. But I was too devastated to care. I had abandoned that baby. It was the first time that I'd done anything like that. The guilt would never go away.

We walked through the streets in silence until Amos said, "You'll join us now?" It was actually more of a statement than a question.

When I'd been stuck in our dark pantry, I'd dreamed of joining Hashomer Hatzair and Amos and showing the whole world that we Jews were not like defenseless animals being led to slaughter, but reality wasn't like that. We'd all been defenseless at the *Umschlagplatz*. Including me. I wasn't a fighter. And I didn't want to be one. I still had Hannah and Mama.

When I didn't reply, Amos got angry, "We just paid a lot of money for you!"

"So you bought my life?"

Amos realized that he'd gone too far and shut up. After a while, he finally said, "It's our mission to seek revenge against the Germans." His eyes were gleaming with determination and hate.

But I didn't have that kind of hatred or determination in me. I couldn't kill anyone. Not even Germans. "My mission is to look after my family," I said.

Amos turned away. This man had saved my life twice, and this was how I was thanking him.

"I . . . I'm sorry," I said. So that he could hardly hear.

His answer was to simply leave me standing in the middle of the street.

33

got to our kitchen.

The dresser had been knocked over.

They were in the pantry:

Ruth.

Mama.

Hannah.

Slumped.

In a pool of blood.

34

screamed like a wounded animal. I screamed until I started to cry. At some stage the crying turned to a whimper. When that stopped, I just stared at the bodies for the rest of the night.

Then hate came.

I was so full of hatred, I wanted kill someone.

Me.

35

wasn't there. I wasn't with them. Not with them. I should be dead with them. I was meant to . . . die.

I went over to the window. It was still dark. There were no streetlights on in the ghetto anymore. There was no one left who could use them. I noticed a small crack in one of the windowpanes. I could see myself breaking the window, picking up one of the pieces of glass, and using it to slit my wrists. Going to the pantry to join the others. Taking Hannah's lifeless body in my arms and slowly bleeding to death beside her.

Being with her seemed right.

I looked around for something to smash the window. The old saucepan in the dresser, maybe? Or the broken kitchen door handle? I could easily pull it off the door. Or I could try to break the glass with an elbow. If I was going to slit my wrists, it wouldn't matter if I cut myself first.

I lifted my elbow and rammed it into the glass, but nothing happened. I tried again, with more force, but the window simply wouldn't break. All I did was hurt my elbow. I went over to the dresser, took out the saucepan, went back to the window, and struck it with all my might. The glass shattered into hundreds of pieces, which all fell out into the street. I should have worked that out beforehand. The pieces of glass didn't make much noise when they hit the ground, but the sound echoed through the empty streets.

If the Germans heard that, they would come, find the broken glass, notice the window, storm the house, and shoot me.

Let them come.

That would be quicker than bleeding to death. I'd sit beside Hannah in the pantry and just let them execute me. Then I'd die the way I was supposed to.

But no Germans came.

I broke off another bit of glass from the window and cut my hand without meaning to. For a moment, I stopped thinking about everything—Hannah dead, wanting to kill myself—and instinctively started to suck the cut to try to stop it bleeding. The blood tasted vile, and I realized I was thirsty.

I stood by the broken window. I could feel the gentle breath of fresh air blowing across my face. The night was cooler than it had been over the past weeks. Autumn was on its way, but it was deepest darkest winter in my soul.

I opened the window wide to breathe in more fresh air, as if it could quench my thirst. Another piece of glass fell out onto the street. Still the Germans didn't come.

I looked down to where the glass had gone, though I couldn't actually see it in the dark. Maybe I should just jump.

Like my father.

I could understand him now.

And I could forgive him.

But if I jumped, I wouldn't be able to lie beside Hannah.

My hand was still bleeding. I kept sucking the cut, remembering I really was thirsty. I hadn't drunk anything for more than a day. I was getting more and more muddled. I wanted to kill myself, but I wanted to drink something, too. My spirit wanted to die, my soul was dead already, but my starving body wanted to live.

There should still be a jug of water in the pantry. I could drink from that if it wasn't shot to bits. I left the window and went over to the three dead bodies. They didn't seem real. As if the corpses riddled with bullets had nothing to do with Hannah, Ruth, or Mama anymore. Their souls were gone. There was nothing left but skin and bones and congealed blood.

The stone jug filled with water stood behind the bodies on the floor. I stepped into the dark room to fetch it and trod on Mama's arm. I stopped and lifted my foot and stared at the body. For a long time.

I never did tell her that I loved her.

My eyes wandered over to all that was left of Hannah, her mutilated soulless shell. Her death was absolutely pointless. So was her whole life.

So was my life.

So was my death.

I leaned over and picked up the jug. I couldn't see if there was any blood in the water in the dark. Some could have splashed in. I raised the jug and let a little bit of water run over my dried lips. It tasted stale, but not like blood. So I lifted it again and drank a bit more water. Slowly, so as not to choke, I took another mouthful. And one more. And another, until the jug was empty.

Then all of a sudden I could think clearly again.

There was no thirst left to confuse me. I still wanted to die. Yes. I did. Even more than before. But I wasn't going to slit my wrists. Or jump. I would die in a different way. A very different way. And not yet. Not today. Suicide was pointless. I wanted my death to have a purpose. It was the only way to give Hannah's death any kind of meaning. Or her life.

Or what was left of mine.

36

"Here are the weapons," Esther said matter-of-factly, and pointed toward a brown bag standing on the floor beside what was left of the printing press. The SS had destroyed it when they arrested Zacharia. There were five pistols in the bag. A real treasure for the resistance. For the Jewish resistance that is. For everyone else, the weapons were a joke. They were from the First World War, and they had cost a lot of money on the black market. The Polish dealers probably still couldn't believe that we had paid fifteen thousand zlotys per gun. I was certain that one of them would jam when we needed it.

"You are to take them to Breul's group on Karmaliicka Street," she ordered. "You'll be given hand grenades in return."

"I'm to go alone?" I asked, surprised.

"Yes."

I didn't like this, but I didn't want to refuse. It was my first mission for the group. At last, I could prove I was useful and show that the money the resistance had paid for me at the *Umschlagplatz* hadn't been wasted.

Esther didn't say goodbye when I grabbed the bag and left the kitchen. She didn't like me. She didn't think that I had what it took to be a fighter. I couldn't care less. I only cared about one last thing these days. When I died, I wanted to take as many Germans with me as possible. I wanted to watch them burn for what they'd done to Hannah.

That was why I didn't like this messenger job. Getting killed taking weapons from point A to point B wasn't the heroic death I had in mind.

Before I went out, I nervously straightened out my new winter clothes. I'd found the thick coat and lined men's trousers in an empty flat last week. The trousers flapped round my skinny legs and ankles. Then I went out into the empty street. Since the end of the *Aktion* two months ago, no one was ever seen in the ghetto during the day. The Germans had allowed no more than thirty thousand Jews to stay alive—or so we reckoned. Another twenty thousand were in hiding. That meant that only one in nine ghetto inhabitants was still alive. One in nine!

Jews only gathered on the streets in the early hours of the morning, on their way to work as slave labor in the workshops and factories, or on the Polish side of the city. And they didn't come back till night. Anyone found on the streets at any other time was executed on the spot by the SS, day or night.

The cold November wind blew feathers up into the air. They floated about like snow. The feathers were everywhere in the ghetto because the pillows and bedding they had previously filled had been collected by the Germans' slaves and taken to the depots along with everything that might make money for the Reich: jewelry, furniture, musical instruments, absolutely everything. The Germans called this pillage of dead Jews' homes *Werterfassung* or the acquisition of "former" Jewish property.

I was living in a city of ghosts where it snowed feathers. The ghosts were the Jews still left alive in the ghetto. We were the living dead. Some of us were kept alive by hatred. The rest just by the bit of watery soup and bread they got at work. Nobody had any hope left. The Germans had halted the *Aktion* for the moment, but everybody knew that even the few of us left alive were going to be murdered. In a month. Or two. Or tomorrow.

I could hear the sound of a car in the distance. The SS was on patrol in another part of the ghetto. So I thought there was no danger. Though it was never a good idea to feel safe in the ghetto.

I turned a corner, and someone grabbed hold of me from behind. Panicking, I tried to get away. But it was no use. I could smell my attacker's foul breath, but I couldn't see him. Was he a German? A desperate Jew? He didn't say anything. Until I kicked him in the shins to get away.

Then he started swearing, "You little slut!"

But instead of letting go, he held me so tightly that I could hardly breathe. While I choked for air, I saw the sleeves of his coat and realized that my attacker was wearing a blue uniform. So he was a Polish policeman. Not a German soldier who was going to shoot me any minute.

I gave up resisting. The Pole loosened his grip slightly, but didn't let go. I could breathe. My chest hurt. It was probably badly bruised.

"What's in the bag?" the Polish policeman asked, and his breath stank like a carrion eater's.

There was no point in lying. Even if I managed to pull away and flee, I would have to leave the weapons we had paid so much money for behind. I couldn't do that. My only chance was to make the policeman fear for his life more than I feared for mine. As I didn't fear for mine all that much, it could just work.

"I'm a member of the Jewish Fighting Organization," I said.

The carrion eater took a sharp breath. Was he scared? He was definitely worried. Unfortunately he didn't let go.

"I'm carrying weapons in the bag. If I fail to deliver them, my people will come and kill you," I said as calmly as possible.

This wasn't a completely empty threat. The resistance had executed several Jewish collaborators. Though no Germans had been killed so far. Much to my regret; I wanted them all to drown in their own blood. Like Mama. Ruth. Hannah.

Also, we hadn't killed any Polish policemen so far, which weakened my threat somewhat. It didn't sound like a joke; it just wasn't quite as convincing as I would have liked. Would he give in, because his fear was greater than his greed? Or would he beat me to death and then enjoy his winnings?

The carrion eater had other ideas. He twisted my arm behind my back. I gasped in pain. But I refused to give him the satisfaction of groaning out loud, or screaming.

"If you try to fight, I'll break your skinny little arm!"

He marched me down the street to the Jewish bank. It was still run by the Jewish council and was where Jews who worked for the Nazis stashed their filthy money. It seemed that the Polish policeman's real job was to guard the bank. He hadn't been on the lookout for Jews. I'd just been stupid enough to run straight into his arms.

"Pawel!" he called. "Pawel, give me a hand!"

Another policeman came out of the bank. He was tall with a beard. He was taken aback at the sight of me. The carrion eater told him, "There's a little treasure here, and I'm not talking about the girl."

"She's too skinny anyway," the one with the beard replied in a surprisingly high-pitched voice. He tore the bag away from me, almost breaking my fingers. Once again I clenched my teeth and merely gasped in pain.

He looked into the bag. "Only Jews would pay anything for this junk," he said.

The carrion eater knocked me over and said, "Tell your friends they can have the bag back for two hundred thousand zlotys."

I looked up at him and saw his face for the first time and his rotten teeth. "Hurry up!" he ordered, and laughed.

I got up and ran off as fast as I could. But as soon as I was round the next corner, I stopped. I could never go back to Esther, Amos, and the others like this. Not having blown a simple mission and cost the resistance even more money. That would be the final proof that I was useless.

I leaned against the house wall and felt a wave of despair. A gust of wind blew feathers in my face. Once upon a time, a Jew had cushioned his head on those. He was probably turned to ashes by now. Thinking about death brought Hannah to my mind again. I closed my eyes, and there she was lying in her own blood. She would never be able to tell another story. But I was going to have to make one up if I wanted to get the guns back.

37

waited a bit because if I was too fast, the story I'd devised for the Poles wouldn't work.

After about half an hour, I went back. The lion door knocker was lying broken on the ground, so I banged against the heavy wooden door with my fist. The bearded policeman with the high voice opened the door, and before he could ask for the money, I walked past him into the bank. It was pretty dark inside; the windows were all broken and had been boarded up. That must have happened some time ago, maybe during the *Aktion* and they'd never been replaced—there was no point in repairing anything in the ghetto.

The cash office was no more than two empty counters. The safes where the Jewish collaborators hoarded their money were obviously kept somewhere else. The bag with the guns was standing on the filthy floor, and there was a pack of cards lying beside it in the dust. The two guards had probably been playing cards—to divide up the money they thought the resistance fighters were going to pay—sitting beside the seized arms.

The carrion eater and the bearded falsetto were both astonished to see me walking through the room as if I owned the place. They were even more astounded when I said calmly, "Give me the bag!"

"Where's the money?" Carrion eater wanted to know.

"You're not getting any!"

For a moment they both couldn't speak. The bearded falsetto found his voice first. "What did you say?"

"We aren't going to give you any money," I explained, and smiled as if I were talking to children who were a bit slow on the uptake.

Carrion eater pulled his truncheon out of his belt.

"You give me the guns and we won't kill you," I explained, not too quickly, but not too slowly, either, to stop him from hitting me. "The ŻOB have surrounded the bank. If I don't get back with the bag in the next five minutes, then our people will come in and shoot you."

They couldn't tell if I was bluffing or not. But they were bound to have heard that the ŻOB had shot several Jewish collaborators in the past few weeks and would certainly not stop at shooting a couple of Polish policemen.

Before their doubts got out of hand, I said as confidently as I could, "So hand over the bag, then!" sounding as if I really did have power over life and death as far as they were concerned.

Instead the carrion eater ran to one of the windows and tried to look out through the boards to see if he could see anything happening outside. Of course he couldn't see any resistance fighters. They were about as likely as a bunch of talking rabbits standing in front of the bank. I was telling a story, just like Hannah used to, only this one was going to save my life.

"I can't see anyone," carrion eater said to the bearded

falsetto. But he didn't dare go outside to take a look. What if everything I'd said was true and he was shot on the spot?

"Five minutes!" I said, ignoring him. "Then the bag has to be outside the door."

I went to the door as calmly as I could. I reached for the door handle, but the carrion eater grabbed my shoulder and said, "You are staying here!"

"You're sure you want me to stay?" I asked, and looked him straight in the eye.

"As a hostage!" he thundered, and his foul breath blew straight into my face.

"And the price for the guns plus you," the bearded falsetto added, "is four hundred thousand zlotys!"

"Okay," I said, freed my shoulder out of the carrion eater's grip, and marched into the middle of the room.

"I'll be your hostage if you want."

They didn't like the way I managed to stay calm.

"And you are our hostages," I added.

Now both of them tried to look through the boarded windows, but of course they couldn't see anything. The carrion eater turned back to me again and raised his truncheon. "If they don't give us the money, I'll beat your brains to mush!"

"If you kill me, you'll definitely die," I said, still bluffing.

The carrion eater beat his truncheon into the palm of his hand. It was supposed to look threatening, but just showed his rising panic. The bearded falsetto had broken into a cold sweat. Although I had no power over the two of them, they were afraid of me. And that meant that I did have power over them. It was the first time that anyone had ever been frightened of me.

It was brilliant.

It was the first time since Hannah's death that I'd felt alive. In fact, I'd never felt like this before.

"Have you got kids?" I asked

How I hoped those bastards had children because then they would be even more scared of dying.

They didn't say anything, so that must mean yes.

I put out my hand. "The bag . . . ," I demanded.

Neither of them showed any sign of giving it to me.

"If you don't mind," I said, and smiled.

The carrion eater picked up the bag and handed it to me. I walked out of the bank with the weapons. Without paying a zloty. Without being beaten by a truncheon.

The person with the least fear wins. I could see that now. Which was why the Germans had won against us.

So far.

But we weren't afraid anymore.

We were already dead.

38

When I got back to our group in the bunker, I didn't feel great, but I felt more useful than I had before. I had completed my first mission.

Of course, I didn't tell Esther, Amos, or the others about what had happened to me. I didn't want them to know how careless I had been. I just reported that I'd delivered the weapons to the other fighting group and had been given the hand grenades in return, as instructed. I stored them in a safe corner of our bunker, which the fighters had dug out in the cellar of the house weeks before. That had been the secret in the cellar that I had not been allowed to know anything about when Zacharia stabbed me in the arm.

This bunker that reeked of earth and sweat was my new home now. I shared it with ten other resistance fighters. Though you couldn't really call us fighters. None of us had actually seen any kind of action so far. The Jewish collaborators had been executed by other groups of the ŻOB.

There wasn't much talking in the bunker. We had all lost

people we loved. What was the point of talking about it to anyone? Each of us bore his fate as best he could. Sometimes at night you'd hear someone crying in their sleep, that was all. Once it was Esther. Not even strong Esther was totally immune to all the pain.

I had woken up one night because of her crying. And had seen her in the dim bunker light twisting in her sleep. But it wasn't my job to comfort her by putting my arms around her to bring her back from the nightmare of her dreams to the nightmare of the real world. Amos did that. He slept side by side with her every night, though not arm in arm. As far as I knew, they didn't sleep with each other; I hadn't even ever seen them kissing passionately. Maybe they did that sort of thing outside the bunker, somewhere else in the house. But I didn't really think so. Esther and Amos were two people who were married to their mission. They weren't in love with each other.

I noticed all this, but really I couldn't have cared less. That wild kiss with Amos at the Polish market so long ago had happened to a different girl.

There was just one other couple living in our bunker. Michal and Miriam. Miriam was a delicate eighteen-year-old, and Michal was a big man, and at twenty-four, he was the oldest of us. No couple could have been more different. Michal had been a bricklayer, and he'd have been the first to admit that he wasn't a great thinker. Curly-haired Miriam wasn't just clever and well read, she was the only person I knew who I could imagine being a university professor of philosophy, history, medicine, or anything she liked.

Michal adored Miriam; she was his whole reason for being alive. He wasn't out to get revenge or kill the beasts. He spent all his time thinking up nice things to do for Miriam, to cheer her up and help her to cope with the pain of having lost her parents.

Miriam on the other hand . . . well, she certainly did like Michal. Who wouldn't have liked such a kindhearted simple soul? In fact she liked him even more than the rest of us. But love? She couldn't really love him. And no wonder. Somewhere out there in the world there were men better suited to a girl like her. Miriam knew it, too, but she was with Michal all the same.

And then one night he proposed.

Michal knelt down on the bunker floor in front of all of us and held out a plain golden ring. It wasn't something he had stolen from an empty flat before the acquisition squads had been to collect everything for the German Reich. No, the ring had been his grandmother's.

"Will you . . . ," Michal asked Miriam in a low voice. He was so excited that he got muddled up, "marry you . . . I mean . . . me?"

Miriam answered without hesitating for a single moment, "Yes!"

Michal put his strong arms around her and held her tight. The rest of us started cheering so loudly, it sounded like we'd just chased the Germans out of Poland or off the planet altogether. None of us had felt this happy for a very long time. We kept up the cheering until Miriam let Michal know that he was nearly suffocating her and he let go.

It was a genuine moment of happiness, and I would never have believed that it could happen in the bunker. But it didn't feel quite right to me. No matter how much Michal loved Miriam, he didn't seem destined for her as far as I was concerned.

Two days later, when the two of us were searching through empty flats for valuables the ŻOB emissaries could use to purchase weapons on the Polish black market, I couldn't stop myself. I asked Miriam, "Why did you say yes?"

Miriam smiled, pushed one of her wild locks away from her face, and told me the simple truth about how she felt. "I haven't got anyone. My parents are dead, and I won't be alive for much longer. So I can spend the rest of my short life alone, or marry a man I don't really love but who loves me. Michal is all the happiness I'm going to get, and that is so much better than none."

I understood. But I could never be like Miriam. And I could never love anyone the way Michal loved her. Had I ever loved anyone like that? Didn't he love Miriam more than I had ever loved Daniel?

There was only one place left where I was able to feel any kind of love. That was the world of the 777 islands.

As I lay awake that night in the bunker, with my eyes closed but unable to sleep, I thought about what had happened at the bank: If I hadn't remembered Hannah and her stories that night, I would never have thought of telling the policemen that the bank was surrounded by resistance fighters. So, although she was dead, Hannah had actually saved my life.

Up till then, all I could see when I thought of her was the picture of her mangled body, but now I could suddenly see my little sister sitting in the pantry in the dim candlelight and remembered the last story she had told us about the 777 islands.

The Mirror King had now dispatched his helper, the terrible Sandman, to kill the Chosen One. Hannah and the crew of the *Longear* knew nothing of the approaching danger and were sleeping peacefully on the shores of Scarf Island, which was ruled by King Scarf I. While Ben Redhead, Hannah, and Captain Carrot snored in unison, the werewolf was on watch. The fog crept up quietly and then took on solid form. It was the sallow-faced Sandman.

The werewolf was caught by surprise. Before he had time to

draw his sword, the Sandman had thrown sand in his eyes. The werewolf managed to grumble, "I'll get you . . . ," but couldn't do anything of the kind because he fell asleep still standing and keeled over on the sand.

Suddenly, I realized that Hannah had never got this far. I had simply imagined her making all this up. I was the one who was keeping the world of the 777 islands alive now.

No sooner had I understood this than I had an exciting idea. If I could imagine myself being in that world, I would be able to see my little sister again.

Of course I couldn't just arrive on Scarf Island from out of nowhere; that wouldn't have made a good story. So I imagined how I came across a copy of the travel guide to the 777 islands in a deserted ghetto flat. And how the one-legged bookseller appeared and tried to take it away from me. The one-legged man was accompanied by two SS men who were also trying to get hold of the book. The Germans didn't just want to conquer our world, they wanted to rule the 777 islands, too. And probably all the other worlds as well: Alice's world and Winnie-the-Pooh's and Lord Peter Wimsey's and even the world in *City Lights*. The beasts wouldn't stop at anything.

Before the SS men had time to pull out their guns, I grabbed a pistol from my pocket and pointed it at the pigs. They backed away. I wanted to kill them. But I couldn't pull the trigger, not even in my imagination.

With my gun drawn, I ordered the SS men to leave the flat. And the one-legged man spat venom and cried, "The world of 777 islands will be the end of you! The Mirror King will destroy your mind!"

I just laughed at him. "I'm going to die soon anyway," I said, "I'm not scared of a mere reflection."

I opened the travel guide and found the page where Scarf Island was described. Before I knew what was happening, I was sucked into the book, transported away from our world, and deposited directly on the island. I could feel the sand beneath my bare feet. The werewolf was curled up asleep beside the fire, and the Sandman was just about to stab Hannah to death with his purple dagger. I grabbed my gun and shot it into the air. The Sandman jumped out of his skin and dropped the dagger.

Hannah, Ben Redhead, and the captain all woke with a start when they heard the shot. Only the werewolf didn't wake up because of the sleep strewn in his eyes. The Sandman stared at my pistol, and his face turned even paler. He asked in a deep melancholic voice, "What kind of magic firework is this?"

"One that will riddle you through and through if you don't disappear."

"Thought so."

He took less than a second to turn back into fog and drift away out to sea.

"Mira?" Hannah asked, and rubbed her eyes. "Mira, is that really you?"

"Of course it is!" I laughed.

"I missed you so much!"

"I missed you, too!"

My darling little sister ran up to me and hugged me and hugged me and hugged me. And I hugged her back. I was so happy. I had been able to save her life here, at least.

39

On the eighteenth of January 1943, when the Germans arrived to finally liquidate us all, it was minus four degrees and the streets were covered in snow. In the early morning, Amos, Esther, and I were standing in the freezing kitchen, printing a leaflet on the printing press, which we had taken days to repair. It was a call for all the Jewish inhabitants left in the ghetto to fight to death. Actually, Esther and Amos did the printing. I tried to keep my fingers warm by rubbing them together. Suddenly, Mordechai Anielewicz stormed into the room. We were all surprised. The leader of the ŻOB never came without letting us know in advance. We noticed that his slender face was very pale this morning. He was normally unfazed by anything. In his midtwenties, he was one of the oldest members of the resistance; he organized the fighters, encouraged us, urged us on, and made us seem far greater than we really were. When he spoke, Mordechai could always convince us that we really would be able to achieve something with our old guns and give the Jews back the dignity they had lost.

Mordechai didn't need a uniform to lead us. He wore shabby knickerbockers and a gray jacket. He simply had far more energy than the rest of us. Even more than Esther, who I looked up to because she worked so hard and dealt with her grief in her dreams.

"Why are you here?" Esther asked Mordechai.

I would never have dared to speak to him. Although he treated us all as if we were his equals, there was no way I would ever feel on a par with this man.

Esther, on the other hand, wasn't only one of the few women who led a resistance group, she also knew Mordechai from before the war. Both of them had been members of Hashomer Hatzair then, too, and the group had gone on summer camps at lakes and even by the sea to be prepared for a life in Palestine.

Were the two of them ever a couple? I wondered. In the days before there was a resistance movement, which was all that mattered to them now, love included?

"The mass deportations have started again," Mordechai explained at once. "The Germans have set up roadblocks already."

This was a shock. We had heard that the SS was hunting for hidden Jews in the Polish part of the city and had assumed that they were concentrating on that, and that we still had some time left to get prepared in the ghetto.

"Anyone with a work permit won't be taken, they say. But no one believes it. Everyone is hiding."

No one was stupid enough to believe the Germans and their promises any longer.

"The Germans are searching the houses. Anyone found will be sent to the *Umschlagplatz*. Anyone who puts up a fight or simply takes too long will be shot."

"What are we going to do?" Esther asked. She understood faster than I did that Mordechai hadn't come just to give us a report of what was happening. We were the group of fighters closest. Mordechai was planning something and wanted it to happen as soon as possible.

"Take your weapons."

"What?" I couldn't stop myself from saying.

Esther gave me an angry look. I shut up at once.

"We are going to join the people being led to the *Umschlagplatz*," Mordechai said. "And on my command we'll draw our weapons and start shooting."

Amos nodded determinedly.

Esther said, "I'll get the others."

And I . . . stood paralyzed.

This was Masada.

Today I was going to die.

Kill someone.

I did my best to hide my fear, as all our group gathered round the printing press and Mordechai asked, "Who is coming with me?"

Everyone lifted their hands. Me too. This was what we had been waiting for. To fight the Germans. It was a matter of honor to be allowed to take part. I only hoped that no one noticed how much my hand was shaking.

"There's a problem," Esther said in a businesslike way as if she were talking about a problem with the printing press. Why was she so much more composed than I was? We both had nothing left to lose.

"What problem?" Amos asked impatiently before Mordechai could do so. Amos was yearning to go out and fight no matter what our leader's exact plans were. Assuming he actually had any.

"We've only got five pistols and one hand grenade. The other hand grenades we got from Breul's group are no use," Esther said.

"I'm definitely going," Amos said, reacting fastest to the fact that there was no point in sending people out unarmed.

"Me too," Mordechai said. He wasn't a leader who would let people die without him. He would lead them, even on a heroic suicide mission.

Michal raised his hand. Miriam, too.

"Don't . . . ," Michal asked her, but Miriam answered, "I go where my husband goes."

There was just one gun left. So only one more person from our group would be able to go. Esther was the logical choice. She was our leader. It was so obvious that she didn't need to say she would be the fifth person, she just asked, "So what is the plan?"

For a second I was relieved that I wouldn't have to join the fight, no matter how it would appear. I would stay alive for a few more hours, a few days.

But the next moment I felt ashamed for feeling like that. In front of the others. And remembering everyone who had died. Why did I hang on to my ghostly existence? Just to fantasize about talking rabbits, Mirror Men, and Hannah each night?

This would have been an opportunity to do something meaningful for once, to give my life and death—and Hannah's—some kind of purpose. But I was too much of a coward to volunteer as quickly as Amos, Miriam, and Michal. And so they would go off to fight together with Mordechai and Esther.

But then Mordechai said, "You have to stay, Esther."

"But . . . ," she wanted to protest.

"This group will continue and needs its leader," he interrupted her with so much authority, Esther couldn't disagree. He obviously assumed that everyone who came with him was going to die. Before Mordechai could ask again who else would join him, I put up my hand.

40

The five of us went out into the cold. Each of us was hiding a pistol in their coat or sweater, and Amos had insisted that he be given the one functioning hand grenade.

I carried my gun in the inside pocket of my heavy coat. The cold metal pressed against my left breast through my sweater and blouse. I would pull it out with my right hand and then start shooting.

We walked down a couple of streets and met a group of about a hundred Jews being led to the *Umschlagplatz* by SS soldiers. The faces of the sentenced people were blank; any hope they may have had of survival had gone ages ago. They bowed to the fate the Germans had in store for them.

We joined the crowd with our hands up so that the SS would think we were just more Jews surrendering. The soldiers signaled to us to get in line and join the march to death. I stared at the ground. I didn't want to see the faces of the men who I would shoot at in just a few minutes' time, and I didn't want to look at the men who were going to kill me.

As planned, we split up in the crowd. Mordechai was at the front, Amos more in the middle of the procession, with me a few meters away from him. Michal and Miriam were farther back.

We walked through the cold together, all doomed to die. I didn't feel weighed down, as I had that other time when I had marched toward the *Umschlagplatz* in the cauldron; I felt all keyed up. I was going to kill someone in a moment. And I was going to die. The blood in my temples was throbbing so hard that I feared a vessel would burst.

We walked and I watched Mordechai, waiting for his signal to attack. I tried to do this without attracting attention, but it didn't really matter. The SS men took no notice of us. They could not imagine that there could be any threat of danger from the people they were leading to slaughter. Hundreds of thousands of Jews had been hounded to the gas chambers without defending themselves already, so why should anything be different for the last few thousand inhabitants of the ghetto?

When we reached the corner of Ziska Street and Zamenhof Street, Mordechai turned round and nodded at Amos. I held my breath. Amos dug into his coat pocket, pulled out his hand grenade in an instant, pulled the ring, and threw it at two German soldiers. Before anyone could react, before anyone even understood what was happening, the grenade exploded and tore the SS men to bits.

The blast frightened the life out of me, although I had been prepared for it, and I squeezed my eyes tight shut. When I opened them again, I saw Amos staring at the dead soldiers. He, too, needed a second to realize what he had just done. He had killed SS men!

I heard shots from Mordechai's direction. I turned round.

He was holding his gun and shooting soldiers. Two of them fell down in the snow.

The crowd dispersed. Panic-stricken people were running in every direction. I could hear shots coming from Amos's direction now, too. The soldiers were shouting, "They've got guns! The fucking Jews have got guns!"

Behind me, Michal and Miriam were shooting at the SS.

And the Germans were shooting back!

"Miriam!" Michal screamed.

She didn't answer.

I looked back. But in the crush of fleeing people, I couldn't see Michal or Miriam. I heard more shots. And Michal screaming. The Germans had got him, too.

Both dead. Both dead. Both dead. That was all I could think. Both dead.

I looked at Mordechai again. He was walking toward three soldiers, pointing the gun at them, shooting and shooting and shooting. When his magazine was empty he threw the weapon away, bent down to a dead SS man, grabbed his pistol, and kept on shooting.

I still hadn't taken a single shot or even pulled out my weapon. As soon as I did, I would be a target for the Germans who were desperately trying to pinpoint the attackers in the crowd.

Amos yelled.

I looked at him, panicked. He was wounded in the arm. Not dead yet! Not dead!

Now I pulled my gun. I didn't know where to start shooting. There were desperate Jews fleeing between all the soldiers. I didn't want to hit any of them.

I ran to the curb where the soldiers Mordechai had mowed

down were lying. Their blood mixed with the snow, turning it into red and white slush. A young wounded soldier was crawling away from me. No idea if he was Latvian, German, or Ukrainian, but he had a beautiful face, like an angel, and he said something I couldn't understand. Was he asking for help? Was it a prayer?

I pointed my gun at him. He looked up at me. Pleading. He didn't want to die.

Why did he hope for mercy? He wouldn't have shown me any. The swine. With his angelic face. My hand shook. I wanted to pull the trigger. I had to.

The soldier started to cry, said something in German, and then, "Marlene . . ."

Like Marlene Dietrich in the American films. Was that the name of his wife or girlfriend? Or of his daughter? Or was he too young to be a father? My hand shook even more. The soldier cried. I bent my finger to squeeze the trigger. Then I heard Mordechai shout, "Mira, behind you!"

I turned round. An SS man the size of a bull was aiming his gun at me, less than three meters away.

I shot at once.

The man slumped down. Lifeless in the snow.

I felt sick.

Mordechai grabbed me by the shoulders and yelled in my ear, "Run!"

We both started running. So did Amos. The two of them shot at the SS who backed off, scared. We ran down two streets, and then Mordechai shouted, "In here!"

We dashed inside and up the stairs. I couldn't breathe, and Amos was bleeding badly. His coat sleeve was soaked in blood, but Mordechai wouldn't let us stop. We scaled up a ladder into the attic, and from there we went through a hole into the next house. The resistance had started building escape routes between buildings. A sort of street system above the actual streets. But the attics weren't safe to hide in. We ran back down the stairs in one of the houses, and into a secret bunker where we fell to the ground, exhausted. I threw up. Mordechai applied a tourniquet above Amos's bleeding wound. No one said a word. We were exhausted and wound up at the same time. Then Amos started to laugh. Hysterically. Mordecai joined in. Hysterical, too. And I laughed with them, and then I cried. For Miriam and Michal.

We hugged one another, feeling happy and sad. Sad because we had lost comrades—friends—and happy to be alive. We had killed SS soldiers. Jews had killed Germans. Nothing would ever be the same again.

41

sther said a few words in memory of those who had died. She did it in Mordechai's stead. He was meeting the heads of the ŻOB in another part of the ghetto, to discuss the new developments. Today, the Germans had retreated out of the ghetto because of us! It was unbelievable.

In her address, Esther reminded us that Miriam and Michal had died for a good cause. Their deaths would be an inspiration to others, she said, and we could all be very proud of them. She really was a great speaker, saying the right things in a quiet, firm voice without a hint of pathos. She insisted that they hadn't just died—they were fallen heroes. Although Esther didn't say so, it meant that the rest of us who had shot at the Germans were heroes now, too.

At the end of her speech, Esther surprised us by sharing a personal memory. Once, at a summer camp, Miriam had sat beside the fire and sung a song that was so beautiful and sad all the children cried. Even the older girls like Esther who would normally have been too aloof.

I had no idea that Miriam and Esther had known each other that long. And I couldn't imagine Esther being moved by anything. And I had never known that Miriam could sing so well. I'd never heard her sing. Not once. Here in the bunker we knew practically nothing about anyone's previous life.

Once Esther had finished speaking, we ate supper. At least, the others did. I couldn't eat a thing. I still felt ill. I had killed someone. It had all happened so fast that I hadn't seen his face. In my memory, my victim—was that even the right word for someone who was trying to kill me?—was a shadowy figure. Instead, I could still see the young soldier with the angelic face clearly, begging for mercy and talking about his Marlene. The soldier's angel face joined the shadow of the man I had actually shot, making a strange mixture of a person. The more this picture filled my mind, the worse I felt. He too kept calling, "Marlene!"

Although I didn't want to think about it, I couldn't stop myself from wondering if the man I had killed had had a girlfriend or wife who would grieve for him, or a child who would have to grow up without a father.

I felt like being sick again.

But then I reminded myself that he didn't give a damn about the people he was marching to the *Umschlagplatz*. What did he care if they'd loved anyone or not. That was the whole point: The Germans didn't think of us as human beings. If they saw us as people, they wouldn't be able to kill us so easily. If I was going to fight against them, I would have to stop thinking of them as people, too. Not the victims of my actions. Just beasts straight from hell. Beasts who could look like angels at times.

I went to bed earlier than usual. Today, everyone could understand that I was feeling tired. The rest of the time, it was frowned upon for a fighter to show any form of weakness. No fear or—even worse—doubt about whether what we were doing made any sense was tolerated.

Before I closed my eyes, I looked over to the corner where Michal and Miriam had slept. With Michal gone there was one person less in the world who was capable of love. And Miriam would never become a professor. How many people would she have been able to teach? How many people would she have touched with her voice? All the songs that would never be sung. All the stories Hannah would never tell. All those dreams. All that love. Gone forever.

I closed my eyes, but the tears welled up. Somehow, I managed not to start sobbing. I didn't want the others to witness my grief and despair on this day of triumph. But I couldn't stop the tears. I let the tears run silently down my cheeks.

Normally, I would have traveled back to the world of the 777 islands, like I did every night for comfort's sake. But I hesitated. How would I be able to tell my sister that I had killed someone? A real person, not some fantasy creature like the ice dragon, Fafnir, who had buried Mongoose Island under a sheet of everlasting snow. We had only managed to get rid of him with the help of the fire elves.

The tubby mongooses organized a great celebration in our honor, and we danced the night away until our feet ached or, in Captain Carrot's case, his paws.

While Hannah danced "the Mongoose" with the tubby mongoose king, she smiled and said, "We are heroes here, and yet they can't stand us on Questionmark Island."

"Questionmark Island?"

"Everybody there looks like one."

"And they really hate the people on Exclamationmark Island."

Captain Carrot, who was gallantly twirling a lady mongoose round, laughed. "Hannah did kick the tyrannical Eminent Questionare way off his mark!"

So a hero wasn't always a hero. It depended on where you were. Mongoose Island or Questionmark Island. Hannah was a happy one here. I was a hero in the eyes of my fellow fighters, but I felt awful.

Hannah would be appalled that I had shot someone.

Or would she understand if I told her that she was dead and I was avenging her? That I was doing all this to give her life and her death some sort of meaning?

But if she found out that she was no longer alive in the real world, wouldn't she want to stop living in my head, too? What purpose would she see in being a figment of my imagination?

No! She mustn't find out that she was dead. Or else I'd lose her forever.

But I would never be able to lie to her. So, for the first time in weeks, I didn't go to the world of the 777 islands. Instead, I cried myself to sleep and was haunted by nightmares. I dreamed about the moment when the young German had begged for mercy. But in my dream it wasn't the German crawling on the ground in front of me in his SS uniform. It was my brother, Simon.

My hands shook again. I didn't know if I should pull the trigger or not.

All at once, Simon stopped begging, pulled out a gun, and pointed it at me. If I didn't shoot him, he would kill me. That was clear. So I pulled the trigger, and Simon slumped to the ground. Just like the SS man I had killed.

I bent down to my dead brother, and right in front of my eyes, he turned into the baby I had abandoned at the *Umschlagplatz*.

I screamed and screamed and screamed, and woke up with a racing heart.

I looked round the bunker in the dark—everyone was asleep. So I must only have cried out in my dream. I stared at the black earthen wall in front of me. It was an endless dark void. I had no one in all the world. Just Hannah. And she only existed in a make-believe world where I didn't dare go. Instead, I'd just killed my brother in my dreams after not thinking about him for weeks. And a baby. And the soldier in real life. I felt like I was losing my mind.

42

I t was my seventeenth birthday, but it meant nothing to me and I didn't mention it to anyone. Four days after the shooting, the SS stopped the deportations. The fact that Jews had killed soldiers had shaken them to the core. Esther hadn't actually called me and the other survivors heroes, but the underground newspapers did. "In the darkest hour of the Jewish people, our heroes showed immense bravery and hit back."

Our triumph was celebrated in glowing terms. Of course no one wrote about how ill I had felt afterward, or that Michal and Miriam would never love or sing again. There wasn't any room for things like that in a hero's story.

During the next weeks, I began to feel more and more proud of what I had done. Not because I was proclaimed a hero, but because our resistance had started to change the ghetto somehow. If all the Jews had felt hopelessly abandoned to fate up till now, suddenly a real jolt went through the ghetto. Everyone knew that the Germans would return, but we had proved that it was possible to fight back. Many young Jews joined the ŻOB. Even those who couldn't fight were no longer prepared to be rounded up like animals and sent to their deaths. Everywhere, people were building secret bunkers in the cellars to hide from the Germans. Anyone with the remotest understanding of architecture was highly sought after. Some bunkers even had running water, electricity, and a telephone. A city arose beneath the city.

The German "supermen" no longer came into the ghetto, certainly not after dark. As soon as there was any kind of resistance they got scared. Cowards!

The ŻOB or "the Party" as the union of fighters was being called everywhere now—the differences between the various groups had whittled down to nothing—was controlling the ghetto. The members of the Jewish council could only report to their German masters that no matter what strings they tried to pull or how they tried to make everyone do as they said, they could no longer influence the people.

Collaborators were executed on a daily basis. The Jewish policemen and the SS were powerless to prevent this from happening. I never took part in any of those killings. I was glad about that. I was a reluctant hero who had had enough for the moment just killing one soldier. I knew that I would have to kill again when the Germans came back to clear out the ghetto for good. And I hoped I would have learned to see them solely as beasts by then, instead of people. Why couldn't I do that yet?

Our group, like all the others, was preparing for the final battle. We practiced shooting in the cellar of our house. Or aiming rather, because we couldn't afford to waste any of the valuable ammunition. We also learned close-combat fighting and how to fill explosives into light bulbs and bottles. It wasn't quite the studies our parents had planned.

Our group also took in new members. And I knew one of

them from before. It was Ben Redhead. All of a sudden, he was standing in our cellar beside me while I awaited my turn to practice shooting. He looked totally different from the way I had imagined him on my journeys to the 777 islands. I had only ever seen the boy once in my life, that time when he was kissing Hannah. So my memory of how he looked hadn't been all that accurate. By now he was almost the size of a man—although he had only just turned sixteen. He had seemed uncoordinated and lanky then, but now he stood straight and tall.

"Ben Redhead," I said, and smiled.

It was good that he was still alive. That would be sure to please Hannah if I ever went back to visit her in the island world. From day to day, I was more convinced that she really did live there, even when I wasn't with her. I was probably out of my mind.

"R . . . R . . . Redhead?" Ben asked, and stuttered as usual. There are some things that don't change, no matter how much you grow.

Of course, Ben didn't know that he was called Ben Redhead in the island world. But if I told him about my fantasy, then he'd realize that I was going mad. So I ignored his question and instead asked him how he had managed to survive. Ben told me that his father worked for the Jewish council and he had started to despise him more and more until he couldn't stand it any longer and ran away to join the ŻOB. He would rather die honorably than live tolerated by the Germans, even if that meant breaking with his family.

I presumed that it had been his father who had stopped Ben from visiting Hannah again after the start of the *Aktion* in the summer, but didn't inquire any further. With his heart in his mouth, Ben asked the question he was so dreading to know. "D . . . did . . . Ha . . . Hannah . . . ?"

"No . . ." was all I could say.

Ben broke down in tears. Uncontrollably. He was still able to do something the rest of us fighters could no longer do. He could let his grief run free.

The others looked annoyed. His tears reminded them of their own pain. And they didn't need that. Certainly not in preparation for the final battle.

I was totally unsure how I should react. His tears annoyed me, too. On the other hand, Ben was the closest thing I had to family. We were bound together by our love of Hannah. So I put my arms round him. He drooped over my shoulder, and I gently stroked his red hair.

"As long as we still remember her," I said to him quietly, "she isn't dead."

It wasn't much, but it worked. Ben stopped crying. He let go of me and wiped away his tears with his sleeve.

"I . . . th . . . think about Ha . . . Ha . . . Hannah every d . . . day," he said. "And I . . . I . . . always w . . . will."

"Me too," I said. "Me too."

But I had a terrible thought. When the two of us were dead, and that would be very soon now—hopefully killed in action and not in the gas chambers—then the memory of Hannah would be completely gone and she would be dead for good.

43

"When you have finished comforting each other," Esther said to me, "I need to talk to you for a moment"—she emphasized the word *comforting* in a disparaging way. Grief was a useless waste of time as far as Esther was concerned. A distraction from what was important. At least she treated me with a little bit of respect, now that I was a hero. And perhaps, or so I thought, she was just a tiny bit jealous because I had been allowed to fight in her place and she still hadn't killed any Germans yet. Though I would have happily swapped places with her if I could. If I'd had a time machine like the hero in the book by H. G. Wells, then I'd have gone back in time with Esther and left it to her to kill the German. She could have had my hero status, and four weeks later, I wouldn't still be haunted by nightmares. Actually— much better—I'd have traveled back in time to save Hannah, my mama, and my papa, and would have stopped Simon from ever joining the Jewish police. Of course the best thing would be to go even further back in time and kill Hitler while he was still a child. That was someone I could imagine killing.

I looked at Ben Redhead—he would always be Ben Redhead to me—and said, "We'll talk later."

Although I had no idea what we would talk about next time. About how Hannah died? Should I tell him how she had lain in her own blood? Then he would cry again and I would, too. Although . . . perhaps it would be nice to be able to share my pain with someone. Maybe I could find some comfort in that. Of sorts.

Together with Esther, I walked up the stairs from the cellar to the flat, and she said, "I don't think boys like him will be any use."

"You thought the same about me," I answered.

Esther didn't deny this.

"And I cost one hundred thousand zlotys," I added without thinking.

"Which were meant for Zacharia," she replied, and her eyes shone with contempt for a moment.

I should have kept my mouth shut. She still hadn't forgiven me for the fact that Amos had got me out of the *Umschlagplatz* instead of her comrade. What could I say? That I thought it would be better if I had landed in the ovens?

Of course I said nothing of the sort. Instead I continued to defend my Ben Redhead. "Ben could simply have stayed with his Jewish council father. That just goes to show how strong his will really is."

Esther didn't reply. It was as if she thought it was useless talking about the boy any longer. Although she had started this. I was beginning to realize that she had seen that something connected Ben and me and she had wanted to hurt me by questioning his abilities.

She pushed open the door of the flat. I wondered if I should ask what she actually wanted me for, but I didn't. I would find out soon enough. If we didn't speak to each other, then at least we couldn't argue.

We went into the kitchen where Mordechai and Amos were sitting at a table beside the printing press. Amos's wounded arm was healing by now. Mordechai jumped up and hugged me like an old comrade. I was one, as far as he was concerned.

Just a few weeks ago, I hadn't even dared look at Mordechai let alone speak to him; now I managed to hug him back so that I wouldn't seem impolite. Once he'd let go of me, he said, "We need more weapons."

"We couldn't own fewer, could we?" Amos joked.

Mordechai smiled, Esther didn't react, and I hopped nervously from one foot to the other. What was our leader planning now?

"We need people to organize weapons on the Polish side. People who live there permanently to liaise with the Polish resistance."

So this was why I was here. I was going to leave the ghetto, to live on the other side of the wall.

"I need really good people," Mordechai said. He looked at Amos and then at me and smiled again, "But all I've got is you."

Jewish humor. Oh, great!

"You two," he was serious again, "are both experienced on the other side, and you could both pass as Poles," he said.

I wasn't so sure myself. It was almost a year since I had been in the Polish part of the city. Okay, so I didn't look as Jewish as Esther did, for example. But I didn't have Amos's blond hair. Just green eyes.

I also had no real wish to go to the other side of Warsaw. Home was home. Even if it was the ghetto. Since the *Aktion*

I hadn't once dreamed of going to see New York's city lights. Those dreams belonged to a different life. The life with Daniel.

Daniel. If Ben Redhead was still alive, couldn't Daniel . . . ?

"Mira and I could be a Polish couple," Amos said, interrupting my thoughts. "We've done it before, haven't we?" He was laughing at me.

What was he playing at? The thought flashed through my mind. Going by Esther's expression, she was wondering the same thing.

"Then," Mordechai said, "tell us what kind of couple you'd be."

"A fantastic one, more gentile than any other." Amos just couldn't stop talking nonsense.

"We wouldn't be anything," I mumbled. All this silly talk annoyed me more than I could say.

Mordechai laughed at our different reactions. Esther did what she always did when emotions were involved. She returned to business and said matter-of-factly, "I'll make sure that the two of them get over to the other side."

"Good!" Mordechai looked pleased and said goodbye to each of us with another hug. Once he was gone, the three of us stood in the kitchen. We didn't speak until Esther said quietly, "He should have sent me."

She'd said it! This strong woman felt degraded by the likes of a young girl like me.

"Mira has green eyes; you don't," Amos said gently, trying to put his arms around her. But she pushed him away and said, "I'm surprised you even know what color my eyes are."

She regretted her outburst immediately and left the kitchen.

Now there were just the two of us. Amos and me. All alone.

"It's just 'cause she loves me," he said. But what he meant was: (1) he thought I was too stupid to see what was obvious, and (2) he didn't love her; otherwise he would have said, "We love each other."

So he was just like Miriam. She'd been together with someone she didn't actually love, she'd even got married, because it seemed better than being alone until she died.

I could just about understand Miriam at the time, but I was disgusted with Amos. Miriam had had no hope of falling in love, but Amos was incapable of loving anyone. He was using Esther, and I stopped feeling inferior to her. All of a sudden, I felt sorry for her.

I left the kitchen, but then just as I was going out, I turned round and said, "If Esther really loves you, I pity her."

As I left, I heard him say, "Ouch!"

44

Esther had organized everything for us, but it was still dangerous to get out of the ghetto. Amos and I were to leave with a group of Jews who were working on the Polish side of Warsaw at Okęcie airport and who usually lived in the barracks on-site. Every two weeks, the workers were allowed to return to the ghetto for a day, and they used the opportunity to smuggle food into the ghetto and valuables out. One of the foremen of the group was a young man named Henryk Tuchner. He was worn down by the hard work at the airport and had deep dark rings beneath his eyes, but he was a member of the ŻOB. He had added our names to the list of workers who would be allowed to pass through the checkpoint to the Polish side, and gave us our forged work permits in the early morning. We walked through the empty streets with him. A half-starving cat crossed our path. A black one.

"That's good luck," Amos said, and grinned at me.

"Idiot!" was all I said.

"Oh, I know," he said, grinning a bit more.

We walked on without saying anything else and joined about thirty workers who were waiting for us at the next street corner. They weren't exactly pleased to see us—we were putting them in danger. The soldiers were prepared to ignore their petty smuggling if they received a share. But ghetto fighters would be shot at once, and if there were bullets flying, no one wanted to be caught in the fray.

None of these men would dare betray us, though. They were too scared of the ŻOB. I was far more worried that they'd do a body search at the gate. Mordechai had given me an important letter. A report for the Polish resistance. It listed exactly how many weapons and what support the ŻOB leaders required from their Polish comrades. This report was hidden under my foot in my sock. When I put it there this morning Amos had grinned and said, "Our Polish friends will be able to smell cheese when they read it."

It was such a stupid remark that I hadn't even bothered to call him an idiot.

The troop of workers went across to the Polish side on a regular basis and our forged papers were excellent, so the chances of being discovered weren't great. But I was still nervous. Who wouldn't be in this situation?

Amos, of course.

He even had a friendly smile for the other workers, though none of them were keen to walk through the gate at Żelazna Street right next to us. When we got there, we had to stop in front of four SS soldiers. A fat German, who had the sort of face friends might call jovial, read out the workers' names on the list. "Jurek Polesch, Shimon Rabin, Amos Rosenwinkel, Mira Weiss . . ."

We reported as our names were called, but while all the other workers were allowed through the gate, the fat German stopped me. Of course I didn't ask what was going on. It would have been foolish to address a German without being spoken to. Foolish and dangerous. A smack in the face was the least you could expect, the lash of the whip likely, and a bullet not impossible.

The fat man pointed at the guardhouse and ordered me to go in.

I looked at Amos, who gave an encouraging nod. I started to move, but I wasn't fast enough for the fat man, and he shoved me along. He didn't make me fall, but he forced me to walk faster.

I hurried into the room. It was sparsely furnished with a table, a chair, and a cupboard, and with temperatures around about freezing it was not much warmer than outside. As soon as we had entered, the fat German closed the door, grabbed his whip, and shouted in German, "*Ausziehen!*"

He wanted me to take off my clothes! I was so scared I didn't react immediately. The man raised his whip and threatened to strike me.

He said it again, "*Ausziehen!*"

I took off my jacket.

And my trousers.

And my shoes.

Now I was standing there with nothing on except underwear and socks, hoping he wouldn't ask for more. Couldn't he see that I wasn't smuggling anything? It wasn't just humiliating to be standing in front of this swine freezing and half-naked. I had to make sure that he didn't find the letter addressed to the Polish resistance that was hidden in my left sock.

If I'd been a real fighter, I'd only have been worried about the report, because it was so important to our cause. If the Germans got hold of it they would know how poorly armed we all were and they would lose the tiny bit of fear we had been able to instill in them. But I was more worried that I'd be thrown into a German prison where SS soldiers would torture all the information I had out of me. I trembled with cold and fear.

The SS man looked me over from every angle. Why didn't he let me get dressed? He could see that I wasn't carrying any valuables hidden under my clothes. Even if I'd been hiding things in my underwear, it would have been visible through the material.

"*Ausziehen, hab ich gesagt!*" he snarled.

What was this pig after? Did he suspect something, or did he just want to see a young girl naked? Or did he want more? I took off my undershirt, shivering in underwear and socks.

"*Alles,*" he barked, and raised the whip again. Everything! Before he could hit me, I took off my underwear as fast as I could. He stared at me naked. He leered at me.

The pig wanted more.

Like those SS men in the camps with Ruth. Like the brutal man everyone had simply called "the doll" who had forced Ruth to sleep with him and worse.

Suddenly, here was something I was even more afraid of than the torture chamber.

The fat German was looking at me as if I were a piece of meat. At his disposal. Even though I tried to hide as much as possible, I couldn't stop him staring at my naked bottom. I had never felt so helpless or humiliated in all my life, or so afraid of the humiliation to come.

He gave me a wet kiss on the cheek.

Now I wasn't just trembling from cold and fear. I was physically shaking, trying to fight back the tears of desperation I felt welling up.

"*Du hast ja noch die Socken an*," he said. And as I couldn't quite understand his German, he pointed at my feet.

I looked around in a hurry. Was there anything I could use to defend myself against this fat pig? The ashtray on the table? Maybe I could grab that and hit him with it. But even if I managed to knock him down, his three colleagues would come in and shoot me. If I was lucky, that is.

Why didn't Amos come and help me?

"I am cold," I tried to explain why I was keeping my socks on in Polish. And so that he would understand, I shivered a bit more.

The SS man simply laughed. I was just a pathetic, naked Jew with socks on.

"*Dich werde ich schon heiß machen*," he said.

I had no idea what he'd said, but his laughter was so obscene that I wanted to throw up.

"*Die Socken aus!*"

I hesitated.

"*Zieh die Socken aus!*"

For a moment I thought about whether I should just let him beat me up. He had no idea about the letter, and once I was lying bleeding on the filthy floor of the hut, he wasn't likely to take off a dirty Jew's socks before he abused her.

Maybe, if I was lucky, he might lose the urge when I was just one more piece of bloody meat.

"*Ganz nackt!*" Completely naked!

A real hero would have cared more about the resistance than her own fate. Even now.

But I wasn't a hero. Just a shaking, frightened thing, wearing nothing but a pair of socks. I started to cry and beg for mercy. "Please," I cried, "please . . . don't . . ."

I couldn't say any more. The SS man slapped me in the face. So hard that I almost fell over and the pain swamped my head. I started to cry. And didn't dare beg for mercy again because I was so frightened of the next blow.

The SS man undid his belt.

My hot tears dripped onto my shivering body.

He undid his zipper.

I cried and cried. So helpless. So wretched.

The man started to take off his trousers . . . then the door opened.

"*Was zum Teufel ist hier los, Scharper?*" said a deep voice behind me.

Although I couldn't understand much German, I could tell that the person speaking was not pleased by what he saw.

I froze and didn't dare turn round or breathe. I didn't even dare hope. I could hear the SS man pull up his trousers and the belt clinking. Perhaps there was hope after all. I stopped crying.

"*Raus!*" the deep voice ordered.

The SS pig hastened past me. Out of the corner of my eye, I saw him do up his belt as he went out of the guards' hut. And I heard the burst of laughter from his colleagues when he stepped outside.

The door slammed shut; I stood up, but didn't yet dare look at the man who had saved me. Because I had no idea if he really had saved me or if he just wanted me himself.

"You can turn round," the man said in broken Polish. He seemed to be one of the few occupiers who had made the effort to learn a bit of our language.

I didn't want to turn round, but was so afraid of being beaten again that I did what he wanted.

A man stood in front of me, maybe in his midforties, wearing an officer's uniform. He had short blond hair showing under his hat, which showed the SS death's-head insignia. His face looked very tired, which calmed me a bit. Such a tired man wouldn't want to abuse me. Or so I hoped.

"The same age as my daughter," he said, more to himself than me and seemed even more tired.

I said nothing. I was still shaking, but more from the cold now than with fear.

"Get dressed," the officer said. It wasn't an order, but it wasn't a request, either. He just didn't want to see me naked.

As fast as I could, I got dressed. I was very relieved once my underwear covered my body again, but even more so when I pulled my shoe back over the sock that contained the letter for the Polish resistance. The dispatch hadn't been discovered.

The officer didn't say anything else, he just fetched a bottle of vodka or schnapps—I couldn't read the German label properly—out of a shabby cupboard, opened it, and didn't even bother to look for a glass, he simply drank straight out of the bottle.

If I had ever asked myself how the few Germans who could still regard us Jews as people of sorts managed to cope with all the murdering going on, this was the moment when I'd have got my answer: They drank.

But I hadn't ever asked myself that question. And I didn't care if one or another of the murderers had a guilty conscience they needed to drown.

The officer took another long draft and then told me, "Go."

I hastened to the door of the guardhouse, relieved to get out of the place that had almost been my personal hell. I was about to push open the door when he said, "Stop!"

I flinched. I thought he was going to shoot me after all. It hadn't felt like it before, but he was a German and he was drinking, and there was nothing more unpredictable than a drunk German.

Carefully, I turned around. The officer was sitting at the shabby table. The bottle was standing on it now, and his hat with the death's-head insignia lay beside it. He looked at me with his tired eyes and said in a low voice,

"I am sorry."

What for? For what the SS man did to me? For what that fat pig had probably done to a lot of other girls in this hut? For all the people the officer had killed himself? Or was he just thinking about his own daughter who he couldn't be with and apologizing indirectly to her because he had caused so much guilt that it would take generations to get over it?

I couldn't help ease his guilty conscience. Even if he had saved my skin. Even if he'd saved my skin a thousand times. They had killed Hannah. I said nothing. Neither did he. Until he realized that he would get no forgivenesss from me and then he said quietly again: "Go."

I turned away, opened the door, and walked out into the open, past the SS men and the fat pig who stared at me angrily, but I looked away. I was afraid of him and felt so ashamed. I couldn't stand the fact that he had made me plead for mercy. The sense of shame made me so angry that I could have killed him on the spot. Or myself.

I joined the labor gang that had been made to wait. Amos was very relieved to see me. Because he had been worried about me, or because of the letter?

The SS men told us to move. As we walked through the gate Amos asked, "Did anything happen to you?"

A lot had happened to me in there. Things that were going to haunt me from now on. But on the other hand, none of the really terrible things that could have occurred had actually happened. I'd been lucky. And I realized that I had done something to make that luck come about. If I hadn't taken so long to get undressed, not kept that one sock on for so long and not risked being beaten, then the SS man would have raped me before the officer came in. The officer would have been bound to find the letter on the floor even if the fat pig didn't notice it, and I would have been taken to prison and tortured to death. By prolonging the start of something that had seemed inevitable, even though there had been no hope of getting out of there unharmed, I had avoided the worst. I was alive and hadn't been hurt. And the letter was still safe in my sock. It meant even more to me now. Resistance was more crucial than ever: The men who had destroyed everything I loved and had almost stolen my honor had to die.

"Mira?" Amos was worried because I hadn't said anything yet.

"No," I said, "nothing happened to me."

"Good," he said, and smiled, genuinely relieved. He didn't ask about the letter. He was worried about me. Not the resistance. Me.

45

On the other side of the gate, an almost alien world awaited us. We had been living in a ghost city for months, but now the world was vibrant all around us. Guarded by the soldiers, we marched with the work gang past shops that were just opening, cafés where people hurriedly downed their morning coffee, and a school with Polish children running to get to class on time. No doubt those children had no idea how lucky they were to be allowed to go to school. I'd had no idea, either, until the Germans came and stopped me from going.

Everywhere, Poles were heading to work. Most of them avoided looking directly at us Jews, but a few stared at us full of contempt. No one showed any signs of sympathy, compassion, or encouragement, although we shared the same enemy, the Germans. Either the Poles couldn't care less or else they hated us.

Suddenly the clouds vanished and the sun came out for the first time in weeks. It was making fun of us, preferring to shine in the Polish part of the city with its Poles and Germans instead of in the ghetto with its living ghosts.

I was mesmerized by everything. The noise on the streets, all the people, the beautiful sky—it was like stepping out of a dark, empty, dead room, like our pantry, into the light.

Amos whispered to me, "Mira, you've got to concentrate . . . come on!"

He didn't say it harshly. Despite the seriousness of the situation, he could understand why I was dazed. He gave me a reassuring smile. And it worked. I managed to block out the foreign-seeming world that had once been so familiar and focus on the soldiers guarding us. The fat pig wasn't with them, thankfully, just two other SS soldiers who looked bored. It was unthinkable that a Jew would try to escape from the troop. The chances of surviving as a fugitive in Warsaw were practically zero. And anyone working at the airport, as this group did, had comparatively good conditions for a Jew because of the smuggling opportunities, so there was no reason to flee.

We walked along a main street with the gang for a while, and then I saw a streetcar approaching on the right. I realized it was heading in the direction of the secret flat that was to be our new home—I still knew my way around the city. I pointed my chin in the direction of the streetcar ever so slightly, and Amos understood at once. If we could manage to jump on board, we could get away.

Even if we blundered and the soldiers noticed us, they wouldn't be able to follow us. For one thing, a streetcar was a lot faster than two heavy-set members of the "master race." And for another, they would have to leave the rest of the workers unguarded if they wanted to chase us. The only real danger was that they might start shooting.

The streetcar drew nearer. We took off our armbands with the Jewish star, let them fall onto the ground, and dropped back from the rest.

The SS men didn't notice.

I nodded to Amos, and we raced toward the streetcar. I didn't turn round to look back. If the soldiers were going to shoot, there was absolutely nothing I could do about it, but I could lose a valuable half second by looking. Following my encounter in the guardhouse no more than twenty minutes ago—was it really no longer?—I wasn't going to forget how invaluable seconds, or even half a second, could be ever again.

I jumped onto the back platform of the streetcar. Amos followed me. I was faster than him. He must have kept looking back; there was no other explanation.

The streetcar moved away, and I watched as one of the soldiers took his gun off his shoulder and took aim, but the other soldier stopped him. He didn't want to risk shooting Polish civilians. Their job was to take a group of laborers to the airport; someone else could worry about a couple of fleeing Jews—who wouldn't get very far, anyway.

Inside, the streetcar was almost empty; the few Poles sitting here took no notice of us. We were shabbily dressed, but a lot of the Polish workers were, too. So as not to attract any attention, I sat. Amos dropped down on the wooden bench beside me and said approvingly, "That was a great idea."

It did me a world of good to hear him say that.

46

A streetcar isn't all that fast, but after having been forced to walk everywhere for so long, the journey felt incredibly fast, even unnatural. I felt at that moment how people must have felt who rode on the very first trains when and wherever that was. Though they hadn't had to worry about being arrested.

After a couple of minutes, I began to relax. We had got away! I almost managed to stop thinking about the fat pig. Then the streetcar stopped again and two SS soldiers got on. Amos and I both knew that even the slightest sign of fear would give us away, but neither of us knew if the other realized this. And so we both whispered, "Don't worry, it's okay." And started laughing because we had both said exactly the same thing at the same time.

The soldiers looked across at us at that moment and saw a happy, fairly shabby-looking Polish couple. They walked to the front of the streetcar where only Germans were allowed to sit, and didn't turn round to look at us again. So we were able to get off the streetcar three stops later at Górnośląska Street without being stopped.

We walked to a five-story house. We were to ring the bell labeled Synowiec, and then a go-between from the Polish resistance would open the door.

I rang the bell. No one opened the door. We waited. I rang the bell again. Still no reaction.

I started to feel nervous. If we stood in front of the door in full view for much longer, we might arouse suspicion. But we couldn't go away, either. Where should we go? As Jews? In Warsaw?

An old man wearing a vest was standing looking out the window of his flat on the opposite side of the road. Watching us closely. Why were two shabby-looking young people hanging around like that? Were they burglars? Or something worse?

"Let's walk round the block," I suggested.

"Good idea." He nodded.

We were just about to set off when a small portly man wearing a flat cap came toward us calling out merrily, "Why, there's my nephew and his brand-new wife!"

The man at the window turned away and went back into his flat yawning.

"You seem to like pretty, skinny ladies, nephew!" the man with the flat cap kept the charade going, and Amos played along, "I like lovely ladies, Uncle!"

Lovely!

Why couldn't I stop lapping up Amos's praise and compliments? What was wrong with me?

"Come on in, I'll make you a cup of tea," "Uncle" said, and I could smell the alcohol on his breath, which suggested he preferred other beverages, even at this time of the morning! That was probably why he was late, instead of meeting us in the flat as agreed.

We entered the house, walked up the freshly polished stairs—I had long since forgotten how cozy ordinary blocks of flats could be—and Uncle showed us into a small two-roomed flat that was almost bare of any furniture but still seemed luxurious to me because there was a real bed in the bedroom.

"The landlord thinks I've rented this flat for my nephew and his young wife who have come up from the country to try their luck in town."

He threw two wedding rings onto the table.

"Your names are Robert and Gabriela Szalach. I'll bring you your papers tomorrow."

Amos put his ring on his finger at once and held it up for me to see, laughing. "Congratulations on getting married," he said.

I gave him a twisted smile.

"And . . . ," he continued, ". . . on your excellent choice of husband."

I pulled a face. "Idiot!"

"But, then, I do have a lovely wife."

Don't go red whatever you do.

"Such a beautiful young lady."

"Idiot," I said again and went red.

"You said that already." Amos laughed, took my hand, and gently put the ring on my finger.

That was the nearest thing to a wedding I would ever know, I thought.

"Can we get down to business?" Uncle asked, sounding annoyed.

"Of course," I answered.

"If we must," Amos grinned.

"You are not to leave the flat. Not even for a second. We will let you know when you can meet with the leaders of the Polish Home Army."

"We need to talk to them as soon as possible," Amos explained; he was totally serious all at once, had turned back into a strong, determined fighter. Amazing how quickly he could switch roles. I wondered what sort of person he would have been if I had really been able to go back in time and kill Hitler. Would there have been an ounce of earnestness in him? Would he have been just another charming daredevil?

"When you are to meet our leaders is for them to decide, not you," Uncle snapped at us. "Just be glad that they are prepared to see you at all."

This man made sure we understood fast just how unimportant we Jews were for the Polish resistance fighters.

I took off my left shoe and sock and handed the dispatch to Uncle. "A letter from Mordechai Anielewicz."

"It smells," he said.

Instead of laughing or saying, "I told you so," Amos laid into the man. "You're not here to make remarks; you are here to deliver it."

"Watch your mouth, Jew!" Uncle said, put on his cloth cap, and left the flat.

When the door closed, Amos sighed. "So these are our comrades," he said.

For the next half hour, Amos berated the Polish resistance for having done so little to help us, giving us the worst weapons, and being riddled with Jew haters who were secretly or even unashamedly pleased that the Germans—the enemies who occupied their beloved Poland—were doing them a favor by getting rid of the Jewish vermin.

I didn't say anything. I knew I was safe here, but I started to feel the fat SS man crawling over my skin until I couldn't stand it anymore and had to wash the spot where he had kissed me. Literally scrub it away.

I left Amos standing in the middle of a rant about how Jews could only ever trust one another, hurried into the bathroom, and turned the taps on as far as they would go. There was flowing water! Hot flowing water!

So there was a God after all!

47

I lay in the bath until I was totally wrinkled, and washed away all the dirt as best I could. I supposed the fat SS man was going to follow me in my dreams, but the warm bath helped me to stop thinking about him for a while. And to stop thinking about the ghetto or our mission or anything else. I blocked out the whole world. There was nothing more wonderful than thinking of nothing at all.

I kept letting water out of the tub and adding more hot water. I think I would have liked to stay there forever, make it my new home. But the most delicious smell floated in under the door. It smelled of bacon. And there was something else in the air: Was it . . . ?

Yes! Fried potatoes and beans!

Smells from another world.

My exhausted soul would have preferred to stay soaking in the bath, but my stomach was of a different opinion and grumbled, telling my soul not to be so selfish. So I got out of my new home, promised I'd be back soon, dried off my wrinkled skin, and felt annoyed that I had to slip back into my shabby, smelly clothes, now that I smelled so good for the first time in ages. The things that annoy us as soon as everything gets just the slightest bit better!

I got dressed except for my socks and shoes—the socks reminded me too much of what had happened in the guardhouse—followed the smell into the kitchen and could hardly believe my eyes: Amos had prepared a feast for us with bacon, beans, fried potatoes, bread, and fried eggs. I was sure he must have used up all the provisions Uncle had left for us at once, but Amos guessed what I was thinking and said, "Don't worry, Wrinkles, there's plenty more where that came from."

I giggled and sat down at the table and said, "You're a wonderful husband!"

"I know," he grinned.

"And so modest."

He laughed even louder. "This is the beginning of a fantastic marriage."

I didn't just eat until I had had enough, I ate until my stomach hurt. And then some.

Amos burped and I burped even louder.

He wasn't going to let me have the final word, though, and burped like a lion. But I was a master at burping.

When we finally gave up, Amos said, half grinning, half-sad, "Sometimes life can be so great."

It was a thought I hadn't had for so long, I'd almost forgotten it existed.

"It shouldn't only be sometimes," I answered, and looked out the window at the afternoon sun. It really did seem to like shining in the Polish part of the city.

"Come on, let's do the dishes," Amos said, determined to not give way to any dark thoughts.

I nodded, went to the sink and started to run the tap, and asked, "What are we going to do all day until we meet the Poles?"

"Ooh, I can think of a thing or two a couple of newlyweds might get up to." He was smiling, teasing me.

Was he really suggesting . . . ? Did he want to deceive Esther?

Even though he didn't love her, she'd be hurt. Not that I liked her very much, but still.

And I would be deceiving Daniel somehow. And I was still a virgin. And I would never want my first time to be with someone like Amos . . .

"Don't look so shocked," Amos interrupted my thoughts, acting the innocent.

"What . . . what did you have in mind?" I didn't want to know, and right away I wished I'd never asked. Why couldn't I keep my mouth shut?

"We could play Rummy."

"What?"

"It's a game of cards."

"I . . . I know that."

"Well, why ask, then?"

"Why Rummy?" I wanted to know, relieved that he hadn't intended anything else.

Amos pointed through the open kitchen door into the hall, and there, lying on a chest of drawers beside a vase with half-dried-out flowers, was a pack of cards.

"That is the only card game I know."

I burst out laughing.

We played cards into the night. I got annoyed every time Amos cheated, and was really pleased when he didn't notice me cheating as I dealt the cards. It was the most untroubled evening

I had spent in a long time. It kept feeling as if I was living a normal life. Almost.

Once I'd beaten him for the seventh time, Amos stretched and announced that he was going to have a bath to get rid of the smell of bacon.

"Then," he said, playing the just-married man so gallantly that I had to smile, "I might smell as lovely as you do, Mira."

He went into the bathroom, and I used my advantage shamelessly. There was only one bed in the flat. But it was a real bed! And I wanted to have it to myself.

I went into the little bedroom, which was practically full with just an oak cupboard and the bed, stroked the feather bed with my fingers, and took off all my clothes except my underwear. I hoped that there would be a nightgown or, even better, a pair of pajamas in the cupboard for me—in the Hollywood films the heroine always wore pajamas that were far too big and belonged to the man she secretly loved. And, of course, she looked amazing.

Unfortunately, there was only a suit for Amos and a long skirt and a blouse for me. Uncle had put them there so that we would be able to walk through Warsaw without attracting attention when the time came to meet the Polish resistance and negotiate about arms. He hadn't thought about nightgowns and pajamas.

So I got into bed in my underwear and cuddled up under the blankets. Lying in a real bed made the illusion of a normal life perfect for a blessed moment.

But the moment only lasted a very short time because Amos appeared, dressed in his shirt and underwear, and asked in an amused sort of way, "So we are going to share the bed?"

"Whatever makes you think that?" I asked.

"Well, you are lying in it."

"You are sleeping on the floor," I explained.

"Whatever makes you think that?" he asked.

"You're a gentleman," I said.

"I'm not, actually. Sorry."

"I know that."

"I know you know."

"But even you would never make your wife sleep on the floor." I smiled.

"You'd never make your husband sleep on the floor." He grinned back and slipped under the covers before I could even say, "Don't you dare."

I was startled to be lying in bed side by side, and a bit surprised that Amos had kept his smelly shirt on. Why didn't he take it off and just keep his underwear on? Was it for decency's sake? Did Amos do decency?

I moved away so that there was as much room as possible between us. But still, here we were sharing a bed, half-naked. And, apart from the shirt, he smelled so good. Soap and Amos. I'd never noticed before, but I liked the way he smelled.

Would it be nice to touch him? As nice as his kiss? Suddenly after more than a year, the kiss in the market had leaped back into my mind. Was he thinking about it, too? But then he started to snore.

He definitely wasn't thinking about that kiss.

I was terrified of falling asleep and dreaming about the fat pig. As long as I stayed awake, I could tell myself that everything had worked out in the end. But in my dreams, the SS man would come back and I wouldn't be able to stop him. I didn't want to be alone with my fear, but I didn't want to wake up Amos, and let him know how pathetic I really was. And if he gave me a hug to make me feel better, I'd start to cry. Because of the fat pig, because of the nightmares that had been haunting me for weeks. And because of Hannah. Once I started crying, I would never stop. I'd go to pieces. Forever! And I'd never be the same again. I'd lose the strength I needed to complete my mission for the resistance.

I fought off sleep as best I could, but I lost. I didn't dream about the fat SS man, though. Perhaps I could have handled him. Instead . . . instead, the Mirror King appeared.

Until now, I had imagined him to be a funny-looking man made of mirrors, the way the scarecrow in *The Wizard of Oz* was made of straw. But in my dream he was a huge, malformed, humpbacked monster made of thousands of razor-sharp mirrors. Mirrors of distortion!

And in every mirror, I saw something horrifying: my brother beating me, a doll raping me, being gassed, burning alive in the ovens, and more and more and more . . . And all the while the Mirror King shrieked, "You must pay, you will pay!"

"What for?" I screamed. "What did I do?" I howled and howled, while the monster grew bigger and bigger, and more and more mirrors sprang open. I watched the barbed wire on the wall come to life and start strangling me; I saw my own father throwing me out the window, and Ruth coughing up more and more ashes until I was buried alive.

"You know very well why you must pay," the Mirror King bellowed.

In his face, I could see reflected eyes, Hannah's, Papa's, Mama's; Ruth's, Daniel's, and the German soldier's. The eyes began to bleed, and these eyes—not mouths for some reason, no, it was the bleeding eyes—all started screaming at me, "You are alive instead of us!"

I woke up screaming. Amos sat up beside me. "What is it, Mira? What's wrong?"

There was nothing I could do, I had to cry. My dreams had defeated me. I was lost forever, and now I knew why. I was paying. For being alive!

But before I could even say, "I was meant to die," Amos said something so surprising that I stopped crying right away, "You know what, Mira? Let's go to the cinema tomorrow."

48

W e put on the clothes Uncle had provided and walked through the streets of Warsaw in broad daylight. I was wearing the smart skirt and Amos had a suit and hat on. When we got to the Schauburg cinema, we joined the line. There were a couple of Poles and a lot of German soldiers out on a date with their Polish girlfriends. None of them would ever have dreamed that there were two Jews in their midst. They didn't even look our way, apart from one or two soldiers who were staring at my bottom to see if I could be a more attractive lover than the one they had already. But of course, I was far too skinny for those soldiers.

Taking me out to the cinema was completely insane, but it was pretty damn wonderful, too. Amos treated me like a queen. He hadn't fallen in love with me or anything, although he kept referring to me as his darling wife. He just wanted to cheer me up. And he wasn't the kind of person who could sit around doing nothing while we waited for Uncle to come. It would have driven him nuts.

We sat at the edge of a row, just in case we had to get away fast—even if we were being reckless, we couldn't ignore the danger altogether—and when the lights went out, my heart pounded with joy. The cinema wasn't showing any of the Hollywood films I loved; they were banned for Germans and Poles, too. Instead there was a funny film called *Quax, der Bruchpilot,* starring Heinz Rühmann as a young man called Quax who was in flight training. It was in German, of course, but I could guess what it was about.

There was a lot of singing, and the hero wasn't a bit like how the Germans usually saw themselves. At the start, he was an endearing, timid little crook. Of course, if you started to think about the film too much, you could tell that the story was a lot of propaganda to encourage young men to join the Luftwaffe. But I didn't want to think about that, I wanted to laugh. And so did Amos. No matter what.

About halfway through the film, Amos suddenly grabbed my hand and didn't let go. After that, I didn't notice what went on, on the screen, and I couldn't care less what Esther would say or what Daniel might think. Sitting in the cinema, holding hands, I realized what kind of person I wanted to be. Someone perfectly normal who led an ordinary sort of life.

After the film, we strolled back to the flat hand in hand. Amos kept laughing and said, "This is part of our cover. We are young and we are in love." I couldn't help thinking that—just now—Amos longed for a normal life as much as I did.

I enjoyed our walk so much that I left it to my "husband" to keep an eye out for Germans or *szmalcowniks.* We walked on holding hands until we saw Uncle coming toward us. "There you are!" he called. Of course his friendliness was just put on. After all, we had deliberately defied his order not to leave the flat.

"I was just coming to get you," he said. "Olga is expecting us and there is plenty to eat. You know what she's like," he laughed, and I could smell the alcohol on his breath again.

"That's our Olga!" Amos laughed along.

Uncle took us to a car, and we climbed into the back. He started the engine and drove off. The reckless way he set off showed us how angry he was.

Well, let him be angry. The outing had been worth it. No one could ever take this memory away from me.

"Where are we going?" Amos wanted to know.

"To the meeting," Uncle snapped.

"That was quicker than we thought," I said, surprised.

"Your stinking letter got things moving."

That sounded like a good sign.

"Where is the meeting taking place?"

"That is a secret. As soon as we are out of town, I'll blindfold you."

"You don't trust us," Amos said, and you could tell how much his pride was wounded.

Uncle burst out, "Of course I don't. You fucking Jews march through town where anyone can catch you any minute, and don't give a damn that you are putting me in danger."

"Who are you calling a fucking Jew, you shithead?" Amos was furious.

"I'm calling you a fucking Jew, you fucking Jew!" Uncle shouted back.

Amos lunged at him. He forgot that he might cause an accident. But I could see it coming, grabbed his shoulders, held him back, and whispered, "Don't!"

Amos stared at me, boiling with rage, but he calmed down a bit and leaned back in his seat.

"The girl's got more brains than you have," Uncle jeered, "not that that's difficult."

I wanted to hold Amos's hand again to show him that we were a team, real comrades, not just a pretend couple, but as soon as I touched his hand, he pulled it away, stuck it in his pocket, and stared out the window.

As we left the city, Uncle threw blindfolds onto the back seat and ordered us to put them on.

"It's a pleasure," Amos said bitterly, "then we won't have to look at you!"

We drove for about half an hour, and then the car stopped and Uncle sniggered, "Let there be light."

We took off the blindfolds and found ourselves in a wood. As we climbed out of the car, my lungs filled with fresh air. All the mingling smells of flowers, trees, and moss threatened to overwhelm me. I hadn't been out in the woods for years.

But I pulled myself together. I wasn't here to enjoy the scenery like some Pole out on a jaunt with her beau. This wasn't the time or place for any semblance of normal life. We were here for the cause. Our cause.

We walked toward a dilapidated hunting lodge that looked deserted. Two Poles were waiting for us at the door. One man had a gray mustache, while the other was clean-shaven with a receding hairline.

"The Jews send us children," the one with the mustache scoffed. But the other man said, "Bravery is not a matter of age."

Both men were wearing dark leather jackets, and the friendlier one introduced them, "I'm Captain Iwanski from the Home Army. This is my commanding officer, Colonel Rowecki." Then he turned to Uncle and said, "You can wait for our guests outside."

Uncle nodded obediently and headed away. No doubt he

was off to sit in the shade of the trees and knock back a couple of drinks.

"Please come in," the friendly captain said.

We followed them into the cabin and sat down at a table. The captain poured out glasses of schnapps and said, "Let's drink, and then we'll talk."

We all raised our glasses, though the frowning colonel with the mustache did so reluctantly.

"To a free Poland," the captain said.

"To a free Poland," we repeated. We clinked glasses and drank. Not being used to schnapps, I shuddered. Amos didn't pull a face, though, and the two Polish officers drank the schnapps as if it were water.

"Let's get down to business," the colonel said. He seemed to be annoyed about this meeting. Maybe he was against it altogether. "You will receive twenty guns."

"Twenty guns?" Amos repeated in disbelief.

It was such a ridiculously small number that the colonel might as well have said: You can have twenty dummies.

"Twenty guns," the colonel confirmed.

"And then we'll take it from there," Iwanski said encouragingly.

"That's not enough," Amos protested.

Iwanski's eyes told us he knew, but his CO explained, "We need the weapons for our fellow countrymen."

"I was born in Poland," I protested. "My parents were born in Poland. And my grandparents, too!"

The way the colonel looked, I could see that he didn't care. This officer had the same enemies as us, and, just like us, he had joined the underground and was risking his life to fight the Germans. Yet he didn't think of us as Poles.

This was when I realized that I wasn't a Pole, couldn't be one even if I'd tried. The Poles would never regard us Jews as fellow countrymen.

"You must help us," Amos implored.

Before the captain could answer, Colonel Mustache said, "We are already giving you more than is wise."

"Wise?" Amos was speechless.

"We need the weapons for our own fight."

"We are all fighting for the same thing," Amos retaliated.

"This is not the time for an uprising," the colonel said coldly. "We must wait until the Russians invade Poland. We can't allow a bunch of Jews to force us to start an uprising before we're ready. We won't let Warsaw burn when we have no chance of beating the Germans."

"A bunch of Jews?" Amos leaped to his feet and leaned on the table, shaking.

The colonel remained unaffected by Amos's understandable anger. And said, "If we support you, we'll be committing suicide."

Iwanski realized that Amos was about to fly off the handle and tried to placate him, "It's not just our opinion. This is what the exile government in London thinks."

"The Germans are slaughtering us!" Amos shouted.

"We know," Iwanski said.

Amos struggled for words, and because I knew that he wouldn't find them, or at least not any that would avoid a further escalation, I said, "We don't have the luxury of being able to wait."

The two officers looked at me, surprised. They seemed astonished that I could actually speak for myself.

"Our people are dying," I said distinctly. It was the first time in my life that I had called the Jews my people. But we really didn't belong to Poland. "We have to fight. Now! Or else we'll all be slaughtered."

To judge by the two officers' expressions, this was perfectly obvious to them both. Iwanski poured himself another glass of schnapps, looking uncomfortable. The colonel couldn't believe that a Jewish girl had spoken to him like this. "Take the twenty guns or do without, as you please."

"If you don't help us, you're as bad as the Germans!" I hurled the words at him.

Iwanski drank.

The colonel's voice sounded as harsh as his words, "I think it is time for you to leave, young lady."

Amos roared, "I think it's time for something . . ."

I knew there was no point in Amos grabbing the colonel and no use talking anymore, either. So I stood up, dragged Amos away from the table, and said, "I'm afraid there's nothing more to say."

We left the hut. Amos smashed his fist against a tree. The tree remained as unmoved as the rest of the world. No one cared about the plight of the Jews. The Polish resistance wouldn't help us, and the Allies wouldn't bomb the railway tracks to the concentration camps.

Defeated, I leaned against another tree. Iwanski came out of the hut.

"What do you want now?" Amos shouted at him.

"To tell you that the young lady is right. You are Poles, too."

"Your colonel made it very clear—" Amos started to say, but Iwanski interrupted, "I will help you, along with a few comrades, as best I can."

So the Jews weren't totally alone after all.

49

We got back to the flat just as it was getting dark. As we closed the door behind us Amos took my hand and congratulated me, "You achieved far more than I did."

I was embarrassed by his praise and confused by his holding my hand. This wasn't a situation where we were pretending to be a Polish couple, and touching was part of our camouflage. This was a moment when we were just being ourselves. Mira and Amos.

"You're a brave woman," he said, and he meant it.

I didn't know where to look.

"I . . . I'm not sure if Esther would approve," I said, and stared at our hands.

"No, I don't think she would," Amos said quietly without his usual grin, and he let go. I was so stupid. Why did I have to mention Esther?

We cooked supper together and talked about what had happened—at the meeting with the Poles, not about our visit to the cinema: That had been a magical outing to an impossibly normal world we would probably never set foot on again. After we'd eaten, we did the dishes and got ready for bed.

"I can sleep on the floor tonight, if you like," Amos suggested when he came into the bedroom and saw that I was already curled up in bed.

"It's okay," I said, and tried to make my voice sound as if holding hands just now hadn't changed anything between us and that we could happily share a bed like we had the night before.

Amos stood there not knowing what to do. In the end, he made up his mind, undressed down to his shirt and underwear, and crawled into his side of the bed.

For a while we lay there in silence, side by side, not looking at each other, and I stared out the window. During the bleak winter in the ghetto, the moon had been covered in clouds most of the time. But tonight it was shining in all its glory, surrounded by twinkling stars. Even the heavenly bodies seemed to prefer to shine on all the world except the Jews.

I turned round toward Amos, who was still awake, and asked, "Why don't you take your shirt off at night?"

He looked like he'd been hit or something. He hadn't expected this question any more than I had. As usual, I'd just opened my mouth and said the first thing that came into my head.

"You don't have to tell me," I said quickly.

"Don't worry, it's okay . . . we are married, remember?" He tried to smile but only managed a tortured look.

He sat up in bed and took off his shirt. It was a good thing that there were no lights on. Even in the moonlight, I could see the awful marks. He was covered in scars. The whole of his back had been slashed open at some stage.

"The Germans?" I asked, sitting up, too.

"The Germans," Amos nodded, and put his shirt back on.

I didn't know if I should ask any more questions, but then Amos started to speak of his own accord. "They caught me smuggling two years ago and wanted to know who my accomplices were."

Despite the dim moonlight, I thought I could see tears in his eyes.

"I . . . I betrayed my friends," he stammered, and now I really could see tears running down his face.

They weren't just accomplices, they had been friends. How could anyone help him?

"They shot all four of them." He tried to take a deep breath, but his guilt was blocking his windpipe and he shuddered instead. He used his sleeve to wipe away his tears. Then he looked at me. He was trying to read my face to see if I despised him as much as he despised himself. Hidden away beneath his clowning facade, I now realized, he absolutely hated himself.

But I couldn't condemn him, with scars like that. Who had enough willpower not to crack? Mordechai Anielewicz probably, and maybe one or two other truly brave fighters. But apart from them, no one could hope to withstand such torture. I couldn't. I had started crying the minute the fat pig had slapped me in the guardhouse.

"I . . . I never told anyone before," Amos said in a voice so low I could hardly hear him.

"Not even Esther?"

"Not even Esther."

He had been afraid that she would despise him.

"Why . . . why me?"

"I don't know. Perhaps because you're my 'wife,' just now . . ."

I held out my finger with the wedding ring to prove it. So he could see that I didn't condemn him.

Amos didn't say any more. He had revealed more of himself than ever before, and it had been a huge effort for him. He crawled back down under the blankets, and so did I.

After a length of silence, I said cautiously, "Amos?"

"Yes?"

"The Germans are responsible for the deaths of your friends. It's not your fault."

"If only that were true," he answered after a while, "it would mean so much."

He didn't believe me. I took hold of his hand and he didn't let go. We held hands like an old couple. Or like two little children. Two damaged souls giving each other something to cling to until they fell asleep.

I didn't have any nightmares that night. The Mirror King left me alone.

50

wanski was true to his word. Together with several comrades from the Polish Home Army, he smuggled crates of weapons into the ghetto. Through the warren of sewers, where you'd lose your way without a competent guide. A mother there begged him to take her two little girls back to the Polish side, and although it was difficult—you couldn't stand upright in the stinking sewers and the little children had to be carried to prevent them from drowning in the water, which was very deep in places—Iwanski had taken them with him and hidden them in his flat where his wife was now looking after them.

The captain told us all this, sitting at our kitchen table. When he was finished, Amos asked, "What is it like in the sewers?"

"It's shit," the captain answered dryly.

"I can smell it," Amos laughed.

It was true. There was still a hint of sewage about him, although he'd had a bath in the meantime and was wearing clean clothes.

"Thanks for the compliment," Iwanski grinned, and got up

from the table. As he made his goodbyes he promised, "I will organize more weapons for you."

We thanked him. I thought about giving him a hug, but then I didn't dare because it might have seemed inappropriate. Once he had gone, Amos summed up my feelings in one crude sentence:

"Thank goodness there are a few Poles left who'll go through shit for us."

"How long do you think we will be able to resist the Germans with Iwanski's weapons and the ones we've already got?"

Amos grew serious again. "A couple of hours maybe, if things go well."

I should never have asked.

"It's hopeless, no matter what we do."

"No, it's not," Amos disagreed. "Just think how proud the Jews in the ghetto are now, ever since we killed the soldiers in January. If we wage war against the Germans, generations of Jews will remember us. We are like the Jews who fought at Masada thousands of years ago. It doesn't matter how long we hold out. A day, a month, or even just a few hours. The main thing is: We will not go like sheep to the slaughter!"

I lacked his spirit. "If there are any future generations of Jews," I said unhappily.

Amos gently touched my cheek. That felt good. "There will be," he said.

He sounded so sure. I smiled.

"Mira, has anyone ever told you how beautiful you are when you smile?"

That wasn't another playful compliment simply meant to cheer me up. Since Amos had confided in me, he was behaving differently. He was more serious than he had been before, and at the same time, he showed more feelings. He'd realized he didn't have to put on an act anymore when we were alone.

"No, no one's ever said that," I answered truthfully. Even Daniel had never mentioned it. He hadn't paid me compliments. What on earth had he seen in me? We'd never talked about things like that. We'd just been kids really. It had been a childish love that never went further than kissing.

I was a very different person from last summer, grown up in the saddest way.

And in the unlikely event of Daniel's still being alive, he would be different, too. With a bit of luck, he wouldn't hate me now, but we wouldn't love each other anymore.

"If no one's ever told you," Amos said earnestly, "then everyone you know must be blind, stupid, or dumb."

I laughed, and I touched his hand touching my face.

"You're good for me," I said without thinking.

"Same here," he said, and he meant it.

We just looked at each other for a moment. Then we kissed. Not like the first time. In the market. This kiss was loving. Tender. More intense. When it was over, we were both trembling. And didn't dare kiss again. Instead, we moved away from each other and got ready for bed without saying anything. When we'd gone to bed we just lay there holding hands. Until Amos whispered, "Mira?"

"What is it?"

"I . . . I'd like to kiss you again."

It was my turn. I said: "Same here."

51

We didn't make love that night, or the next. Somehow it felt like we had a guardian angel. Like there was all the time in the world. Although everything was against us. I had never felt as happy as in those few days when we were the go-betweens with the Poles round Iwanski. My nightmares stopped for a while. And I even went back to the 777 islands again.

The *Longear* sailed across the sea on a lovely sunny day. The waves rocked the pirate ship gently, and you could hear the sound of music and dancing. We loved to party in this world. To be fair, the sailors' singing could be so dire that the dolphins would flee at times, but everyone really did enjoy themselves.

Hannah and I danced up and down the deck to the were-wolf's accordion music and she asked, "Where have you been?"

"I . . . I was back home," I said, dodging the truth.

"You should not always leave me for so long."

"No, I shouldn't."

"How are things in the ghetto?" Hannah asked. She was all excited. "Have things changed much?"

What was I supposed to say? That Mama was dead? That she herself was dead?

I knew she had the right to know everything, but I didn't have the heart to tell her. So I said, "It's complicated. I'll tell you all about it, but not right now."

"When?" Hannah asked suspiciously.

"As soon as . . ." I was searching for a ploy. "As soon as we defeat the Mirror King."

"That's not going to take much longer," Hannah cried. "We wangled the third magic mirror off the Sandman, and we are on course for Mirror Island right now."

I swallowed. I banished all thoughts of the monster. I tried to stop feeling guilty about being alive. Instead we danced round and round the deck and celebrated the third magic mirror. It was such fun. Life was wonderful. On the islands and in our little flat.

Until we heard that the Germans were transferring more troops to Warsaw.

52

"I'm going back to the ghetto," Amos said that evening, telling me what I already knew. "When the fighting starts, I want to be with our comrades."

"But someone has to stay here to liaise with the Polish resistance," I said.

If we stayed on the Polish side, we could stay alive. At least for a while. I wasn't afraid of dying, but in the past few days, I had found something worth living for. I didn't want to lose Amos. I couldn't stand the thought of losing another person I loved.

"You can stay if you like," Amos said, and his eyes flashed angrily.

That look shot right through me. And made me feel ashamed. The resistance should mean more to me than our love, but it didn't, not right now.

"I can't stay here by myself . . . ," I started to argue.

"Mordechai will send someone," Amos interrupted. He was angry with me. And I was angry with him. How could he think of leaving me behind?

"Mordechai can send someone for me, too," I snapped, "I'm coming with you."

I would rather die fighting by his side than live a single day in the Polish part of the city without him.

"Okay," Amos said, and his face relaxed a bit.

"Okay."

Without saying a word, we cleared the table, did the dishes, turned off the light, and lay down in our "marital" bed, all for the last time.

Amos stared at the ceiling in the dark while I looked out the window at the sky. There was a half-moon. I probably wouldn't live to see another full one.

Then Amos said, "I'm sorry."

I turned round to face him. "What for?"

He turned toward me, too. Our faces were almost touching.

"Everything," he said.

"Everything?"

"And nothing."

"You could be just a tiny bit more specific . . . ," I said.

It took him a moment, and then he said, "Mira, I think I love you."

"You think?"

"It's the only thing I believed in all my life." He smiled.

And then we made love.

53

Mordechai seemed perfectly calm when we all met up on the stairs in 29 Miła Street. But he must have been feeling as tense as the rest of us. The Germans would be marching into the ghetto any moment now. The SS had deliberately chosen the beginning of the holy Jewish Passover festival for their final operation.

"The moment we have all been waiting for has arrived," Mordechai said to us. "We will wear down the enemy, attacking constantly, from doorways, through windows, out of ruins, day and night."

Amos was standing beside me. His eyes shone. Esther looked wildly determined, too. She had managed to ignore the fact that Amos and I were a couple now. There were far more important things than love. For her. For Amos. And even for me.

"The Germans," Mordechai went on, "will have to fight continuously for months. If we get all the weapons, ammunition, and explosives we need, the enemy will drown in a river of blood."

We weren't going to get the weapons. I'd known this ever since our mission to the Polish side, and Mordechai knew it, too. But what else could he say to rally the troops before the battle? The truth? That we'd all be dead in a couple of hours?

We were a group of no more than fourteen hundred untrained fighters, spread out throughout the ghetto. We would have to face the Germans and their tanks with little more than a gun per person. We had a few hundred hand grenades and Molotov cocktails. There was going to be a river of blood, all right. But it wouldn't be a river flowing with the blood of German soldiers—it would be our own.

I felt it would have been easier to die if spring hadn't just arrived. On the 19th of April 1943, the sun shone over the ghetto with an assurance that made our life and death harder to bear.

After Mordechai's speech, our group took up positions behind the designated windows, balconies, and up on the roof. Several other groups had dug in, in six surrounding houses, so about a hundred fighters had the crossroads at Zamenhof Street covered from all sides. The Germans would pass this point as soon as they invaded the ghetto.

Like most of us, I was armed with a gun and a hand grenade. Only Ben Redhead owned a rifle. One night, a couple of weeks ago, he had ambushed a soldier near the wall and taken his gun. Since then, he guarded it like a treasure.

I took up position beside Amos at a window on the fourth floor. At first, I'd not been sure if I shouldn't choose a different position. Did I really want to fight and die beside the person I loved? Wouldn't it be better not to know when the bullets hit him?

Amos didn't worry about things like that. He was completely focused on his imminent revenge. If I'd tried to say goodbye before the Germans arrived, he wouldn't have noticed. All I could do was say goodbye to my little sister.

"We'll be reaching Mirror Island soon," Hannah said, sounding pleased. She was out on deck. The *Longear* was sailing through a choppy sea. I hadn't dreamed about the Mirror King in the past few days, probably because I'd stopped feeling guilty about being alive, seeing as I was going to die today.

"And then," Hannah chatted away excitedly, showing me the three magic mirrors that were sparkling like diamonds, "we'll defeat all evil."

"But not," Captain Carrot boasted, "without giving it a great kick in the backside first."

"And in the groin!" the werewolf added.

I smiled. At least one world was going to be free.

"They are coming!" I could hear Esther shouting. "The Germans are coming!"

Her voice reached me in the world of the 777 islands.

I wanted to tell my sister so many things, but there was no time left. I hugged her and whispered, "I love you."

She protested, "You are squashing me!"

"Because I love you so much!"

She returned the hug.

"Now you are squashing me!"

"Because I love you so much!" Hannah laughed.

Tears welled in my eyes.

"Why are you crying?"

"Because I have to leave."

And then there was nothing left to say. It took all my will-power, but I let her go and left. Probably forever.

54

peered through the broken window. I had a perfect view of the street and an excellent shooting position, assuming I actually managed to shoot.

The Germans were able to gas us so easily because they didn't regard us as human beings. We knew exactly what kind of people they were, though, and that was why the other fighters were burning to kill them. But I could still see the face of the young soldier begging for mercy, and I still didn't know if I was going to be able to kill anyone.

In the distance, we saw a tank rolling into the ghetto followed by about twenty members of the Jewish police. Behind the traitors, the soldiers had shouldered their arms and were marching in rows of four. It was unbelievable, but they were singing!

Im grünen Walde, da steht ein Försterhaus,
da schauet jeden Morgen,
so frisch und frei von Sorgen,
des Försters Töchterlein heraus . . .

The swine were belting out a marching song.

They thought they could wipe us out and sing while they were at it . . .

Lore, Lore, Lore, Lore,
schön sind die Mädchen
von siebzehn, achtzehn Jahr . . .

The SS men marched with every confidence, without even one of them holding a gun at the ready. They obviously weren't expecting any resistance. They were so used to leading Jews to the gas chambers without a battle that they weren't even on the lookout for signs of an ambush.

We all waited for Mordechai's signal to start shooting. But right now the soldiers weren't close enough.

Der Förster und die Tochter, die schossen beide gut . . .

The tank rolled toward our window.

Der Förster schoss das Hirschlein, die Tochter traf das Bürschlein . . .

Jewish policemen walked past. Miserable creatures.

Tief in das junge Herz hinein . . .

Now the first soldiers marched past, right under our window. Amos couldn't wait to start shooting, but Mordechai still didn't give the order. He waited until enough soldiers were within shooting distance.

Ta-ra-la-la, ta-ra-la-la,
tief in das junge Herz hinein . . .

At last, our leader gave the signal by throwing a hand grenade out the window right into the bulk of the men.

Lore, Lore . . .

As it exploded, the soldiers screamed and a barrage of Molotov cocktails, grenades, and bullets rained down on them from the roofs, out the windows, and off the balconies.

The Germans and their Jewish helpers started to panic and broke formation. The German *Übermenschen*—the supermen—knocked one another over as they sought cover in empty shops and house entrances, or behind mounds of rubbish.

All over the place, soldiers were struck by bullets and collapsed to the ground, while others ran through the streets, burning alive, until they fell down on the cobblestones and didn't get up again. Their screams were barely audible in all the din of the explosions. No one went to help a fellow soldier. And no one was singing now. No more *Lore, Lore . . .*

Amos was standing beside me shooting. It was strange to see him like this. Fulfilled, exhilarated, avenging his friends and himself at last.

The first Germans started to shoot back. Bullets hit the wall behind us.

I crouched down beneath the window.

"Mira, shoot!" Amos hissed at me and threw another hand grenade down into the turmoil raging on the street.

But all I wanted was to scream. I was so scared of dying. And of killing someone else.

"Mira!" Amos shouted.

Black smoke was billowing up from the street.

"The tank, I took out the tank!" Esther whooped.

I stood up and stared down at the street. The tank was in flames, and I watched a soldier crawling out covered in blood. There was just a bloody stump where his right arm had been. He fell off the tank and hit the ground. The rest of the crew didn't get out. They burned to death inside the vehicle.

A Jewish policeman lay bleeding to death beside the soldier. The two of them shared the same fate. But the Jewish policeman accepted death. He called out, with the last of his strength, "Jewish bullets! Thank you! Thank you!"

He was able to die knowing that we had given him back his dignity in the final moments of his life.

"Mira!" Amos was outraged.

I couldn't shoot. Until . . . until I spotted the fat pig from the guardhouse in all the chaos, standing beside the burning tank. I remembered what he nearly did to me, what he had likely done to so many other girls. I pointed my gun at him and my hand shook.

The window next to ours was hit by a volley of bullets. It burst into thousands of pieces, but I didn't duck away again, because the fat pig from the guardhouse was aiming his gun at someone. He'd shoot one of our comrades throwing Molotov cocktails from the roof. Or Ben Redhead, maybe, who was up there, too. I envisaged Hannah lying in the pool of blood in the pantry. And shot.

The SS man fell to the ground.

It was the first time I'd shot someone deliberately, not in self-defense but in battle. I kept on shooting, shooting, shooting. As if I was intoxicated. And I didn't feel guilty, at all. Every soldier I killed was one SS man who would never kill children again or sing while he was doing it.

55

fter about half an hour, any soldiers who could still run fled out of the ghetto past their dead comrades and the burned-out tank. It didn't matter if they had been ordered to retreat or had simply fled in panic. What mattered was that German soldiers were running away from the Jews! It was unbelievable! They were running away from us!

And there was something even more amazing; once the chaos abated a little, and we got the reports on losses in from all the groups positioned at the crossroads, we discovered that there weren't any! All the fighters had survived.

We couldn't believe our victory, our luck, our survival. We fell into one another's arms. Hugged, laughed, cried, whooped for joy. A few fighters even started singing and waltzed round and round.

I'd have loved to dance with them but I still didn't know how.

Mordechai gave me a huge hug. So did comrades I hardly knew because they had joined us while I was in the Polish part of the city with Amos. Even Esther threw her arms around me.

"Did you see the tank burn?" she asked, beaming.

Our triumph was bigger and more important than anything that had gone before.

Ben Redhead looked even happier than everyone else. Still holding his rifle, he came up to me at the shot-up window and shouted, "Eight!"

He had been counting.

"I got eight of them!"

He'd stopped stuttering. He had probably always felt guilty because his father had collaborated with the Germans, and now he felt free. "For Hannah," he said seriously, and he seemed grown-up all of a sudden.

I wasn't sure if I should reply, "For Hannah," even though I had joined the resistance to give her death a purpose. But my sister would be forgotten forever when Ben and I died. And we would be dead very soon—tomorrow or the next day—despite today's triumph. No, we weren't doing this for Hannah. Amos was right. We were doing this for future generations. We would live on in their thoughts.

I stroked Ben Redhead's cheek. Even if he seemed grown-up and had stopped stuttering—maybe for the rest of his life—I would never forget the boy who had been kissed by my sister.

Amos came up to me, laughing. "We're alive!"

"Yes, we are," I agreed. It was a miracle.

And we kissed each other as if we hadn't been fighting for future generations at all, but simply for this one kiss.

56

When it got dark, we went out onto the street and looked at the dead, bullet-riddled, broken bodies of our enemies. The air smelled of smoke and charred flesh. Not just here, but all over the ghetto. Everywhere, fighting units of the resistance had forced the SS to retreat. And you could smell alcohol. The Jews were celebrating. Fighters and civilians alike came up out of the bunkers in the safety of the dark.

Esther climbed onto the burned-out tank. It was her trophy. Mordechai and the others collected the weapons of the dead soldiers.

I was starting to hope that tomorrow wouldn't be my last day on earth, that we would be able to hold out for one or two days longer or even a week, perhaps. I knew that we could never win the physical battle in the long run, but we had already won morally today.

Amos came to me. "Mira . . . ," he said, but his voice broke.

"What's wrong?" I asked, confused.

"Look!" he said quietly, and he was fighting back tears.

He pointed toward the roof of a house at Muranowski Square, and I realized he wasn't sad; he was deeply moved. Two flags were being hoisted. The red and white Polish flag and the blue and white flag of the resistance.

There were tears in my eyes, too. The flags made me think of the one carried by the children from the orphanage on their way to the cattle trucks.

The tears for the dead children mingled with tears of joy. Germans, Poles, Ukrainians, Latvians—all our enemies and our few friends beyond the wall—could see these flags.

I'd never been prouder than at this moment when those flags fluttered in the gentle breeze and hundreds of Jews started cheering. I had always thought that the story of Masada was about Jews dying in honor.

But it wasn't. It was about being alive. We had driven the soldiers away. The ghetto belonged to us. Maybe just for this one night. But we were free. And we would be free for the rest of our lives!

57

At first, we were all far too excited to fall asleep at our posts in the various houses. Everyone had stories to tell of their own and other people's acts of courage and heroism, "Did you see Sarah throwing the hand grenade that hit that officer?" "All the workers in the brush maker's district have gone into hiding; they are refusing to be resettled. One of the fighters shot the owner of the brush factory in the hand."

But bit by bit the voices grew quieter and people became more serious.

"How long will we be able to survive?" "What are the Germans going to do next?" "I hope I get shot and don't die in the flames."

Amos and I lay side by side. Holding hands. We didn't say anything, we just looked at each other in the light of the moon. On top of the world because we'd been granted a little bit more time together. No, not granted—we had won this in battle.

Amos smiled at me. "I can die happy now," he said.

I didn't know what to say. I felt happy, and free, but I didn't want to die. I did not want him to die!

I was so energized that I thought I would never get to sleep, but I was overwhelmed in the end. I slept deeply and didn't dream a thing, which was a blessing for me.

When I woke up toward the end of the night, Amos was still asleep. He looked so peaceful. I'd never seen him like that before. He seemed to have been released from the pain he had been carrying for so long. His friends were avenged.

Mordechai came over and woke Amos up. He opened his eyes, and it didn't take a second before he was wide awake and jumping up. As I struggled to get up, too, Mordechai called Esther and Ben Redhead over to join us and said, "You four must go over to Nalewki Street and support our people there. We think there will be even heavier fighting than in Miła Street."

A few moments later, the four of us left the building. The air felt colder than it had yesterday—the day of great triumph—but the sky was still clear and cloudless. The sun was rising over the ghetto, and I tried not to think about whether this was my last sunrise. I just wanted to enjoy the beautiful play of colors. Then Ben Redhead laughed. "They are even more beautiful in daylight," he said.

He pointed over to the building at Muranowski Square where the two flags were flying.

It was still amazing. At this moment, the ghetto wasn't a prison anymore; it was home.

58

We reached the junction where Gęsia, Franciszkańska, and Nalewki Streets met up, and heard music coming from 33 Nalewki. A fighter was playing the accordion, and the beautiful sounds filled the ghetto. A home with music. Could there be anything more wonderful?

"Schubert," Esther said.

"The Germans can compose almost as well as they can kill," Amos said, and opened the door of the house on Nalewki Street. We climbed the stairs, past shot-up windows, and reported to Rachel Belka in the top flat. She was a woman so determined, strong, and harsh, even Esther looked like a little girl next to her. Rachel was one of the oldest fighters. At twenty-nine, she was actually five years older than Mordechai.

We gave her the latest news, and she told us where our posts were. Amos and I were on one of the top balconies. From there we could see the Germans gathering at the ghetto gates. Jewish policemen were with them again, acting as human shields this time. Each bullet that struck a collaborator couldn't reach a German. Two tanks took up position in front of the gate.

"They're going to fire at us," I said, stating the obvious.

"They're going to try," Amos replied. "They are too far away, and they won't dare come any closer."

That must have been the worst thing for the SS: Jews had destroyed one of their tanks, the Germans' favorite weapon.

"Are you sure they can't get us?" I asked.

"We'll find out soon enough," Amos smiled.

I took a pair of binoculars, looked through, and realized that in the Polish part of the city, life was going on as normal: Just a few hundred meters away, people were on their way to work, traders had opened their shops, and cars were driving through the streets.

There was a war going on right under their noses, and the Poles were behaving as if it were happening on a different planet. Mars. Jupiter. Uranus.

If anyone had still been suffering the illusion that our actions would inspire the Poles to join us and resist the occupiers, he or she would have been disappointed now at the very least.

A black limousine stopped outside the ghetto gates. The driver got out and opened the car door for a stiff-looking German wearing an SS uniform. The huge man put on a pair of leather gloves once he had got out of the car, as if he didn't want to get his hands dirty.

Amos turned to me. "Give me the binoculars," he said.

I did so.

"SS Major General Jürgen Stroop."

So the head of the SS in Warsaw had arrived to supervise the mission personally. His first name was Jürgen now, but we had heard that his real name had been Joseph and he had changed it several years ago because he hated the Jews so much.

Stroop was the closest thing to Hitler, Himmler, or Goebbels that I'd ever seen face-to-face. Himmler had visited the ghetto a couple of months ago, but none of us had actually met that monster—apart from a few Jews working in the acquisition department, and none of them had had the guts to attack the beast.

Amos got up to leave the balcony.

"Where are you going?" I asked. "We're supposed to stay here!"

"Not anymore," Amos said, and grinned before he disappeared.

I didn't understand. I had thought the two of us were going to fight side by side on this balcony and maybe die together. But Amos had been so energized, he hadn't even said goodbye.

I debated whether I should follow him or not, but only for a second.

Just as I was heading out of the flat, Esther tried to stop me. "Why are you two abandoning your post?"

"That's what I'd like to know, too," I said, and pushed her out of the way.

As soon as we reached the roof, Stroop commanded his soldiers to invade the ghetto.

This time they used mattresses that had once belonged to Jewish inhabitants of the ghetto to make a barricade and opened fire from there. We fighters on the roof shot back. I still didn't know why Amos wanted to be up here, but didn't bother asking. I'd stopped asking myself or anyone else questions. Shooting and being shot at wasn't something I had to think about anymore. I was just full of adrenaline.

Some of us lit gasoline bombs and threw them at the soldiers. The mattresses caught fire and the men lost their cover. We shot at them.

Then the tanks started firing at our positions from the Polish side, but they missed. As Amos had predicted—they weren't close enough. And I found myself thinking: The "master race" can't hit us because they are so scared of us.

Amos jumped up and ran over to the comrades throwing the bombs. Below us the soldiers were hiding in doorways and shooting and shooting and shooting, just like yesterday. Unlike us, they didn't have to save on ammunition.

Amos didn't care if he was an easy target. He pointed his gun and fired. Not at the soldiers or the tanks, but precisely in the direction of SS Commander Stroop, who was sitting behind a command table. So that was why Amos had run up to the roof. He wanted to kill the leader of our enemies all by himself.

The bullet struck less than two meters away from Major General Stroop. The giant SS man jumped up from his chair and hurried away from the table as fast as he could. It was almost funny.

Amos cheered loudly and so did I. Although he hadn't actually got Stroop, seeing this man flee was more humiliating for the Germans than the burning tank had been.

Then I heard Ben Redhead calling from the balcony below, "The house is burning!"

59

D own on the street, soldiers had thrown incendiary grenades into the entrance of our house, and the first flames were already shooting out of the burst windows on the ground floor.

"We can't stay here," Amos said, and everyone agreed. There was no point in dying in the flames. We would have to flee and look for a new position to continue fighting.

We hurried down from the roof and ran out onto the stairs. Of course there was no way we could just run out the front door. Even if we managed to get through the flames unharmed, the Germans would be waiting to mow us down outside. Rachel's fighters had prepared a retreat, though. We would escape into the house at 6 Gęsia Street through the holes in the attics and continue the battle from there. Rachel had sent someone to see if the coast was clear.

It wasn't.

The scout was a man called Avi, who used to be a Jewish policeman. He had joined the resistance when the first trains started out for Treblinka—why, oh why had my brother not had the decency to do the same? Avi was standing in front of us sweating and stroking his red beard nervously. "The Germans have occupied 6 Gęsia."

We all stared at one another in desperation. The flames were creeping up the stairs step by step, and there was no way out.

Rachel was the only one who stayed calm. "You . . . ," she pointed at Avi, "and you," she pointed at Ben Redhead, "try to find an escape route that's safe."

She probably didn't realize that she had picked the only two redheads among us to get us away from the fire. The two of them ran off, and the rest of us gathered in a dark attic room. The heat of the fire made us all sweat; the smoke made breathing difficult. We smashed the little attic window but that didn't help at all. In fact it only made matters worse. The smoke from outside poured into the room. We coughed, and I was so scared that I blurted out, "Now we are going to be gassed and burned after all."

Amos grabbed me. Instead of trying to calm me, he shook me hard and said sharply, "Shut up!"

He was right. I needed to pull myself together and not infect the others with my panic. At that moment, Avi returned.

"Well?" Rachel asked.

"Nothing," he said, defeated. "There's no way out."

The smoke got thicker and thicker every second. Our eyes were streaming. But Ben Redhead wasn't back yet, so there was still a chance.

Like everyone else, I couldn't stop coughing. Even Amos, who was trying not to show any kind of weakness, was gasping for air.

The soldiers had thrown firebombs onto the roof, too. Burning timbers rained down on us. But no one screamed, although everyone wanted to. Not even when the floorboards started to twist.

"Over there!" Esther cried.

Through the little window we could see SS men in the house opposite. Without hesitating, Esther, Rachel, and Avi, who were close to the window, started to shoot at the soldiers. They fired back without hitting anyone and then retreated. The exchange of fire diverted us from the fact that we were surrounded by the flames.

Ben Redhead stormed in. "I think I've found an escape route into 37 Nalewki," he said.

"You think?" Rachel asked coughing.

"I couldn't go all the way. It would have taken too long. There's not enough time."

"It's better than nothing," Rachel decided.

We all left the attic slowly. Then went onto the stairs where you couldn't see anything because of all the smoke and where breathing was virtually impossible. From there we went to another attic room where there was a little hole in the wall leading to the next house. This wasn't one of the prepared escape routes. It was just a chance hole in the wall of a damaged building. The hole was so narrow that I thought at first we'd never fit. But, one by one, the fighters squeezed through. When it was my turn, I got stuck. I'd caught my shoulder and started to panic. I screamed, "I can't . . . I can't . . . !"

"You can!" Amos shouted, and shoved me through the hole. I thought my shoulder would break, but then I stumbled into the house next door. Only, there was smoke there, too. The SS had set the building on fire as well.

We moved forward, feeling our way rather than actually seeing anything, and held our breath so as not to burn our lungs.

We managed to find another gap into the attic of the next house, but even here we still weren't safe. The fire would jump to this house next.

We climbed through a skylight onto the roof, and we stayed low and crawled to the next house—we didn't want to be moving targets for the soldiers—then from there, we jumped onto the roof of yet another house.

"There must be a bunker here somewhere," Avi said.

The members of the ŻOB hadn't built extra hideouts. When the civilians had started digging out bunkers everywhere in the ghetto, we had concentrated on preparing for the uprising: getting hold of weapons, killing collaborators, training to fight . . . We hadn't even thought seriously about additional hiding places. Why should we have? We had not expected to last more than a single day. No matter how much some of us had gone on about Masada, not even the most daring dreamers had any kind of pretense that we were in the same league as our ancestors in the fortress against the Romans.

How I wished we were fighting the Romans. Their persecution of Christians seemed almost civilized in comparison to the Nazi persecution of the Jews.

Was Avi sure there was a bunker here somewhere, or did he just have an inkling? We didn't really want to know. We swarmed out of the house into the yard to hunt for a concealed entrance. And it was Esther who found the hidden door to the cellar. Without knocking or asking permission, we tore the door open and entered a stuffy bunker where about twenty civilians including a number of children were hiding. We all flung ourselves onto the ground, exhausted. Until now, I'd fought back the smoke in my lungs, but now I coughed and choked until I threw up. I couldn't care less. We were safe for a moment. I hadn't burned to death.

"Get out!" a woman screamed at us. She was holding a starving child in her arms and was little more than a ragged skeleton herself.

"Go away! You are putting us all in danger!" shouted a haggard old woman. Another one of the living dead.

Before we could say anything, people started shouting at us from all sides. "We don't want you here!" "You'll be the death of us all!" "If the Germans catch you here, they'll kill us, too!"

It was unbelievable. We were fighting for the whole of the ghetto, and these people were so scared of dying that they hated us.

From a corner where a number of children were gathered, a young man came forward and declared, "The fighters stay!"

It was Daniel.

60

ven in the dim candlelight I recognized him at once, although his head was close-shaven and he was thinner than he used to be.

"Were you in Treblinka?" I asked. I was shocked and couldn't help coughing again. Partly because of the smoke still burning in my lungs and partly because I remembered Ruth's cough. She had got out of the camp because her lover had been prepared to pay for her. But no one would have paid anything for Daniel, and according to everything we had heard so far, no one was ever able to escape a concentration camp. Our scouts, who had approached Treblinka a few months back, had reported seeing prisoners running into the electric fences to put an end to their torturous lives.

"I had lice," Daniel answered.

I was relieved at that. And I finally managed to stop coughing.

Amos looked over at me. I'd told him as little about Daniel as I'd told Daniel about him. He didn't join in our conversation and turned to look at the hysterical civilians who had crept into the corners of the bunker after Daniel's intervention and were now staring at us with hatred, as if we were the ones trying to kill them.

"You fight?" Daniel asked, looking at the gun in my hand.

"Yes," I answered, not sure what he would say. He wasn't armed, so he obviously didn't belong to the resistance fighters.

"And you kill people." It was as if he was disappointed in me.

Who did he think he was? Why was he condemning me? I could just as easily judge him for not helping us. Daniel noticed that I was angry, and he softened his expression. "It is so wonderful that you are alive, Mira."

Of course he was right. It was silly to be angry. This was a moment of happiness. "You too, you too . . . ," I said, and we hugged each other. It felt very familiar.

We didn't let go until Amos came over to me and said, "I'm not sure how long we can stay here. At some stage soon, the Germans will burn down this house, too, and we will all suffocate in here."

"It will be your fault if they send us to the ovens!" the skeleton woman cried while her little boy stared at us as if his soul had been burned to cinders long ago.

Before Amos or I could tell her to shut up, Daniel went to her and took the boy into his arms and promised softly, "We won't die here."

The woman believed him. The child in his arms closed its eyes. Then I realized:

In this bunker, Daniel was a young Korczak.

61

While my comrades gathered in a corner of the bunker and worked out what we were going to do now, I sat in another corner with Daniel. They didn't mind. Not even Amos. It was so unusual, such an incredible piece of good luck to meet someone from the past, everyone was happy for me.

"This is some Passover," Daniel said, holding the sleeping boy on his lap.

"How did you manage to survive?" I asked.

"My girlfriend knocked me out."

I could tell by looking at him that he wasn't angry with me anymore.

"That was good of her . . . ," I said. I still didn't know if I'd done the right thing back then.

"Yes," he said, and gave me a friendly, almost loving smile. "It was."

Another child was leaning against him. She was about eight years old and wore a ragged dress. Her hand was curled into a fist, as if she was holding something tight. She reminded me of someone.

"This is Rebecca," Daniel introduced us.

"Hello, Rebecca," I said.

The little girl looked at me warily.

"She doesn't speak," Daniel explained.

Now I recognized her. It was the little girl who had stuck out her tongue at me in the orphanage. She still wore the polka-dot dress, only it was so filthy by now that the pattern and the color were gone.

"Rebecca hid in the orphanage when the Germans came."

I didn't tell her that she'd been very clever. But I thought so. It was much better than climbing into a cattle truck waving a flag.

"What has she got in her hand?" I asked instead.

"Her favorite marble. She never lets go of it."

The eyes of the girl glistened angrily, as if she wanted to scratch my face if I got too close to her marble. No, not as if. She definitely would.

"Have you been together all this time?" I wanted to know.

"I hid her and worked at Többens so that we both could get something to eat."

I wanted to know if he had tried to find me in the meantime. But then I'd have had to admit that I hadn't tried to find him.

"How about you?" Daniel asked.

"After the *Aktion*, I joined the underground resistance."

"And Hannah?"

I couldn't say anything.

"I . . . I'm sorry," he said sincerely, and went to take my hand to comfort me. But I pulled it away. Daniel noticed that I was wearing a wedding ring.

"You . . . you got married?" he asked, and although he tried not to let it show, he was hurt by that.

"Not really," I said.

"What do you mean, 'not really'?"

"It's a disguise."

"But the two of you . . . ?" He pointed toward Amos, whom he had rightly assumed to be my "husband."

"Yes," I said. "The two of us . . ."

Daniel was upset.

And I was upset, too. Had he expected me to go on loving him forever, even though I thought he was dead?

"Are you going to join our fight?" I asked. I didn't want to talk about Amos and me.

"No," Daniel said immediately.

"Why not?"

"I don't believe in killing."

"You don't believe in killing? You don't believe in it? Well, the SS does!"

"I know."

"And a least we can give our people some dignity by defending ourselves!"

"There are more important things than dignity."

"Name me one! Just one!"

"Survival."

I shut up for a moment, but I simply couldn't understand it all. "You would have gone to the trucks," I said, "and then, all of a sudden, your survival is more important than everything else?"

"No, not mine," he answered, and hugged little Rebecca. So she was the reason why he wouldn't fight? As if the two of them could ever survive! Should I say it out loud? But the girl was so small. So frail. It would be awful to let her know that we were all about to die, including her. On the other hand, there was no point in lying, even to a child. She must know? At least she must have sensed it.

In the end all I said was, "We are all going to die. The question is, how?"

"Die like a hero?" Daniel asked sarcastically.

"If that's what you want to call it."

"It's what the underground newspapers say," he retorted. "There's nothing heroic about killing people."

"Oh yes! It's far better to climb into a cattle truck with a flag held high, isn't it?" I answered angrily.

Daniel got angry now, too. "Korczak was there for the orphans until the very end. And that is a lot more than you'll ever do."

I'd gone too far. I had no right to attack the old man. And perhaps, just perhaps, Daniel was right. Perhaps it really was the bravest thing to die with loved ones, instead of with a gun in hand.

Would I have had the guts to die by Hannah's side? Or would I have run away, given the opportunity?

"I will do everything I can to make sure that she survives. We don't have to die," Daniel explained, looking at Rebecca, who was busy staring at the treasure lying in her open hand. A blue and white marble.

This little girl was the only survivor of Daniel's orphanage family. She was his sister. That was why he couldn't bear to think that he might lose her, too. I could understand that. If Hannah were still alive, I would feel the same.

"You could defend her better with a gun," I said quietly.

Daniel just shook his head. There was no point in talking about it. I scrambled to my feet and went back to my comrades. They had decided that we should spend the night looking for food and that we needed to contact the other groups.

Rachel called me over. "See if the coast is clear."

Amos jumped up, "I'll go," he said.

No way! I was a fighter. Just like him. Not some princess who needed a prince to protect her.

"I'm going!" I said determinedly, left the bunker, and went upstairs. Most of the windows were still intact here, and I stared out at the street cautiously. There were no soldiers to be seen. But, of course, I couldn't see the whole street. I'd have to go outside for that.

I drew my gun—not because I hoped to defeat a whole SS patrol single-handedly, but perhaps the weapon would allow me to get away in an emergency. But . . . if the Germans saw me, I mustn't run in the direction of the bunker or I'd be leading the SS to the hideout. If I was captured, the SS would definitely torture me until I betrayed my comrades. And the civilians. Amos. Daniel.

Before that happened, I'd use the weapon on myself.

Carefully, I crept out the door. The air stank of smoke. Farther down the street, ashes glowed on the remains of a house that had been completely destroyed by fire. Only the foundation was left. There was no one to be seen anywhere. I went as far as the next crossroads just to make sure. No SS. And I couldn't hear any sounds of tanks or cars. I looked over to Muranowski Square. The flags were still flying high. The ghetto still belonged to us.

62

That night we learned of the losses the other groups had suffered but gave one another courage as we ate; we had survived two days already; we had defied the Germans for two days and we'd manage a third.

Early in the morning, we moved into position on the fourth floor while the civilians stayed in the bunker. But we didn't engage in any fighting. There were only a few sporadic sounds of shooting in the ghetto.

"The Germans don't dare fight anymore," Esther said around midday, looking pleased.

"We're not that lucky," Amos answered.

Of course he was right.

Half an hour later, we heard the sound of trucks. One of them stopped farther down the street. SS men jumped out, too far away for us to shoot. The soldiers rolled barrels in front of the houses.

"Those are barrels of gasoline," Amos realized.

The soldiers got back into the truck, threw burning torches, and then raced away. The barrels caught fire and exploded. Within seconds, the first houses went up in flames.

"Oh no . . . ," Esther gasped.

No one else said a word.

Civilians ran to the windows and out onto the balconies of the burning houses. There was no choice but to jump. The SS men had gathered in front of the burning buildings and took turns shooting at the civilians as they jumped. When they hit someone as they fell, the SS all cheered. Someone earned an especially huge cheer when he shot a mother holding her baby.

An old woman fell from a balcony onto a heap of burning rubbish. But she was injured and couldn't get down. She was on fire in a matter of moments and screamed and screamed, begging the soldiers to put her out of her misery, "Shoot me, please, please, please, shoot me!" But the soldiers didn't do her the favor. They preferred to shoot the jumping Jews. That was as much fun as a shooting stand at a fair for them.

We watched, shocked, unable to move. Rachel was the first to find her voice again. "We need to get closer."

But before we had time to get close enough to shoot the bastards and be shot ourselves, soldiers went from house to house and threw firebombs into the doorways.

I grabbed Rachel. "We've got to get the civilians out of the bunker," I said. "They'll set this house on fire, too!" I was mainly worrying about Daniel and his little sister.

"You are right." Rachel nodded. Her desire to seek revenge was not as great as the desire to help others.

We rushed down to the cellar and just as we tore open the door to the bunker, we heard an explosion. The Germans had thrown a firebomb into our house.

"Hurry up!" Rachel called to the civilians. "We have to get out of here!"

The next moment, a hand grenade rolled down the cellar steps.

"Take cover," Amos yelled.

We all ran. Most of us ran back into the bunker. Only Esther . . . Esther headed for cover in another room in the cellar. The grenade rolled in that direction and exploded.

"Esther!" Amos screamed above the noise of the explosion, and ran out of the bunker through the flames to help her. But all he found was her body, torn to pieces.

Amos screamed like an animal.

"The stairs! My God! The stairs!" Avi yelled.

The soldiers' grenade had destroyed the cellar stairs. Above us the house was on fire and we couldn't get out! We were trapped in a hole in the ground like rabbits in a blocked burrow.

"We'll burn to death! We're going to burn to death!" Avi screamed hysterically.

"We need a ladder or a plank or something!" Rachel shouted. She was the only one who seemed to be able to think clearly.

We all started looking. Except for Amos, who stood staring into the flames where Esther's body was burning.

"Amos!" I shouted.

He didn't react.

"Amos! We need something to help us get out of here!"

Slowly, very slowly, he managed to tear himself away from the terrible sight.

In the bunker, people were starting to scream. Daniel tried to calm them down. "We'll get out," he kept saying, "we'll find a way out."

But it was no use. There was nothing he could do. The people were panic-stricken.

"This'll do!" Ben Redhead shouted. He pointed at a long plank that was lying in a corner. We propped it up where the steps had been just two minutes earlier. It stood upright at an extremely steep angle. You couldn't just run up it; we were going to have to climb up the plank to get out.

Daniel came over to me and said, "The old and the sick will never make it out."

We let the civilians go first and helped them as best we could. Even Amos, though he stared back at the flames that had engulfed Esther's body every other minute. I tried not to look.

At last there were about a dozen people still left in the bunker: old people, the sick, the wounded, the weak. Including the skeleton woman and her child.

"We can't leave them behind," Daniel said.

"We have no choice," Rachel insisted.

The people in the bunker were calling, "Don't abandon us! Please don't abandon us!"

Some were weeping. Some didn't move at all. Would they have hidden here for so long, survived for so long, only to be burned to death now?

The fighters climbed up the plank, one by one, and so did Daniel, who had decided to remain alive for his little sister's sake instead of staying with the doomed people we had to leave behind.

There wasn't a moment left to grieve for them, or for Esther. When we got into the yard, the fire-lit sky was glowing red. Towering tongues of flame devoured the houses all around us.

"This is what hell must be like," Ben Redhead said.

We went through hell. Twenty fighters and maybe forty civilians. We ran through the burning streets. The Germans had retreated so as not to be caught in the inferno themselves.

Buildings collapsed. The surface of the road beneath our feet started to melt. I was certain my shoes would stick to the ground. The roar of the flames was deafening. Any moment now, I feared the pandemonium would make my head explode. Burning timber rained down on us. One civilian was killed when he was struck by a falling beam. Another was hit by a barrage of falling roof tiles.

Daniel didn't let go of Rebecca the whole time, and she held on to her glass marble. She knew that if it were to fall onto the road, her treasure would melt.

The things people cherish in the face of death.

We made our way to a part of the ghetto that wasn't burning, and which might be spared as long as the wind didn't shift. In the early evening we reached a courtyard where about a hundred civilians had gathered, all of them with the few possessions they had been able to save from their burning houses and which still seemed to mean as much to them in all this madness as Rebecca's marble did.

This time, no one swore at us. It was the reverse. They begged us to help them. "Get us out of the ghetto!" "Save my child!" "Help!"

Everyone gathered around us. But we had no idea what to do, either.

"We can't take all these people with us," Avi said.

"Well, we certainly can't leave them!" Rachel retaliated.

And I realized they were both right.

"We'll have to find a new hiding place." Rachel said what we were all thinking. "A bunker large enough for all of us!"

"And just pray that the Germans don't come back tonight!" Avi added.

"I don't pray!" Amos and I both said at the same time.

The fighters split up into groups of scouts. Amos and I headed off at once. The night sky was glaring eerily above the ghetto. I stared at Muranowski Square and could still see the flags flying there. But they were a small comfort now. We had seen people die. Seen Esther die!

Amos didn't say anything as we walked through the streets.

"Esther . . . ," I said.

"Died honorably," he said curtly, stopping the conversation at once.

Honorably! To be torn to pieces by a hand grenade didn't seem like an honorable way to die to me. No matter how hard I tried to think otherwise, I felt she had died as miserably as any other Jew in the ghetto.

We didn't say anything else. We combed through the houses in silence, hoping to find a bunker. We just stopped once when we found water in an abandoned flat and drank. We drank until we weren't thirsty anymore. It took about another hour, and then we found a bunker under the rubble of a half-demolished house.

"There is no way we can all fit in here," I said while I stared at the squalor. The bunker was already crammed with people. Sweating. Despairing. Terrified.

"There's enough room for our unit," Amos said.

"We can't leave the others behind," I shouted.

"Let's let Rachel decide," he said, and I agreed. I had no idea if Rachel would leave the civilians behind or not. What about Daniel and Rebecca? I couldn't stay with them, could I? No. One fighter would not be able to help them, anyway.

It was almost midnight when we got back to the courtyard. We were surprised to see that everyone was getting ready to leave. Before we could ask, Daniel told me, "Your people have found a bunker."

"For all of us?" I asked.

"That's what they said."

"That . . . that's a miracle!" I stammered.

"I said we weren't going to die." Daniel smiled.

He believed in survival. Against all odds.

63

The bunker in Miła Street belonged to Shmuel Asher and the Chompe gang. The mafia boss was a lot thinner than he had been a year ago, and there was a scar across his face, no doubt from his time in prison, but he had been able to buy himself out one more time. With the rest of his money, he and his friends had built this immense bunker. There were wells for water, electricity, a perfect kitchen, stylish sofas, and even glass cabinets. An elegant parlor hidden beneath the city.

Crime paid. Not just for German industrialists.

Asher came up to me, having recognized me at once, and asked immediately, "Have you seen Ruth?"

Should I let him know that she had coughed ashes, that she had been raped by "the doll" in Treblinka, and that she had sung *Lulay, lulay, little one,* half-crazed?

"She loved you," I told him.

That was all Asher needed to know. He closed his eyes for a moment. He had loved her, too.

When he opened them again, he went up to our leaders,

including Mordechai who had joined us here, and welcomed all the fighters and civilians.

"We will fight and die together," the mafioso promised. "We are all Jews, after all."

That was something the Germans hadn't bargained for when they devised their plans of destruction. They had turned people who had never cared so much about their Jewishness into proud fighting Jews!

Our group was assigned a chamber with the name of Auschwitz, along with a few civilians. Asher had given all the rooms names of concentration camps: Treblinka, Sobibor, Mauthausen . . .

Auschwitz had belonged to a man called Izak, who had lived there by himself with his family until now. He was a little man who reminded me of a weasel, and he wasn't one bit pleased that his boss had opened the bunker for all of us. He had been expecting to die in relative comfort, at least. But there was nothing he could do about it.

We let him and his wife keep their bed. Amos and I sat against a wall. He fell asleep quickly, but kept twitching in his sleep nervously. No wonder, after he'd seen Esther die today.

Daniel and little Rebecca were lying opposite. I felt jealous when I looked at them. Not because Rebecca was curled up beside Daniel or anything like that. But because Daniel still had his little sister with him.

In the world of the 777 islands, the *Longear* had landed on Mirror Island. Surprisingly, the island wasn't made of mirrors, it was rocky. In fact it was really just a gigantic mountain that reached up to the sky.

"Up there, above the clouds must be where the Palace of Mirrors is," Hannah said. "That's where we have to go."

"Well, that's bloody brilliant, isn't it?" the werewolf growled. "I'm no mountain lion, am I?"

"Which is a shame," Captain Carrot sighed.

"Why?"

"Because you'd be a lot nicer to look at."

"I love you, too, ugly butt-face," the werewolf just growled.

I was nervous, too. I was terrified of the Mirror King. And I feared that Hannah would be killed in battle, which would mean that I would lose her forever.

"We've got this far," Hannah said cheerily. "We're sure to manage the rest." She strapped a bag, containing the three magic mirrors, to her back and started to climb the mountain.

"Sure," the Captain sighed.

"Hmm," grumbled the werewolf, and both put on thick caps. The captain had trouble stowing his ears underneath his one.

It was great to see Hannah again. I had said goodbye to her, but I was still alive after all, and so she was, too.

I felt a small ray of hope. What did she just say? We've got this far, we're bound to manage the rest! Perhaps, just perhaps that applied to life outside the 777 islands, too.

64

ny hope I had brought back from the 777 islands vanished the next morning. The flags were gone. Our comrades at Muranowski Square had been defeated. Fighters were being killed everywhere in the ghetto. We couldn't stage any more massive attacks now. We weren't strong enough and had less and less ammunition. Also, the SS had changed tactics. Rather than marching into the ghetto with troops in formation, they now sneaked through the streets in small units.

We switched to guerrilla warfare and attacked SS patrols herding Jews to the *Umschlagplatz*. Sometimes we managed to overpower the soldiers and give the Jews a few more hours to live; sometimes they fought back and we lost comrades. Avi was badly wounded in the leg by grenade shrapnel; we only just managed to drag him back to safety.

I got used to the fighting on a daily basis, the danger, even killing and the fact that after each mission fewer people returned. But the fact that I survived from day to day was something I could never get used to. At the beginning I had felt exhilarated, but soon I was simply exhausted.

Our leaders hoped that we would be able to inspire the Poles to join us, and published an appeal for a united struggle, which they smuggled out of the ghetto. But the Poles simply ignored it. Some Poles watched the Jew hunt from the windows of their houses close to the ghetto wall. As if this was a modern version of the Roman circus. They would probably have applauded if the SS had sent in hungry lions, too.

Instead, the SS was using tracker dogs. When they weren't busy setting houses on fire, the German soldiers used the dogs to search for bunkers. They were supported by collaborators. Even now, there were still people willing to betray us because they believed they could save their own skins that way. Even children were sent out by the soldiers to search for the bunkers. They were given bits of food as a reward.

In the crammed bunkers, the people were as quiet as mice all day long. No one dared even speak or cough.

Ben Redhead, Amos, and I were on our way back from a gunfight near Leszno Street, where we had not managed to take out a single German and had wasted valuable bullets, to the bunker at 18 Miła Street.

"Look," Ben Redhead whispered as we reached the cellar steps, and pointed to a boy with a flat cap who seemed to be searching for something in the cellar.

"He's looking for somewhere to hide," I whispered while we watched him from the stairs.

"The question is, is he on his own or is he working for the SS," Amos whispered back. "One block away, there's a patrol."

"He's found the bunker," Ben Redhead said.

The boy stood directly in front of the bricks we used to disguise the entrance to the bunker. But he didn't go in; he hesitated.

"He's going to sell us out," Amos said.

I wanted him to wait a minute before he judged him. If the boy made a move to go away, then we could be sure that the SS had sent him. But Amos didn't wait and called, "Hey, kid!"

The boy looked dismayed. Not like someone who was just looking for a place to hide and had been surprised by a friend. He looked more like someone who was about to betray a secret and had been caught by the enemy.

We went down the stairs and stopped in front of him.

Slowly he put his hands up.

"What . . . what are we going to do with him?" Ben Redhead wanted to know.

"Shoot him," Amos said.

The boy went white.

"You don't mean that," I said.

"There's no choice," Amos insisted, and took out his gun.

"Of course there is."

"He'll betray us."

"You don't know that!"

The boy was too terrified to defend himself. "Please . . . ," he begged.

But the fact that he didn't defend himself didn't look good.

Amos pointed his gun at the boy.

Who couldn't speak.

"Are you completely mad?" I yelled at Amos. "You can't murder a child!"

Amos didn't say anything. His hand was shaking, but he pressed the gun to the boy's head.

"This makes us as bad as the Germans!"

Amos's hand was shaking violently now. There was sweat on his forehead.

"If I don't, then everyone in the bunker will die."

"We don't know that!"

"Can you take the risk, Mira?"

I couldn't, of course, but I wanted to so badly that I said, "We'll just have to."

The boy started to cry silently and wet himself in fear.

"What kind of human do you want to be?" I asked Amos frantically. "Someone who kills children?"

Amos battled with himself. There were tears in his eyes. His hand was shaking like the hand of a sick old man.

"Amos . . . ," I begged, "if we want to stay human . . ."

Amos was crying now and finally lowered the gun.

The boy started sobbing in relief.

I started to cry, too.

I wanted to hug them both. Amos. And the boy.

Then a shot rang out.

The boy slumped to the floor at our feet.

Amos and I stared at Ben Redhead, shocked, who was holding his rifle and stuttered, "He . . . he . . . w . . . would h . . . have b . . . b . . . betrayed us all!"

All three of us started to cry.

65

"So, you've started killing children now?" Daniel came over as I crouched on the floor of the bunker cleaning a gun we had captured.

"It was the Germans' fault," I said without looking up at him.

"They didn't kill that boy," Daniel answered.

"Oh yes they did. They sent him to us." I stood.

"You killed him, no matter how you look at it."

Daniel's talk made me furious. Amos, Ben, and I were suffering enough because of what had happened. I didn't want to listen to any more reproaches. I felt like hitting him. Instead, I said, "There was nothing else we could do."

"There's always a choice. In any situation. You made the wrong choice."

I knew that, too.

"I didn't want . . ." I tried to convince him and myself.

But he interrupted me, "You let it happen, didn't you?"

Now I did hit him as hard as I could.

I was only sorry that I hadn't hit him with my fist instead of just the flat of my hand.

Daniel stared at me so angrily that I thought he was going to hit me back.

"I thought you wanted to survive," I hissed. "Every second you stay alive is because of us!"

"Thanks a lot," Daniel said bitterly.

"The boy would have betrayed us. We would all be dead by now, or at the *Umschlagplatz*."

Daniel didn't say anything. He knew I was right.

"Him or Rebecca? Who would you choose?"

Daniel still didn't say anything.

But I wanted him to. So that I could hit him again. And so that I wouldn't start crying. Above all, so as not to cry. But he still didn't speak.

"I . . . I tried to prevent it . . ." I battled with my tears.

Daniel's anger disappeared.

"You have to believe me. But I couldn't . . ."

"I . . . I'm sorry," Daniel said.

"Why? Because I didn't stop it?"

"Yes . . . and because you are hurting so much."

He wanted to take me in his arms and comfort me.

And I wanted him to.

But then Amos suddenly stepped between us and said, "There's going to be a miracle tonight."

"What?" Daniel and I both asked.

Amos ignored Daniel, like he always did, and pulled me away to another part of the bunker. To a man with a curly beard.

"This is Leon Katz," he introduced us. "Leon, this is Mira. She's just volunteered to help us."

I wondered what I'd just volunteered for. A surprise attack on the Germans?

"Tell her what we're going to do," Amos said to him.

"We're going to bake bread."

"You're crazy!" I laughed.

"Leon is a baker," Amos explained.

"This is some kind of joke, isn't it?"

"No, really!" Amos insisted.

"I've found a bakery in the yard next door," Leon told me excitedly. "With sacks of flour. And there's enough water. All that is missing is sourdough."

"Sourdough?" I couldn't quite understand what he was telling me.

"So we'll use onions instead."

"Onions?"

"There are still plenty of those in all the flats," the baker laughed.

I grinned. His enthusiasm was catching.

"Tomorrow the whole ghetto will have bread to eat!" Leon promised us. And that really did sound like a miracle.

66

H alf an hour later, Leon was already charging round the bakery giving us orders. He was wearing a white apron and looked at least as proud as any soldier in uniform. "You've got to knead the dough more quickly." "Chop the onions into smaller pieces." "That's not how you stoke a fire!"

All of us "baker's apprentices" laughed and joked, "Mind your beard doesn't fall into the dough." "Glad you weren't commanding the Polish army, they'd have lost even faster!" "It's not the onions making me cry, it's you!"

We enjoyed ourselves. In the middle of the war we were baking bread! I even managed to forget what we had done to the boy for a little while.

Leon was busy weighing dough when Rachel came up to him and asked, "Does it matter if the loaves aren't all the same size?"

Leon slapped his head. "Of course you're right! I'm an idiot wasting precious time."

Although we were all lighthearted, time was an issue. The bread had to be done and handed out before dawn.

"I hope no one sees the smoke," Rachel said as the first loaves went into the oven.

Amos and I went outside to check. Of course you could see the smoke rising from the bakery into the sky. If the Nazis decided to search the ghetto tonight, they'd find us at once.

"It's worth it, though," Amos said.

"Yes," I agreed.

"For once, it's not just about killing," he said quietly. He was guilt-ridden about the boy we had shot. After all, he'd drawn his gun first. Before Ben.

"I thought I would be able to redeem myself in battle," he confessed as we watched the smoke rise up to the stars. "But fighting the Germans just means there'll be more shame and guilt every day until I die."

I took hold of his hand and said, "Until we die."

Three hundred loaves of bread.

That was how many we had baked by dawn.

Because there was no sourdough, the loaves were pretty flat, but they still looked amazing. We handed them out to the people in the bunkers who couldn't wait to eat the warm bread.

"Look at their eyes," Amos said, watching a group of children stuffing themselves.

"Oh yes!" I whispered, hardly able to speak.

Their eyes were shining.

That morning we hadn't given the Jews dignity or honor, we'd given them joy.

67

"We should have dug tunnels over to the other side," Mordechai said regretfully when all the fighters met in the bunker at Miła 18 for our next briefing. It was the first time I had ever heard our leader sounding despondent.

"If we could just get out of the ghetto," he continued, "then we could hide in the woods and continue to fight the Germans. What is the point of burning to death here?"

"The fact that the SS are turning the ghetto to ruins could be a chance for us," Asher piped up.

We all turned to look at the mafia boss in surprise. Unlike some of the members of his Chompe gang, he had never once complained that his luxury bunker had been turned into a crowded stifling hellhole.

"The fire has spread to the workshops," he continued.

"We know that, what are you getting at?" Amos asked impatiently.

Asher explained. "The Germans are using Polish firemen to put out the fires. If . . ."

". . . we could bribe them, they might smuggle you out of the ghetto!" Avi said, realizing what Asher meant.

His leg was still badly injured, but Avi was excited by this idea even though he knew that he would never be able to hide in the woods with his injury.

Mordechai liked the idea, too. So it was agreed that we'd approach the firemen. Rachel, Leon the baker, Amos, and I headed off to a burning factory that same night. We slunk through the destroyed streets quietly, on our guard. The SS had started coming back into the ghetto at night to patrol the streets.

It took us about twenty minutes to reach the workshop area where Polish firemen—guarded by a handful of Latvian SS men—were fighting a blaze, trying to save what they could. We hid behind a destroyed wall and watched the firefighting operation.

"Do we shoot the soldiers?" Amos whispered.

"The firemen would flee, and more soldiers would arrive in a matter of minutes." Rachel sighed.

"So what do we do?"

"Wait."

"We just sit here and hope that one of the firemen walks over?"

"We deserve a bit of luck," Rachel answered, and smiled ever so slightly. But I was sure we'd used up all our luck over the past few weeks of the uprising.

We waited behind the wall and only peered out every now and then. The firemen slaved away in vain. After about half an hour, during which Amos had become more and more impatient and checked his pistol over and over, an exhausted fireman came away from the blaze for a cigarette and headed in our direction.

"I think we might be lucky after all," Rachel whispered to us.

When the man was no more than five meters away, she gave

us a signal and we rushed round the wall. Leon grabbed the man from behind, and I pointed my gun in his face. The fireman realized what was happening and let us lead him away to a burned-out house without resisting or alerting the soldiers. As soon as we were inside, he groveled in front of us and started whining, "I've got nothing against Jews!"

He would be covering himself in ashes off the floor next, if we weren't careful.

"That's good to know," Amos said, grinning.

Rachel told him what we wanted. "Next time you're deployed here, we want you to smuggle our fighters out of the ghetto in the fire trucks. And you will need to get in touch with the Polish resistance. They can get us to the woods and show us where to hide. We will continue to fight for our Polish homeland from there."

I no longer felt as if Poland was my home. I wanted to fight the Germans in the forests, but not for my country.

"You will be paid well," Rachel continued. She was telling the truth. Although a lot of the money the resistance had collected was gone by now, we still had more than enough to pay off a few Polish firemen.

"I'll do whatever you want," the man promised. He was clearly relieved that we weren't going to shoot him. He staggered to his feet and went back to the fire.

"Are we really going to trust our lives to a coward like that?" Amos asked. "What happens if he double-crosses us?"

"We'll find out soon enough if he does," Rachel answered.

We stayed in the building. Ill at ease. With our arms at the ready. But no soldiers came. The man hadn't betrayed us so far.

"He's after the money," Leon said, relieved.

And I tried to get used to the prospect of maybe getting out of the ghetto alive.

68

We spent long hours in the bunker, where the air was getting more and more stifling because of the fires. Amos imagined what it would be like in the woods. We would join the Polish partisans and ambush German troops together with our new comrades, paving the way for a Russian invasion that would hopefully happen next year or the year after.

When I mentioned that our Polish "comrades" hadn't exactly supported our uprising and might not be too pleased to have a whole load of Jews joining them, I only boosted his imagination. He talked about a purely Jewish group of partisans who would strike blow after blow against the Germans and who were feared throughout all the SS. A sort of Jewish death's-head commando.

He was still planning to redeem himself if he could.

Looking around the bunker, I couldn't help thinking that there was no way we would be able to smuggle all these people out to the woods. We would have to leave them behind. And they would end up burning to death either here or in the ovens. More people to feel guilty about, even if it wasn't my fault.

They must never know about our plans to escape, but I did tell Daniel. I felt indebted to him somehow, and so I told him about our encounter with the fireman.

"So you do want to survive," he declared, and sounded pleased.

"Survive to fight," I explained.

"Till death?"

"It seems so."

"You could hide and try to make it through to the end of the war somehow."

"My place is with my comrades."

"With your 'husband,' you mean!"

Daniel sounded jealous.

"With Amos," I confirmed.

He didn't like my answer, but he didn't pry. Instead he said, "Take Rebecca with you."

"What?" I was astonished.

"Take Rebecca with you when you escape."

He wasn't thinking about himself, he was thinking about her.

"We can only take fighters with us," I said.

"She's so small, she won't take up any room."

"How can a child survive in the forest?"

"You could find someone to hide her."

I looked at the little girl who never spoke. She was sitting on the floor playing a game with her marble that only she could understand.

"I . . . I can't see how that would work," I said, dodging the issue.

"You'll find a way."

I didn't think so.

"If you try."

I didn't say anything.

All at once Daniel blew up, "All you ever think about is killing people!"

I didn't know what to do.

"All you ever talk about is death, death, death . . ."

He stormed off. Back to Rebecca.

And his words echoed in my head, "Death, death, death . . ."

69

That evening, Mordechai put a new team together to meet with the firemen and finalize the details of our escape. Ben Redhead was joining us instead of Amos, who was to go over to the other side of the wall. His task was to persuade Polish canal workers to show us a route through the labyrinth of sewers. That would give us an alternative escape route if the plan with the fire engines failed.

Ben Redhead had not gotten over killing the boy. He had started stuttering again, when he spoke at all. He had also stopped eating and hardly drank anything. He was intent on fighting.

Death. Death. Death.

Amos came over to me and said, "Get back safe!"

"Same here!" I said, and we both smiled.

He kissed me on the lips for the first time since we'd shot the boy.

It was a short goodbye. Especially considering that it might be our last. Amos's chances of surviving weren't exactly great.

I watched him as he crawled through the exit to the bunker.

Then Daniel came up and asked, "Have you decided about Rebecca yet?"

I hadn't even thought about it. It was obvious that we wouldn't be able to take civilians with us.

"I can't talk now . . . ," I said.

"You're going to leave her behind," Daniel realized, and looked weary for the first time. As worn out as Korczak had been in the end.

I wanted to stroke his cheek, comfort him somehow, but he turned away. He didn't want comfort, he wanted me to help the girl.

Without saying anything more, I pushed my gun into my coat pocket and our group headed off to 80 Gęsia Street where we were to meet the Polish firemen. We had to dodge a German patrol on the way, and so we got to the building a few minutes late. The firemen weren't there.

"The question is," I said, "have they been and gone, or aren't they here yet?"

"We'll wait," Rachel said. "There's nothing else we can do."

So we waited. Five minutes. Ten.

"They aren't coming," Leon swore, "those stinking bast—"

"Psst!" Rachel hissed. "Footsteps!"

Let it be the firemen.

Rachel crept to the window to see what was happening.

A shot shattered the window and hit her in the forehead.

Rachel collapsed on the spot.

I screamed.

Germans were shooting at us with machine guns.

Leon pulled me to the floor as bullets flew over our heads and hit the wall behind us. A cupboard hanging on the wall was riddled with bullets and fell down with a crash.

"That swine betrayed us," Leon said, outraged. Ben Redhead was lying on the floor, firing back although he couldn't see the enemy and probably didn't hit anyone.

"We've got to get out of here!" Leon yelled above the noise.

We crawled out of the room, got up, and stood there for a moment not knowing where to go.

Up the stairs and onto the roof!

But then we heard the front door being kicked in. The Germans began shooting wildly into the house.

"Through there!" I said, pointing at a window in a room that was facing the backyard.

"But we'll be trapped out there," Leon argued.

"Not if we can manage to get into another flat first."

I opened the window and jumped out into the yard. Leon and Ben followed.

"Search the yard!" We heard an SS man barking orders at his men.

"Oh hell!" Leon swore.

"I . . . I . . . I'll h . . . h . . . hold them off," Ben Redhead said, and stopped running.

"But that's suicide!" Leon shouted at him.

I realized that that was exactly what Ben Redhead had in mind. He wanted to die a hero. He couldn't stay alive racked with guilt any longer. There was no way we would be able to stop him. No matter how much we wanted to.

I grabbed Leon's arm and charged on without looking back.

Behind us, I heard Ben Redhead shouting at the soldiers, "Die, you bastards!"

He shot in the direction of the staircase, and the soldiers shot back.

I grabbed a stone and smashed open a window.

Behind us, Ben stopped shooting.

He had fallen.

Don't turn round, I thought, *don't turn round. Don't waste another vital second!*

The soldiers shot at us.

I climbed through the window and jumped into the flat.

Behind me, Leon screamed.

Twice.

And then he was silent.

Don't waste a vital second!

I charged through the flat. Opened a window into the next street and leaped out. I landed badly and twisted my left ankle. I swore, but tried to run on regardless. The pain was terrible, and I could only hobble along. The soldiers would come out onto this street any minute now, and I would never be able to get away.

"Damn, damn!" I gasped, but then I reminded myself that I was only wasting valuable time by swearing. And that could be the difference between dying or seeing Amos again.

I disappeared into a house and started to limp up the stairs. Maybe I could get away over the rooftops.

The front door was forced open.

I stopped, hardly daring to move. I could hear footsteps, but it couldn't be more than two soldiers. My pursuers had obviously split up to search the houses. And that meant they didn't actually know I was here.

As quietly as possible, I opened the door to one of the flats and crept inside. I started to move down the hall, but I had only gone a few steps when the door slammed behind me with a bang. I hadn't thought about the draft!

I heard the soldiers charging up the stairs.

I tried to think. What could I do now? I was on the fourth

floor so I couldn't jump out of a window. I'd break my neck. I had to hide. But where? I rushed through the flat. It was practically empty. The acquisition squad had done well. Every single bed, cupboard, or decent piece of furniture had been hauled to the depots. They had taken everything.

The footsteps stopped outside. The soldiers had reached the flat.

"Come out with your hands up!" one of them shouted through the shut door.

I would never surrender. Surrender meant certain death.

I pulled my gun, hobbled toward the door, and started shooting in the desperate hope that I might hit the bastards, although I couldn't see them.

The soldiers screamed. I threw myself to the ground to duck any return of fire, but no one shot back. Did I get them?

I stood up carefully. I couldn't stay here. Other soldiers were bound to have heard the shots and would surround the house in a few minutes. I had to get out of here.

I hobbled to the door and pulled it open. Two soldiers lay on the floor in front of me. One was dead, the other was holding his bleeding stomach, unable to shoot. He was in agony. If I'd been merciful, I would have put him out of his misery. But the SS hadn't done that with the old woman on the burning balcony. I stepped over him. Let his comrades give him the coup de grâce.

I limped up the stairs to the attic and climbed onto the roof from there. When the soldiers reached the house, I was already four buildings away. At the next street corner. All I had to do was simply get round that corner, then I'd be able to get away. Unfortunately, the two corner houses weren't adjoining. There was a gap of about three meters. I could normally jump that far. But I wasn't sure I'd make it with a sprained ankle.

I'd rather fall to my death than be shot by a German bullet.

I jumped as best I could, but my aching ankle hindered me and I wasn't fast enough. I fell through the air . . .

And realized that I wasn't going to make it.

I missed! Instead my body crashed against the edge of the roof. I was winded but, instinctively, I fell forward while my legs dangled in the air unable to get a grip anywhere on the house wall.

I used the last of my strength to pull myself up and lay there gasping for air. It took me a moment to come to and then another one before I could manage to get to my feet and duck away across the roofs.

A few houses farther on, I saw a mound of feathers in a backyard. A good hiding place at last.

I climbed through a skylight into the attic and nearly screamed in pain when I landed on the floorboards, but I bit my lip instead, so hard it started to bleed.

I reached the heap of feathers in the yard and managed to hide. But that was all. I had no strength left. Physically or mentally. I closed my eyes. I couldn't even stay awake to see if the soldiers would come.

70

I woke up to the smell of someone smoking a cigarette. Someone was here in this yard. Another Polish fireman? Pausing for a break while putting out the fires? Or a German taking time out from the hunt? Or was it a fighter? A comrade? A friend? Not likely. I'd used up all my luck for today.

Judging by the light that fell through the feathers, dawn was breaking. So I would have to get back to Miła 18 quickly or else stay hidden where I was for the rest of the day. With nothing to eat or drink. And what would I do if the Germans decided to set fire to the buildings here?

I listened for a moment and then decided to risk it. The man seemed to be alone. I leaped out, holding my gun. If I wasn't wrong, there would still be one or two bullets left.

I was standing in front of an SS soldier. He jumped and dropped his cigarette.

I was startled, too. I knew this man.

It was the officer who had saved me from the fat pig in the guardhouse. The German who could speak some Polish and had more or less resembled a human being.

It was the first time that I had ever stood facing an SS man like this. One who was in my power. I had to make use of it. To try to understand.

"Why?" I asked him.

He was confused.

"Why . . . what?"

"Why are you doing this to us?"

He thought about it.

"Your life doesn't depend on your answer."

I wanted him to tell the truth and not just say something to save his skin.

He nodded. He understood now.

"Do you want to know why I am here, or why my superiors are doing this?"

"Both."

"Himmler and the others are mad."

"And you?"

"I wish I could say the same." He laughed bitterly.

"That's not an answer."

"I wanted a better life for myself and my family."

"They are better off if you slaughter people here?"

"Rubbish!" he snapped. He seemed to have forgotten for a moment that I was pointing a gun at him. Then he remembered and got more factual. "I've got a good position in the SS, money—"

"So you murder for money," I interrupted.

"That was not the plan. I didn't look that far ahead. Who could have imagined anything like this?"

"Hitler never mentioned that he hated the Jews?" I asked sarcastically.

He didn't answer. Instead, he said, "My family doesn't have a better life. Hamburg is being bombed, and I'll return home with my wife and daughter emotional wrecks. If they are still alive."

Part of me hoped they weren't.

"And," he continued carefully, "if you let me live."

"Why should I?"

"I saved you from Scharper. You should have seen what he did to the other girls."

"The ones you didn't save."

"I don't have all that much room to act. I can't save hundreds of Jews."

"There's always a choice."

"You think so because you've got nothing to lose."

"Thanks to you."

"As head of a family, I stand to lose a lot."

The longer I let him speak, the more human he seemed and the more I detested him.

"If you kill me, my family will lose the father, the husband—"

"Shut up!" I snapped, and pointed my gun at his head.

The officer stopped talking. He tried to look calm. But his hands were shaking.

"Turn around."

He did as I had ordered. He was shaking all over now.

"Bitte," he pleaded in German.

"I said: Shut up!"

He began to cry.

I wanted him to stop.

He cried even more.

And I struck him with the handle of my gun as hard as I could.

The officer fell to the ground. The back of his head was bleeding; he couldn't move but he moaned. He wasn't unconscious yet.

So I struck him again. And again. Until I'd knocked him out.

I let him live. Not because he had saved me from a worse fate in the guardhouse. Or because I felt sorry for him. Or his family. I let him live because the sound of a shot would have alerted his comrades.

71

When I got back to Miła 18, the building had been destroyed. *Dead, they're all dead*, I thought, but I forced myself not to give up quite yet. I'd learned this much. As long as I didn't find any bodies or signs that they had all been driven to the trains by the SS, there was still hope.

Desperate, I searched for one of the five entrances beneath the rubble, found a hole at last, crawled through, and was overjoyed to find the others still alive. The fire hadn't reached the bunkers, and the SS hadn't found them.

The mood in the chambers didn't match my joy, though. It was like being in an oven; everyone was wearing nothing more than underwear, and Asher was the only one who managed to muster any kind of humor. "I always wanted to have a sauna down here," he said.

My comrades became even more despondent when they heard that the Polish firemen had betrayed us.

"Now we can only hope that Amos finds a way through the sewers," Mordechai sighed.

Avi, whose leg had become infected and who was feverish, rubbed his red beard and said, "Others have tried and failed. Shit happens!"

So far, no fighter had managed to get through the sewers. Two had even been killed when soldiers had heard them and thrown hand grenades at them through a drain.

"Amos," Mordechai tried to sound assured, "will find canal workers to show us the way."

"If he is still alive," Avi groaned.

"Don't say that!" I snapped.

I twisted my wedding ring nervously. It meant as much to me now as Rebecca's marble did to her.

Why hadn't Amos and I simply stayed on the Polish side and tried to remain alive? But I knew the answer. Because we couldn't desert our comrades.

"I'm sorry," Avi said. "Of course Amos is still alive."

"It's okay," I answered, and slipped away to the chamber called Auschwitz. I took off my trousers, blouse, and shoes, and inspected my swollen ankle. It would have been good to be able to cool it, but water was too precious. I lay down and tried to not think about Amos, tried to ignore the pain. Instead, I wanted to travel to Hannah. But before I could set foot on Mirror Island, we heard the sound of footsteps above us.

Immediately, everyone in the bunker was silent. Most of us actually held our breath. Some people started to mumble prayers softly. Fighters grabbed their weapons.

Then the hammering started.

They were using heavy tools to try to drill through the debris. Did the Germans know that we were here? Or were they searching at random? For a horrible second, I imagined that they had captured Amos and tortured him until he had betrayed our hiding place. Ending his life in guilt. Dust trickled down on us.

After an eternity of fear, the hammering stopped.

Had they discovered us?

More and more people were praying, more and more quietly.

The footsteps moved away.

You could see that a few civilians wanted to cheer. We fighters were relieved, too, but now we knew for certain that our time had almost run out. We had hardly any ammunition left, practically no food, and it was almost impossible to find anything to eat in the ruins of the destroyed ghetto.

Even Daniel had lost his courage. He crawled over to me and said, "You were right."

"What?"

"You said we'll never survive."

Daniel looked over at Rebecca. She was staring at her blue and white marble again, as if there was a whole world hidden inside. It was a miracle that this little girl was still alive.

Daniel whispered, "Korczak would start getting her ready, telling her that there is another, better world to come . . ."

That was what the old man had done with his play on the day when the Germans had come to fetch the children.

". . . but I'm not Korczak," Daniel said sadly.

"Only Korczak is Korczak," I said kindly.

"I wanted to be like him all my life. And how have I ended up?"

"Daniel!"

He looked miserable.

"I'm not even that," I said.

Daniel didn't know what I meant.

"You have achieved so much more than me!"

He looked surprised.

"You gave this little girl almost a year. We fighters could only add a couple of awful days."

He had made the miracle of her survival happen.

His answer was to kiss me gently on the cheek.

I was so surprised I didn't know what to say.

Instead Daniel said, "Don't listen to Avi. Amos will be back."

And for that I kissed him on the cheek, too.

We were standing in the snow and looking down on the clouds that circled the mountain like a snugly fitting ring. About fifty meters above us the mirrors of the palace reflected the light of the sun.

The crew of the *Longear* was tired. Not as tired as the fighters in the bunker at Miła 18, but tired enough.

Captain Carrot swore, "These blasted mountains! I know why I chose to be a seaman."

"You're a seaman because you won this tub gambling," the werewolf reminded him.

"Ah yes, I should gamble more."

"Our whole life is a gamble."

"In that case, we are the best gamblers in the world."

Hannah wasn't part of that conversation. She was smiling at Ben Redhead. The real Ben was dead. The real Hannah was, too. But because I couldn't bear the thought of death and because Amos wasn't with me, I surrounded myself with phantoms less and less like the real people they thought they were.

I didn't want to die by myself.

I was all alone in my corner of Auschwitz. I got up, hobbled over to Daniel and Rebecca, and asked, "Can I join you?"

The little girl rolled her marble over to me. I picked it up carefully, as if it were the most valuable treasure. Which it was. It was incredible that it was still in one piece after all this time. It lay snug in the palm of my hand, and I could suddenly feel that there was more to the world than death.

Daniel pointed at the marble and smiled at me. "That's an invitation," he said.

I gave the marble back to Rebecca, cuddled up to the two of them, and felt less alone.

72

The next morning the hammering started up again. The Germans had discovered the bunker. How? Dogs? Traitors? Listening devices? It didn't really matter.

All the fighters pulled their guns. Civilians started to cry. Some even screamed with fear. Shmuel Asher ran around telling everyone to be quiet. But people like Izak the weasel wouldn't shut up. "They've come to get us! They've come to get us!"

"There's still time for a miracle," his boss insisted.

The Germans had not only turned him into a proud Jew, he even believed in miracles!

The hammering stopped.

Silence.

Waiting.

Fear.

"I'm one of you," we heard the voice of a Jewish collaborator. He was standing on the mountain of rubble above our bunker. "You can trust me! The Germans will send you to work. But if you don't surrender, they will kill you."

Mordechai signaled to Pola, a fighter who had once wanted to be a ballet dancer, to go to one of the entrances. Pola knew exactly what she had to do. She ran to a hole, moved away some rubble, and shot.

That was our answer.

Pola moved away from the entrance, as it was perfectly clear what would happen next. The Germans threw a hand grenade into the bunker through the hole. The explosion scared everybody, but no one was hurt.

The Germans continued digging with their heavy tools. The traitor pig called again, "Surrender! Surrender! I swear to God nothing will happen to you!" No one believed a word he said.

"What's that?" Izak asked suddenly.

I didn't know what the weasel meant at first.

"What is it?" he asked again, sounding hysterical.

Then I smelled it, too.

The smell wasn't very strong at first.

But it grew stronger.

And we all realized what it was.

"Gas!" someone shouted.

"Out of here. Get out!" Asher ordered his men.

"I thought you were going to stay here till the end," Avi called weakly from his sick bed.

"We will die here; outside there is still the tiniest chance we might survive!" Asher replied, and left the bunker along with about one hundred coughing and choking civilians.

The Germans didn't shoot them. They were destined for the gas chambers.

The fighters and some civilians stayed in the bunker that was rapidly turning into a gas chamber of its own. Daniel and little Rebecca stayed, too.

There were about one hundred people left.

"What are we going to do?" Pola asked.

"We'll shoot ourselves," Avi answered.

"What?" I said. I couldn't believe what he was saying, and Pola looked shocked. "Are you crazy?"

"We'll do it like the people at Masada. They won't get us alive."

"They mustn't take us alive," Pola agreed, "but we should die fighting! I say, let's go out shooting and be killed fighting!"

Avi retorted, "They are blocking all the entrances. We can't sneak out and attack without being seen. We can just go out one by one through the guarded entrances. You'd have one shot and then be shot. And we don't have enough ammunition to fight. Only enough to kill ourselves."

"We should still try," Pola said.

I didn't like either option. Although I realized that the end I had been expecting all these months had finally come, I didn't want to die. Neither fighting, nor by killing myself, and certainly not by being gassed. Amos wasn't with me.

Mordechai didn't approve, either. "We shouldn't choose to die as long as there is still a chance . . ."

"But that's one in a million!" Avi cried. As far as I could tell by looking at them, about half the fighters approved of his plan while the rest supported Pola's suggestion to die in a hail of bullets.

"It is better than nothing," Mordechai said decidedly. "As long as there's any possibility of fighting, we will not go to our deaths. Not either way."

"But what about the gas . . . ?" Avi and Pola asked at the same time.

More and more was pouring into the bunker. Our eyes were streaming with tears.

"Water can weaken the effect," Mordechai said. "We'll soak cloths with water and hold them in front of our mouths."

He did this himself, dipping a bit of cloth into a murky puddle. And I followed his example. Some of the others did, too.

With the cloth over his face, Mordechai told several fighters to try to find an unguarded way out, although he knew there wouldn't be one.

Avi sat up and climbed out of his bed. He headed into the Mauthausen chamber, pulling his leg after him. We heard a shot.

Other fighters followed suit.

A pale, beautiful fighter named Sharon handed out the last of the cyanide capsules to some of the children. They all swallowed them. Their little bodies shuddered and jerked, then life left them. It was less torturous than death by gas.

Sharon approached Daniel and Rebecca.

She was a beautiful angel of death.

Daniel hesitated to take the capsule for the little girl. Finally he did so and was about to give it to her . . .

"No!" I cried.

He did what I said. Gave the capsule back to Sharon and she passed it on to a mother and child. Then she took her gun and shot herself. Seven times! Until she was finally dead.

I ran to Daniel and Rebecca and gave them both wet cloths. I sat down by them. We huddled together. If I couldn't die with Amos, then at least with them.

The gas slowly filled all the chambers of the bunker. More and more fighters took their lives. Others like Pola went out shooting and were shot by the enemy. It was hard to imagine that they actually hit anyone before they were killed.

Daniel grabbed my hand.

I tried to travel to the 777 islands for the very last time, but

I couldn't concentrate. There was practically no air left. With all the gas, I was coughing so much I couldn't manage to picture Hannah climbing up the stony mountain path on her way to the Palace of Mirrors.

All I could see was Hannah in the pool of blood.

I held on to Daniel's hand as tightly as I could.

United in death.

Then someone shouted, "There's a way out!"

I didn't understand at first.

"There's a way out!"

A skinny fighter was standing in front of me. Someone I'd never really noticed before. I didn't even know his name. He was one of the fighters Mordechai had sent off to look for a way out. I could hardly breathe because of the gas and assumed he must be mad. There couldn't be any more exits. But I let go of Daniel's hand nonetheless—he was almost unconscious—and got up.

"We can get out! We can get out!" the fighter shouted.

Mad or not, there was nothing to lose by following him. I bent down to Daniel and started to shake him.

He didn't open his eyes.

"Daniel!" I gasped.

He still wouldn't wake up.

I looked around for the skinny fighter. I couldn't risk losing sight of him, as I had no idea where the supposed exit was—if it existed at all and the comrade wasn't simply mad.

The skinny fighter told as many people as possible about his discovery, but he was too late. Nearly everyone was dead. They had killed themselves, or gone out shooting and been shot by the Germans, or they had already choked to death. Just a few of us, like Daniel and Rebecca and me who were holding the damp cloths over our mouths, were still breathing. Daniel only just.

"Wake up," I screamed, and nearly threw up coughing.

No reaction.

I slapped him, once, twice.

At last he opened his eyes. I dragged him to his feet. And Rebecca, too. Then I looked for the skinny fighter. He had assembled a group of people and led us to a back corner of the bunker. There was a hole the Germans hadn't discovered. We removed the rubble, crawled through, and hid amid the debris and ashes. Fourteen people. Dressed in underwear. The last survivors of 18 Miła Street.

Mordechai wasn't among us. I had no idea if he had been killed by the gas, or killed himself, or if he had shot at the Germans one last time. The Jewish Fighting Organization had lost its leader. And nearly all of its remaining fighters. We had lost Miła 18, and we had lost all hope.

73

n the night, I heard footsteps. I was far too shaken to think of fleeing. So were the others. Daniel still had so much gas in his lungs that he couldn't stop coughing. We heard guns being leveled behind a mound of rubble. The skinny fighter who had saved us put his hands up to surrender. The rest of us did so, too. Those of us who had any strength left, that is. Daniel wasn't one of them. He was sitting motionless in the debris.

People were climbing the mountain of rubble from the other side. Any minute now the SS would be towering over us and either arrest us or shoot us. Who cared! It didn't matter either way.

"Hands up!" a voice called in Polish.

I looked up. These weren't Germans, or Latvians or Ukrainians. They were three comrades. Two men and a woman.

We stared at one another.

Seventeen Jews met up in the debris of the destroyed ghetto.

It took a while before we finally realized who they were and lowered our hands. And even longer before anyone managed to speak and we could answer the comrades' questions. When they discovered that everyone else in 18 Miła Street was gone, their eyes brimmed with tears.

Only Samuel, the leader of the other group, refused to cry for anyone who had killed themselves. "There is no point in killing yourself as long as you can still fight. Their deaths were pointless," he said.

What death ever made sense?

What life?

Mine?

No.

No one's.

When another survivor recounted how Sharon had shot herself seven times, Samuel just said, "Six wasted bullets."

I was too exhausted to yell at him and point out that he hadn't been there. He wouldn't have listened to me anyway. He and his comrades started searching the rubble for weapons. But there was no point. The SS had blown up the bunker. The bodies of our comrades were gone.

We headed off through the destroyed ghetto, across mountains of ash and stone, trying to find somewhere to hide. A group of people as destroyed inside as the streets and houses around them.

We got to 22 Franciszkańska Street. Another bunker. Probably the last one left. More a sick bay than a sanctuary. Full of wounded, burned, and dying people.

I didn't think about food. Or my injuries. Or about Amos. I closed my eyes. I just wanted to sleep. Sleep forever.

Peace.

What kind of a person did I want to be?

One who could be put out of her misery.

74

"Anyone who doesn't look Jewish, come over here!" Samuel called.

I wanted to stay where I was, sleep, die . . . So I told myself, *you don't look Aryan, Mira. They don't mean you, sleep . . .*

. . . but Mordechai had chosen me to go over to the Polish side of the city because he was sure that I could pass for a Pole, and I had proved him right time and again. If Samuel, who was leading us now, wanted Aryan-looking people, it must mean that we were to go over to the other side, and then . . . then perhaps I could see Amos again.

Only when he was dead would I truly be able to sleep forever.

I forced myself to get up, and limped over to Samuel and a blond fighter who looked more manly and Nordic than most of the SS men.

Samuel looked at me skeptically until he noticed my green eyes. Then he asked me, "Are you okay?"

"No" would have been the honest answer, but this was my very last hope of ever seeing Amos again. So instead I said, "Yes."

"There's no point in dying miserably in this bunker," Samuel explained. "You have to contact the comrades on the other side, and together you must get us all out."

"How are we supposed to do that?" the blond guy asked.

"You'll have to think of something, Josef," Samuel answered, and chucked me some clothes to wear. A blouse with a torn sleeve, a pair of men's trousers that were too big.

"How do we get to the other side?"

"Through the sewers."

We didn't say anything. It was a desperate plan. Without any knowledge of the layout, we would be lost down there. Amos had probably never made it out. Why else hadn't we received a message from him by now?

"Abraham here," Samuel pointed to a man whose left cheek had been badly burned, "knows his way around the sewers. He'll lead you to a place where you can climb out on the Polish side of the city, and he'll come back here to let us know you got through."

Abraham nodded so hard we had to trust him.

Less than half an hour later, he lifted a drain cover, and we climbed down into the sewer, one by one. Abraham had a torch; Josef and I were carrying candles. At once, we stood knee-deep in waste water. The stench was beyond belief. If I'd had anything to throw up, I'd have done so.

Abraham took the lead. The farther we got, the deeper the water. In some places, it came up to my neck.

We were in a tunnel where the foul water merely went up to my chest when Abraham suddenly shouted, "Look out!" A gigantic wave of waste water was surging toward us.

The wave broke over my head, tore me off my feet, and I went under. The filthy brew poured into my nose before I could manage to hold my breath. Desperately, I tried to find my footing again. I struggled and struggled, and then, at last, my feet touched the ground.

I surfaced and threw up at once. So did Josef. Abraham was gasping for breath, but he helped me along until I could walk by myself again. The candles had gone out, and we were left with a single torch.

None of us said anything. No one mentioned the fear of drowning down here. We just kept going. Step by step. Going left or right at each junction. Sometimes the water rose, sometimes it was no more than knee-high. Another two waves of sewage washed over us, but we were better prepared than the first time and managed to hold our breaths.

When we reached the next turnoff, Abraham, our leader, seemed uncertain, looking this way and that. I knew what that must mean. "Are we lost?"

"No, no, it's okay," he tried to calm me, "we need to go left."

Abraham tried to look confident. We followed him, but my courage started to fail. We would never get to the other side. I was going to perish down here.

A few minutes later, Josef also realized that our leader didn't know where we were anymore.

"I . . . I am sorry," Abraham said.

"You're sorry? You're sorry?" Josef shouted. "If we don't get over to the other side, we'll die!"

"I know." Abraham started to cry. "What can I do? What?"

I leaned against the wall. Exhausted.

Then I saw the flash of a torch.

It was coming from around the corner.

"Germans!" Josef hissed quietly.

The cone of light grew larger and larger. The soldiers were approaching.

We stood there frozen. There was nowhere to flee to in this stinking hell.

The light came round the corner and blinded us. We were in shock. Caught like animals.

Someone shouted, "I'm one of you!"

"It . . . it's not possible," Abraham stuttered.

"Amazing," Josef laughed.

I laughed even more. It was Amos!

As fast as I could, I waded toward my husband—yes, that's who he was—and he took me in his arms. We stank of excrement and worse, but the feeling of joy was indescribable. I had never expected to feel this happy again.

Amos told us that he had bribed a Polish canal worker to lead him through the sewers to the ghetto. The canal worker had gone down with Amos, but had tried to turn back at some point. Amos had pulled his gun, and the man had decided to choose to live. He showed Amos a way through the sewers to get into the ghetto and out again safely. But when Amos got to Miła Street to fetch everyone, the bunker had already been destroyed.

"I thought I'd lost you forever," he said, squeezing me even tighter.

"That's what I thought, too," I said. I never wanted to let him go again.

"You can't get rid of me that easily," he grinned.

I started to laugh. Amos handed out sweets and lemons he'd been carrying in a little bag.

"I . . . I can't remember the last time I saw a lemon," Josef stammered.

"Here of all places!" Abraham laughed. He was so relieved! We wouldn't end up drowning in the sewers because of him.

"What are we going to do now?" I asked Amos while I sucked a sweet and the wonderful flavor got rid of the foul taste in my mouth.

"We need a truck."

"A truck?" I asked, surprised.

"You all climb out of the sewers on the Polish side of the city. I organize a truck, pick you up, and we drive to the woods . . . ," he told us, brimming with enthusiasm.

I couldn't really see this plan working. But I didn't say anything. Amos's eyes were shining so brightly.

75

When Josef, Abraham, and I returned to the bunker at Franciszkańska Street, the comrades were past cheering. They were far too exhausted and dejected to muster any kind of hope of being saved.

"If this had happened just one day earlier," Samuel couldn't help saying, "then a hundred friends would be able to go with us."

"We need to let the comrades at Nalewki Street know," Josef said, and looked wildly determined.

"It's getting light," Samuel objected. "If we try to get to them, we'll be caught and then we'll all be lost."

"We can't go without them," Josef said, and a lot of us agreed.

"Even if Masha is still there—is it worth the risk?"

Josef struggled with his conscience.

I realized this poor guy might have to leave the person he loved behind so that we could survive.

What kind of human do you want to be?

We would all have supported Josef if he had insisted we stay and get the others. I would have taken the risk if it had been me. I couldn't have been as rational. Not even for the cause. Not anymore.

But Josef said sadly, "You're right, Samuel."

He was willing to sacrifice his wife for us.

There were about fifty of us who made our way through the sewers. Daniel and Rebecca walked behind me. Daniel carried her if the water got too high. The hope that his sister would be saved and he could hide with her till the end of the war had revived him a bit.

Others were even more exhausted than he was. When the water reached his neck, Abraham begged, "Leave me behind, I can't go on."

Samuel snapped at him, "Shut up! If we leave you here, you'll drown!"

So Abraham dragged himself on. The farther we got, the more cramped and narrow the hideous tunnels became. In the end, we couldn't stand upright. My damaged ankle hurt with every step. People kept collapsing and had to be dragged out of the water. One woman could only be revived when Josef threw waste water in her face. What kept us going were the arrows Amos had left for us. At least we always knew we were going the right way. Away from the destroyed ghetto toward the Polish part of the city and from there to the forest.

I thought about the trees I had seen when we had met the Polish resistance to negotiate an arms deal. The thought of lying beneath a tree with Amos gave me enough strength to go on.

At about midday, we finally reached our destination. An exit from the sewers at Prosta Street. We could stand upright here. Sunlight shone down through the drain, and above us everyday life was in full swing. Children played, cars drove by, a married couple argued about smacking their son for his naughty behavior—no one appeared to have noticed that a huge part of the city had just been destroyed. And no one noticed that people were waiting beneath the street to be rescued.

We stayed there for more than an hour before a note was thrown down to us. A message from Amos. I was standing right beneath the drain cover and I caught it, although it very nearly slipped through my fingers and fell into the water. I read the note, but I couldn't believe it. The truck wouldn't arrive before dark.

That meant that we would be stuck down here for another eight hours, although most of us were nearly done for.

My husband was standing above me, and all I could see were the soles of his shoes. I couldn't call to him, couldn't let him know how desperate we were, how much I yearned to be with him. I would give us all away. Amos walked off, and I had to tell the others the soul-destroying news.

"I can't stand it any longer, I can't stand it," a little man whined. He was bald civilian wearing a vest.

"Well, I can't stand your moaning!" the skinny fighter who had led us out of Miła Street said angrily. Normally it would have been impolite for a younger man to speak to an older man like that, but down here he only said what we were all thinking.

"Shoot me, then," the bald man said.

"I'd love to," the skinny fighter retorted, "but I won't do it for nothing."

"What did you say?"

"One hundred zlotys. Bullets aren't cheap, you know."

The bald man was quiet for a moment, then he laughed and said, "I'll give you fifty!"

Even I had to grin at that.

"Two hundred," the skinny fighter said.

"Hey, you just said one hundred."

"That was before you offered me fifty."

Their insane banter made more and more of us smile.

"Thirty!" the bald man offered.

"Three hundred," the skinny fighter demanded.

"Twenty, that's my final word."

"I want fifty!"

"Fifty?" the bald man seemed surprised. "But that's what I offered to start with."

"I'm just trying to confuse you!"

Some of us actually managed to laugh.

Despite everything.

If my wish had been granted in the Franciszkańska bunker and I had fallen asleep forever, I would have missed this rare moment.

The happiness didn't last very long, of course. One civilian collapsed from exhaustion. Another was so thirsty he drank waste water and was terribly ill. But we all managed to stay alive until evening. When it started to get dark and we could hear only the occasional sound of people or cars, I saw Amos's shoes again at long last. He had come to lift up the drain cover! We would finally get out of this sewage hell, climb into the waiting truck, and leave the ghetto once and for all.

Amos stood above us, but he didn't move. Why didn't he lift the damned drain cover?

A note sailed down to us and got caught in my hair, which was dripping with dirt and sweat. I took it, but I didn't want to read it if it meant we would have to hold out even longer. How long? An hour? Two? Not any longer, surely? More starving people would collapse. More thirsty ones would try to drink the waste water.

Finally, I unfolded the note and read it out loud. "The soldiers are patrolling all the exits to the sewers during the night. We can't get you out before tomorrow morning."

Tomorrow morning!

I looked up. Amos had already disappeared. I passed the note on. Samuel started to crack up. "We'll never hold out that long!" he said. "We'll have to climb out now and start shooting. That way at least a few of us will manage to survive."

I looked at Daniel and Rebecca, sitting there, worn out. They would definitely die if we did as Samuel suggested. I turned to him and said emphatically, "No! We won't do that."

"Giving up is not an option," he snapped.

"This has nothing to do with giving up; there is no truck waiting for us up there! We will all be killed. The SS will shoot the civilians and all the fighters as well. Just like the comrades who left Miła 18 shooting."

Samuel hesitated.

"We've got to wait," I said.

Unwillingly, Samuel had to agree.

An hour later, the drain cover was lifted.

Amos made use of a moment when the SS was patrolling elsewhere to pass down two buckets of soup and lemonade. It was so little that our mouths stayed dry, but it was enough to stop people from drinking the waste water in desperation and gave us courage to hold on. Me most of all, because I could see Amos's face for a few precious moments.

"I'll get you out of here," he said. His eyes shone more brightly than ever before.

And now I believed him.

76

The only person who seemed remotely happy about the developments was Josef. He hoped to be able to save his wife now after all. "I'll go back to the ghetto and fetch our comrades from Nalewki Street. If I hurry, I should be back here with them by tomorrow morning."

The rest of us decided to spread out to various exits for the night. If the Germans discovered us all hiding in the same place, we feared they might kill us all with just one grenade.

I moved two streets away with Daniel and Rebecca. We were able to sit in the cold waste water here—though there was the danger that the little girl would drown if she fell asleep.

Daniel kept her awake by telling her the stories about King Macius that Korczak had written. He told her about Klu-Klu who knew 112 European words, the hermit in the tower, and how the little king tried to flee from the dungeon and realized that the outcome wasn't the most important thing in life, it was the decision to act.

Rebecca was only half listening. She kept nodding off, for

one thing, and Daniel spoke more and more slowly and quietly. The gas in the bunker at Miła 18 had affected him far more than me.

Rebecca turned to me looking dog-tired and said, "Can you tell me a story?"

It was the first time she had ever spoken!

I was so surprised that I couldn't say anything for a moment.

"Daniel always tells stories about Little King Macius," she complained. "I know all of them."

Daniel managed to smile.

"I . . . I," I stammered, "I can think of one."

Beside me, Daniel closed his eyes gratefully, and I started to tell the story of the 777 islands, about how Hannah and Ben Redhead had discovered the book, Hannah's claim to be the Chosen One, how she had discovered the three magic mirrors that would defeat the Mirror King, and on and on . . .

Sometime past midnight, I reached the point where the crew of the *Longear* reached the mountaintop.

Tonight in the sewers, the fate of the islands would be sealed. So would Hannah's and mine. Would I dare face the Mirror King?

77

The Palace of Mirrors in front of us seemed to be never ending. The real size was impossible to guess as the reflections mirrored one another infinitely. Perhaps it had no size at all. There were no gates or doors; no entrance or gap to be seen. Only mirrors. Shiny polished mirrors everywhere.

"A door would be useful," Captain Carrot said. Despite his fur coat, he was shivering in the cold at this height far above his beloved sea.

As if we had said the magic word, a mirror disappeared and revealed a long passageway leading into the depths of the palace. Of course, the walls, floor, and ceiling here were all made of mirrors.

"Do we really have to go in there?" The werewolf's teeth were chattering. More from fear than from cold. The rest of us were feeling uneasy, too.

"I am afraid the answer is yes," the captain said.

"I should never have left my pack of wolves."

Hannah did her best to calm us all. "It's a good thing the tyrant is a king of mirrors and not of manure."

"Thank heaven for small favors." The captain smiled.

Even the werewolf managed to grin, and his teeth stopped chattering.

We entered the hallway. Our distorted reflections were all around us—fat, thin, ugly, pulsating.

"One thing I hate even more than the Mirror King . . . ," I started to say,

". . . is his sense of humor!" Hannah finished my sentence for me.

We smiled at each other. Two sisters who knew each other inside out. Here even more than in real life.

Step by step, the pictures became more and more menacing. After fifty meters, our reflections looked truly gruesome, like monsters with eyes bulging out of their sockets, crippled limbs, and faces rigid with hatred.

The Mira staring down at me with a vile expression was the one who shot soldiers. I closed my eyes. I couldn't bear to look at her. And I didn't want to be her ever again.

I felt my way along behind the others. And then I heard Hannah calling, "Oh, this is beautiful."

I opened my eyes again. We were standing in a great hall filled with glass crystals, diamond flowers, and mirror chandeliers. Beams of light were dancing in the glass. Everything sparkled. The play of colors was so magnificent, it took our breaths away.

A funny-looking man who seemed to be made totally of mirror glass climbed down from his mirror throne and came toward us. The Mirror King looked nothing like the monster I'd seen in my nightmares.

"So you are the Chosen One," he said to Hannah in a friendly sort of way.

"Yes, I am," Hannah answered, and grabbed Ben Redhead's hand.

"And you want to break my hold over the islands?" His smile looked a little bit less friendly all of a sudden.

"I don't just want to—I am going to," Hannah said.

The Mirror King opened his arms wide, presenting himself as a target, and laughed. "Do what you must!"

Hannah let go of Ben Redhead's hand, opened the knapsack quickly, and took out the three magic mirrors, although none of us had any idea how they were supposed to work. She pointed them at the Mirror King and hoped that something would happen, that the mirrors would make him disappear or at least paralyze him.

But the Mirror King seemed to relish reflecting the three mirrors on every part of his body until all of them were filled with images of him laughing. "The three magic mirrors," he taunted, "don't you know I created them?"

"You . . . ? Why?" Hannah asked.

"So that you would look for them!"

None of us knew what he meant.

"I also allowed the story of a Chosen One to spread throughout the world of the 777 islands."

"Are you saying . . . ," Hannah asked, "that there is no Chosen One?"

"Clever girl."

"But why . . . ?"

"As long as all the creatures in my kingdom believe that they will be rescued by a little girl with three magic mirrors, they will never try to fight me by themselves."

"So it was all a lie . . . ?" I couldn't believe it.

"The second-most deadly weapon of a tyrant is the lie," the Mirror King said triumphantly.

"And the first?" Hannah asked.

"Fear."

Suddenly, he started to grow and expand in all directions.

"I wish she hadn't asked that," the captain groaned.

The tyrant continued to swell and bulge, sprouting more and more mirrors with razor-sharp edges that could cut you to shreds. He was the monster from my dreams after all. His grotesque head touched the ceiling. The mirror chandeliers crashed to the ground and shattered into thousands of pieces. In them, I could see myself shooting at the Germans, leaving the baby behind at the *Umschlagplatz,* and Mama lying dead in her own blood. With Ruth beside her. And Hannah beside them both. Hannah was in thousands of mirrors. Hannah was everywhere.

"What . . . what is this?" Hannah asked me. Her eyes wide with horror.

"Didn't you tell her, Mira?" the monster asked in a cutting voice.

"Tell me what, Mira?" Hannah asked frantically.

I couldn't say a word.

"Mira managed to survive," the Mirror King said, "but you, my little Chosen One, are—!"

"Fight," I shouted to stop him telling the truth, and pulled my sword.

"You can't defeat me, Mira," he laughed, "I am part of you."

"Fight! Fight!" I cried desperately.

Then I heard a little girl calling, "No, please don't."

I looked at Hannah, but she was as confused as I was. It wasn't her calling. The voice came from nowhere.

"No fighting!"

Then I recognized it. It was Rebecca calling from the dark stinking sewage canal where I was telling her the story.

"I don't want there to be any more fighting," she begged.

She was right. I lowered my sword. Let the Mirror King destroy me if he liked! If he killed me, I could stop feeling guilty for being alive, at least.

But no sooner had I lowered my sword than he started to shrink. He grew smaller and smaller, and when he was my height, he looked me in the eye and whined, "Fight is my elixir of life . . ."

Without it he would fade away, I realized.

Although he continued to shrink, my feelings of guilt didn't completely disappear, and he didn't vanish altogether. We could still see the horrifying pictures showing in his mirrors. There was still something I was fighting with.

"What didn't you tell me, Mira?" Hannah asked again.

"You . . ." I admitted and my voice faltered, "Oh, Hannah! You're all dead!"

Hannah was so stunned she couldn't speak. Instead the captain asked, shocked, "I'm dead?"

"I am not feeling too bad," the werewolf said.

"No, not you sailors . . ."

"Ah . . ." The werewolf wasn't sure quite what to think.

"You never existed," I explained.

"Well, that's not much better," the captain said. He could sense that I was telling the truth.

"D . . . d . . . d . . . ?" asked Ben Redhead.

"We're dead?" Hannah asked, and took hold of Ben's hand again.

"I've brought you back to life in your story," I tried to explain.

She didn't blame me for not having told her the truth all this time. She just asked, "Whatever for?"

"I didn't want you to be gone forever," I tried to explain, heartbroken.

"But this isn't me! I'm not a chosen hero. I never was." Hannah pointed at the mirror showing her lying in the pool of blood and said sadly, "I'm just a girl who got killed . . ."

"But I . . . ," I was all choked up, "I don't want to remember you like that!"

"It's the truth . . ."

It felt as if a mighty weight had landed on my chest, which was stopping me from breathing.

"But I'm far more than just a hero in a story," she continued. "Remember me how I was."

Pictures shot through my mind. Pictures of the real Hannah: Hannah eating, kissing Ben Redhead, looking at me angrily, being cheeky, telling me stories when I wasn't well, and, yes, lying dead in the pantry.

"Promise me that, Mira?"

"Yes," I said quietly, and the weight on my chest fell away. "I promise."

Hannah hugged me. "I'll always be with you."

"So will I," the little Mirror King laughed behind me with a squeaky voice.

But I hardly noticed him.

I could live with the guilt of being alive if I let myself remember how things had really been. Hannah gave me a kiss, and I left the world of the 777 islands.

Forever.

I was back in the sewers, sitting in the water with Daniel, who was very weak now, asleep against the wall, and with Rebecca, who was staring at me.

It took me a while before I could say anything or give the story I'd just told the little girl some sort of meaning she'd understand.

"That was the story about how I found my sister again . . . ," I tried to explain.

"There's no more fighting, is there?" Rebecca asked.

Stories are like that. They work differently for different people.

"No more fighting," I promised the little girl.

And then I kissed the top of her head.

78

The next morning, the three of us made our way back to the drain cover in Prosta Street. Rebecca could manage to wade through the water by herself, but I practically had to carry Daniel. When we got to the exit, we waited for Amos and the truck again. In vain. Again.

Instead, Josef returned from the ghetto. His face was all swollen from crying. "The SS . . . is blowing up the entrances to the sewers in the ghetto . . . no one can get through to us now. Everyone in Nalewki Street is lost . . ."

His Masha was lost.

And we could not go back to the ghetto if the pickup failed. The truck had to take us to the woods or else we would die down here.

It was past nine when Amos came back again, at last. I was standing directly beneath him. He pretended to tie his laces and whispered, "You've got to wait again."

"What is wrong?" I wanted to know.

"I couldn't get a truck—the bloody Poles didn't keep their word."

"We . . . we can't last any longer," I protested.

"Mira, darling! I'm going to get you out."

I still wanted to believe him.

"Give me till tonight," he asked.

"Don't you understand? This is the end."

"Mira, any sooner is too dangerous."

I looked at Daniel slumped against the tunnel wall, unable to sit up straight.

"You have to get us out now, Amos. Or else we'll die down here. There's nothing more dangerous than that."

Amos understood. He worked out what he was going to do and said, "I'll have to hijack a truck."

"Then do it."

He hurried away, and I looked at all the people standing round me or sitting in the stinking water. Not everyone had come back from the other entrances yet. I hoped they would be back before Amos returned.

If he returned.

Hopefully Daniel would last that long.

It was another hour later when I heard a truck stop beside the entrance.

Amos.

It had to be him!

The drain cover was dragged away. Amos stuck his head down and called, "Everybody out! Now!"

Although there were more escaped Jews than there had been an hour ago, not everyone was back yet. Samuel ordered Josef and Abraham to fetch the rest, but Abraham refused. "You'll all be gone before we get back." Josef obviously shared his doubts.

Samuel insisted, "There's a risk and I can't make you go. But it is worth it. Their lives are at stake."

That was enough to make Josef start running. But not Abraham. "I'm not crazy!" he said. Samuel realized that there was no point in discussing it and looked at the skinny fighter. He just nodded and headed off at once. Samuel was the first to climb out of the sewer to coordinate the escape. I saw him and Amos hug each other briefly. Then Amos leaned down and shouted, "Go! Go! Go!"

He waved to me to come up next, but I looked over to Daniel and hesitated. He was only semiconscious and hadn't noticed what was happening around him. Rebecca was clutching his hand and her marble as tightly as she could.

"Please get the little girl out," I asked the bald man who was next in line to climb out after me.

"I promise," he said.

I climbed up the rusty metal ladder step by step, dragging my hurt ankle behind me. As I crawled out of the hole, I was blinded by the sun. After more than a day in total darkness, I could barely see Amos. He helped me out, kissed me on the cheek, and said, "We have to hurry!"

My eyes grew accustomed to the daylight in a few moments. There was a covered truck waiting, and Amos had put up a barrier behind the drain cover. Polish passersby were standing staring at us. The fact that dirty smelly ghosts were emerging from the sewers astonished them. Some looked shocked, some suspicious.

The smallest ghost was Rebecca. Blinded by the sun, she staggered across the cobblestones with no sense of direction. I grabbed her and carried her to the truck as fast as my damaged ankle allowed. I set her down in the back.

"Daniel," she said quietly.

He hadn't emerged yet.

"I'll go and get him," I told her.

More and more people stopped to see what was happening. The Poles watched silently as one by one the living dead crawled up out of the earth . . . eleven . . . twelve . . . thirteen . . .

To try to placate their suspicion, I called out, "This is an action of the Polish Home Army."

They would betray Jews, but not fellow countrymen. Or so I hoped.

"This is your chance to be heroes," I shouted. "Support your countrymen."

They didn't help us. They didn't believe me. But they didn't call the Germans. Not yet.

"We have to go," Amos said. "They won't stay quiet much longer."

"But there are still people down there," I replied.

Sixteen . . . seventeen . . . eighteen . . .

Josef and the skinny fighter were still in the tunnels fetching the others. And Daniel was down there!

An old woman started hissing, "Are those cats?"

Cats were what Poles called fleeing Jews.

"Two more minutes," Amos said. "That's all!"

"As long as it takes," I said.

"Two minutes," Amos insisted.

I hurried back to the hole while Samuel and Amos helped everyone climb into the truck. More and more Poles were calling, "Cats, cats!"

I was just about to climb down when I heard Amos swearing, "Oh shit!"

At the end of the street, a single Polish policeman wearing a smart blue uniform was walking toward us. He hadn't noticed anything yet. He was even eating an apple. But he would see us in a moment, hear the catcalls, and fetch the SS.

Amos ran over to him without hesitation.

I made my way down the hole. Before I disappeared underground, I checked to see what Amos was doing. He was talking to the policeman. What was he thinking? I was so afraid that he would be arrested on the spot. But Amos showed the policeman the gun he was hiding inside his jacket without attracting any attention. If Amos pulled it out and pressed the trigger, the crowd might start to attack us and the Germans would definitely be alerted.

I climbed down the metal rungs and waded through the water to Daniel. More comrades and civilians hurried past me.

There were still so many down here. Fifteen, twenty people—maybe even more. Most of them were still making their way over from the other entrances.

Above me a Pole started shouting, "Jews! They're damn Jews! Get the SS!"

I took hold of Daniel's hand and tried to pull him up out of the water.

"Leave me," he said, and started coughing. "You need to go."

"Not without you."

"I'll die anyway . . ."

"We don't know that," I told him.

I dragged him to his feet, put my arm around him, and supported him as best I could. I needed all my strength to drag him the last few meters to the ladder.

Samuel yelled down, "We are leaving!"

Daniel and I were the only two left by the drain. I could hear the sound of footsteps coming nearer, hurrying through the tunnels. That must be Josef and the skinny fighter with the comrades they had fetched from the other entrances. They were going to be too late.

Daniel couldn't stand. He was too weak. There was no way he would be able to climb up the ladder. And I didn't have enough strength to climb up with him on my back. It was hard enough just supporting him.

"Go!" Daniel said. "Don't die with me."

I heard the truck engine start.

"You need to be there for Rebecca," Daniel insisted.

The engine revved up.

Josef and a few other figures turned into our tunnel. They were a hundred meters away.

"Please, Mira!" Daniel pleaded. "She can't survive without you."

It was right to listen to him, but it felt so wrong.

"I'll look after her," I promised.

I let Daniel sink back down to the ground as gently as I could. He was almost lying in the water now.

Don't waste any more vital time, I thought, *don't waste a single precious moment.*

I leaned down and kissed Daniel.

The most precious moment of all.

I hurried up the ladder. As I scrambled out of the hole, Samuel leaped onto the back of the truck just as it was about to move off.

The comrades still in the tunnel weren't going to make it. Perhaps I wouldn't, either.

I ran toward the truck, my injured ankle a ball of pain.

It started moving.

Samuel reached out to me. I ran as fast as I could. The pain nearly made me faint.

Samuel grabbed my hand and pulled me onto the truck. I looked round. Amos wasn't with us.

He was still standing beside the Polish policeman.

"Amos!" I screamed.

He yelled at the policeman, "Get out of here, or I'll shoot!" The man ran away, and Amos started running, too. Toward us. The truck wasn't going fast yet, he could still make it.

Two Poles who wanted to cash the ransom money blocked his way.

"Amos!" I screamed again. I wanted to jump off the truck, to help him, but Samuel grabbed hold of me from behind and wouldn't let me go.

Amos pushed the two Poles out of the way. He had about twenty meters to go.

I struggled to free myself from Samuel's grasp. But I couldn't.

The truck gathered speed.

More and more Poles got in Amos's way.

"Amos!"

He took out his gun and shot into the air.

The Poles ran away.

Our truck turned the corner.

I couldn't see Amos anymore.

I screamed!

Samuel tried to calm me. He kept telling me, "We'll come back and get him. We'll fetch them all!"

I screamed and screamed and screamed.

Then Amos headed round the corner. He was running for his life, getting closer. The comrades reached out their hands toward him. To pull him up.

Amos tried to grab Samuel's hand.

The truck drove faster.

Amos dropped back.

I couldn't even scream anymore.

Amos made a last desperate effort and ran even faster. I put out my hand. So did Samuel.

Amos reached for mine . . .

. . . and grabbed hold of it.

Don't let go, don't let go. Never let go.

Samuel grabbed his other arm, and together we pulled Amos into the back of the truck.

As soon as he was on board we all crawled farther in, closed the tarpaulin, and drove out of the city.

79

I was too distressed to fall into Amos's arms. I lay exhausted on the floor. The other survivors were quiet all around me, each of us lost in thought. Thinking of those who had died, the comrades we had left behind, the ghetto and the danger that awaited us in the forest.

Rebecca crawled over to me and asked, "Is Daniel still coming?" She was frightened.

I could have lied to her and told her we would go back to get him. But even if we went back to Warsaw in an hour—which was out of the question—Daniel and the others would have been caught or murdered by then. And I didn't want to lie to her. So I said, "I promised Daniel that I would look after you."

Her eyes filled with tears.

"Forever?"

"Forever."

She wept for Daniel, and I held her tight.

80

Half an hour later, we stopped in Łomianki woods and got out in a clearing. The fresh air was like a drug. After all the hours in the sewers, all the days in the burning ghetto, all the months, even years with practically nothing green, I was intoxicated by the scents of the forest.

People fell into one another's arms, sank to the ground, by themselves or together, some cried with happiness. Others laughed. I saw Abraham stroking the moss as if he had never touched anything like it before.

My ankle hurt so much that I lay down in the warm grass. Rebecca lay down beside me, her tears dried by now. She put a hand in her pocket, brought out the marble, and held it out to me. The marble rolled round the palm of her little scratched hand and came to rest in the middle. The sun shone through the trees right onto the marble, and it sparkled in every direction just like a diamond. It looked more magical than ever. A real treasure.

"For you," Rebecca said.

"I . . . I can't take that," I stammered.

"Please . . . ," she said.

"It is the nicest thing anyone has ever given me."

"I know." She smiled, and the dried tears round her eyes sparkled in the sun, too.

To feel the marble in my hand, to smell the wood, the little girl's smile . . . there was so much more to the world than my fear.

Rebecca pointed at the marble, and said, "You know what . . . ?"

Her eyes could hardly stay open. I should have let her fall asleep, but I was far too interested to hear what she wanted to tell me about the marble, so I asked, "What do I know?"

"A deer lives in there . . . ," she mumbled with her eyes closed, "and a unicorn and three fairies . . . and . . . a . . ."

Her voice dropped to a whisper . . .

"teddy bear . . ."

. . . and she fell asleep.

The little glass ball was a world full of friendly creatures.

A world of peace.

Rebecca slept tranquilly, and the sun shone down on us. Amos came over and lay down on the other side of the girl. We watched her like my parents used to watch me when I was little.

"She's beautiful," I said.

"A miracle."

A miracle, indeed.

We couldn't stop looking at her. For a moment we were the family each of us had lost.

After a while, Amos said in awe, "Twenty-eight days."

"What?" I asked.

"We resisted the Germans for twenty-eight days."

Had it been twenty-eight days? Was that really true? I'd never counted. I didn't have a clue what the date was. Not even what day. Monday? Wednesday? Was it summer yet?

"We held out longer than France!" Amos said proudly.

Something else meant far more to me. We had saved people from hell.

Saved Rebecca.

This wasn't another Masada where everyone—fighters, women, children—perished and only the legend survived.

It was bigger.

We were alive.

"Amos?"

"Yes?"

"I won't fight a twenty-ninth day."

He didn't know what I meant.

"I'm going to find somewhere to hide with her."

Then he understood, but he didn't say anything. He wanted to continue fighting. "Till the end." The question was, did he want that more than he wanted to be with me?

I hardly dared ask, but I needed to know, even if his answer was going to break my heart. "Will you come with us?"

"Hiding somewhere is dangerous . . . ," he said slowly.

"More dangerous than fighting to death? I don't think so!"

Amos struggled to make up his mind. Played with the wedding ring on his finger.

"You've repaid your debt . . . ," I started to say.

"I haven't . . . ," he interrupted me.

". . . as best you can," I continued speaking.

No one could ever completely defeat the Mirror King.

Amos didn't say any more.

I couldn't breathe. It was like being back in the ghetto I'd left forever—only worse.

Here was a kind of fear I had never felt before.

The fear that he would leave me.

"I . . . ," Amos said, "I don't want to abandon our comrades . . ."

I closed my eyes.

It was so painful.

"But I can't live without you."

I kept my eyes closed.

Amos kissed me. He didn't care how much I stank.

With this kiss in the clearing in the forest in the warm sunlight, I knew what kind of person I was going to be.

One who lived life to the fullest.

Dear Reader,

In the history of the Warsaw Ghetto you can see how truly terrible and how truly magnificent humans can be. All the Jews there were victims of the Nazis, but they acted differently. There were some who sacrificed their own parents just so they could stay alive themselves for a few more days. Yet others, who could have saved their own lives, stayed with their children to their death. There were heroes who took up arms, and heroes who taught the children even though it was punishable by death.

All of these were one part of what inspired me to write this book. The other part was the story of my own family. None of them were in the ghetto of Warsaw. But my father's father died in the concentration camp at Buchenwald in 1940, and my grandmother died in 1942 in the ghetto of Łódź. As a young man in 1938, my father had to flee from Vienna to Palestine. He had to make similar decisions to those Mira has to make in this novel. He did not fight in the ghetto, but he did fight for Israel's independence, first in the underground, and later in the military. At some point he decided to no longer bear arms, and he committed himself to the love of his life. He adopted a small girl, my older sister, and he built a family. Despite all the loss and suffering he'd witnessed, he chose life.

Mira, Amos, Daniel, and Hannah are invented figures, but this novel is based on historic facts and eyewitness testimony. Real people did experience things similar to those you have read about. Mira also meets some historic figures, such as the ghetto fighter Mordechai Anielewicz, the fool Rubinstein, and Janusz Korczak, who stayed with the orphans in his charge to their—and his—deaths. I hope that through Mira you experienced a bit what it was like to live and love and fight in the ghetto of

Warsaw. That you learned what extraordinary acts humans are capable of, even in the most terrible circumstances. But most of all, how they were still capable of love, just like my father, whose capacity for love could not be destroyed by the Holocaust.

That's why *28 Days* is not just about the past. It's about all of us. It's about love, and it's about those universal questions we all should ask ourselves: What would you do to survive? Would you sacrifice your life for others or would you sacrifice others to save yourself?

And what it really is about is: What kind of human, what kind of *mensch* do you want to be?

Yours,
David Safier

Thank you for reading this Feiwel and Friends book.

The friends who made

28 DAYS

possible are:

JEAN FEIWEL, *Publisher*

LIZ SZABLA, *Associate Publisher*

RICH DEAS, *Senior Creative Director*

HOLLY WEST, *Senior Editor*

ANNA ROBERTO, *Senior Editor*

KAT BRZOZOWSKI, *Senior Editor*

ALEXEI ESIKOFF, *Senior Managing Editor*

KIM WAYMER, *Senior Production Manager*

EMILY SETTLE, *Associate Editor*

FOYINSI ADEGBONMIRE, *Editorial Assistant*

RACHEL DIEBEL, *Assistant Editor*

ERIN SIU, *Assistant Editor*

MALLORY GRIGG, *Art Director*

Follow us on Facebook or visit us online at mackids.com.

OUR BOOKS ARE FRIENDS FOR LIFE